THE

LAST REBEL

THE
LAST REBEL

After Bosworth: Lovell Fights On

NIGEL GREEN

STELLAR ★ BOOKS

Published in 2015 by:

Stellar Books LLP
Dunham Gatehouse
Charcoal Road,
Bowdon
Cheshire,
WA14 4RY
UK

E: info@stellarbooks.co.uk
W: www.stellarbooks.co.uk
T: 0161 928 8273

ISBN: 978-1910275054

A copy of this book is available in the British Library.

Typeset in Perpetua, Palatino Linotype and Trajan Pro by Stellar Books LLP.

FSC is a non-profit international organisation established to promote responsible management of the world's forests. Products carrying the FSC label are independently certified to assure consumers that they come from forests that are managed to meet the social economic and ecological needs of present and future generations.

Printed and bound in Great Britain by TJ International Ltd, Padstow, Cornwall.

For Michael Colin, Nicki and Jonah.

ACKNOWLEDGEMENT

My thanks in particular go to my editor Patricia Byron. It is due to her objective criticisms and helpful suggestions that this book has become infinitely better.

At all stages of the book's development, Patricia managed to combine a fine eye for detail with a view to the broader scope of the novel and it was these skills especially (combined with a lively sense of humour!) that I came to appreciate and value.

My thanks to you, Patricia.

Nigel Green
March 2015.

THE RELEVANT PART OF THE

HOUSE OF YORK IN 1486

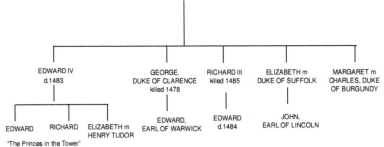

EDWARD IV
d.1483

GEORGE,
DUKE OF CLARENCE
killed 1478

RICHARD III
killed 1485

ELIZABETH m
DUKE OF SUFFOLK

MARGARET m
CHARLES, DUKE
OF BURGUNDY

EDWARD   RICHARD   ELIZABETH m
HENRY TUDOR

EDWARD,
EARL OF WARWICK

EDWARD
d.1484

JOHN,
EARL OF LINCOLN

"The Princes in the Tower"
Both killed 1483

PROLOGUE

Hitherto, I believed that I had chosen the location of my command post wisely, since it afforded me a clear view of the whole battlefield. But as I looked towards the southwest and saw the final stages of the vicious skirmish by the edge of the great marsh, I realised that I had been foolish to select a spot that provided me with such good visibility.

Most of Richard's knights who had followed him in that fatal charge against the usurper Henry Tudor were already dead. A handful might have got away, but the majority had been hacked down by the troops of a traitor. With bitterness I cursed Lord Stanley; he had sworn to fight for Richard against his Lancastrian rival Tudor, but he had betrayed him. Immediately after Richard and his knights had charged, Stanley rushed men forward to rescue Henry. Now, due to their intervention, not only was Tudor saved, but a mere twenty or so of Richard's knights survived out of the elite force which thundered down the hillside following their King in his quest for eternal glory.

But there was to be no glory for the survivors. They fought on foot, since their horses' steaming flanks had long since proved highly vulnerable to the cruelly sharp billhooks of Stanley's infantry. Since they had unhorsed Richard's knights, it was Stanley's men who now held the advantage. Being more manoeuvrable than the heavily armoured knights, they used their greater numbers to swarm around them.

Despite the odds, the knights had no thought of surrender. They were the household companions of a King and had pledged him their undying loyalty. Since he had been killed, their last duty was to avenge him by killing as many of his murderers as they could. The knights ignored the greater numbers of their enemies and fought on bravely. They might have been a dwindling band of doomed men, but they were proud of their loyalty to the dead King.

However nothing less than the death of these men would satisfy Stanley's billmen. Hunting like wolves, they separated the knights from each other. Encircling their victims, they moved in, their blows falling randomly so that, with vision already restricted by the narrow slits of their visors, the knights were unable to guess at the direction of the next attack.

The billmen pressed remorselessly forward. The pace of their assaults quickened. They stopped using the points of their weapons to probe for weak sections in their enemy's armour, instead using the cutting edges to systematically bludgeon the knights.

I tried not to imagine the knights' suffering but failed. They would know too that this ceaseless pounding would continue inexorably until a sudden blow would detach a part of their armour and a razor sharp bill would plunge into their exposed flesh.

What would make it worse would be their constant fear of falling. A bill is a formidable weapon with its point, cutting edge and vicious hook, but even the shaft is deadly. In expert hands it can easily be used to trip a man. Once unbalanced, the knight is finished; his visor would be quickly wrenched open and the point of the bill thrust down into his terrified face.

Provoked beyond the point of endurance, one knight decided to break out of this circle of death. As his comrades were being savagely beaten to the ground, he somehow found the strength to make a lumbering charge. Heedless of the danger that he might fall, he hefted a heavy mace and launched himself directly at the billmen opposite him, smashing his way through them. For a moment the knight's tactics dumbfounded his opponents, but they rallied swiftly – he could not be allowed to escape. More manoeuvrable in their lighter jacks, the pack rushed after him, adjusting their encircling formation to replace their dead. Angered by the knight's defiance, they jabbed and hacked at him furiously, but still he fought back fiercely, his solid mace cruelly emphasising the weakness of the billmen's breastplates, mocking their paucity of armour.

The knight swung his weapon more confidently now; a billman in front of him crumpled, his helmet no match for the crushing weight of the mace. Seeing this, the other billmen hung back and, sensing them wavering, the knight stepped forward triumphantly to deliver another devastating blow.

But it was to prove to be his downfall. Even as he raised his mace above his head, a well-aimed billhead tore into his exposed armpit and, as the point seared into his chest, the knight crashed to the ground. I looked on in disgust as, like ravenous beasts, the soldiers flung themselves on the dying knight using their daggers to jab and slash. A moment later fighting began between the looters, even as their wounded prize moaned feebly blow them. Seeing them distracted, others rushed in to rip the armour off the knight and, heedless of his bloody wounds, raked his body for coins. Within minutes it was over and, having acquired the bulk of their spoils, the handful of men hurriedly withdrew to argue over the apportionment of their loot. Even as they scurried away, still more scavengers skulked towards the carcass to gather the remaining scraps.

And this would have been Richard's own fate, I guessed miserably. Superbly mounted, his glittering armour would have made him a natural target for looters, even before the incredulous infantry noticed his distinctive battle crown. For a brief moment Stanley's men must have gaped in amazement at their luck for, if a knight or lord was worth a fortune, the value of a king was unquantifiable. From the moment that he was first spotted Richard would have become every man's focus and, against a horde desperate for wealth, he would not have stood a chance.

How badly I had failed him.

'There's Tudor!'

A great shout went up.

'By the marsh!' Richard pointed excitedly down the slope. 'Francis, you see him? There can't be more than forty or fifty with him.'

But why was Tudor exposing himself to such danger, I wondered?

xiv

'Bring up all my household knights!'

And why was his small force moving so slowly?

'We've got him now, the battle's won!' Richard smiled ecstatically. 'Francis, you guard our northern flank while we charge them.'

'Wait Richard!' I said urgently. 'It's too obvious…'

But he brushed past me shouting for the trumpets to be sounded while messengers flew in all directions and squires helped eager knights onto their horses.

I ignored them and concentrated on Tudor. Was the man a complete fool? He must have known that his action of exposing himself to a hostile force was highly dangerous. His main force in the north was too far away to come to his assistance and, while admittedly Stanley's division was moving up slowly from the south against us, they were mainly infantry. Our heavy cavalry would surely crush Tudor long before they reached him.

Tudor's action made no sense and made me feel uneasy. I sensed a trap, but I could not identify its nature.

The massive warhorses seemed to sense their riders' excitement as they neighed loudly and jostled each other in their eagerness to gallop off. Holding their banners aloft, the knights fought frantically to control their bridling beasts and collided with each other as they attempted to form a crude line.

I passed through them hastily until I came to the place where Richard was.

'Let me lead the charge', I begged him. 'You stay here.'

His savage laugh cut me off.

'No, Francis. God has delivered the usurper into my hands and I will personally slay him.'

He lowered the point of his lance and slammed his visor shut; with a final flourish of the trumpets, the King and his household knights thundered down the slope.

That had been my mistake. What I had sensed but had not been able to understand had come grotesquely true. Richard and his knights had charged down the slope but, instead of galloping to victory, they had stumbled into a trap devised by traitors.

I was to blame for Richard's death. I should have used my experience and obeyed my instincts. I should have forbidden my headstrong King from charging. Eventually he would have agreed with me, not just because he trusted me but because he valued my military skills. Dear God, he had rated them sufficiently high enough to make me his general.

I clenched my fists in anger. My leadership had proved totally inadequate and Richard's trust in me had been wholly misplaced. I had failed him completely.

'My lord?'

I looked down at the shocked face of my squire and was abruptly reminded of my duty to what remained of our army. With Richard dead and two out of the three divisions of our original force turned traitor, only the Earl of Surrey's men could still oppose Tudor's main army. But with Stanley's force creeping stealthily northwards to mount a cowardly attack on Surrey's left flank, it was clearly time to extricate his division. But even as I started to give the order to conduct an immediate fighting withdrawal, I heard the noise that I had dreaded most coming from Tudor's army. There is no sound more terrifying than the beginning of the rolling roar of the victorious enemy. Of course, all battles start with sound. From the very moment that both sides face each other, they will look to bolster their own confidence and intimidate their opponents with a barrage of insults and threats. This cacophony grows louder as the two forces edge together, climaxing in a great shout as the armies finally crash into each other, but after that there is no time for speech. Men will make no sound unless it is to moan in exhaustion or to cry out in pain. A knight or man-at-arms, sweating profusely in his armour, has neither the energy nor the inclination to waste his ragged breath on mindless curses or useless exhortations. Besides, who would hear him? A helmet with visor closed leaves a man frighteningly alone in a disorientated world of his own. He will be conscious of his own panting and aware of the incessant clanging but he will be oblivious to all other sounds. Because of this, it is usually the more lightly armoured archers who are the first to catch the start of the enemy's rolling roar; it is from their sudden agitation that knights sense, rather than hear, that disaster is about to strike.

There was nothing triumphant about that sudden roar from Tudor's army, I thought grimly. Indeed the sound itself was pitched so deep that there was an almost bestial quality to it. Instead of joyous cries of victory, what I heard was an ominous rumble. While muted, no one could fail to discern the dark malevolence of that low growl with its awful promise of total destruction.

My shoulders drooped as I turned towards the sound that was already starting to swell. I was at too far a distance to see much on that dust-filled plain, but I guessed that Tudor's troops had finally found a weak spot in Surrey's line and had broken into it.

By now they must have exploited their penetration and would be surging into the widening breach. Fanning out quickly, they would waste no time in attacking the exposed flanks of Surrey's men.

I groaned quietly. Instinctively, Surrey's troops would have flinched away allowing still more of the enemy to pour into the growing gap. Swiftly, Tudor's encroachment would become ever deeper and that great rolling roar still more intimidating.

The dust cleared momentarily and I winced; already Surrey's line was buckling under the weight of the sustained assaults. A trickle of men began to slip away from the rear and, as the rolling roar grew even more menacing, so the trickle became a stream. Sensing the final breakthrough, Tudor's army braced itself ready to tear through the ever increasing gaps in Surrey's division to wreak havoc on their foes. The battle was lost now, I knew, but nothing in my experience prepared me for the sheer scale of the disaster that followed.

Even as Surrey's front began to crumble, some of his men must have spotted Stanley's men approaching from the south and, for Surrey's panicking division, the threat of an additional attack on their flank was simply too much. Within minutes the troops lost all semblance of military cohesion and degenerated into a mob. They turned to fly in all directions, frantically discarding their heavy weapons and armour. The very things that had kept them safe all morning were now liabilities.

I watched in horror as Surrey's men collided together in desperate confusion. They mindlessly trampled over fallen comrades and struck out wildly at those who blocked their paths. Tudor's army rolling roar rose to a paean of savage exultation and their men moved grimly towards Surrey's terrified troops. But still a few brave souls fought on. Perhaps they were unswervingly committed to the House of York or, conceivably, they wished to settle an old score with a particular opponent. More probable was that they were sufficiently experienced to recognise the futility of flight under such circumstances or were simply too stubborn to bother. Whatever their motivation, their resistance caused Tudor's army to hold back for fear of a trap.

For the fleeing troops the reprieve proved to be short lived. Tudor's captains advanced their Welsh archers and, for a short while, volley after volley rained down on Surrey's defenceless troops. The maelstrom of arrows having subdued the opposition, Tudor flooded all his troops forward. It was then that the final butchery began. Hopelessly out of their protective formations, already partially unarmoured and largely without weapons, Surrey's men were easy prey for the sharp swords and vengeful poleaxes of Tudor's killers.

I turned away numbly. A lucky few might escape, but most would not be so fortunate and would suffer grievous wounds to their exposed heads and unprotected arms. Some of the wounded might be able to crawl away but most would not survive.

Curtly, to hide my distress, I ordered for the horses to be fetched. There was no reason to remain any longer. The army that I commanded had ceased to exist; my King was dead and our defeat total. But for all that, my feelings of guilt and grief had to be suppressed. All that mattered was the future and a promise that I was now duty-bound to honour.

It was, of course, no ordinary promise, but then the man to whom I had sworn the oath was no ordinary man. He had, I knew, regarded me as his friend. Indeed twice he had declined the formal oath of loyalty that I had offered him – firstly when he ruled the North as Duke of Gloucester, just as he later rejected it when he ruled

England as Richard III. On both occasions he declared my offer to be superfluous, as he already had my friendship.

How great a friend I proved to be, I cannot truly say. Except for my obvious failure today, I believe that at all times I had acted in a manner that served his interests best, even if that meant opposing his will. Such instances invariably provoked his wrath, but that never concerned me. True friendship demands that you do what is best for the other person, even if that differs from doing what he wants.

In time, Richard came to understand this belief of mine and, even if it angered him, I think he respected it. Indeed he even joked about it once, pointing out that when I infrequently viewed a matter in the same light as himself, he did not have to worry that I was merely nodding along like another sycophant.

I winced at the memory, as the point at which I had made my promise was one of those rare occasions where we had been as one in our thoughts. I knew that he had hoped to manage the business himself but, conscious of his own mortality, he had begged me to undertake it if he proved unable to.

It was a simple matter: Richard's own son had died the previous year and he had no other lawful children. To make amends to his dead brother Clarence, he determined that his son Edward, Earl of Warwick, should be the next king and rule England after him. Since by blood and natural inheritance the young Earl of Warwick was Richard's natural successor, I willingly swore the oath to make him king when Richard died. But Richard's plan was upset by Henry Tudor, the Lancastrian claimant to the throne. Despite having no right to the crown, he had invaded

England with a largely French army to stake his own claim. A number of malcontents had joined him, but it had been the treachery of Richard's own supposed supporters that had given Tudor his victory here today. And with that victory and Richard dead, Tudor would contemptuously dismiss the wholly lawful claim of the young Earl of Warwick and go on to proclaim himself King. With our defeat today, I was powerless to prevent this, but even as I strode towards the waiting horses, I felt a curious sense of detachment from the battle and its outcome.

Tudor would not rule for long; I would ensure that. My failure today may have lost Richard both his crown and life, but I would not fail him again. He had entrusted me with this duty and I would not let him down. I would create another army. It would be a good army, fiercely loyal to the House of York. When they were ready, I would lead my men against Henry Tudor and sweep him from his throne. Then I would make Richard's chosen heir, the young Earl of Warwick, England's King.

I dismissed all but two of my aides and rode away. Not once did I look back. There was no reason to now.

PART I

1485 - 1487

CHAPTER 1

Colchester, 1485.

'You appear somewhat healthier than you did when you first staggered into Colchester!'

Gravely, Walter Stanstead, the grey-haired Abbot of St John's, indicated that I should be seated. I sat down gratefully. While I was able to walk again, it was still an effort.

'I have no recollection of coming here.'

'Given that you were close to death that is not altogether unexpected,' he replied with a touch of asperity. 'Do you have any recollection of your flight from Bosworth?'

It had been a nightmare as Tudor's men had been everywhere.

'I can remember getting to Huntington; Cambridge was too dangerous so we skirted round it. By the time we got to Bury St Edmunds we were weak from hunger and the horses were exhausted.'

'You were trying to get overseas?'

'Yes, but we were spotted and shortly after we ran straight into one of Tudor's patrols. He must have had the whole of East Anglia watched to prevent fugitives escaping. Anyway, a running fight ensued.'

'Leaving you badly wounded. You were fortunate to

have such a loyal attendant who was quick-witted enough to bring you here to claim sanctuary.'

Abbot Stanstead rose stiffly and moved towards me. He gestured for me to bend my neck as he carefully removed the covering to inspect the wound.

'Now that all traces of the arrow have been extracted, the injury appears to be healing satisfactorily,' he murmured. 'And your arm?'

I extended my arm tentatively. Each day now I could raise it a little higher.

'It's better.'

The Abbot washed his hands fastidiously in a large silver dish.

'You have, I trust, given thanks to God for your preservation?'

'I will.'

'Additionally there are the healing brothers here to whom you owe your life.' Abbot Stanstead hinted at where my thanks should lie.

'I will make a gift to your abbey once I am in a position to do so.'

He nodded sagely.

'Not many men would survive such wounds.'

I smiled grimly recalling how many times over the past few weeks I had felt that I would welcome death. The herbs, which the brothers prepared, helped to dull the pain to an extent but careless movements produced moments of searing agony in my neck. Nor had the nights proved any better. The drugged wine that I was given eased me to sleep, but all too frequently my slumbers led me into a terrifying world where I was pursued by nameless foes. On one occasion I recall that I had a companion. Tired of flight, he urged me to turn and fight them with him. His opponents were too many, so I reluctantly abandoned him.

'*But I trusted you Francis!*' Richard's anguished tones echoed after me.

I shook my head to rid myself of my nightmares.

'How long have I been here?'

'You have been in sanctuary these past three months,' the Abbot replied quietly. 'St Denis' fair has long since passed and our new King's coronation is now but a memory.'

Abbot Stanstead's eyes lit up happily as he recalled the occasion, while I sat silent, shocked by the length of my illness. But even as the Abbot extolled the great pageantry of Henry Tudor's crowning, two thoughts struck me. The first was, as the good Abbot had attended the coronation, it was probably fair to assume that he was a mitred prelate with a seat in the House of Lords. As such, he was presumably a supporter of Henry Tudor now. The second thought was even more worrying. I must have been in the Abbey of St John's for over three months. Yet, by law, the maximum period you could remain in sanctuary was forty days. After that time you were supposed to hand yourself over to face justice or flee overseas.

I glanced at Abbot Stanstead. Now that I was over the worst of my injuries, doubtless he would wish to ingratiate himself with his new King.

'Are you going to evict me?'

For a moment he sat deep in thought while I gazed at him apprehensively. Then, to my surprise, he rose.

'May I show you something of our abbey?' he enquired.

Confused by his offer and uncertain of his purpose, I slowly followed him out of the chamber. My bewilderment increased as he made no effort to show me any of the abbey's buildings nor did he seek to make me known to any of its inhabitants. He even ignored commenting on the great abbey church with its imposing central tower and four spires and led me instead towards a vast gatehouse. My shoulders drooped wearily; plainly I was to be evicted but, weak as I was, I could probably reach the coast and, with luck, I might be able to find a ship.

'I fear that the climb will fatigue you.' Abbot Stanstead apologised as he indicated the steep stairs. 'However, I do believe that you will find the view from the top worthwhile.'

Courteously, he slowed his pace as we ascended and, slightly to my surprise, I managed the climb. He led me forward and, from our vantage point, I could easily see much of the small walled town of Colchester. Abbot Stanstead began to point out those parts of the town that the abbey owned but, after a few moments, I lost interest and I was still staring at the small castle when he tugged my sleeve.

'I believe that those men might interest you, my lord,' he murmured.

I followed his pointed finger down to the street below us where a small group loitered. There seemed to be little remarkable about them except that they all wore similar tunics. Then my heart sank: green and white were Tudor's colours.

I glanced left and right quickly. About four hundred paces in both directions were other such small groups. Presumably Tudor's men ringed the entire abbey. I was trapped.

'Shall we descend?' the abbot enquired politely.

I hesitated.

He gave a small smile.

'And return to my chambers.'

* * *

4

'You will try these oysters, my lord? They are from our very own River Colne.'

With a smile, Abbot Stanstead proffered the dish.

'Thank you.'

I was in no mood to dine but I had to discover what the Abbot had planned for me.

'Perhaps we might serve ourselves,' he suggested. 'There are but the two of us and I expect that the servants will have other tasks with which to occupy themselves.'

I took the hint.

'Of course.'

He waited until they had gone and then leant back in his chair.

'Doubtless you are wondering why a notorious traitor such as yourself has been allowed to remain in sanctuary for so long.'

'I am no traitor!'

'But you are!' he reproved me. 'His Gracious Majesty King Henry has seen fit to date his reign as commencing on the day before the Battle of Bosworth. Therefore, it must surely follow that anyone who fought against him at that battle is a traitor?'

I silently cursed Tudor's duplicity.

'But His Majesty can be merciful to traitors,' Abbot Stanstead continued quietly. 'Even to those who were closest to the tyrant Richard of Gloucester...'

'King Richard!'

'Our gracious monarch is known to be willing to deal sympathetically with them. Those who throw themselves on his charity may have no fear of death for it is his express wish that the wars should end and the country's wounds healed. This is to be a time of peace and reconciliation for all men, even those who misguidedly fought against him.'

He eyed me hopefully, but I made no comment. Henry Tudor had seized the crown by force and ruled by right of conquest, not by natural inheritance. It surely followed that he would be desperate to bolster his flimsy regime by winning over as many people as he could. He could hardly do otherwise.

'I am given to understand that your wife's brother, Lord Fitzhugh, has been given posts and honours in the North,' Abbot Stanstead added silkily. 'Doubtless there are many others who, by now, have happily accepted the sheer inevitability of our blessed new King's position and are content to live in peace and tranquillity.'

My brother-in-law's defection did not surprise me for he was a peaceful man. But I found it hard to believe that support for the House of York would have eroded completely.

'Naturally His Majesty cannot be seen to make the first overtures to his former foes,' the Abbot continued smoothly, 'but, as with our dear Saviour, all those who come forward freely and penitently to confess their sins and beg for forgiveness may be assured of his loving mercy.'

He leant forward expectantly.

'Might I be permitted to pass on the joyous news to His Majesty that I have one such repentant sinner in my very own abbey who desires to come to grace?'

Tudor's offer was undoubtedly sincere and, were I to accept, I could return to my lands and see my wife Nan again. How long had it been since I had seen her, I wondered. It had been months since Bosworth now and I had been apart from her long before the battle. Sadly I calculated that we had not been together for the best part of a year. Nor had I had news of her. I had no idea how she was coping in Yorkshire or even if she was well. The more I thought of her the greater the urge to see and talk to her grew irresistibly.

With an effort I opened my eyes and traced the outline of the ring that hung on a cord round my neck. It had been a gift from Richard and I wore it as a reminder of my promise to him. And because I had made that promise I was bound to overthrow Tudor and not to submit to him.

Hesitantly I turned to face the Abbot.

'Repentance is only of value when it comes from the heart as well as from the lips,' I said slowly. 'My feelings of loyalty to my dead King are still too fresh in my mind for me to make a sincere submission to King Henry. May I not reflect on the matter for a few more days?'

Abbot Stanstead nodded in understanding.

'Take all the time you need, my lord…'

'Thank you.'

He rested his chin on his hands.

'After all, it's not as if you are going anywhere.'

I had assumed that I was the only Yorkist fugitive to have found safety in the abbey but, to my surprise, a day later I saw two familiar figures emerging from the abbey church.

'Francis!' boomed Sir Humphrey Stafford. 'How long have you been here?'

'Over three months.' I glanced around to ensure that we could not be overheard. 'And you?'

'We've been lying low since Bosworth,' Humphrey's

younger brother Thomas replied. 'We thought that we had actually managed to find a ship to take us to Burgundy last week, but we were betrayed.'

I sympathised with the pair but clearly their misfortune was my gain for, having been at liberty these past few weeks, they would know what was going on in the world outside the abbey.

I questioned the red-faced Humphrey eagerly on how the country had reacted to Henry Tudor's seizure of the throne. He pulled his cloak closer round his burly frame as he considered the question.

'I think that by now people are used to the fact that Richard is dead,' he said at last. 'As a matter of fact, many see his death as God's natural justice.'

I looked at him incredulously.

'Why?'

He shrugged awkwardly.

'Well, they might believe the rumours that not only did Richard steal his nephew's crown but subsequently had the young prince and his brother put to death.'

'That said,' Thomas broke in awkwardly, 'it doesn't necessarily mean that England will accept Henry Tudor. Alright, for the moment everyone has given in to him because there is no other candidate, but if there was another claimant from the House of York, everyone would rush to him...'

'Where is the Earl of Warwick?'

'Imprisoned in the Tower of London.'

'The Earl of Lincoln?'

'Richard's other nephew has already surrendered to Henry Tudor.' Humphrey grunted. 'Anyway, it hardly matters about him. Our men want the Earl of Warwick to replace Tudor and there are a lot of them. Don't forget that many of the supporters of the House of York did not manage to get to Bosworth.'

'There's another reason that men doubt Henry Tudor,' Thomas broke in. 'He promised to marry Elizabeth, the eldest daughter of the late King Edward, and so unite the rival Houses of York and Lancaster. Well, he's been crowned and he still hasn't married her.'

'There was talk that the revolts would force Tudor to marry her quickly; some say as soon as January. I heard that...'

'What revolts?' In my excitement I seized Humphrey Stafford's arm roughly and he winced.

'Have you not heard Francis? The North is already up in arms, there's trouble in Cornwall and opposition to Tudor elsewhere.'

I waved away these minor activities. What mattered was the opposition to Tudor in the North, where the bulk of support for Richard had always been and it was the part of the country that I knew best.

'How widespread is the northern revolt?'

Sir Humphrey Stafford tugged his grey moustache thoughtfully.

'It's hard to distil the truth from rumours.'

'Particularly when you are a fugitive!' his brother observed wryly.

'But it must be fairly widespread. I heard that the Lords Fitzhugh and Strange were unable to deal with it. Tudor's been forced to release the Earl of Northumberland from the Tower of London to try to overcome the rebels.'

Alone in my chamber, I lay quietly as I thought about all that I had heard these past two days and tried to separate truth from wishful thinking. I started with my own grim situation. I would never submit to the usurper, but he had me trapped and his guards would be particularly vigilant. Undoubtedly Henry Tudor would have given clear orders that under no circumstances should the man who had done his best to defeat him at Bosworth be allowed to get away again. Yet somehow I had to escape as soon as humanly possible in order to honour my promise to Richard. After all, fairly shortly Henry's offer of clemency would expire and I would be taken from the abbey and executed.

I mulled over what the Stafford brothers had told me. The obvious question to consider first of all was how reliable their news was. As a man Humphrey Stafford had lacked the brains to ever be more than on the fringes of government, but he was solid and widely respected in his native Worcestershire. It seemed probable that he was not inventing stories, but was genuinely reporting what he and his brother had heard. So how far could I believe all these rumours and tales? Most of them, I knew from my own time in government, could be discarded as irrelevancies. News travels slowly, particularly from far-flung places like Cornwall, and once the matter had been twisted and distorted by itinerant peddlers and gossiping friars, it would bear little resemblance to the original events. As such I dismissed all that I had heard except for one key point: due to the failure of Lord Stanley's son, Lord Strange, to crush the northern revolt, Henry Tudor had been forced to release the Earl of Northumberland to deal with the troubles. From that one simple statement, I knew that the situation for Tudor in the North was critical. He would have no more trusted Northumberland than anyone else would following his incredible conduct on Bosworth Field, for, at the key point of battle, not only had the supposedly loyal Northumberland refused to engage the opposing forces of Henry Tudor, he had then marched his men off the battlefield completely.

But if Northumberland had both unexpectedly and devastatingly proved to be a traitor to Richard, he had also made it perfectly clear that he was not prepared to back Henry Tudor. He made no attempt to align his division alongside Tudor's troops or to attack any of our troops. Instead, he simply withdrew from the field, seemingly wholly indifferent to the battle's outcome.

Henry Tudor was apparently so mistrustful of Northumberland that he locked him up immediately after the battle was won and kept him in prison, preferring to have more loyal men control the North of England. But, with their failure to manage the region, Tudor's hand must have been forced. The only man with the power and the influence to bring order there was Northumberland. So Henry would have had to take an enormous gamble and send a man whom neither he nor anyone else trusted back to the very area where his power and prestige were second to none. It would have been the very last thing that Tudor would have wanted to do.

A few nights later, I stood on top of the massive gatehouse looking out into the darkness. Next to me, the bulky shape of Humphrey Stafford was trying to adjust his cloak to keep out the cold but struggling to suppress his shivering.

'I can't think why you wanted us to meet here,' he grumbled.

'There's no danger of being overheard up here, and we will be totally alone, since your brother is guarding the stairs.'

'Well, let's talk then,' he said gruffly. 'Have you decided yet whether the situation in the North is worth exploiting?'

I had thought of little else this last week. It had been a difficult decision because of the lack of information, but on balance the troubles in the North appeared to offer the quickest way to dethrone Henry Tudor. It would however be extremely risky to rush into conflict without proper planning.

Humphrey Stafford pointed out the sentries by the camp fire in the street below us.

'They won't be there tomorrow night,' he grunted.

'Why not?'

'Haven't you heard? Tomorrow Henry Tudor is marrying his Yorkist wife. Everyone will be celebrating all day and, by nightfall, the whole town will be a senseless, carousing rabble.'

My heart raced – events were conspiring to make my final decision for me.

I took a deep breath.

'We'll break out of here tomorrow,' I said. 'I'll go north and proclaim the Earl of Warwick to be the rightful King of England. You and your brother head to Worcester and create a diversionary revolt there. That way we'll force Tudor to divide his forces.'

Humphrey Stafford's dark form remained very still as he thought my proposal over.

'You're right,' he said at last. 'Now how do we go about escaping from Colchester?'

I smiled in the darkness.

'There are four things we need to do before we can escape,' I told him.

The next night I slumped miserably in my saddle as Tudor's captain led me through the packed streets of Colchester. My wrists ached and I had no feeling left in my fingers. Tudor's men had done a thorough job when they had bound me, I thought bitterly. Despite the lateness of the hour, drunken laughter, shouts and raucous singing spilled out of the alehouses. In the streets, men capered inanely or vomited violently by the side. They would be easy pickings for thieves this night, I reflected sourly. The point of a sword jabbed me in the back, and I turned to remonstrate with the green-and-white tuniced soldier who rode behind me. He leered at me.

'Keep moving traitor!'

I glared at him until a sharp pull on the heavy chain that linked my wrists to the captain's horse pulled me forward again and we resumed our slow progress. Men were starting to leave the taverns now and the narrow streets were clogged with groups of people arguing or laughing together, their drunken swaggering blocking the captain's progress. With a loud curse, he reined in his horse and glanced around. Then he saw what he wanted.

'You men!' he called out sharply. 'Over here now!'

It was too dark for the men-at-arms emerging from the inn to make out the captain's badge of office, but even in their befuddled state they recognised the natural authority of the officer's voice. Six or seven of them stumbled towards us and blearily regarded the captain who towered over them.

He scowled at them.

'Where's your officer, you drunken scum?' he demanded.

They looked at each other owlishly.

'Don't know, sir.'

For a moment the captain's mouth worked furiously as he contemplated them. They shuffled uneasily.

'He's probably drunk like the rest of you!' the captain bellowed. 'You are a complete disgrace. I'll have you all flogged when this is over.'

'But it's the King's wedding!' one of the men-at-arms shouted truculently.

Shortly after, he screamed in agony as the flat of the captain's sword hammered into his shoulder. He collapsed instantly. The captain glared at the other men-at-arms.

'The next man to argue with me gets the point of this through his guts,' he snarled. 'Now clear a way through that mob!'

Moving quickly, the soldiers began to push their way through the crowd ahead of us. I glanced around in despair. My chances of escaping were growing lesser with every step we took.

I was jabbed in my back by the sword again.

'Don't even think about it,' my guard grunted.

I bit my lip in frustration, but then I had an idea. As the captain's horse halted, I took advantage of the loosening of the chain to move closer to the guard.

'Listen,' I said urgently. 'I can help you. I'm a rich man...'

'Captain, sir!'

Tudor's captain wheeled his horse round.

'Prisoner attempting to bribe me, sir.'

Fury blazed in the captain's eyes and, without warning, he back-handed me hard across the face. I yelled out in pain and slid to the ground. The captain gestured to the men-at-arms who had turned back at the sound of my cry.

'Get him back on his horse, you scum!'

I was man-handled back into the saddle and the captain gave my horse a vicious yank, so that we were now very close.

'Try that again, Lovell and you are a dead man,' he hissed. 'Remember the bounty on you is the same amount – dead or alive.'

One of the men-at-arms glanced up at me.

'It is Lovell!' he shouted excitedly. 'The last time I saw him he was...'

His recollection was not to be relayed. In a lightning move, the captain jerked his foot out of the stirrup and kicked violently. There was a shriek of pain and the man-at-arms fell to his knees clutching his head.

The captain glared at the remaining men.

'Of course, this is Lovell,' he said savagely, 'but keep your stupid voices down. There has already been one attempt to rescue him and I do not want any more. Now, fall in around the prisoner.'

The sword jabbed my back again.

'Move it, Lovell!' my guard jeered softly.

I slumped down helplessly until we came to the west gate, where the captain signalled to the solitary guard squatting on the ground.

'Open the gate!' he commanded.

Unsteadily, the guard rose to his feet and peered at us.

'Who the hell are you?' he demanded belligerently. 'It's forbidden to open the gates before dawn.'

'God damn all peasants!'

The captain shouldered his horse forward, pulling me after him. His sword rose and fell and the guard slumped to the ground with a hollow thud. The captain gestured to the gate with his blood-stained sword.

'Open it!'

The five soldiers rushed forward to remove the heavy crossbar and pulled open the heavy wooden gate. To my surprise, Tudor's captain made no move to leave the city. Instead, he beckoned the soldiers to him. They obeyed his summons nervously.

The captain looked them up and down contemptuously.

'You're drunken fools and you know it!' he snapped. 'But as you are soldiers, for formality's sake listen to what I have to tell you and repeat it to your officer when he eventually emerges from his drunken stupor. Do you understand?'

His sword swept in front of them.

'I said – do you understand?' the captain asked menacingly.

There was a frightened murmur of assent. The captain smiled thinly.

'I doubt it, but no matter. Now, the prisoner Lovell was detected and apprehended while trying to escape from the abbey earlier tonight. Together with his fellow traitors, Sir Humphrey and Thomas Stafford, he was arrested. Is that all clear?'

The captain's sword glittered in the moonlight as he held it against the throat of one of the men-at-arms.

'I asked – is that clear?'

There were instant sounds of comprehension. Satisfied, the captain lifted his sword.

'Good. Now following a rescue attempt that killed five of my men, the two Stafford brothers managed to escape. Tell your officer to send word to the ports on the east coast, since the two traitors will have tried to reach there to escape to Burgundy. Tell them also that I have taken the most dangerous traitor, Lovell, to London.'

He lowered his sword as he looked at them.

'Now repeat all that!' he barked.

He listened to their incoherent mumble disdainfully.

'You're drunken scum!' he sneered. 'You'll never amount to anything, nor will that officer of yours. Tell him that, had he been sober, we would have shared Lovell's bounty. As it is, I'll get to keep it all to myself.'

There was a discreet cough from the guard behind me and the captain turned around.

'I'll see that you get something too,' he added, 'I'm going to need you to get Lovell to London.'

Then he paused and thought for a moment. His hand dug into his purse.

'You're all a shame to the profession' he snarled, 'but it's probably fair that you have something to drink with. Here, this is for your work tonight.'

With a vicious jerk to my wrists, the captain spurred his horse through the gates as the men-at-arms scrambled on the ground hunting for their share of the captain's coins.

We rode in silence for an hour or so. Finally, the captain pulled up on the bank of a stream.

'We'll water the horses,' he muttered.

I awkwardly dismounted and glared at him.

'Why did you hit me so hard?' I demanded.

Sir Humphrey Stafford's teeth gleamed in the moonlight as he started to remove his green and white tunic.

'I thought I better make it look realistic,' he said with relish.

He did have a point, though I thought he had overplayed the role a little.

'And why did you have to keep jabbing me in the back?' I asked Thomas.

He grinned.

'Same reason. Anyway, your plan worked. No-one's following us now.'

'Well they won't until they discover those four in the porter's lodge in the morning.'

'Were they four or five?' Thomas interrupted me.

'I thought there were three!' Humphrey boomed.

I sighed. While excellent bullies, the Stafford brothers were not overburdened with brains.

'There were four,' I explained patiently. 'The groom and the porter who we overpowered, and left bound and gagged after we had taken the horses from the abbey stable...'

'And then there were those two men-at-arms that Thomas and I knifed.' Humphrey Stafford finished my sentence triumphantly. 'Now let me see, that is, um, one, two... yes, you are right Lovell, there were four.'

I glanced up at the stars. I would need to plot my course north; I needed to be as far away as possible before daybreak. I ignored Thomas, who still seemed to be doing mental arithmetic and held up my wrists for Humphrey Stafford.

'Would you mind untying me?' I asked impatiently. 'We need to go our separate ways now.'

A few moments later, I was leading my horse alone through the darkened countryside in a northerly direction. It was cold but I was pleased with our escape and full of hope for the future. My revolt had begun.

CHAPTER 2

Yorkshire, 1486.

B ut three months later I had reason to doubt my optimism. Ahead of me the giant captain of archers, John Fennell, raised his hand. I halted and reached for my sword. There were the sounds of bows being notched. Fennell beckoned me forward.

'We'll be out of the forest in a moment, my lord,' he muttered.

I glanced around – sure enough, in front of us was a patch of light.

'There is a slight ridge after this wood,' Fennell went on. 'You might just be able to make out the city of York in the distance.'

'Alright. Tell the men to rest here while you and I scout ahead.'

He grunted in assent and we cautiously emerged into a clearing. There was indeed a ridge before us. We hiked our way to the top and surveyed the scene. The ground was thickly wooded. Occasional hamlets could be seen, and to my left grazing cattle indicated the presence of at least one farm. On the horizon, I thought I could just make out the city walls of York. Beside me Fennell stiffened.

'Enemy horsemen, my lord.'

I narrowed my eyes as I followed his pointed finger – a long way off I could discern tiny forms moving between the trees. He pointed again.

'Another group there, my lord – and another there.'

So Tudor had sent his scouts to look for us. Presumably he had rushed men up to York and they were now probing in a westerly direction to discover our position. By the look of things, they appeared to be advancing on a broad front.

'Do you want to retire, my lord?'

'Yes. Rejoin your men and I will be with you in a moment.'

Fennell nodded and moved down the slope as I moved behind a tree and waited for Tudor's outriders to come closer. With twenty or so archers firing from a partially concealed position, I would be able to inflict considerable damage. But then I stopped to think: what had I been reduced to? The men I was planning to ambush were not Tudor's main army or even a part of it; they were merely lightly armed scouts whom I could kill because I possessed the advantage of surprise. I was being vindictive. It was my bitterness and resentment alone that had led me to contemplate such a cowardly action, I realised. How had it come to this? I thought back to the time when I had returned to the North. The rebellion had spluttered out by the time I arrived, but I had moved around secretively and talked to men quietly. Soon I became convinced that it would take but a spark to reignite the blaze and make it burn so fiercely that it would be impossible to extinguish. I hoisted my colours of revolt and called on my followers to fan the flames of rebellion. Within a few weeks, I had over a thousand men.

All the while during this time I sent out messages; messages designed to win over the men of substance of the

North that reminded them of their past loyalty to our friend and leader, Richard of Gloucester. My words invited them to help right a terrible wrong by sweeping Tudor off his throne and replacing him with the lawful heir, the Earl of Warwick. I waited in anticipation, confident of their support, and still I waited. Incredulous at their lack of support, I despatched still more urgent summons commanding them to fight for their lawful king – commands which were duly ignored. I rounded on Thomas Broughton when he returned from delivering my instructions.

'What's the matter with them all?' I demanded. 'When I spoke to them only a few weeks ago they promised me both men and money, but now they are all just skulking away.'

My best friend pulled at his long, straggly beard and glanced uneasily at Edward Franke who stood beside me.

'I heard that they are all afraid,' Edward said heavily. 'They fear Tudor. Apparently he's threatening to move against us and they do not believe that our own force is strong enough to withstand him.'

'But their loyalty…'

'Counts for nothing!' barked Broughton.

I tightened my mouth at the thought of their cowardice. Broughton regarded me evenly.

'I would have to say that theirs is an opinion which both Edward and I now share, Francis.'

I reeled in amazement. I had known Broughton and Edward since we fought together in the West March and I had always valued their military acumen, but surely it was inconceivable that on this occasion their assessment was correct.

'You're misreading the situation here,' I protested.

Edward shook his head emphatically.

'We're not, Francis. Our own presence here owes more to loyalty to you rather than any conviction that we can win.'

'The same applies to most of our force,' Thomas agreed.

He plucked at his straggly beard and glanced up at me.

'By my reckoning it's time for you to repay that loyalty,' he said quietly. 'You see, Francis, you can't go on asking your men to sacrifice their lives in a war that they cannot hope to win.'

He paused for a moment.

'Why not have a think about it and Edward and I will come back later.'

I watched them go and sat down shakily. Was my revolt failing? There had been reverses admittedly and the recent attempt to kill Henry Tudor at York had not succeeded but I had always been optimistic of our venture's ultimate success. But how well-founded was my belief? I had not questioned it before as a leader who lacks confidence is a poor one. However, confronted by the candid opinions of my two friends, it was clearly time to do so. Unhappily I forced myself to make an honest appraisal of our chances of victory. It was several hours later that Broughton and Edward returned to my lonely campfire. Broughton eyed me quizzically.

'Have you seen sense yet?' he asked.

I spread my hands ruefully.

'You're right and I'm wrong,' I said simply.

Edward eyed me sympathetically.

'Well we tried and we failed, but we have to look forward. So what do you want to do now?'

I stared at him blankly. Having only just conceded that this particular rebellion was not going to work I had not thought of the next move against Tudor. Edward nodded when I told him that I had no plan.

'I don't suppose any of us do,' he admitted slowly. 'But there is one thought I've had, although I have no idea how feasible it would be.'

He fell silent and stared into the fire while Thomas and I waited patiently. At length Edward raised his head and smiled apologetically at the two of us.

'Can we just test out a theory of mine?' he asked. 'What would you say was the reason that our rebellion has not succeeded?'

'It's obvious,' Broughton quickly responded. 'Insufficient numbers joined us. Men weren't prepared to risk their lives and lands.'

'I think that we would all accept that,' agreed Edward. 'But now let us look at the deeper issue – was there one thing which might have swayed them sufficiently to take that risk?'

It was the same question I had asked myself earlier. As soon as I had come to the painful conclusion that our revolt was failing, I had gone on to try to see why men who might have joined us had not. There were a number of reasons of course, but by the evening I believed that I could identify the two major ones. The first was simple: there were simply not enough men in our force to start with. I had instigated a spontaneous revolt with my own followers as the nucleus of our army, but while I might have been satisfied with their numbers, clearly no one else had been. In their opinion my force was too paltry to risk supporting. With the benefit of hindsight I realised that I should have had a far greater army right at the outset of the revolt. Men who were sympathetic to my cause might have been tempted to join me had I had thousands before I approached them.

The second major reason why men had shied away from me was that I had no visible leader to display. My claim that

I intended to overthrow Henry Tudor and replace him with the Earl of Warwick had been received favourably but not sufficiently to make men join me. How much more impactive it would have been, I reflected, had I actually been able to show them the young Earl. The more I had brooded on this the more important the physical presence of the Earl of Warwick appeared. Had I been able to parade the young Earl about instead of just talking about him, I believed that support would have come flooding in. Confronted by the rightful heir to the throne, men would have been swayed by his impassioned appeals to their loyalty and seeing him in person would have brought back memories of their previous service to King Edward and Richard of Gloucester. Sentimentality might have played a part too, I had reflected. Warwick's youth and orphaned status would have given him a certain vulnerability which would have moved men and, in their emotional state, they would have thought less of their lives and their lands and more of where their duty lay.

I relayed my thoughts to Broughton and Edward. Thomas grunted agreement but Edward stroked his chin thoughtfully.

'That's interesting,' he said at last, 'I had not thought of the need to have a large body of troops before you start a revolt but I agree that it makes sense. I could not agree more with your point about having the Earl leading the army.'

'But that advantage is always denied to us,' Broughton pointed out. 'May I remind you that Henry Tudor had Warwick arrested immediately after Bosworth. Since then he has been incarcerated in the Tower of London.'

Thomas poked moodily at the spluttering fire.

'And since the Tower is impregnable we'll never get him out,' he continued. 'So we'll have to manage without him.'

Edward jerked his head up excitedly, his eyes gleaming.

'Not necessarily Thomas,' he said quickly.

He turned to me.

'Francis, as I said earlier, I have an idea which might or might not work. Will you allow me to try it? I will need to go away for a month or so.'

I had always trusted Edward.

'Of course.'

'So where shall I meet you?' Edward asked.

'How about my house in Cumberland?' Broughton proposed. 'It's quiet and discrete so we can plan our next attempt in secret.'

Broughton Hall would be an excellent venue and such was Thomas' influence in the region that his men would ensure that no spy of Henry Tudor's could get close.

'Do you want to go there now?' I asked. 'It will take me a while to disband our force since they are widely scattered, but I'll join you there afterwards.'

'And I'll come to Broughton Hall when I return from the South,' Edward added.

That conversation had taken place three weeks ago and it was time for me to move on from this minor skirmish. I gestured to Fennell,

'We'll retire and pay off the remaining troops now.' I told him.

We returned to camp and I thanked them for their service before riding on to Broughton Hall. For the hundredth time I wondered what Edward was planning.

'A pretender!'

Broughton smiled at my astonishment as he nudged his pretty young wife.

'Only Edward could have come up with that idea,' he murmured.

Marguerite smiled back at him.

'It is a brilliant idea, isn't it? It's not as if we can get the real Earl out of the Tower, so we have no choice.'

'What's so brilliant about it?' I demanded. 'Marguerite, we can't use someone to impersonate the Earl of Warwick!'

Her fiery temperament rose to my challenge.

'Why not?'

I looked at her in exasperation.

'Because he would look nothing like the real Earl,' I explained patiently.

I expected her to argue, but unexpectedly she smiled.

'What exactly does the Earl of Warwick look like, Francis?' she asked sweetly.

I stared at her. It had been some time since I had seen him of course and, frankly, one small boy is pretty much like another.

Marguerite's smile grew a little wider.

'He's like his father,' I blustered. 'Tall and fair-haired. Come to think of it, he has blue eyes too.'

'Actually he's short, brown-haired and has hazel eyes,' Edward corrected me. 'By the way Thomas, how old is he?'

'Um... about twelve or thirteen?'

'Closer to ten in reality.'

Edward paused for a moment and looked round the table commandingly.

'Let us agree on two points,' he said. 'Firstly, do we all concur that we need a visible leader?'

We nodded in unison.

'Then the issue of what our pretender looks like is irrelevant,' Edward continued. 'As you have just demonstrated, very few people know what the real Earl looks like.'

I nodded, carefully ignoring Marguerite's eye.

'Our own endorsement of the boy will count for a great deal,' Thomas volunteered. 'Mind you, the snag is that everyone knows the Earl of Warwick is locked away.'

Edward narrowed his eyes.

'I've been thinking about that. It seems best if we fabricate a story about how he escaped from the Tower.'

'But what happens when Tudor shows off his prisoner?' Marguerite objected.

'We will say that the boy with Henry Tudor is a fake,' Edward said calmly, 'and that we have the genuine item.'

Edward's words carried conviction but there was one major element of his plan that I did not like at all, namely the length of time it would take to transform a normal boy into a plausible pretender. Indeed the more I thought about it the harder the potential transformation seemed since the sons of nobility are raised so differently to those of others from ordinary stock. There would be months, if not years, of training before our young lad could act and speak convincingly. Also, the boy would need to know about the real Earl of Warwick's family and the Earl's own childhood and that was not going to be an easy matter either. I explained my concerns to the others. Edward shot me a triumphant look.

'If we were only just starting to train our pretender I could not agree with you more,' he said. 'It would take two or three years at least to make the lad plausible and in that time Henry Tudor would build up his power even more.

But in this case the situation is very different.'

'How so?' I demanded.

'In this instance we have a head start, Francis. You see the pretender we will be using begun his training over two years ago when Richard of Gloucester was King.'

The stunned silence was broken at last by Broughton.

'But why was the boy being trained to be the Earl of Warwick in 1484?' he asked. 'At that time people either supported King Richard or Henry Tudor. There were no other candidates for your loyalty.'

'If I had not prevented it there might just have been a third,' Edward replied slowly. 'You see the boy who was being used in '84 was not being trained to impersonate the Earl of Warwick. The aim was rather to use him to play the role of King Edward's younger son...'

'One of the Princes who was murdered in the Tower of London,' Marguerite interrupted excitedly.

'Precisely,' Edward concluded.

I reeled in amazement. There had been all sorts of rumours flying about after the deaths of the two princes. Men had mostly spoken of them being killed but others had claimed that one – if not both – had escaped. Well clearly someone had sought to profit from those rumours and somehow Edward had latched onto him.

'Let's hear your story then, Edward.'

Edward's blue eyes met mine.

'But a question for you first, Francis. Do you remember where I was sent to be the sheriff after Buckingham's revolt?'

Once again I thought back. After Buckingham had so disloyally turned against Richard of Gloucester, he had rebelled. His revolt had failed of course, but it brought home to our regime how unpopular Richard was in the

South. Under the circumstances, a great many crown officials there were replaced by loyal northerners.

'Of course I do,' I told Edward. 'You were sheriff of Oxfordshire and Broughton here went to Cornwall.'

'I did,' Broughton recalled. 'Mind you, Francis, I'm not sure that I did much good there. The local people viewed me as a complete outsider and had as little to do with me as possible. To find out what was going on, I needed to use paid informers.'

'I had to do the same,' Edward concurred. 'In fact that is how the priest Symonds and his protégé, John Verney, came to my notice. There were a couple of snippets that I picked up on and I got my people to investigate. After a little while I discovered what Symonds was up to.'

'So what did you do?' Broughton asked.

'I warned the priest off,' Edward replied. 'To my mind treason was probably being planned but the fact was that it had not actually taken place. Since the rumours of the fate of the Princes were dying down it wouldn't have made any sense to restart the whole business by arresting Symonds and the young boy.'

'So that's why you went south again. Did you find the priest Symonds?' Marguerite asked eagerly.

Edward drew himself up proudly.

'Indeed I did. He was still at Oxford. I have agreed a deal with him and we'll get a first rate pretender. Young John already acts and looks the part of a young noble, so all we have to do is to teach him about his family.'

'Where are Symonds and the boy now?' Broughton wanted to know.

'On their way here,' Edward replied. 'I thought you would want to see them for yourselves.'

It was amazing to reflect how much Edward had achieved in so little time. It looked now as if we had a visible leader.

'There's more,' Edward announced. 'After I left Oxford I went to visit your friend, the Abbot of our Lady in Abingdon.'

'He's your friend too!'

Edward shook his head with a smile.

'John Sante has known you for much longer. He's forever telling me about all the occasions when you've helped him.'

Then it was my turn to smile as I remembered the kindly white-haired Abbot who had always been so good to me.

'Is John Sante still as short-sighted as ever?' I asked Edward. 'I believe that the last time I saw him was just before Bosworth.'

'He is,' said Edward, 'but he manages enough. Anyway he knows that you are well and he is eager to help you in whatever way he can.'

I glanced up excitedly. John Sante had access to funds and many powerful friends within the church.

'He will be a considerable help to us,' I told Edward. 'Thank you for everything you've done.'

Edward waved away my words.

'It was nothing,' he demurred, 'but now let us move onto the second thing that we need to begin a revolt...'

'Thousands of troops from the outset!' growled Broughton. 'Just like Tudor had before Bosworth.'

He turned to me.

'You've had a month to think about it Francis, so what's your plan?'

I had indeed had sufficient time to outline my strategy for overthrowing Henry Tudor and after this recent discussion it was all looking more substantial.

'My plan is the same as it was after Bosworth,' I told Thomas. 'I will go to Burgundy and enlist the help of the Duchess. After all, as sister of both King Edward and King Richard, her sympathies are bound to be for the House of York. With her help I will get mercenaries to serve as a nucleus for our new army.'

Broughton nodded.

'Burgundy has always been sympathetic to the House of York so it seems sensible to try them. But how many troops will you look to get from Burgundy, Francis, and what type?'

'I want about five thousand pikemen.'

He whistled softly.

'Tudor's men have never faced a block of men wielding eighteen-foot long weapons. They will be slaughtered.'

'So what do you want Thomas and I to do?' Edward asked. 'Do we come with you?'

It would have been comforting to have travelled together but there was more than enough work for the two of them here so I shook my head.

'Not on this occasion. It would be useful if you could prepare the ground in the North. Talk to people who you know and trust and tell them that next year the Earl of Warwick will come in person to claim his natural inheritance. Tell them that he will be backed by a large army and that the venture is well funded.'

'Are you referring to the Abbot, John Sante?'

'I am, Edward. He knows you and trusts you. Take him into your confidence as our plan develops and he'll ensure that we get what we need.'

'As soon as we know when you are coming we can prepare supply points and mustering areas,' Edward added.

'We'll have to secure the landing point first,' Thomas added dryly.

I glanced at the two of them.

'We'll keep in touch by confidential messengers. Do you have any questions?'

They shook their heads, but, having fallen silent during the discussion on military matters, Marguerite leaned forward to speak.

'It is not a question but rather a suggestion,' she began. 'Do you want the pretender John Verney to come to Burgundy?'

I had not thought about it but of course it made perfect sense. The Duchess Margaret would know more about her brother Clarence's family than anyone.

'That's an excellent idea,' I congratulated her. 'The Duchess of Burgundy can train up her pretend nephew.'

Marguerite grinned at me.

'Not only that but if you get her to swear that the pretender really is her nephew Warwick, no one will accept that Henry Tudor's prisoner in the Tower is anything but a fake.'

It was a brilliant idea and I said so.

'So one way or the other it does not matter whether the pretender looks like the real Earl of Warwick,' Marguerite concluded wickedly.

I inwardly winced but after a moment joined in the general roar of laughter.

CHAPTER 3

Burgundy, 1486.

I estimated I was still a few miles from Malines when I saw a small number of horsemen approaching. I cautiously moved my hand to grasp my sword but then relaxed as I recognised their leader, Thomas David. We greeted each other warmly, as I had not seen him since we had fought the French together at Guineagate. With a smile, he explained that my messenger had arrived in Burgundy and that the Duchess Margaret had instructed him to watch out for my arrival.

'Instructed?' I asked curiously.

'I am in the service of the Duchess. I was in the Calais garrison at the time of Bosworth. I would not serve Henry Tudor and refused to take the oath, so I was ejected from the garrison. Two hundred others joined me, so now the Duchess supports us along with a number of others who fled here after Bosworth.'

'Will you take me straight to the Duchess?' I asked eagerly.

Thomas David shook his head.

'I'm a soldier, my lord, not a courtier. But I know that there is a special way of doing things here. "Protocol" they call it. I'll take you to the house of Sir Richard Harliston; he will explain the way they operate.'

We chatted about other matters until we approached Malines. It was a large walled city and Thomas insisted that we rode round it, so I could gain an idea of its strength. It was an impressive town, with strong walls protected by a moat.

'There are twelve gates, my lord. This one is the Brussels Gate. Just look at the strength of those two towers.'

I followed as he slowly pushed his horse through the throng of people in the corn market. Eventually we arrived in a large market square and I looked up in awe at a large church. Thomas David followed my gaze.

'That's St Rombout's Cathedral. They are still working on the spire, which is why it looks odd, but when it's finished it will be the tallest in the world. Now let me take you to Sir Richard's house as you will be lodging with him.'

I pondered about Sir Richard Harliston as Thomas' men led our horses through the busy streets. I had never met him, of course; he had served as the Governor of Jersey these past twenty years but I knew him to be a devoted servant of the House of York. It was presumably that loyalty which made it impossible for him to accept Henry Tudor as his King and explained his presence in Burgundy.

My favourable view of him was strengthened within minutes of our arrival and it was easy to see why the Duchess Margaret had decided to make use of him. Harliston's commanding height, piercing blue eyes and white hair gave him a natural air of authority; he was knowledgeable and pleasantly spoken. He explained that he would be serving as the intermediary between the court of the Duchess and myself.

'But why?' I asked naively. 'Why can I not tell her myself what I need?'

He shook his white head slowly.

'They do things a special way here, my lord. There are rules and protocol that govern all aspects of court life and diplomacy.'

He followed this statement with a brief lecture on the pomp of the Court of Burgundy, which had reached its apotheosis under Duchess Margaret's father-in-law, Duke Philip. However, even Harliston admitted that the ceremonial aspect of court life was excessive and the laws of etiquette which governed it were at times absurd.

'Why, every time the Duchess' late husband, Charles, dined it was a state occasion,' he remarked with a laugh. 'Food and drink were all brought in in a solemn procession. The cup bearer had to hold the Duke's jewelled drinking vessel up in the air so that he wouldn't pollute the wine with his breath and when the food was finally presented, six physicians who were in attendance advised the Duke what meat would be especially suitable for him that day.'

He chuckled gently.

'Of course the Duchess Margaret has brought all her dead husband's rules and regulations to her little court in Malines, which explains why she wishes me to act as an intermediary.'

'So what is her current thinking?' I probed.

Harliston narrowed his eyes.

'Favourable to you, I would have said. The Duchess fears that since the French backed Henry Tudor at the time of Bosworth, it will not be too long before both England and France threaten Burgundy.'

'Well that, as well as the Earl of Warwick being her nephew, should make her support a certainty.'

Harliston shook his head.

'Until I came to know the Duchess, I would have agreed

with you instantly but she is a complex character and follows governing principles in her life and policies. Her overwhelming aim is to maintain the total independence of Burgundy; she would do nothing to jeopardise that. She will not for instance instigate actions that would cause her larger neighbour France to invade. Nor would she wish to have England as an enemy.'

'But with the Earl of Warwick on the throne of England she would have a friendly ally.'

'Assuming you succeed. If she backs you and you fail, you will have upset Henry Tudor, who may wish to have revenge on Burgundy, together with his ally France. The second principle that dominates her thinking is religion,' continued Harliston. 'She firmly believes that God will help to direct her thinking in all things.'

'So when can we start negotiations?' I asked.

Harliston pursed his lips.

'I have a lot to do in order to prepare the ground first. In the meantime, have a look at Malines. The city is full of lawyers but the cathedral is beautiful. Did you know that when the spire is completed it will be the tallest in the world?'

Throughout July and most of August, Harliston and I were subjected to a number of fairly intense interrogations. The Duchess' financial man, Hippolyte de Bertuz, conducted them mostly. There were others too, whose names I forget now, but I grew tired of the repetitive nature of the Burgundian questioning.

'Is this their normal way of conducting affairs?' I asked

Harliston as we made our way back from the palace one day. 'We seem to be achieving absolutely nothing.'

He thought for a while as we approached the bustling market square.

'I would say that your plan interests them deeply but remember that they have to be certain that you will succeed; they cannot afford to antagonise the French or Henry Tudor, so we will just have to be patient. The work on the spire seems to be coming on. Do you know that when it's finished it will be...'

'... the tallest in the world,' I finished his sentence. 'By the look of things I'll probably still be here when they complete it.'

But this was not to be the case. A few weeks later the Burgundian terms were presented. The Duchess Margaret was prepared to publicly acknowledge the young pretender as her nephew, Edward Earl of Warwick, and his training could be completed at her court. Additionally Burgundy would fund the costs of two thousand mercenaries for the campaign and had sent messengers to the Irish so that they could contribute troops towards the downfall of the common enemy. Finally, the Duchess would send secret envoys to well-wishing churchmen, such as John Sante, and she would invite her nephew John, Earl of Lincoln, to come to Burgundy to join the venture.

After such a long period of waiting, to receive all of this news in one simple statement was slightly bewildering. On the downside, the number of Burgundian troops was less than I had requested, but then I had not thought of involving the Irish. On the upside, the Duchess' endorsement of our pretender was very welcome, particularly also as she had persuaded her nephew, John of

Lincoln to join our army. Lincoln's royal blood and connections would add weight to the cause and his men would swell our numbers.

But there was more. Lincoln's defection would prove hugely embarrassing to Henry Tudor. After all, the Earl of Warwick was Lincoln's cousin and Lincoln knew him well. As a result, everyone would believe that Lincoln was joining us because he knew that our pretender was in reality the true Earl of Warwick.

'How well do you know Lincoln?' Harliston asked later as we reviewed the Burgundian terms.

'Reasonably well. We served together when Richard of Gloucester was King. Lincoln's no soldier of course but, in many other respects, he is like his Uncle Richard.'

Harliston nodded thoughtfully.

'His rank does however entitle him to lead our army,' he said delicately.

'Of course it does, but in reality I'll be advising him.'

Harliston gave a relieved smile and our talk drifted onto military matters and the likely calibre of the Irish troops.

'Men say that they are not very good,' I admitted, 'although I don't suppose anyone really knows much about them.'

Harliston made a note.

'I'll try and find out more,' he said. 'By the way, it is excellent news about the Duchess Margaret using her influence with sympathetic churchmen in England, isn't it? That will be a real bonus in terms of wages and supplies, won't it?'

It certainly would, but what had truly impressed me was the scale of the Duchess's influence among the prelates in England. One name in particular had caught my attention.

'I didn't know that the Duchess knew Abbot John

Sante,' I remarked. 'He's a friend of mine and I have already involved him in the plot.'

Harliston fell silent as he thought about it.

'It's a coincidence but a fortunate one,' he said at last. 'I heard that the good Abbot visited the Duchess a few years ago and was greatly moved by her piety. It seems that the pair of them have been in constant communication on ecclesiastical matters ever since. It is good however that both of you know him. After all, if John Sante is already working hard for you, he will redouble his efforts once he hears from his spiritual ally, the Duchess Margaret.'

That sounded encouraging, but then another thought struck me.

'What did you think of the Burgundian idea to give our venture a coded name?'

Harliston laughed.

'The Symbol of Lambert? It's a bit fanciful but Tudor's got spies in Burgundy so it's probably sensible.'

His lips twitched mischievously.

'Mind you, if, like you, Tudor's spies have no idea that St Lambert is Burgundy's favourite saint it's probably more than sensible. In fact it's positively inspired. None of them will decipher the code name.'

I flushed and decided to change the subject.

'So what happens now that we have an agreement? Do I go to Bruges to secure my troops?'

'No.'

The sharp reply was at variance with his normal emollient style and I stared at him in consternation. Harliston hastened to explain.

'If the protocol of Burgundian diplomacy runs true to form then it is now that you face the hardest part,' he said grimly. 'You see, Francis, up until now Duchess Margaret has been working behind the scenes. The people we have been dealing with are her agents, reflecting her doubts and passing on her queries, but now it will all climax in a private meeting between you and the Duchess. Convince her of your sincerity and the agreement goes ahead, but if you can't then you will get nothing.'

I had believed that all negotiations had been satisfactorily concluded and said as much. Harliston narrowed his eyes.

'They may yet be Francis. But it is all down to you and the Duchess Margaret now.'

For all Harliston's talk of the importance of the meeting, I found the Duchess's library a gloomy place. The thick dust on the leaded windows did little to illuminate the heavy wooden panelling which provided a backdrop to innumerable crucifixes. Solid tomes rested on the shelves, save one which was laid open on the table. Predictably it turned out to be an illustrated Bible. I glanced with curiosity at the only picture on the walls. It depicted a young-looking man dressed in black with tousled hair. The only bright colour in the picture was the man's gold chain. I guessed that this was the late Duke Charles, Margaret's husband.

The sound of footsteps outside announced the arrival of the Duchess, her financial agent Hippolyte and a priest. Upon entering the library, Hippolyte quickly summarised the major points of the agreement, which I swore to uphold. Satisfied, he rolled up his scroll and gestured to the cleric. They both bowed deeply as they withdrew.

I glanced at Margaret, Duchess of Burgundy with interest. My initial impression was that she was tall and fair-haired and seemed to resemble in height her brothers Clarence and Edward more than Richard of Gloucester. I swallowed nervously, for while all three brothers had been shrewd and astute I had never seen on their faces the cold, calculating look which I saw on their sister's now.

The meeting began. There were matters to be discussed, the Duchess explained, for which no witnesses should be present. Nor, she added, would I refer to our conversation with anyone else.

'Of course, my lady.'

'Good. Now you must understand also that ever since my brother King Edward gave me away to be the bride of Duke Charles, I have come to love my new country. Indeed, perhaps love is a wholly insufficient word, since I have realised that it is my divine duty to protect Burgundy against its more powerful neighbour, France.'

Her hand slowly stroked the plain gold cross that she wore as she looked at her long dead husband.

'Had he lived longer, no doubt the Duke would have dealt with the French but since God in His wisdom has seen fit to take him to lead the armies of Heaven, it falls to those who are left behind to carry on this divine duty on earth.'

'Of course, my lady.'

She favoured me with a sour smile.

'So you will naturally agree that it is essential that at all times England should help to protect Burgundy?'

Harliston had warned me about this and I had my answer ready.

'Assuming that we are successful, my lady, it would be in England's interest to ally with Burgundy. But obviously once we have put the Earl of Warwick on the throne, his council would need to draw up a proper treaty.'

'And the new king's council will be strongly influenced by what you and my nephew Lincoln tell them?'

'I believe so.'

Still caressing her little gold cross, the Duchess moved over to stand below her husband's portrait. She gazed at him in silence as if she was seeking guidance or inspiration.

I waited until she was ready.

'Then let us reach an agreement, Lovell. In return for my help now and in the future, both you and the Earl of Lincoln will swear at all times to do all that you can do to support Burgundy.'

Harliston had cautioned me about this. I remembered his words:

'It's a favourite tactic of the Duchess, Francis. The Burgundians will sign an agreement and then, at the last moment, she'll make an extra demand. If you don't accept it, they will tear up the original agreement.'

There was too much at stake.

'I accept and will swear the oath.'

Her long white fingers continued to play with her cross.

'You will have cause to regret it were you ever to break your oath.'

I looked at her angrily.

'If it wasn't for my oath to your brother Richard I would have no cause to be here today. I don't break oaths.'

She smiled thinly.

'That is possibly true. And from what I hear you are honest so I will not dwell on the matter. Now onto more agreeable matters; tell me what you know about St Rombout?'

In spite of the solemnity of the occasion, the commonplace

answer about the potential height of the cathedral's spire sprung mischievously to mind but wisely I did not voice it.

'Very little I fear, my lady.'

'St Rombout was one of the early Irish monks, a great man of God and a zealous missionary. He came to bring Christianity here long ago and is buried in the cathedral.'

She picked up a small wooden box and passed it to me.

'In the box is one of the saint's bones. You will take it to our allies in Ireland. The relic will serve as a token of our common links that go back centuries.'

'I need to see about organising my troops first,' I told her, 'but thank you for your backing in this venture.'

She made no response but signalled for me to depart as once again she moved over to commune with her long dead husband.

Ignoring the noise from the street below, I frowned at the blank parchment. This would be my final message to Thomas Broughton and it was essential that I provided him with the information that he and Edward Franke required.

I reviewed what I needed to tell them. The first and most obvious point concerned the landing site. It had always been my strategy to begin the campaign in the North of England where our supporters were more numerous, but until the Irish involvement had been mooted, it had been my intention to land on the east coast. Now of course it was self-evident that we would need to sail to Dublin and collect the Irish troops and land on the west coast, probably in Cumberland since it would be easy for Broughton to secure a beachhead in his own area of influence.

Satisfied I moved onto the question of timing. If all went smoothly I saw no reason why we could not be in England in May. That said, the voyage could be disrupted by bad weather so it would be more prudent to indicate June and send a more definitive estimate of our landing date once we had arrived in Ireland.

I pondered on the other points to include in my missive until at last I reached for a pen and started to write.

A couple of hours later I sat back satisfied. Presently both Thomas and Edward would be fully aware of both the strategy and the timings. Equally importantly they would know what was expected from them in terms of supplies and equipment. But had I been sufficiently explicit? Their roles were crucial and we could afford no mistakes. I pulled the parchment towards me and started to read the relevant sections.

I would add, Thomas, that their leader is known to you already. No doubt you will recall Martin Swartz from the last time we fought here. With regard to the numbers to be supplied I confirm that I will be bringing out of Burgundy a force of not less than two thousand, two hundred. Of these, the majority will be pikemen. Since they cannot march carrying their pikes it is essential that you provide carts for the pikes as well as for their supplies. As well as these, Swartz will be bringing gunners and his shock troops whom he calls his Berserkers.

Thomas would not have forgotten Swartz; of that I was certain. He, like I, had been amazed by the intellect he had displayed prior to Guineagate. Indeed, had it not been for his remarkable powers of perception the French plan would have succeeded and the Burgundians would have been defeated.

To that which you already know about Swartz I would add that he has used the intervening years to build up considerable experience and I consider us fortunate to have gained the services of such a professional captain. To come now to the Irish contingent: I expect them to number around four thousand. Contrary to my previously held belief, it would appear that in the main they are of reasonable quality with their elite warriors rather grandly referred to as the 'Fraternity of Arms'.

Thomas would find that last part amusing, I reflected. Equally he would have been reassured since like me he would have heard adverse stories of the Irish military capability. Yet Harliston's report had been reassuring. The Irish troops in the main were not wholly dissimilar to their English counterparts with only the poorly armed Irish kerns being of a noticeably lesser quality. I turned back to the letter.

Their light cavalry is unusual in as much as they do not use spears, preferring instead to employ bows and arrows. Thus it is that they do not charge directly at the enemy but rather fire at them and wheel away. I hope to secure at least three hundred of these but they will require mounts once we arrive in England.

It would be simpler to provide horses for the Irish cavalry in England rather than shipping them over the Irish sea and Dick Middleton could probably arrange this when he bought his Carlisle horse volunteers down to join the army. I chewed my lip thoughtfully. All told, we would probably have a reasonably potent cavalry force.

And so, on to what Thomas and Edward needed to do. I pulled the parchment closer to me.

Accordingly I expect to land in England with over six thousand men. The force is overall a strong one although we will be short of archers. This deficit, I believe, can be easily made up in England although I would ask you to pay it special attention. It is also essential that you and Edward prepare mustering and supply points between Cumberland and York so that we can enhance our strength before we swing south to confront Tudor.

I skimmed through the rest of the letter and sat back satisfied; I knew that Thomas and Edward would not fail me. By my reckoning we probably had a larger force than Tudor had when he had invaded England and, with Swartz's pikemen, we probably had troops of a better calibre. Moreover, unlike Tudor, who had not attracted much support after he had landed in Wales, I knew that our numbers would swell as we advanced on York since we had eradicated the causes of our previous failure. With the presence of the young Symbol of Lambert, we had a visible leader and our numbers would be sufficiently great to give men confidence to join the force that Lincoln, Harliston and I would bring to England.

Idly I traced a circle over where Richard's ring hung on my chest. If all went as I expected, in a few short weeks Tudor would be defeated and the young Earl of Warwick would be England's King. And I would have honoured my promise.

CHAPTER 4

Cumberland, 1487.

Broughton had done his work extraordinarily well. By occupying Piel Castle he had ensured good protection for the seasick troops as they staggered ashore. To secure the landing area further, he had posted sentries in all directions while, on the beach, his men stood ready to help the newcomers towards the blazing fires.

I sniffed the air keenly. Already the smell of roasting meat was cutting through the salty tang.

'That was clever of you, Thomas,' I told him. 'Everyone will feel better once they have eaten.'

He nodded agreement.

'You'll find that once we move off this bridgehead that everything has been arranged,' he said. 'Edward Franke has organised all the other mustering and supply points along the way to York.'

He broke off, his eyes widening in amazement.

'Who in hell's name is that?'

I followed the direction of his finger. The Irish were splashing ashore now and in the fore was the gigantic Thomas Fitzgerald.

'That's Fitzgerald. He commands the Irish troops.'

'God help anyone who has to face him in battle,'

Broughton grunted. 'So, what's he like?'

'He's good, Thomas. A bit unimaginative perhaps, but he's shrewd enough and his men respect him.'

Broughton nodded thoughtfully and then his lips twitched.

'I suppose you could say that he's our biggest asset then.'

I groaned and in companionable silence we watched the long files of infantry scrunch their way up the beach. As more and more passed us, I felt my spirits soar. Not only had the army landed safely and intact but more men were waiting to join us. I smiled as I envisaged our ever-growing numbers advancing unopposed to York. As usual Broughton sensed my thoughts.

'We'll get plenty more recruits there,' he said easily. 'All of York is certain to support Gloucester's heir.'

'Of course. And when they do it will be time to turn south and confront Tudor,' I agreed.

Thomas grinned as he contemplated the forthcoming battle.

'You've no objection if Marguerite comes along with us?' he asked suddenly.

I blinked in astonishment. It was unconventional, to say the least, to take one's wife on campaign.

'Why?'

Broughton's foot dug a furrow in the pebbles.

'She claims I'm neglecting her;' he said awkwardly, 'particularly over the past few months.'

I stirred guiltily. Broughton had been working tirelessly to ensure the safe arrival of the army in England and the fact that we were now on shore was testament to his efforts.

'So she wants to accompany me,' Broughton continued. 'She sees this as a great adventure.'

It went against my better judgement but Broughton's

love for his young French wife was legendary and I was not prepared to be the cause of further strife between them.

'Of course she can come with us,' I told Thomas.

He nodded in a relieved way.

'I thought she could help on the translating side,' he suggested.

I thought briefly. Some of the mercenary officers spoke French but, with the exception of Martin Swartz, none spoke English.

'That's an excellent idea,' I said. 'Now let us go and see if Edward Franke's preparations are as good as yours.'

They were very thorough and our numbers swelled as we advanced towards York. Among the first to join us was my boyhood friend, Dick Middleton, together with a sizeable contingent of the Carlisle horse. I embraced him warmly and mingled happily with his troopers, pleased to recall familiar faces from my time in the West March. Dick smiled as he indicated his cavalry's ostentatious saddle cloths.

'They are wearing those to remind you of the time when you commanded us there,' he explained.

My own men had converged on Bedale and it was from there that my former steward brought them. Typically conscientious, Rowland Robinson had ensured that they were exceptionally well provisioned.

'Although, given that we are now so close to York, I'm not sure that it was necessary to bring so much,' Rowland admitted.

He glanced round our teeming camp.

'So how many of us are there, my lord?'

'About ten thousand.'

Rowland's heavy features creased into a smile.

'And that's before we get the men from York. I can't say that I envy Henry Tudor.'

I grinned back at him.

'Nor do I Rowland.'

Our optimism proved to be ill-placed. That very evening we received news of the worse possible sort. Contrary to all expectations, the City of York would neither support us nor would it grant us access. It was a crushing blow. York had been fiercely loyal to Richard when he ruled the North as Duke of Gloucester and after when he became King Richard III. Not for a moment had anyone believed that the city would not support his heir. However clearly the city's Mayor and Aldermen were afraid of Henry Tudor and municipal self-interest had prevailed over what should have been natural loyalty. Not only had we been denied a fertile recruiting ground but the chance to replenish our supplies had been snatched from us. But there was little time to brood on York's treachery. Our strategy had to be reconsidered and quickly. I was still weighing up our options when still more bad news arrived: there were hostile troops now in York. Once I heard this I immediately joined the crowded throng in Lincoln's tent.

'Lord Clifford is already in York with his horsemen,' Dick Middleton reported breathlessly. 'On top of that, the Earl of Northumberland is moving south with another three thousand.'

Lincoln looked at me anxiously.

'What should we do, Francis?'

I ignored the babble of shouted suggestions. The key thrust of our strategy was to advance on Tudor and force battle upon him before he could muster all his support. Any other proposals, therefore, whether for an assault on York or an attack on the Earl of Northumberland, were time-wasting diversions.

'We'll break camp immediately,' I snapped. 'Forget about York. We'll by-pass the city and head south as quickly as we can.'

I saw hesitation in Fitzgerald's eyes, but Swartz rose to stand next to me.

'It is essential to reach Tudor as quickly as possible,' he said quietly but firmly. 'We must march quickly and attempt to throw both Clifford and Northumberland off our tail.'

★ ★ ★

Clifford's horsemen could move faster than our lumbering army though. Two days later a distraught Fitzgerald reported that one of his Irish foraging parties had been cut up by Clifford's men. Some had been killed immediately, but the rest had not been so lucky. Thinking to celebrate Trinity Sunday in a novel manner, Clifford had rounded up the survivors and forced them to kneel with their necks exposed. Each was then executed by three blows of a blunted sword.

The news of the massacre drove the army berserk. So incandescent were the Irish that it took all of Fitzgerald's authority to prevent them from abandoning the campaign altogether and hurling themselves on Clifford. But while

Fitzgerald eventually persuaded his men to resume their march south, I knew that for the sake of their motivation I would need to deal with Clifford. I wanted Broughton's ideas to discuss how we might achieve this, but he seemed to have hidden himself away. It was odd that I rarely saw him these days. Failing to find him, I took the problem to Martin Swartz. Unsurprisingly, he agreed on the need to crush Clifford. Additionally he pointed out that the immediate proximity of enemy horsemen was impeding the progress of the army.

'Coming to the greater issue of morale,' Swartz continued, 'I believe that it is essential that you personally lead the attack on Clifford's men. Our troops will want to know that you feel so strongly about the massacre that you see the need to involve yourself. Secondly use the Irish for the attack. Was it not the Irish kerns that Clifford attacked?

'Yes. But how do lightly armed infantry attack cavalry?'

'At night. Get Middleton to find out where Clifford is camped and hit them when they are resting.'

We talked together some more and then I left him. As I rode back along the sprawling column to find Fitzgerald, I was amused to see Broughton's wife, Marguerite, riding on a cart next to the Swiss troops. She seemed to have become a particular favourite among them. She waved gaily as I cantered past.

'Clifford is based four miles east of us,' I told Thomas Fitzgerald that evening. 'He's made camp next to the river. It's a strong defensive point because the river curves sharply there which is probably why originally someone built a castle there.'

'On which side of the river has he placed his men? Is it possible to cross the river there?' asked Fitzgerald.

'The south side and Dick Middleton reported that the water is too deep to be crossed.'

Fitzgerald grunted.

'That makes it harder. But tell me Francis, why does Swartz recommend that we use the kerns for the attack? Why do we have to use the worst troops in the army?'

'Because a victory by the kerns will boost them immensely. Men mock them now because they have no armour and poor weapons. But I doubt that they will laugh at them when the kerns are marching along wearing Clifford's men's armour and brandishing their captured swords.'

Fitzgerald nodded in reluctant agreement.

'But how do we get past Clifford's sentries?' he asked. 'He'll suspect that we are camped nearby. He'll have an outer cordon of guards and an inner one. The alarm would be sounded before we could get close,' he glanced up at the pale disc in the blue sky, 'particularly as it is a full moon tonight.'

'We'll need to create a diversion,' I told him. 'Clifford's men need to be facing the other way when we attack.'

Fitzgerald glanced at me keenly.

'So what is your plan?'

I scowled because I had been unable to think of one.

'I hoped that between us we could come up with something.'

'We are going to have to!' Fitzgerald exploded. 'No one in their right mind would launch a night attack on a cautious enemy under the light of a full moon without one. An attack incidentally which you insist is to be carried out by the worst troops in the army and in a few hours' time. It will be a disaster unless Clifford's men are distracted.'

A number of men nearby turned curiously at the sound of his raised voice and conscious of this, Fitzgerald shrugged apologetically.

'Let's sit down quietly and see if we can come up with something,' he suggested.

I did so and let my mind tease at the problem. The biggest issue, of course, was the river which guarded nearly three quarters of Clifford's camp and was too deep to cross. Given that obstacle, it followed that we could only attack Clifford from the south. But how to create a diversionary attack when you can only approach the enemy from one direction? I worried at the question but could find no plausible solution. I looked round the Irish camp moodily. Someone was playing a pipe and a number of soldiers were gathering to listen. Some traders were selling food and drink. The women, however, were selling other things.

'We need a diversion before we attack,' Fitzgerald observed somewhat obviously.

I rubbed my hands and waited expectantly for his suggestion but none came. We relaxed back into silence. We must have sat there for some time, lost in thought, before the sound of shouting roused me. I glanced up; there were many camp followers gathered now. I guessed that most of the whores from York had arrived on site. Indeed, there seemed to be too many of them, as they were competing fiercely among themselves for the available soldiers.

One such conflict was going on close to where the piper was trying to play. Shouting between a pair of girls had degenerated into a scrap and the crowd started bellowing raucous encouragement. This continued for a few moments before a grinning officer hurled a large bucket of water over both women to quieten them. The women had not been overdressed before being drenched in water, so the effect of being soaked only made their natural contours more apparent and both were propositioned quickly.

Then I stopped and smiled broadly. I prodded Fitzgerald, who was either asleep or deep in thought. I gestured at the women.

'They are the diversion we need.'

He thought about it.

'It wouldn't work,' he grunted; 'It's too obvious. Anyway, even Clifford's sentries would not be tempted by that crowd of drabs when they see them close at hand.'

'But they won't be close at hand!' I protested, getting up quickly.

He frowned and then, after I explained the plan, he began to laugh. He was still chuckling as I walked away to find my steward. Rowland Robinson would certainly be able to handle the required negotiations better than I. He listened attentively to the scheme and then grinned.

'It's probably best if you try to find someone who is in charge,' I said quickly. 'It would take too long to negotiate with thirty women one by one.' He leapt up. 'I think that the one we need is called Cherrylips. I'll sort out your plan with her, my lord.'

★ ★ ★

I was astonished how quickly men could advance without the burden of armour and supplies. Fitzgerald's kerns glided along easily and quietly behind their guides, clutching their spears and long knives.

I ambled along beside them, smiling as I recalled Rowland's account of his agreement with Cherrylips. She was initially horrified at his proposal, which had surprised him. Knowing her to be a leading authority on her profession, he assumed she would be used to unusual requests from men, but it seemed Rowland had proposed something that not even Cherrylips had come across before.

'YOU WANT WHAT?' she had shrieked at him.

'Thirty of your girls to disrobe by the river and jump in – splash about a little, make some noise and...'

'MY GIRLS WOULDN'T GO NEAR A RIVER!' Cherrylips' shocked voice became even shriller. 'God knows they'll do most things... But jump into water? It's not natural!'

'They'll be guided to the right place because it will be at night. There'll be a full moon, of course, that...'

'You want them to jump into a river? At night!' The obscenity of Rowland's proposal hit Cherrylips. 'What would happen if someone saw them?' she demanded, horrified.

'Well, there will be about four hundred men watching,' Rowland admitted.

'FOUR HUNDRED!' Cherrylips' shriek could have been heard in York. 'You want my girls to undress and get into the water in front of four hundred men! At night?'

Roland smiled at her. Cherrylips was speechless for a moment, but she recovered quickly.

'It's indecent. It's immoral. It's perverted. It's...'

'Worth four pence to every woman,' added Rowland.

'Six!' Cherrylips snapped back instinctively. She eyed him shrewdly for a few seconds. 'You don't look like some sort of deviant, so it's got to be something else. It's Clifford and his army, isn't it? You want his men looking at us while you attack them, don't you?'

Rowland admitted this was true. Surprisingly, Cherrylips smiled at him knowingly.

'I'd heard you were a bit worried about him. I can't say that I'm overly fond of him myself. His men weren't so pleasant with my girls in York last week.'

Rowland said he was sorry to hear this.

'Mind you, they didn't ask my girls to go jumping into rivers,' Cherrylips added fair-mindedly. 'I hear your leaders are all a bit angry with the City of York because it wouldn't support you?'

Rowland confirmed this.

'Can't say I blame them,' she said moodily. 'Mind you, I've got a bone to pick with the town officials myself. Do you know they tried to kick me out of the city four years ago?'

She sat silently considering Rowland's proposition. At last she looked at him and got up briskly.

'Alright, we'll do it. But it's six pennies per girl and in advance. There's another thing too: I want all these other women out of your camp at once, then my girls can make more money. The less competition there is, the more we can charge.'

'Did you agree?' I asked Rowland.

'Of course but then I asked her how she would ensure that her girls remained naked for as long as possible. She thought about it for a while and then she just smiled.'

'Why was that?'

'I think Cherrylips was quite keen to do the job by that point. While the nature of the task was unusual, she stood to make a lot of money by having the monopoly on the camp, so she explained that she and the guides would conceal the girls' clothing once they were in the river. She pointed out that Clifford's men would be gawping at the women, whether they were in the water or running around looking for their clothes.'

Thus an agreement had been reached and our small force moved towards Clifford's camp. The right flank comprised myself, Fitzgerald's kerns and their captains, and we advanced on the south bank of the river. The left flank was made up of Cherrylips, her girls and their guides, who had already crossed the river and were thus on the northern bank. A guide halted and pointed to the moonlit river.

'Eight hundred paces or so to Clifford's camp,' he muttered.

Fitzgerald signalled and the kerns began to drop silently to the ground. Ahead of us, I could make out the mound where the walls of the old castle stood. In the distance, I could hear the sound of horses in the camp. We should be very close to the outer cordon of sentries by now, but there was neither sight nor sound of our army's left flank. By now the girls should have been splashing about and shrieking at the coldness of the water. The riverbank should have been lined with Clifford's men enjoying the surprising, albeit welcome, scene.

Could Clifford have put patrols out on the north bank, I wondered. As the river was too deep to cross, there didn't seem much point, but clearly someone had detected Cherrylips' force, as on the far side of the river there was total silence. I cursed quietly; without our diversion we would lose the element of surprise.

I gestured to Fitzgerald and, crouching down, the two of us advanced a further two hundred paces. Ahead of us now, I could make out the dying fires of Clifford's camp. Slightly to my right and in advance of me, I noticed a sentry huddled against a tree. He appeared to be asleep. We dropped to the ground again.

'We'll have to rush them, Francis,' Fitzgerald whispered. 'It looks like our left flank has deserted us.'

I had not considered that possibility. Payment had been in advance, so there was nothing to prevent Cherrylips' contingent heading back to York instead of coming here.

I glanced up at the sky; clouds covered the moon but they were drifting over it. I guessed that the sky would clear in a moment. At that point, the whole scene would be bathed in moonlight. Instead of revealing Cherrylips' troop though, it would render us visible to the sentries. The obvious thing to do would be to advance while there was still some cloud covering the moon but I gestured to Fitzgerald to wait. My gut feeling was that Cherrylips hadn't deserted us.

'She'll be waiting until the clouds move away,' I whispered, 'the more light, the more impact they'll make.'

He snorted disbelievingly but a few minutes later when the sky was clear we heard a shout from Clifford's camp. And then another. Then shrieks from women came from beyond the camp. Shadowy sentries in front of us moved back towards the riverbank to investigate.

I counted to fifty slowly. Next to me Fitzgerald shuffled restlessly. I nudged him and he rose to his feet swiftly.

All eyes were on his huge frame as he waved his sword

in the direction of Clifford's men and speedily, the vengeful kerns began to run towards them, screaming wildly.

Clifford's men wheeled round and shrieked in terror as the kerns raced towards them. Instinctively they huddled together for protection, their swords useless against the six foot Irish spears.

The kerns halted and moved into crescent formation easily outflanking Clifford's troops. At the sight of this a number of Clifford's men threw their swords to the ground and raised their hands into the air, but to no avail. Remorselessly, with spears outstretched the kerns advanced. A few of Clifford's men tried to parry the spearwall but most inched backwards towards to the river.

As Clifford's soldiers moved back their grouping became even more compact and they found themselves hemmed in by the kerns. Sensing that the moment of revenge was at hand the Irish pushed forward, their jabbing blows became faster and their savage shouts were now so loud as to almost drown out the shrieks of their impaled victims.

The semi-circle of kerns around Clifford's troops tightened inexorably. Animalistic grunts of satisfaction now replaced their shouts as their spears thrust at the packed mass of soldiers. Splashing sounds from the river told me that Clifford's men were being forced back into the dark waters.

Still the kerns pressed forward. Baying for blood, they hunted down the survivors on the river bank and cleared it completely. What remained of Clifford's force huddled in the shallows, trapped between the depths of the river behind them and the glittering spears of the kerns.

Relentlessly the Irish advanced into the river, spears outstretched and, panic-stricken, Clifford's men retreated further into the deep dark waters. There was a cacophony of screams and cries for mercy which gradually diminished into frantic splashing.

It was not until there was almost total silence and the water calm that the Irish spearmen halted their advance.

★ ★ ★

'The attack worked brilliantly.' I told Broughton the next day, as we made our way to the meeting with John, Earl of Lincoln and the other army leaders.

He grunted but did not reply. He seemed to have something on his mind these days, although I was unsure what was troubling him. Still, no doubt he would tell me when he was ready.

'Now the kerns have won an outstanding victory and they have weapons, so their morale is justifiably sky high.'

A glance at my comrade's face told me that his own was not. I took his arm.

'Thomas, is there anything?'

Broughton gestured to the men surrounding the Earl of Lincoln.

'We're late,' he said with a heavy heart.

CHAPTER 5

Central England, 1487.

John, Earl of Lincoln, looked at me enquiringly.

'But why do you say that Francis?' he asked.

I bit my lip in annoyance. At every other meeting of the leaders of the army, I had managed to brief Lincoln in advance in order that his inexperience would not be too obvious. On this occasion though I had been unable to do so and it would now appear that I would be telling my nominal superior what to do. However in that crowded tent and with Lincoln being steered in totally the wrong direction, I had no choice.

'With Clifford's force destroyed, my lord, we still have the problem of Northumberland following us. Now I agree with those here who say that he is a nuisance, but I totally disagree with the proposal that we should halt the army and wait for him to find us.'

'But we would slaughter him!' Fitzgerald shouted.

I ignored him and looked at Lincoln.

'It's not Northumberland that I want to fight John,' I told him, 'it's Tudor. An attack on Northumberland would merely delay us and give Henry Tudor more time to build up his army. As I said before, the correct thing to do is to try and throw off Northumberland.' Next to me Swartz nodded emphatically and, seeing this, Lincoln relaxed.

'So how do we do that?' he asked.

'We create a diversion. We detach a small part of the army to double back to York and mount an attack on it. The city leaders will panic and beg Northumberland to come to their assistance and he will be only too happy to oblige.'

'But why?' Harliston asked sceptically. 'Militarily, Northumberland would be far more useful to Tudor if he continued to shadow us.'

He was right of course. Indeed had anyone else been in Northumberland's position, that would have been what they would have done, but my plan was based on the certain knowledge that Northumberland's foremost loyalty was to himself. Theoretically Northumberland was Henry Tudor's man just as he had been Richard of Gloucester's, but as Richard discovered at Bosworth, it would be an extremely rash move by anyone to put the Earl's loyalty to the test.

'Northumberland believes that he should rule the North,' I explained to Harliston, 'and I very much doubt he is sincerely loyal to Henry Tudor. Provided we give him a credible excuse, he will happily take it. That way he does not have to support either us or Tudor. He'll wait for us to take on Tudor and come along later to congratulate the winner.'

'Just like he did at Bosworth,' Broughton added.

There were expressions of disgust at Northumberland's treachery, but Lincoln gestured to the elderly Lord Scrope to speak. He rose slowly.

'I agree with Francis, my lord. With your permission, I'll take my contingent to threaten York while the rest of the army advances south.'

Swartz got up impatiently.

'Then the sooner we continue to march, the better,' he concluded briskly.

★ ★ ★

Our advance resumed. Middleton despatched part of the Carlisle horse to watch Northumberland's army as we marched. He was also experienced enough to place scouts far in advance of our army, which was fortunate.

I was with Swartz that evening when Middleton found us and brought bad news. I had hoped Broughton would have joined us but he was still brooding on something. I never seemed to see him these days.

'There are about one thousand mounted infantry south of us,' Dick reported. 'They're commanded by Sir Edward Woodville. Judging by their northerly direction, I would say that Tudor is sending them as reinforcements for Northumberland.'

He looked at me.

'Your orders, Francis?'

I cursed quietly. My plan of luring Northumberland back to York had been previously sound as it gave him the perfect excuse to avoid committing his men to fight for Henry Tudor and I had little doubt that he would seize it readily. But the arrival of Sir Edward Woodville would be as unwelcome to Northumberland as it was to us. Without Woodville, if we were defeated in battle by Henry Tudor, Northumberland could always excuse himself by exaggerating the threat to York. He could lie about the numbers of Lord Scrope's force. He could talk regretfully of his immediate priorities, and no one could contradict him. But, as soon as Woodville joined him, Northumberland had an unwelcome witness. As a soldier, Woodville would quickly realise how unreal the threat to York actually was. He would insist on Northumberland returning to his pursuit of our army. I looked at Swartz and Middleton who were waiting patiently.

'We have to stop Woodville joining up with Northumberland,' I said. 'We'll use our cavalry to defeat him, while the rest of the army continues to march south. Let's keep in contact with each other and meet up in two days' time.'

Swartz smiled. It was evidently the correct military solution. Middleton moved away to organise the Irish cavalry and Carlisle horse. After a moment, we followed him. As we came out of Swartz's tent I was amused to see the normal cluster of his officers around Broughton's wife by the campfire.

'I'll break the news of Woodville to Lincoln now,' I said.

But Swartz merely grunted. His eyes were on the group by the fire; I guessed his thoughts were elsewhere.

★ ★ ★

We found Woodville by Hatfield Moors. He had done well to advance his troops so quickly. By now he was close to York, where he must have expected Northumberland to be. Approaching Woodville from the south, our scouts had gained sight of his force earlier.

'He's split his men into four groups, Francis.' Dick told me, 'It probably makes for faster progress. Anyway, they are spread out now so we'll take the last two groups today. If you take the Carlisle horse, I'll go with the Irish. I want to see what they are like before we face Henry Tudor.'

'Alright,' I agreed. 'You take Woodville's third group with the Irish and Captain Appleby and I will manage the fourth one. We'll make camp here when we're finished.'

I watched Dick and the Irish ride away shortly

afterwards, I talked through the situation with Appleby. He was dubious about our chances.

'It's more or less open ground, my lord,' he said gesturing to the moor in front of us. 'Woodville's men would have clear sight of our approach. They'd merely dismount and form a defensive position. Their archers would shoot us to pieces before we could close in on them.'

'I agree with you,' I told him, 'but there's no time to shadow them until we find a better place.'

'They'll know our army is round here somewhere,' he persisted. 'They'll see us and know from our lances that we are not mounted infantry. They'll assume we are Yorkists so, naturally, they'll adopt a protective formation as we approach them.'

I looked at the white rose standards that two of his men bore aloft. He followed my gaze.

'As soon as they see those, they'll know us to be hostile.'

I looked at the flags. He had a point.

'I mean, if they didn't have archers it would still be difficult,' Appleby continued gloomily. He looked puzzled when he saw my expression.

'Why are you smiling, my lord?'

A short while later, I led the bulk of the Carlisle horse – without their ostentatious saddle cloths – after Appleby's small group. As we galloped over the moor, I tried to put myself in the mind of the enemy commander. If I were him, what would I do when I saw Appleby's small force? And what would I do if I saw, in the distance, another body of horsemen pursuing Appleby? The obvious thing would be to adopt a defensive position. The men should dismount and the horses sent to the rear. The men-at-arms should be stationed so that they could defend the bowmen. All archers should be ready to fire at anyone who approached their position. This would be the safest course of action; no one would be rash enough to approach three hundred men in this formation. But while this was the most prudent tactic, it would take time to execute and would disrupt the progress of the mounted infantry. Woodville was clearly in a hurry to reach Northumberland. The group of men we were targeting were already last in his small army. Unless their commander could hasten his troops, they would find themselves arriving at camp with all the best places already taken, and he could expect a tongue lashing from Woodville for his tardiness too. The enemy commander might risk it and keep moving.

We thundered over the crest after Appleby and, for the first time, spotted the mounted infantry far to our right. At the sight of a second body of charging cavalry the enemy came to an abrupt halt. We followed each of Appleby's twists and turns. When he turned left, I did the same. When he swerved right, I moved in the same direction. With each mirrored move, we were establishing our credentials as pursuers and all the time were edging closer to Woodville, whose men were still motionless.

'Come on Appleby!' I willed him. 'Show them your flags.'

I shot a quick glance at the column as we charged after Appleby. A number of men seemed to be gesticulating, but so far no one had dismounted. Pray God they had identified the standards that Appleby was waving! Eight hundred paces from the column, I signalled for the Carlisle horse to spread out as we closed in on Appleby. Six hundred paces from the still immobile column, Appleby feinted to his left but we were widespread now and, with my left wing fully extended, Appleby found himself herded back to his original course. Four hundred paces from the column and the Carlisle horse, on the right flank, caught up with two men at the rear of Appleby's band. There were swift jabbing movements with spears and now two riderless horses followed the others in Appleby's group. Two hundred paces from the column and they were caught between Woodville's men and us. Appleby wheeled to the right in sheer desperation. His path would take him parallel to Woodville's men, who sat enthralled watching the chase. This time I did not follow him but halted my troops and signalled for them to form a line. Our horses jostled one another as we mingled in broad formation, lances aloft facing the flank of the enemy column. Clearly our halt caused some consternation, as two horsemen detached themselves from the column to trot towards us. I moved forward a little and signalled to the men at the far left of the line to start the Gloucester salute.

To an enemy, the Gloucester salute is both terrifying and beautiful. One moment he is facing a number of horsemen just milling about, the next he sees the line of cavalry who, one by one in quick succession, lower their lances from the upright to the charge position. The enemy would be entranced by the ripple effect of the lances' movement, but he is unlikely to have time to react. As soon as the last lance is in the horizontal position, without giving an order, the Carlisle horse breaks into a charge.

Woodville's men were perhaps a little quicker than other opponents, as I saw some movement in their column. Men were trying to push their way out; gaps were appearing but they were too late. A moment later, spears outstretched, the Carlisle horse slammed into the flank of Woodville's column.

'I hear you did the Gloucester salute?' asked Dick, as we sat in our makeshift camp that evening.

'It seemed a good idea to practice it before we meet Henry Tudor.'

'So what happened when you struck the column?'

I clapped him jovially on the shoulder.

'What do you think? They were in a state of considerable confusion. Some tried to flee but Appleby's men picked them off. How did you fare?'

Dick pointed at a horseman who was coming down the hillside towards us, the last of the sunlight causing his saddlecloth to glisten.

'It seems that Lincoln is sending us news, but, to answer your question, the Irish are good. We came up behind that group ahead of yours as they were entering the woods by the river. The Irish mounted archers shot up their rear as they went in and ambushed the head of their column as it emerged. Quite a few of them fled; I reckon by now Woodville will know that he's got a problem.'

'Do you think he'll turn north or south back to Tudor?'

'The obvious thing would be to head north,' said Dick, 'but Woodville will want to tell Tudor our location, so he'll flee south and we'll be waiting for them as they come back this way. We'll catch them tomorrow.'

We discussed tactics for the morrow, but were interrupted by the messenger from the main army.

Middleton took the scroll and looked at me enquiringly.

'You read it,' I said easily.

'It's from Swartz,' he said and then grinned delightedly. 'Northumberland has abandoned the pursuit of our army. He's turned back to help York. Swartz says that it's essential that Woodville does not get through to assist Northumberland.'

'He won't.' I laughed.

'There's more,' chuckled Dick. 'Henry Tudor's approaching Nottingham or has already arrived there. There is no sign of the Stanleys having joined him.'

I grinned with delight and sat up quickly.

'We need to move fast. In three days we can be on him before they arrive. What does Swartz say about Tudor's numbers?'

'He says that there are around twelve thousand.'

I got up.

'Well our nine thousand or so should prevail over Tudor's twelve thousand, but what is important is to hasten the speed of our advance. We must close on Tudor quickly. I think I'll return to the army to hurry them along. Dick, what is the matter?'

He rolled up the scroll and looked at me, stony-faced.

'I think you may need to return anyway,' he said quietly, 'Broughton's been arrested.'

I looked at him in amazement.

'What do you mean, arrested?' I stammered. 'You mean Tudor's men have captured him?'

Dick stared into the fire.

'No, he's been detained in the camp.'

'But why?'

'He tried to kill someone!'

CHAPTER 6

Approaching Stokefield, 1487.

We never reached camp. Somehow we got lost in the darkness and it was Harliston, commanding the forward scouts in Dick's absence, who found us.

'What's this about Broughton?' I asked him directly.

Harliston waited for my escort to withdraw.

'Keep your voice low, Francis. Swartz wants the whole matter to be hushed for the moment.'

'What matter?'

He sighed.

'Broughton appeared in the German camp the other night. He demanded to see Swartz's lieutenant.'

'Hans Kuttler? But why?'

'And when Kuttler appeared, Broughton just went for him. It took four of them to drag Broughton off him; he'd gone berserk.'

Dear God, what could Kuttler have done?

'Hans Kuttler's good looks have been spoiled for a while,' Harliston went on, 'but he's not too badly injured.'

I licked my dry lips.

'Why did Broughton attack him?'

'Keep your voice down,' he hushed me. He glanced

round and nudged his horse closer to mine. 'It seems that Broughton's wife…'

'Marguerite.'

'It seems Marguerite has fallen for young Kuttler. She told Broughton that after the battle she wished to return to Burgundy with Kuttler. She was sorry for her husband, but now she had found true love.'

I groaned. I should have followed my instinct and refused to have Marguerite with us.

'Can you get a reliable guide to take me back to the army?' I said abruptly.

He raised his sword into the air and, as one of his scouts trotted towards us, Harliston deftly turned the talk to other matters. The army was set to cover thirty miles today. Swartz wanted to close in on Henry Tudor quickly, so he'd ordered a start to the march before daybreak. The lack of supplies was becoming more of an issue. He asked me how I had fared against Woodville but I was in no mind to talk and left him quickly.

Exhausted, I followed the scout back to the army. I cursed Marguerite's foolishness and the pain she had caused Thomas. I guessed that Kuttler had just been amusing himself and Marguerite had convinced herself that this was true love. I even felt a little sorry for her for a moment.

'He does have a weakness in that direction,' Swartz admitted a short time later. 'That's probably why he has to keep changing his name – to avoid jealous husbands.'

'So what happens now?'

'Nothing. Lady Broughton has been placed in charge of your young Symbol of Lambert and has been told to stay away from my officers until the battle has been fought. Thomas is being guarded but I think he is resigned to the situation.'

Swartz sounded callous and I told him as much.

'Francis, we have to make light of this matter. I'm told that we are two or three days away from Henry Tudor and, despite the fact that we are almost out of food and we didn't gain many reinforcements after York, all our men are in surprisingly good spirits.'

I shrugged impatiently.

'I intend to keep it that way,' Swartz continued. 'One sure way to wreck morale is to let the men know that their captains are fighting among themselves.'

'I want to see Broughton!'

'I imagine you'd see him, even if I forbade it,' Swartz commented dryly. 'You'll find him at the rear of the march, but don't mention it at Lincoln's Corpus Christi meeting tonight.'

So great had been my worry for Broughton that I had forgotten about the scheduled session to plan our forthcoming strategy; I shrugged impatiently.

Swartz looked at me angrily.

'Strategy is vital at this stage, Francis,' he snapped. 'It is essential that we formulate the right tactics.'

He was right of course, but for once I had no desire to think of warfare and I turned away to find Thomas.

He was riding slowly between two men-at-arms by the wagons. Even at a distance, I could see that his shoulders were hunched and his head bowed. I moved towards him and dismissed his guards then guided his horse away from the marching army.

Thomas made no remark but eyed me bleakly.

'I'm sorry I didn't help you when you needed me.'

'It doesn't matter,' he said distantly.

We rode together in silence.

'I wanted to kill him, Francis, do you know that?' he said angrily. 'But now, I think — what would the point in that be?'

I kept silent. I should have made him talk long before.

'If it had not been Kuttler, it would have been someone else,' he said in a resigned tone. 'If your wife's unfaithful, just let her go. She's not worth the trouble.'

We rode on, without speaking.

'What can I do for you?' I asked at last.

Broughton gave me a wan smile.

'There's nothing. Perhaps I should have talked to you before, but I felt I could manage this by myself. Stupid, really.'

He paused in thought for a moment.

'There is *one* thing you can do for me, Francis,' he said.

I turned to face him.

'Of course.'

'When it comes to the battle, make sure I'm placed in the front row opposite the fiercest enemy troops.'

'I won't do that Thomas,' I stammered out.

He gave me an angry glare.

'Call yourself a friend!'

I signalled to his escort and rode away sadly. Whether we won or lost the battle, I had to help Broughton through this.

In contrast, the mood at Lincoln's tent was jovial as we sat outside after Corpus Christi prayers. Middleton had returned to announce a further defeat of Woodville's force.

'They are fleeing south,' he told the leaders of the army cheerfully. 'That won't do much to encourage Tudor's troops when they scramble into camp.'

I smiled with the others. This was the third victory we had gained in a few days. With the threat from Northumberland being averted as well, it seemed that our momentum was unstoppable. Even the lack of food did not seem to be worrying our men too much and in a day or so we would be up against Henry Tudor.

I surveyed the happy faces of the others and suddenly felt guilty about Broughton. He should have been here now, not languishing in a tent by himself. I had taken him some wine before prayers. He took the wine, but refused to talk, only serving to further increase my guilt. Harliston's arrival made everyone lean forward expectantly. His message was terse.

'Tudor's about a day away. He knows where we are and he's moving to intercept us.'

A cheer greeted this announcement. Harliston held his hand up.

'There's more! Henry Tudor was reinforced this morning by Lord Stanley and five thousand men. His force now numbers seventeen thousand.'

His words were met with general silence and a few groans; our happy mood was shattered. Stanley had beaten us to Tudor by just one or two days. We were now outnumbered almost two to one.

Swartz rose to address the meeting and everyone looked to him trustingly.

'We must force battle on Henry Tudor immediately. Once our army hears this news, desertions will increase. We should attack while we still have some supplies and morale is high.'

His eyes met mine.

'You agree, my lord?'

There was no other alternative. If we fled, Tudor would hunt us down remorselessly and, even if some of the English troops escaped, there was little chance of Swartz's men or the Irish making it back to their homelands.

'We have no choice,' I told him.

Swartz nodded.

'Then we'll continue to advance towards Tudor. When we have more information, I will devise a strategy for the battle.'

★ ★ ★

I did not have long to wait as we only had a short march that next day, which culminated in the crossing of a wide, albeit shallow, river and the ascent of a steep wooded slope. At the summit, the army stopped.

Swartz asked for me as camp was being made. I forced my way through the mass of soldiers to find him. He pointed back in the direction from which we had just come.

'Our line of retreat, if we need it.' He gestured at the river. 'The ford at Fiskerton is wide but, as you have just experienced, is easy to cross.'

'You're intending to fight here?'

He swung round and looked at the track which ran from west to east at the bottom of the hill.

'That's the road to Newark, Francis. Newark is to the east of us.'

'Is that where Henry Tudor thinks we are going?'

'It would be an entirely logical deduction,' Swartz explained seriously. 'Tudor's spies will have told him that we are low on supplies and greatly outnumbered, so he will believe that we are heading there to get reinforcements and food. To prevent that, his army will take this path in pursuit of us.'

'When?'

'My informers tell me they will come tomorrow,' Swartz said quietly.

'Then I want Broughton released,' I said after a minute.

'Of course. Keep him away from Kuttler and let's meet in one hour with the others.'

I moved off to find Thomas. To my relief he was more talkative today and he was no longer orchestrating his death in battle.

'If I'm killed, I'm killed, but I won't be seeking my own death. No woman is worth that.'

I listened to him and tried to console him without success. Like him, I was at a loss to explain the suddenness of Marguerite's change of affection.

'I can't understand it either, Thomas, but what I do know is that you can't just stay here. You need to be involved with the army.'

'To take my mind off it?'

I sighed.

'Look, what has happened is in the past now. You can't undo it.'

'I can!'

'By killing Kuttler? Thomas, you have to hope that you can win Marguerite back of her own free will. You can't just kill everyone who looks at her.'

'Looks at her! Kuttler's done a lot more than just look at her.'

He leapt to his feet and stood in front of me. His face was red with anger.

'Look,' I said reasonably. 'It's not just Kuttler, is it? You said it could be anyone. You said that...'

He punched me hard on the chin. The blow hurt; while only of medium height, he was immensely strong. I wiped the blood from the corner of my mouth slowly and gave him a crooked smile.

'I'm sorry,' I said. 'I probably didn't put that very well.'

He took his seat again and covered his face with his hands. I moved over and put my arm around him. His shoulders shook as he sobbed. I gave him some of the wine that Edward had provided. After a while, he gestured at my mouth.

'I'm sorry.'

'That's all right. It made me appreciate what Kuttler must have felt. But Thomas, you can't stay here; you have to go on with your life. Swartz will have you back in the army.'

Broughton mumbled something.

'I didn't hear that?'

He looked at the ground.

'I would rather stay here.'

I looked at him blankly.

'But why?'

He didn't answer. Then I began to understand. Broughton had been embarrassed by the mocking laughter and cruel jibes from the other men. He was a man who had lost his wife in public to another. Nevertheless, he could not just wallow in this tent.

'Come on!'

'I told you, I'm not coming.'

I hauled him upright.

'Yes, you are. You and I are going to walk through the

camp together. If men jeer you, they are only doing it to hide their own thoughts of how faithless their wives really are. And they won't anyway.'

'Why not?' he muttered.

'Because there's a battle tomorrow. Most of them will be thinking of that. Now forget Marguerite and come with me.'

He hesitated for a moment.

'Alright I'll come with you but I'll not fight with the Swiss or the Germans tomorrow.'

'They probably would not want to fight with you either!' I pointed out. 'Kuttler's face is still a mass of scars and bruises.'

A flicker of a smile crossed Broughton's face. I took his arm and led him back into camp.

That evening, we sat together by the fire. Lincoln was quiet and subdued, Fitzgerald, happy and confident. Harliston, having seen more warfare, was probably dubious of our chances but hid his thoughts behind an urbane smile. Broughton and I sat next to each other. Unsurprisingly, Martin Swartz had not invited Hans Kuttler.

'I have already explained my reasoning why Tudor's army will pass this way tomorrow,' Swartz continued, 'so now it is time to explain the tactics we will employ in the morning.'

Swartz gave a little smile and looked around our circle.

'Our most recent information tells me that Henry Tudor believes us to be much further east than our present position. It is his intent to reinforce Newark and to bring us to battle as quickly as possible.'

'That suits us!' Fitzgerald laughed.

'Accordingly tomorrow he will march east but, being unaware of our own proximity, he will spread his army out in order to march quicker.'

'We even believe that we know his order of march,' continued Swartz. 'First comes the Earl of Oxford with around eight thousand men, then Henry Tudor with four thousand, and Lord Stanley comes last with the remainder.'

'So what's your plan?' asked Harliston.

'When the Earl of Oxford passes this way tomorrow, he will see a small army on this hill. They will be less than his own number and will have poorer weapons and armour.'

'But our army numbers more than Oxford's!' Lincoln objected.

'It does, my lord, but since you and two thousand men will be concealed on the far side of the hill, Oxford will not see them,' Swartz replied.

'Do you think he would be tempted to attack you?'

'He might Francis, but I think it is more likely that he will wait until the rest of Tudor's army reinforce him. But while he is waiting I'll attack him.'

Swartz looked straight at me.

'The only way we can beat a larger army than our own is to defeat them piecemeal. Francis, I want you to take all our cavalry and delay Tudor, while I defeat Oxford.'

'Horsemen alone are not going to delay Tudor significantly; I would need archers as well,' I said thoughtfully.

I turned to Broughton.

'Will you take charge of those?'

Broughton shook his head.

'You need a captain of archers, not me. I'll put my men

and myself under your command, my lord,' he went on, looking up at Lincoln.

Harliston nodded.

'It makes sense for the English contingent to fight as one unit. I'll arrange that for you, my lord.'

Lincoln swallowed nervously.

'I have some wine still – Sir Richard, Sir Thomas? We might, perhaps, finish it while we discuss tomorrow?' He hesitated and then spread his hands. 'Well I would welcome your advice.'

The three of them left us. A moment later, Fitzgerald departed to see his troops. Swartz's brigade were to be the vanguard of our army but Fitzgerald had placed himself and his men under Swartz's direct command. His Irish troops would serve directly behind the mercenaries. Lincoln's rearguard would support both bodies and attempt to supply cover for the flanks.

I was left alone with Martin Swartz.

'Shall we walk?'

He rose and we strolled in the direction of the evening sun, until I turned and gestured to the slope behind us.

'Your plan won't work,' I told him.

'Why not?'

I pointed to the top of the slope and then to the road at its foot.

'You'll be at the top of the slope and Oxford will be at the bottom?'

'Correct.'

'He won't attack you; you know that. So you will have to descend the slope to reach him.'

'While you delay Tudor and prevent him from reinforcing Oxford,' Swartz agreed calmly.

'I understand that,' I said irritably, 'but your plan still won't work. Oxford's army will have far more archers than we have. Now, how long will it take you to descend the slope?'

He narrowed his eyes.

'Four minutes, perhaps?'

'So for two, maybe three, minutes you'll be in the range of his archers. Assume he has about three thousand. They will be firing eight, maybe ten arrows each minute – your force will be decimated before it even comes close to Oxford.'

'Part of it will be,' he admitted, 'but the rest of us will arrive intact.'

The setting sun was casting long shadows across our little hill and the small village at the end was almost out of sight by now. I tried to follow Swartz's thought processes, but then gave up.

He linked his arm through mine.

'Our advance will be preceded by the kerns,' he said quietly.

They would be massacred, I shouted in my head; when attacked, archers shoot at the enemy closest to them. Some of them have the armour they had taken from Clifford's men, but every arrow in Oxford's army would target them. Swartz was right: the remainder of his force would close on Oxford's men more or less unscathed. But in order to do this Swartz was sacrificing the kerns.

'Is that why you got them to launch the attack on Clifford's camp?'

'It was an excellent way to build up their morale,' he replied softly. 'Now they think they are the best troops in the army and can beat anyone.'

'But they will never have seen a massed volley of arrows

before. They'll have no idea what they are about to face!'

'Arguably that's better for them, Francis. If we do it this way, at least the rest of the army will stand a chance of reaching Oxford and you can have hope of winning the throne for your young king.'

I fell silent. Ruthless though Swartz's plan was, it offered a chance to our army. By sacrificing four hundred men, he was saving eight thousand.

'How long do you want me to try and delay Tudor for?'

'He'll probably be half an hour or so behind Oxford. Hold him off as long as you can.'

I grunted. I had no idea of how I was going to achieve this. I was still thinking of how best to use my archers and cavalry together when I noticed that Swartz was gazing at the darkening track at the bottom of the slope. He was probably visualising the battle tomorrow.

'Assuming I can stop Tudor from reinforcing Oxford, do you think you'll win tomorrow?' I asked.

'I'm not sure, Francis.'

I wheeled round to face him.

'But... your numbers are equally matched.'

'They are not.'

'But... but back then with the others, you said Oxford had eight thousand men.'

Swartz gave a sad smile. 'I know I did but, the fact is, Francis, I wanted to keep up the morale of the army. In reality, the Earl of Oxford leads over ten thousand men.'

My heart sank. These would undoubtedly be the best of the Tudor forces. Swartz was badly outnumbered; moreover, his force would be without my cavalry and archers. He shot me a sideways glance.

'After the battle you can tell your friend Broughton and

I how you overcame Tudor's force.'

I was about to point out that the odds of my small force of archers and horse had not the slightest chance of doing anything except delaying Tudor's advance, but I stopped myself. Swartz was a professional and a realist. He knew better than anyone that the odds were heavily stacked against us but, despite the situation, he was prepared to put a brave face on it. I admired his courage.

'Hmm, well I suppose I'll have to get Broughton to tell me how you defeated Oxford while I'm dealing with Tudor,' I grunted, 'I know you will be too modest to tell me afterwards how you managed it.'

He managed a faint smile. 'Well, shall we go and drink to our respective victories?' he suggested.

I nodded agreement and resignedly we began to trudge back up the slope.

CHAPTER 7

Main Battle, Stokefield, 1487.

The rising sun picked out a small number of scouts approaching Swartz's army from the west. Behind them a large mass of men was just visible. Broughton knew that this had to be Oxford's army.

'What's he doing now?' demanded Lincoln.

Broughton peered down the path.

'Those are Oxford's outriders,' Broughton told him. 'They will have spotted us. Oxford's halted while they report.'

The Earl of Lincoln swallowed. Broughton had forgotten that this was his first battle.

'Are your men concealed my lord?' Broughton asked.

Lincoln nodded curtly and swallowed again; his eyes were still on where he supposed Oxford's troops were. He had to be kept occupied, Broughton thought. It would be at least two hours before Oxford came upon them.

'It might be an idea for you to walk round your troops, my lord,' Broughton suggested. 'Some may be frightened and they will appreciate a word of encouragement from you.'

Harliston turned to Lincoln.

'That's undoubtedly true. I'll come with you.'

'You'll send word Sir Thomas if anything develops?'
Lincoln asked.

'Of course.'

★ ★ ★

Lovell's Ambush.

I gestured to Dick Middleton to move away from his horsemen and my archers who were resting in the wood. It was better that they did not hear their commanders quarrelling.

'It's a coward's way of fighting!'

Dick's voice was angry in the cool morning air. A lack of sleep was beginning to make me irritable.

'Act your age!' I said shortly. 'Henry Tudor's got about four thousand troops in his contingent; we've got six hundred. We need to delay Tudor from joining Oxford to allow Swartz to overcome him. Does the method we use matter?'

He glared at me.

'Look, I know what we have to do and I understand, but I still maintain that ambushes and attacks at the rear of the enemy are not an honest way to fight!'

I glared back at my oldest friend.

'What are you proposing then – a charge across open countryside dodging their arrows? A suicidal attack on troops who know you're coming? Perhaps you would like to do the Gloucester salute before our whole force is wiped out?'

He rose in anger.

'Look, I'm not that foolish!' he shouted. 'But, given the odds we face, I tend to look on this as my last battle. Under the circumstances, I would have to say that I – for one – would not mind fighting with honour.'

Even I could spot the weakness in that argument.

'So you'll fail but you'll die with honour? What about the rest of our army? They will be delighted to learn how your honourable death has caused their certain demise.'

I took his arm and pulled him round to show him the ambush point.

'Dick, we'll have archers on this side in the trees firing at random into Tudor's troops. Then, with the Irish attacking them further down the column and the Carlisle horse attacking the rear, we'll create havoc.'

He kicked a stone in frustration; he couldn't counter the argument but he still didn't like the plan, I could tell.

Main Battle.

There was movement on the hillside now as Swartz's army began to ready itself. Men started to stumble into attack formation. A few swore loudly to conceal their fear, but most were silent. Oxford was moving. The priest Simmons and the young Symbol of Lambert retired back to the camp.

Around him, despite the fresh dawn, the air was fetid. The sour smell of men grew stronger as Oxford's dust cloud began to move towards us. On either side of Broughton, soldiers twitched their rosaries, stroked lucky charms and checked their weapons. It was time to brief Lincoln. Broughton left two of his people on the brow of the hill and descended to the trees on the far side of the slope.

'Oxford is approaching, probably in close-order formation,' Broughton told him.

'Marching together, not spread out,' Harliston explained.

'His numbers?' Lincoln asked.

Broughton frowned. Judging by the size of the dust cloud, he thought there were many more than eight thousand. Lincoln must have noticed Broughton's expression; when he opened his mouth to speak, Harliston smoothly interjected.

'If we may speak a little about the order of the battle today?'

John of Lincoln gestured for him to do so.

'Oxford will line up to face us on the other side of the track below,' Harliston explained. 'It will be the usual formation: archers, then behind them men-at-arms with cavalry on both flanks.'

'He'll move over to give Henry Tudor space to come up on his left,' Broughton added.

'Precisely,' continued Harliston. 'Now our formation is fairly simple. The kerns advance in front to... um... absorb the enemy arrows, then come Swartz's own pikemen and hand-gunners. The pikemen will advance in lateral formations with the Irish men-at-arms behind.'

'Our role is to guard Swartz's flanks and to supply reinforcements when required. We'll watch for weak points among the Irish and push our men in there.'

'The enemy line will outflank ours, my lord, due to their greater numbers and their horsemen. We are vulnerable at the sides. Oxford will try to swing his men in behind Swartz's force. It is our role to prevent that.'

He paused and smiled at the Earl of Lincoln.

'Shall we return to the top to see?'

If food was in short supply in the army, it was plain that drink was plentiful. The stench of ale and cheap wine was pervasive. The kerns had obviously been given their special drink, a curious Irish brew which appeared to be intoxicating and extremely potent, as already they were leaping around wildly and yelling incomprehensible curses at the oncoming Oxford. They waved their captured swords, as they were ushered into the front of the army by the heavily armed soldiers of the Fraternity of Arms.

'Oxford's stopped.'

Harliston pointed down and Broughton could clearly see that Oxford's men were beginning to deploy on the far side of the track below them.

'There's no sign of Tudor,' observed Lincoln tightly.

Broughton looked down the path that Oxford had marched along. He guessed that he could see for three or four miles. There were no dust clouds or glints of sunlight on armour.

'They must be quite a long way behind,' repeated Lincoln, trying to conceal his nervousness.

The noise around them was beginning to increase as Fitzgerald and Kuttler began to spread their men. Oxford's line was eight hundred paces below Broughton and his archers were planting arrows in the ground, ready for the attack. It was evident that he would not attack them, but equally he would defend his position until Tudor arrived to reinforce them. As Broughton watched, he saw Oxford increase the weight of horsemen on his right flank.

'I would suggest that we place the majority of our archers on our left-hand flank,' Broughton told Lincoln.

'Now?'

'In a moment. We'll keep the men behind the brow of the hill until Oxford is totally ready,' Harliston said. 'If I take the left flank, Thomas, will you take the right?'

Already the Yorkist army was straining to move forward. Below them, Oxford's troops formed neat lines under their colourful banners. The men around Broughton lurched forward again.

'And I?' asked Lincoln, having to raise his voice, as by now the curses and yells of contempt for Oxford's men roared from the hillside.

'Bring your men up now, my lord,' Broughton told Lincoln. 'We'll split them between us. Keep them in the centre, support Swartz when he needs reinforcements and, if either Harliston or I fall, keep the flanks of the army safe.'

Lovell's Ambush.

Appleby gazed round the ambush point in the clearing until he spotted Middleton and I, then he trotted over as the remainder of our scouts dismounted wearily. He was adamant. Compared to Oxford's men, the force commanded by Henry Tudor was a mob. Oxford had passed us by in tight formation with scouts and outriders up ahead.

'But not Tudor's men,' Appleby told us. 'His men are spread out and jumbled up with their own baggage, as well as Oxford's.'

'Scouts? Outriders?'

Appleby dismounted.

'None that I saw. Tudor probably assumes that he's quite safe now that Oxford is ahead of him.'

'What of Stanley?' asked Dick.

'Not with Tudor,' Appleby said happily. 'They must still be breaking camp or else they're behind Tudor's march.'

Thomas David emerged out of the trees.

'It's thirty paces from the edge of the wood to the road. We'll be comfortably in range. I've spread the men out and they know to keep silent.'

I turned to Dick and Appleby.

'After we attack, you'll see men fleeing in all directions,' I said grimly. 'That's when you get in among them.'

'And after that?' Dick asked.

'Get straight back to Swartz. Use your men to protect his flanks.'

'And you?'

I glanced up at the sun.

'If I can, I'll try a second ambush. If not, I'll bring the archers back to the main battle.'

Main Battle.

A huge roar erupted as Swartz's hand swept down. With a jolt, the pikemen began to descend the hill. A few minutes later, Broughton led his small force out to the right flank. He positioned his handful of archers and men-at-arms and glanced down the track. There was still no sign of Tudor.

Oxford was extending his line of battle. The cavalry on his right flank were edging up the slope. The smaller number on his left flank was likewise moving forward. Broughton signalled to the men to advance slightly. If the horsemen tried to encircle Swartz's advancing men, the archers would have to be in range of them.

Ahead of Swartz's line, the kerns were running to close in on Oxford's men. Their excited yells could be heard above the measured tramp of the Germans and Irish infantry behind them. They were brave, those kerns, but they were ignorant of the dangers of mass arrow fire.

There was no retreat, even as the fearsome arrow storm swept through them; they just kept running until they fell in swathes. None of them reached Oxford's line. Swartz's pikemen faltered for a moment at the horrific sight in front of them but, a moment later, they recovered and quickened their pace. Leaving his archers in their position, Oxford ordered his men-at-arms forward to engage the pikemen. A few moments later, the two lines slammed together.

Lovell's Ambush.

I counted quietly; it was essential that our ambush was launched at the centre of the enemy troops who straggled along the path in front of us. I nudged Thomas David to fire the first arrow. It was a signal for all the concealed archers to begin firing.

The effect was devastating. What had been an untidy mass of troops ambling along peacefully descended into a mob. Men shrieked with agony as they sought to flee; yells and moans from the injured were heard. The agonised noises of wounded oxen added to the cacophony.

No fire was returned. Even if anyone had been brave enough, it would have been folly to stand on the exposed road and try to shoot at a concealed enemy.

I pushed my way to the edge of the wood and peered out at the chaotic scene in front of me. Men and beasts mingled together in total confusion as they sought to escape the arrows that still rained down on them. As they ran they collided with one another and stumbled on the dead and wounded.

'Advance the archers!'

Tudor's men were now a leaderless rabble. They rushed frantically towards the open ground, away from the woods.

'Increase your range!'

Closest to us, a number of the enemy were using their own bows to support themselves as, with pitiful slowness, they hauled themselves away. Our archers ignored them. Instead they concentrated on the dark figures silhouetted against the golden fields. I heard their grunts of grim satisfaction as, one after another, Tudor's men slumped to the ground.

Thomas David found me. He pointed to the track.

'Do you want their wounded killed?'

Few of their wounded would be able to fight today, so I shook my head.

'We'll leave them as a warning for the rest of Tudor's army,' I told him.

Broughton could see Oxford's mistake at once. By advancing his infantry, he had made his archers impotent. As his men-at-arms engaged Swartz's force, his archers could not fire for risk of hitting their own men. What he needed to do was get his archers out to the flanks and start shooting in from both sides.

It was a grave error. Already the momentum of Swartz's advance was pushing his men-at-arms back. Having advanced over the track towards the slope, Oxford's men were beginning to retrace their footsteps. But his horsemen were beginning to move now. They were clearly going to make a flank attack to relieve the pressure on their army's centre.

Broughton signalled for his archers to fire.

Lovell's Ambush.

I could vaguely make out the remainder of the Tudor army. For all their caution, they were still moving purposefully towards our second ambush position. Behind us I could just discern the sounds of battle. Clearly Swartz had not defeated Oxford's troops yet.

'They are coming on slow and steady,' Thomas David commented thoughtfully. He peered at the distant soldiers. 'I thought you said Henry Tudor had about four thousand men?'

'Well, originally…'

'There are more than four thousand there. Don't forget

that we must have taken out about a quarter of Tudor's force an hour ago. So who are all those?'

'I think Stanley has caught up with Henry Tudor. Our attack delayed Tudor by an hour or so. In that hour the Stanley army kept moving. Now they are joined together.'

'So what do you want to do now?' asked Thomas David. 'The advance guard will be upon us soon.'

My second ambush plan was not going to work. The outriders of Tudor would spot us on the hill or they would see our horses. Archers would be sent to pin us down as the rest of the united Tudor and Stanley army marched on disregarding us. I looked up at the sun. We had probably delayed Tudor for as long as we could.

'We'll rejoin Swartz,' I resolved.

★ ★ ★

Main Battle.

Broughton knew that Oxford's next attack was going to be a nightmare. Not only had Tudor's general taken men from the right wing of his army to reinforce the cavalry on his left wing, but Oxford had additionally decided to move his archers up from the rear of his infantry. Now his bowmen were acting as a shield for his advancing horsemen.

Broughton sent a messenger to Lincoln for reinforcements and more arrows. Men reappeared with the arrows, but there were no more archers; Harliston had them all. Wearily, Broughton told his men to spread out.

The enemy's first volleys coincided with their cavalry charge. Broughton's force responded by aiming at horsemen and archers indiscriminately, but this time they could not stop Oxford's men from surging into the side of our lines.

When the enemy fire slackened, Broughton risked a quick glance at Oxford's cavalry and groaned deeply. The sheer momentum of their charge had driven the horsemen deep into the Swartz's army creating an open wound on its exposed side. Being tightly pressed together, the large number of infantry had slowed the impetus of the charge, but they had not stopped it.

Broughton watched horrified as Oxford's horsemen rained down blows on the exposed heads of Fitzgerald's men. A man, his face sliced open, stumbled blindly into the path of one of the great horses and was instantly flung to the ground. In front of the advancing horsemen, there was frantic movement as panic-stricken men sought to flee. In such congestion, there was no escape. Broughton glimpsed the horsemens' blurred swords rise and fall as they scythed their way through the Irish, their bloody harvest trampled underfoot by the massive hooves of their maddened horses.

The sergeant grabbed Broughton's arm.

'More horsemen approaching from the west, Sir Thomas!' he yelled. 'There are hundreds of them!'

'Sweet Christ, Tudor must have sent reinforcements!' Broughton quickly gestured to his men to rise and face this new threat.

Lovell's Ambush.

We rode fast along the track, heading east towards the battlefield. Stragglers or deserters from Oxford's force leapt from the path at the sound of our hooves. We had to halt to water the horses and I was concerned by the delay. Certainly Tudor was behind us but, with no opposition, he would increase his pace. Swartz had to break Oxford before he arrived. I remounted and urged my tired archers on.

★ ★ ★

Main Battle.

Somehow, the Irish had repelled Oxford's horse, as they came streaming back out of the battle in groups of threes and fours. Noting their retreat, their archers began to retire step by step.

The fresh enemy cavalry were close now and Broughton ordered his archers to stand to face them. Their thin screen was all that remained of the western flank.

The enemy commander wheeled his men, who seemed to be in two groups, straight towards the battle and began to charge. Arm aloft, Broughton waited for them to come into range.

'Don't fire!' Broughton yelled. 'Don't fire!'

The Carlisle horse swept past them, taking Oxford's retreating cavalry on the flank and sweeping through them. The unsuspecting enemy archers were spitted as they started to flee. The Irish cavalry ignored both enemy horse and archers and continued down the slope to fire into Oxford's infantry.

Within minutes, their flank was clear. Broughton signalled to one of the horsemen.

'Tell Middleton to help Harliston on the left!' he shouted.

The trooper raised his lance in acknowledgement and moved away. Broughton went to find Lincoln. His numbers had reduced substantially but all trace of his fear had departed.

'Harliston is still holding the left flank!' he shouted. 'He's taken most of my men. What's Swartz doing?'

Ahead of them the track was clearly visible and Swartz's men were still pushing the greater number of Oxford's troops back, but their progress was being stoutly contested. As they watched, the two lines seemed to fall back from one another, as if by mutual consent.

'They keep doing that!' Lincoln said irritably.

'It's exhaustion,' Broughton pointed out sharply. 'Men can't fight forever.'

A squire appeared and stood before Lincoln.

'Sir Richard Harliston advises that his flank is now clear. All enemy horsemen have now retired,' he announced.

Lincoln looked at Broughton curiously.

'So, what do we do now?'

Broughton pointed to the scene below them.

'We'll collect all the men we have left and reinforce Swartz,' he told them.

'Welcome Francis!'

Edward Franke helped me put on my full armour in the almost deserted camp.

'Where is Tudor?' he asked.

'He'll probably be here in two hours.'

'Has Swartz broken through yet?'

He shook his head.

'Oxford kept mounting flank attacks. Broughton and Harliston were hard pressed as Oxford's line was longer. But the Irish and the Carlisle horse helped our archers drive them off for the moment. Lincoln sent a message – he's taken the remainder of the men to reinforce Swartz.'

I grunted. We had to break through very quickly indeed. He handed me my helmet and hammer.

'Take care of yourself, Edward.'

With my helmet on I couldn't hear his response, so I raised my gauntlet and turned to descend the slope.

At least half of Swartz's pikemen were dead or wounded, it seemed to Broughton. Being in the front line, despite their longer weapons, they had suffered heavily. They no longer appeared to present an unbroken front against the enemy; rather they fought in isolated groups.

There was no sense of time down there. Ahead of Broughton, the heavy infantry of the Fraternity of Arms pushed and swayed. While there was movement, he had no idea whether they were advancing or retreating. He was thirsty and beginning to feel weak.

Men came and went on either side of him. At one point Broughton saw Kuttler, who was urging a party of his pikemen forward. He made no move against him as he couldn't cause him any grief now. If Marguerite had been unfaithful, did it matter with whom?

It was hard to Broughton to keep upright in a constantly milling body of men, but to fall would be the end, as he would be instantly trampled to death. He was close to the enemy now, so he raised his sword, but he was flung to the side as huge men with scarred faces and swathed in wolf-skins pushed through his ranks towards the enemy. They must be the Berserkers, he thought; Swartz's shock troops used to overcome particularly stubborn resistance.

He watched awestruck as they charged straight ahead into the troops in front of them, axes flailing.

There were probably only twenty of them but, within minutes, the pressure in front of them diminished, and they swirled forward.

'Surely Oxford must break soon?' Broughton thought exhausted beyond endurance.

I glanced around me as I came out of the camp and started to move down the slope to the rear of Swartz's army.

To the west, sunlight glinted on the armour of Tudor's approaching troops. I judged that they would send forward mounted infantry to reinforce Oxford, whose battle line was now distinctly bowed but Oxford's cavalry was approaching again from the east. The remains of the Carlisle horse were moving out to oppose them and the Irish horse seemed to have disappeared.

I found Swartz behind the lines.

'You're wounded.'

A trickle of blood ran down his forehead. He ignored my concern, but pointed to the two groups of Berserkers, whose shoulders were heaving.

'Tudor will be here soon,' he panted. 'We must make the final breakthrough now.'

He turned to the huge men beside him and snapped

something that I did not understand. The Berserkers had formed a protective circle around Swartz. I gripped my hammer and tramped after them.

★ ★ ★

Broughton's thirst was intolerable and his body soaked in sweat, he swung his sword mechanically as he stumbled forward.

Again and again, he tripped on bodies underfoot, but somehow he kept upright and moving. He had no idea who his companions were on either side of him. They all just kept hacking at whichever faceless armoured figure appeared in front of them.

Finally he sensed that the pressure ahead of him was slackening slightly. He didn't trust himself by now so he hung back. To advance in front of your companions leaves you dangerously exposed. But then the man on his right was ahead of him and, a moment later, so was the man on his left. Oxford's army was pulling back. No, they were breaking.

★ ★ ★

Oxford's line disintegrated; Swartz's final surge forward saw to that. Whether it was the troops from the Fraternity of Arms who finally broke the enemy line or the Germans I will never know, but men saw Swartz advance and they followed him.

For a few blessed moments I was able to lower the heavy war hammer and stand still panting loudly. Then I raised my visor and looked for Swartz. We would need to realign the men to confront Tudor himself.

With the line broken, Oxford's men started to flee. Our men did not follow – they were too exhausted. They sank down among the dead and wounded, too spent even to loot the corpses all around them. But we needed to turn Oxford's retreat into a rout. Even a small number of horsemen charging after retreating troops can quickly create complete panic. Where was Middleton and where was the Irish horse?

Kuttler appeared and silently gestured for me to follow him. Apprehensively, I walked after him through rows of prone men to the place where Martin Swartz lay. He was dead.

His face was peaceful in repose. His warped armour made it clear that a mace or war hammer had struck him. A number of the Berserkers lay next to him. I gazed down at him guiltily, my heart full of pain and remorse. His death was my fault for I had brought him here.

'Francis?'

I turned slowly. One arm dangling uselessly, Dick Middleton approached. He gestured to the men strewn about us.

'We've probably lost half the army,' he said uncertainly.

He seemed to be shivering or shaking, despite the heat of the day.

'Can your horsemen pursue them?' I pointed at Oxford's men.

He looked at me in amazement and started to laugh in a high-pitched, shrill tone. I glanced at him and it was only then that I noticed how pale his face was and how feverish his eyes.

'The Irish horse has been wiped out completely,' he stammered. 'If I've got thirty left from the Carlisle horse, I'll be lucky. Men I've known for ten years or more are dead and you're talking about pursuing the enemy? Francis, we could not even defend ourselves now, let alone pursue Oxford.'

He glanced at the soldiers slumped around us.

'I doubt that you will get these men to fight Tudor.'

I pointed to where the remaining German and Swiss were filing past Swartz's body.

'If it had not been for him, we would not have defeated Oxford. We will get men to carry down whatever ale or wine there is in camp. Then we'll order the men to rest.'

'But Tudor will be here soon!' Dick objected.

'We have a bit of time,' I told him. 'Then, when everyone is rested and some of the more lightly wounded have been treated...'

'Francis, our army is probably less than four thousand in number now,' he said quickly. 'Tudor's got double that.'

'We can't flee! His cavalry would ride us down.'

He considered that. An army is at its most vulnerable when it starts to break up; men in armour seldom managed to escape. Besides, where would the Irish flee to?

'So, we'll establish a fresh line facing west,' I said. 'Then straddle the road. We'll need a screen to try and stop...'

'A screen? With thirty horsemen? I suppose it will be a way to fight with honour at last.'

There was little or no order to the army. Men were not fighting as part of the northern levies or as a member of Fitzgerald's contingent, they were muddled in a crude line facing the fresh troops of Tudor. Their line more than doubled Broughton's.

Predictably, for each archer they had, the enemy boasted ten. The opposition's tactics were simple – they pounded Broughton's line as they advanced towards them. Broughton sustained a heavy blow on his upper arm and fell to one knee as others passed by him. As he slowly rose, he realised that his troops were being pushed back again. Step by step, he inched his way backwards up the slope.

Tudor did not follow. The enemy waited until they were some distance away and then advanced their archers. Around Broughton men dropped steadily. To advance would spell destruction but to remain here would mean a slow death. They moved back out of range.

Tudor was waiting for what remained of Oxford's men to come up again. He could probably defeat them now but he would lose fewer men if he attacked from two sides simultaneously.

The last of Broughton's men were retreating from the Tudor line and he found himself next to John of Lincoln. He stood upright between his two household knights and raised his visor as he recognised Broughton.

'Swartz is dead,' he said. 'Lovell too, I believe.'

Broughton's heart sank. For a moment he even forgot Marguerite.

'We'll fight here to the end,' Broughton said.

He was not afraid; he had nothing to live for now.

Risking the arrows, Broughton kept his visor up, watching his troops struggle and limp back to position. But then he frowned. One of the last men to retreat was a tall man carrying a hammer in one hand. He was staggering and seemed unable to walk straight, as if he was dazed or wounded.

As quickly as his armour permitted, Broughton moved

down the slope to help him. Behind the Tudor line he could see movement. Clearly the reserves were being moved up for the final assault. A sufficient number of Oxford's troops had been rounded up for their flank attack.

The enemy archers ceased firing. Except for Francis and a few others, most of what was left of the Yorkist army must be out of range by now. Tudor probably wanted to conserve his remaining arrows for the last attack.

★ ★ ★

Broughton took my hammer and placed his hand on my shoulder. Unsteadily, we turned back up the slope.

I was silent as he removed my helmet. Carefully, Broughton lowered me to the ground.

'I can't see properly,' I said. 'What's happening?'

Broughton removed his helmet.

'Tudor's waiting for Oxford's men. They look as if they will come this way soon. Tudor's using his horse to encircle us and cut off our retreat.'

I closed my eyes with a sigh, but then I heard Lincoln's voice. I opened my eyes. He limped towards us.

'He's safe, Thomas,' he croaked.

'We all are for the moment but our line of retreat is cut off and we face superior forces to the front and the flank,' I heard Broughton reply.

'With Lovell wounded, it seems a good time for me to assume command,' Lincoln continued confidently.

I thought of the few thousand battle-weary men huddled on the slope. Listlessly, they awaited the final onslaught. They were doomed and they knew it, but a few would fight to the end.

'In these circumstances, you hardly need to be a great general,' Lincoln observed. 'Now Broughton, Lovell has to get away. He's the only one who men will follow. He can unseat Tudor at another time.'

'I'll get a horse for him,' Broughton said slowly.

'He'll never make it on his own,' snapped Lincoln. 'Look at him. Harliston's brought down two horses.'

'But what about you?'

Lincoln drew himself up proudly.

'We will fight the last battle here. When men come to speak of this battle against the usurper Tudor, they will say that John of Lincoln died fighting bravely at the head of his army. They will say that of me, as they said it of my Uncle Gloucester.'

Broughton was amazed at how completely Lincoln had conquered his fear.

I groaned which made Broughton glance down. I was trying to get up. At length, I rubbed my head and examined my hand, which I found to be bloody.

With great effort, I manage to stand up despite my swaying. Broughton grasped my shoulders.

'It looks as if the remainder of the Carlisle horse is going to make a last attack on Tudor's cavalry,' muttered Lincoln.

Broughton glanced up. Sure enough the pitifully small remnants of Middleton's men were milling about. Sensing this, Tudor's fresh horsemen began to extend their lines to outflank them.

'Well, at least that will give you and Lovell a chance to slip away,' Lincoln added thoughtfully. 'Now Thomas, this is no time for drawn-out farewells, so mount up.'

Broughton hesitated. It seemed wrong to desert his comrades.

'Don't disobey your commanding officer!' ordered Lincoln.

Broughton sighed and helped Lincoln's squire heave me onto my horse before mounting his own. He started to lead me away glancing back as he did. Already the forward elements of Oxford's division were closing on Lincoln's flank while Tudor's men were edging forward threateningly.

A sudden burst of sunlight illuminated the silver saddlecloths of the remnant of the Carlisle horse. The twenty or so beleaguered horsemen jostled around making a brave display as, with ragged pennants streaming on their lances, they confronted the mass of cavalry in front of them. He watched as one by one they lowered lances but as they broke into their last charge, Broughton had to turn away as his eyes suddenly filled with tears.

PART II
1487 - 1489

CHAPTER 8

North Lakes, Westmoreland, 1487.

'Scotland?' said Broughton.

'Well, where else?' I answered impatiently. I had been thinking of little else since we had fled north. 'We cannot remain in England. The Irish would not welcome us and nor would Burgundy.'

Broughton was silent. I watched him as he pondered. Having spent much of his life fighting the Scots, it would undoubtedly seem strange to live among them. Equally, he knew that I was right; we could not remain concealed in England for too long. He also needed to be free in order to stand a chance of winning back Marguerite.

'I hear that the Scottish King James is an ally of Tudor,' he grunted at last.

'Yes, but there is opposition to that policy. We can take refuge with Henry Lovell. He can arrange for us to have access to the King's Chancellor, the Earl of Argyll, as my kinsman Henry is his man.'

Broughton looked dubious, so I smiled confidently at him.

'Think about it, Thomas. If we can enter Scotland, we will be safe there. Then we will be close enough to rebuild our support in England and we can persuade the Scots to give us an army.'

'Scotland's a poor country!' Broughton objected. 'It's also not strong enough to invade England by itself.'

'I agree, but we will have support in England and we could purchase mercenaries.'

'With what? We still owe Burgundy for the last effort.'

'We'll get the money,' I said easily as I toyed with the ring I wore on a chain around my neck. 'Thomas, I promised Gloucester that I would put his nephew Warwick on the throne of England. I cannot break that promise. I accept that our support in England is in disarray after our defeat at Stokefield. I accept we have to start again and rebuild that support and I accept that it will be difficult. I see too that it is doubly hard for you because of Marguerite – but I am not giving up.' I stopped and looked at him nervously. 'Will you not come with me?'

Broughton shrugged his shoulders.

'I have neither home, lands nor wife, Francis. I've probably been declared a traitor by now. If you take all that into account, I don't suppose I have too much choice.'

'Have you got a reliable man who we can send to Henry Lovell at Ballumbie?'

He nodded. From then on, in daily fear of discovery, we awaited the response.

It was early October when the messenger returned from Cousin Henry. His master, the Earl of Argyll, would welcome Lord Lovell and his companion into Scotland. He would meet us to discuss matters of mutual interest at a suitable time. The Earl would provide an escort to ensure that we would be able to travel from the borders to Henry's home in Ballumbie safely. Henry added that we should reach the Debateable Land on All Soul's Day. We would be found and brought to him.

I smiled at Broughton.

'Well, that sounds encouraging.'

He sighed morosely. Marguerite's desertion plunged him into fits of deep depression. He tried to conceal his sombre temperament but at times he was unable to do so.

'Anyway,' I said looking round our ramshackle hut, 'I won't be sorry to leave this.'

'It depends where we're going,' came the gloomy response.

The Debateable Land was as bleak as I had remembered it. No men or animals dwelled there. No one had attempted to regenerate the place after Skiam and his followers had been driven out. It had been a brutal campaign, I recalled, but an effective one.

'I assume we just wait to be found then,' Broughton muttered.

I looked around the empty landscape.

'Well, they shouldn't have too much trouble finding us,' I pointed out. 'No one else is going to have lit a fire here.'

He slumped down and gazed into the flames. I guessed that he was thinking of his wife so I wrapped myself in my cloak and we sat in companionable silence until at last the Scots arrived. There were six of them – four were men-at-arms wearing a black and yellow livery with the image of a sailing boat on it. A slight figure pushed his way through their horses towards us.

'Brian Emslie,' he announced cheerfully. 'So you must be the hated English – Lord Lovell and Sir Thomas Broughton, I presume?'

We nodded in unison. He cocked his head and regarded us with amusement.

'You don't look as frightening as people say you are. Still appearances can be misleading.'

He chuckled and clicked his fingers.

I glanced at his hulking companion: a vast man who was heavily bearded, covered in furs and unkempt; he dwarfed his horse. He glowered at us.

'And this is Mulvanie,' Brian Emslie continued happily. 'He'll see to our needs on the journey. He speaks no English, so you'll be spared his lively sense of humour. Now, shall we be moving on?'

The men-at-arms left us as we came out of the Debateable Land and began to move into Scotland. The journey was the stuff of nightmares. There were few tracks, so most of the time we rode over sodden moors with low clouds obscuring our vision. We skirted innumerable marshes, waded through swift-flowing streams and trailed over endless hills. My abiding memory, though, was of being constantly buffeted by strong winds, carrying either sleet or heavy rain. At night, we entered small hamlets, which rarely contained more than a dozen families. We sheltered in one of the larger huts, although after the first few nights we ceased to complain. Emslie had taken my comments to task after I had remarked how much better off the English peasants were.

'Do you think so, my lord? Yet these are the people to whom you have come for help. You say that the peat fire creates smoke but no heat. Doubtless these people would prefer wood but there are no trees around here. Then you complain that there is no salted meat. My lord, these people cannot afford to purchase animals for husbandry.'

Mulvanie interrupted him by muttering something.

'He says he can tell from your tone that you must be whining about something else,' Emslie translated. 'He's pointed out that all these people can grow here are oats. They cannot sell or exchange their products, as there is no market nearby. He is asking whether you saw the plough outside this hut. That's the plough for the whole village. These people have no wealth and no security, since their homes or hovels as you describe them, are leased to them by their laird or by the church.'

Mulvanie eyed us contemptuously and spoke again.

'If you are cold, my lord,' Emslie translated, 'think of these people when the heavy snow comes. During that time they cannot get peat for fuel and have to heat their own manure.' Emslie clicked his fingers. 'You say that the peasants in England are better off. Well, maybe that's so, but remember that you have come to us for aid, so stop complaining and try to learn a little of the people who'll be helping you.'

Suitably chastised, we refrained from making further comments.

The journey continued slowly. We were always wet and Broughton brooded endlessly. For my part I tried not to dwell on my wife Nan in order that I could comfort Broughton but to little avail. For never a dreary day passed, when Nan did not walk through my thoughts and there were times when my longing for her became so great that I had to force myself to go on.

At times, we talked of our prospects in Scotland but in depressed tones. I was increasingly beginning to think that Scotland lacked the resources to provide us with an army. When we did talk, it was in a desultory fashion and only when Emslie was not nearby. We paid no heed to Mulvanie, who usually rode next to us or else just behind, since he ignored us. We went on in the same fashion day after day, following the cloaked figure of Emslie and watching his horse's steaming flanks.

My mood of deep depression reached its nadir on the night we stopped in a cottage in an even more isolated position than we were used to. We ate the normal gruel from the common pot with our fingers, but the meal was frequently interrupted by cries from the child of the house. The boy was evidently very ill. I felt his forehead while Broughton put his fingers to the lad's wrist.

'It's fever, no doubt,' I whispered.

He shook his head.

'It's worse than that,' he said in a low voice. He put his hands on the child's chest and frowned. 'It's no use, Francis.'

The boy began to shiver violently, so I laid my cloak over him and he seemed to be comforted by its warmth. He opened his eyes and stared at us. Behind him, Mulvanie looked at us impassively. To cheer the lad I took the chain from my neck and showed him Richard of Gloucester's ring and his eyes lit up at the sight of the gold, but then he fell back to sleep.

Emslie looked at me curiously as I put my chain back on.

'Why do you wear that?' he asked.

'It was a present from a king to remind me of a promise.'

Mulvanie gestured to me and held out his hand. I shook my head.

'He only wants to look at it,' said Emslie.

Reluctantly I handed it to him. He squinted at it by the light of the wax taper he had lit and grunted. He spat on the floor, then he handed it back with a scowl.

The child was still alive when we left and Emslie gave me a sheepskin jerkin to replace my cloak. The next day an itching on my back and chest told me that I was not the only inhabitant of the jerkin. Emslie grinned as I scratched furiously and he nodded at the ox-like Mulvanie.

'It was one of his,' he laughed.

It was a little better in the couple of small towns we passed through. There were no walls, of course. One had only a crude ditch, the other a wooden palisade. Neither of the towns had markets, but business was conducted in the little alleys that ran off a single street.

We passed kilns for drying corn and barley and tanning pits, before we came to large wooden houses, which fronted onto the main street. Behind them were long gardens with busy workshops and outbuildings. When I saw these I began to feel more confident about being able to raise an army from Scotland. There was evidence of some prosperity here: one man wore a velvet cap, another leather shoes. Emslie told me that there was a thriving guild system and pointed out evidence of trade to me: crude woollen cloth, fish stalls, pottery-making, and an occasional iron worker. There was trade with foreign countries, he added, mainly with Germany and the Baltic. It was for that reason that the major ports – Edinburgh, Perth, Dundee – were all on the east side of the country.

'But what do you export?' asked Broughton. It was one of his better days and he was being relatively communicative.

'Wool, skins, leather-workings,' said Emslie, 'fish too, of course.' He looked up at me. 'Doubtless, you'll be comparing us unfavourably with England, my lord, but we poor Scots manage as best we can.' He gave one of his little chuckles and clicked his fingers.

Sullenly, Mulvanie muttered something to Emslie.

'We should be in Ballumbie in two days, he estimates,' Emslie said. 'You'll find something fresh to complain about there I expect, my lord.'

He walked away smirking. I was beginning to dislike Emslie very much indeed. Taking advantage of Broughton's comparative cheerfulness that day, I turned to him as we rode along.

'I cannot say that I will be sorry to arrive at Ballumbie.'

He nodded.

'Not to mention, losing our genial companions,' he added.

Ballumbie Castle sat menacingly at the head of a slope, so it was easily visible. Even at this distance, it looked formidable with its high inner walls and large rounded towers at each of the four corners. As we approached, I noted that the building also had an outer wall, although curiously this had no towers for archers. I pointed this defect out to Broughton.

'You don't need them. The ground's been cleared in all directions. The chances are that you would pick off any attack long before they even came close.'

Emslie, who was riding nearby, joined in the exchange.

'On the far side of the castle, you'll find there's a small tower on the outer wall, Sir Thomas. On that side the ground is not so open and the climb up from the stream there is not a steep one. Three or four miles that way is the sea. You have now travelled the breadth of Scotland.'

'It feels like it,' Broughton said unenthusiastically.

Emslie clicked his fingers, a habit that irritated me immensely.

'You sounded just like Lord Lovell then, Sir Thomas. I wonder why, if all the English hate Scotland so much, they keep attacking us and trying to steal our lands? Why would you want to possess something that you do not want?'

He let out a crow of laughter and turned to face me.

'But it's a different story when you need our help, isn't it?'

He clicked his fingers in amusement again and we entered the outer courtyard. Turning to his right, he led our little group through the main gate and into the small inner courtyard.

Henry Lovell was as wiry as ever and grinned at our appearance. He nodded to us and, ignoring Mulvanie, led Emslie off for a brief discussion. We waited patiently while Mulvanie glared at us. The desire to part ways was obviously mutual. It was shortly afterwards that Henry and Emslie re-emerged. Emslie mounted this horse.

'Keep them safe!'

'As the Earl has ordered,' agreed Henry. 'Has he said when he might send for them?'

Emslie laughed.

'You know better than to ask that, Sir Henry. When he's good and ready he'll send word. Maybe one or two months from now.'

He looked at me.

'It grieves me to be leaving you, my lord, and I'll miss your kindly observations on Scotland and its people, but you will remain here until you're sent for.'

He gestured to Mulvanie, who gave us a final malevolent look and then they clattered off. Henry watched as the hulking Mulvanie waited for his superior to ride out of the gate before him, then he looked at me.

'Welcome to Ballumbie then, Francis and Sir Thomas. This will be your home for the next few weeks or months. It's not grand, but you'll be able to rest and recover from your recent misfortunes.'

He pointed to the hall, which lay opposite the gateway.

'We'll eat in there later and you'll meet my parents.'

He pointed to a small building on the right.

'There's the chapel, if you need it, and I have put two chambers in that tower there at your disposal. I'm sure you'll want to rest but come to the solar and have some wine first.'

We eagerly followed him into the little room. It was plainly furnished with just a couple of benches. There was no attempt at either comfort or luxury but for all that it was the most wonderful room I had ever been in, since it contained three of the things I had been longing for most these past three weeks.

'It's warm and dry in here,' Broughton said delightedly. He then looked at the wine. 'And so is my palate.'

I moved closer to the fire, while Henry poured us wine, which Broughton duly drained.

'So Henry, why are we to remain here?' I asked. 'Of course, we are grateful to you for your hospitality but why does the King's Chancellor want us to be hidden away from court?'

Henry smiled.

'More wine, Sir Thomas? Now Francis, the answer to your question is simple – I don't know. What I can say though is that when your messenger arrived I reported the matter to the Earl of Argyll. He thought for a while and then summoned Emslie. "Bring them into Scotland," he told him, "but manage it in a way so that they are not noticed but allow them to see something of the country. Mulvanie will give them the protection they'll need.'"

'Then the Earl told me my part,' continued Henry. 'But before I tell you about that, let me explain how matters are here. My father's too old and infirm to manage the estate, so I am the Master of Ballumbie. Accordingly, you'll be my guests until the Earl sends for you or gives me further instructions. Sir Thomas, some more wine?'

There seemed to be a degree of secrecy in all of this which was puzzling, but I was growing tired with the wine and the heat of the fire.

'As your host, I have two responsibilities – your safety and your comfort. Let me start with your safety: you may roam anywhere in the castle but not outside it unless I am with you.'

'So we're prisoners,' I said with distaste.

He shook his head.

'No, but the conditions I have referred to are there for three reasons: the English are hated here and, secondly, you two are wealthy and the people here are very poor and thirdly, the Earl has instructed me to keep you safe.'

Next to me Broughton began to snore and I nudged him awake.

'I'm confused. What does the Earl want?'

Then fatigue seemed to overwhelm me.

'I don't understand.'

Henry laughed.

'Look at you man; you're all worn out – to bed with both of you. We'll talk in the evening, but for now let me attend to my second duty as a host. I am neglecting your comfort.'

★ ★ ★

Being older, Broughton had suffered under the privations of our journey more than I. Or perhaps he was in a dark mood. Either way, he begged to be excused that evening. Dressed in the new clothing that had been provided, I followed Henry down to the hall alone.

His parents and son were already present. I was introduced to his father, a tall, stern old man, who welcomed me to Ballumbie. As an afterthought, he thanked me for ransoming Henry. His wife Katherine was everything that he was not. Her bright blue eyes sparkled under an unruly mop of white hair; she had an enchanting smile and engaged me in a cheery babble of conversation.

'For shame, for shame!' She turned on her husband in mock anger. 'You and I have but one son and him born to us late in life. Your son goes to war and gets himself captured by the English. Then he's returned to us in a smart new gown, riding on a fine horse with a purse in his hands. All of these things were provided by a distant kinsman, who paid his ransom. And what do you say? All you can say is "I thank you for Henry."'

Her mimicry of her husband's gruff manner was so exact, and her expression so stern, that we all burst out laughing. Even her husband's rigid expression softened into a smile.

'Aye, welcome Francis. I'll not call you 'my lord' as you are kin, albeit from a long way back. I've heard a little of your troubles and doubtless Henry here, along with the Earl of Argyll, will make matters worse for you. You're with family again, Francis. Sit and eat. But what of Sir Thomas?'

To avoid any future embarrassment, I explained how Broughton's wife had departed and the effect this had had on him. There were sympathetic nods and Henry indicated that we should be seated.

Henry's son, Andrew, had carved the meat in a corner of the hall near the great fire and carried a portion to his grandfather. The old man cut some of it into small pieces and passed the trencher to his wife. With a jolt, I suddenly realised that she had only one arm. She must have heard me gasp, as she smiled at me.

'There's no cause for concern, Francis. It happened over fifty years ago and I've managed well enough since.' She gave her husband a loving look. 'With the help of my new right arm.'

'I am sorry,' I said, embarrassed at my clumsiness. 'It must have been a terrible accident.'

'It was no accident. I lost my arm trying to protect King James. Not the current King, Francis, but his grandfather. It was at the time when he was killed by his rebellious nobles.'

I sat open-mouthed as Henry and his father exchanged glances.

'Why do you not tell Francis the tale, mother?'

'Oh Henry, Francis would have no interest in such matters.'

'Please my lady, please.'

The request was from young Andrew; clearly the story was a great favourite of his. Still she hesitated; I added that I would be most interested to hear the tale. The Lady Katherine went a little pink.

'Well it's not much of a story – Andrew did you use a knife when you cut this meat? A long time ago when I was a wee lass, I was at the King's court, Francis.'

'He had a terrible life did he not?' Andrew chimed in. Obviously he knew the story by heart. 'He had been marooned on a rock, captured by pirates and then held prisoner in England for eighteen years. Then he had to pay an enormous ransom to regain his liberty and throne.'

'Silence!' Henry cuffed his son lightly. 'Certainly, he was ransomed; but his ransom was paid by his people and the remainder of what was raised was squandered by King James on his own pleasures.'

His mother turned on him indignantly.

'After all that captivity and deprivation, do you begrudge the poor man a few simple pleasures?'

'Simple pleasures?' Henry retorted. 'King James wasted money on buying foreign artillery, jewels and luxuries for the court, royal residences, a new palace at Linlithgow and...'

'Enough!' his mother interrupted. 'King James did good things for Scotland. He tried to weaken those lords, who had too much power, so the country could become peaceful. But, for all his goodness, his nobles did not support him as they had supported his father, Robert III, who, let me tell you Henry, was a truly incompetent King.'

'So I have heard, mother. But at least he consulted with his nobles and they tolerated his weakness. King Robert's son James was like his grandson, our present King. He chose his own way and would not be guided by his nobles. That was folly on his part. By birth and experience, his nobles have a natural place in the ruling of the country.'

His mother sniffed.

'That is incorrect. But you are right to say that our present King James III is similar to his grandfather, but not for the reasons you said. The reason that they are similar is that both of them were ordained by God to be our Kings and, whether you or your precious Earl of Argyll like it,

He has sent them to rule over us.'

I had kept quiet during these heated exchanges. Clearly, the Ballumbie Lovells had differing views of their monarchs and it is never advisable to interrupt a family argument. Perhaps they felt my silence, as Henry turned to me,

'Your pardon Francis; we're unearthing old battles. Mother, forgive me – please continue your tale.'

His mother smiled at him.

'There is not much more and you know it already. But rather than let Francis see us squabble, let me finish the story.'

She frowned in thought and then looked at me.

'That year, Francis, we were at Perth for Christmas. Naturally the court was spread about the town but the King and the Queen needed to be in a secure place, due to the enmity of a number of nobles led by the Earl of Atholl. So it was that the royal family was lodged at the Priory of Blackfriars, since it was sturdy and even had a little moat around it.'

'You were in attendance on the Queen?' I asked.

'Yes, I attended Queen Joan. There were not too many of us lodged in the priory, just a few friends and trusted servants of the King or so he thought. We spent Christmas there which lingered on into February.'

She broke off and smiled at the memory of that long distant time.

'They were such happy times, Francis. Until the night when they came for the King.'

'What happened madam?' Andrew had heard the story countless times but still he sat with eyes wide open listening intently.

'Well Andrew, it had been a quiet evening with just the King and the Queen and three of her ladies. Earlier, we had heard some very pleasant music and had played chess. But then all of a sudden we heard cries from outside and a scream. The shouts grew louder and I heard cries of 'Treason!' Men were coming for the King.'

'But there was only one door to go in and out of the room, wasn't there?' panted Andrew.

'Certainly, there was only one door and the window was too small for a man the size of the King, so he seized the tongs from the fireplace to lever up the floorboards so he could drop into the vault below. The Queen was screaming by now, as there was the sound of swords clashing on the other side of the door. The King was covered in sweat as he raised up the boards and lowered himself down below. The Queen and the other ladies helped put the floorboards back and I flew to the door to secure it.'

'Then what happened?' I asked excitedly.

'There was no bar on the door, Francis.' Katherine's husband took up the story. 'It was discovered later that King James's own chamberlain, Sir Robert Stewart, the grandson of the Earl of Atholl, had removed it. He had also instructed a makeshift bridge to be laid over the moat to allow Robert Graham and three hundred other traitors to enter in order to kill the King.'

'The men burst into the chamber,' continued his wife, 'demanding to know where the King was. They were coarse and abusive and some had blood on their swords. The poor Queen was struck dumb with terror but, after subjecting us to insults and pawing at us, they left to look elsewhere for the King.'

She smiled at her husband.

'Will you finish it, my love?'

'It is not known how the murderers discovered that the King was hidden in the vault but they returned a while later and went to the place where he had dropped down. They began to rip up the floorboards with their swords and, of course, they found the King. One of the murderers – Sir John Hall, I believe – climbed down with a large knife. Another climbed down at the other end. Naturally King James was unarmed, but for a while he managed to hold them off; he was a big strong man, but his arms and hands were covered in blood. Then the leader of that pack of wolves – the cursed Sir Robert Graham – drew his sword and climbed into the vault. Opposite him stood his monarch, bleeding and defenceless.'

I shuddered at the vision, but the old man continued proudly.

'It was at this point, just as Graham was preparing to strike the fatal blow that a young girl leapt down into the pit. She screamed, "Cowards and traitors!" and stood in front of her King. Robert Graham pushed her aside and made to smite the monarch. But as his sword curved through the air, the young girl struck out her right hand to block the blow. His sword cut cleanly through flesh and bone, severing her arm completely.'

I gasped. Even Henry and young Andrew sat motionless.

'Many men might have stopped at that point, but not Robert Graham. His next blow killed King James and then the other "heroes" jumped down to desecrate the King's body. Finally, when it was all over and they had departed, Lady Katherine was lifted out. For a year or more she hovered precariously at death's door. But finally she recovered.'

He glanced at me under those bushy eyebrows.

'Even cowards, such as Graham and his men, felt guilty

about mutilating a woman and tried to play down the incident. They claimed that Lady Katherine had merely put her arm in the place of the bar on the door. They argued that the arm had been unfortunately broken when they pushed on the door to open it. Well, you're a soldier and know what a sword cut looks like, don't you?'

I nodded slowly.

'I have never heard of such bravery.'

★ ★ ★

'A remarkable lady,' I said to Henry, as we sat by the fire after the others had left.

'Hmm... yes.'

After watching the flames for some time, he turned to me.

'But you see, Francis, the problems we had then are not so different to the problems we face now. As you witnessed earlier, even within families people hold opposing views about our kings.'

'James I was proclaimed a martyr by some, yet others thought Scotland better off without him. That is history, you may say, but maybe our current King will come to share the fate of his grandfather.'

He gave me a sidelong glance.

'It's late, but you're here to look for support and an army. To get these things certain other actions need to be undertaken and you need to understand what they are. Do you want to know now or at another time?'

I had slept the day through and was impatient to hear how I could get the help I needed.

'No, let's talk now.'

Henry got up and poured wine for us both.

'The problem which you have, Francis,' began Henry slowly, 'is that you've come to Scotland to look for an army.'

'And money for mercenaries.'

'Alright, you want an army and money to overthrow Henry Tudor. But Scotland has a King, who believes that his interests and those of his country are best served by having peace with England. In fact, King James believes that it is good to come as get as possible to King Henry.'

This was not encouraging. Clearly, if the Scottish King wanted peace with England then he was not going to help me as a rebel against Henry Tudor.

'On the other hand,' my cousin continued, 'the problem that we have here in Scotland is that there are a great many people who do not want James to be our King.'

'Go on,' I said hopefully.

'Yes. In fact they would rather have him replaced by his son. He, of course, would be strongly advised to reverse his father's policy towards England.'

Excellent, I thought, but Henry was not finished.

'Of course, King James still has much support in certain quarters.'

He poked at the fire and the sparks flew upwards.

'It's all rather complicated,' he said gloomily.

He thought hard for a while and turned to me.

'Probably the simplest way to explain the situation is to start at the beginning. Tell me, what do you recollect of the situation in Scotland when Richard of Gloucester invaded?'

I thought hard. I had not been with Gloucester's army for much of the campaign. Indeed, I had spent nearly all the time at Berwick, which was how I had come to meet my Cousin Henry. Fortunately, Lord Stanley, who resented having to do the hard work there, had agents who reported the news to him. This information he shared freely with me.

'The purpose of the invasion was to install James III's brother on the throne in place of him,' I said at last. 'His brother, the Duke of Albany, had reached an agreement with the English. After the successful invasion, he would become King Alexander IV.'

'So those were the English objectives at the time of the invasion. But what did you find out when you actually invaded?'

'Our information was that James III was moving south towards us. Obviously, we expected the Scottish army to force battle on us south of Edinburgh but then we heard that a number of the Scottish nobles had seized King James, had imprisoned him in Edinburgh Castle and some of his favourites had been hanged. Inexplicably, the Scottish army had then withdrawn.'

I stopped and looked into the blazing fire. The news had been disastrous for Richard of Gloucester, who had wanted a decisive military victory to boost his reputation. Worse still, with the Scottish King imprisoned and his government scattered, there was little chance of installing the pro-English King as Alexander IV or of making the peace treaty work. The only real gain in the campaign had been Berwick, I reflected. None of the other objectives of the invasion had been attained. Henry poured me some more wine and settled himself comfortably.

'So that's what happened. But Francis, would you not say that the situation was somewhat unusual? After all, the hated English – whom we've been fighting since time immemorial – invade. So what do we do? We raise an army to oppose the English but then we refuse combat, imprison our own King and hang a number of his favourite servants. It's not exactly the conventional response to an invasion from your oldest enemy, is it?'

I laughed.

'No, I suppose not. So why did you do it?'

'I suppose it all started a long time ago before the invasion. The truth is that our nobles here have been used to having things their own way. Both James III and his father had long minorities before they came to reign and in those periods the nobles got used to ruling. I don't suppose James helps himself much either.'

'Why is that?'

'He is aloof; he doesn't seem to like mixing with people. He is always making plans to travel outside Scotland so folk didn't believe that he likes his own country. But that didn't matter too much – the real issue is that he is proving to be a poor King.'

'In what way?'

'We're a fractious lot, we Scots. From time to time we need a firm hand but King James refuses to travel out and about to administer justice or resolve local feuds and, as such, murder and robbery have become widespread. He has taxed heavily, but has not spent the money wisely. He used it for buildings, the court, jewellery and other fripperies.'

It sounded disastrous, but Henry was not finished.

'He upset the church too and ruined the currency.'

'Why do you still put up with him?'

'We've had bad kings in Scotland before, Francis, and doubtless we will again. In the past, the bad kings survived if they listened to the bishops and took advice from the nobles. But James is opinionated. He won't take criticism, despite being totally out of his depth running the kingdom. So he doesn't listen to the nobles who could help him. Instead, his advisors are commoners – a musician, a tailor, a shoemaker.'

I sensed his anger was rising, so I kept silent. He gave a small apologetic smile and shrugged his shoulders slightly.

'I'm not saying that he wasn't unfortunate with his family. Albany was a self-seeking traitor and their other brother was possibly the same – but at least they were men. Albany commanded the Eastern March against the English and was a soldier. But King James does not like soldiers. He does not even like horses. He wanted peace with England, while a lot of the nobles wanted war.

'Then the rumours began. They were probably untrue but they did not help him. He was supposed to have killed his brother, Mar, and committed incest with his sister, Margaret. Mind you, that last one didn't catch on.'

'Why was that?'

'Well, it was rumoured that he preferred men to women. I don't know the truth of it and I don't want to but the fact was that King James was proving a disastrous and unpopular king.'

'So when we invaded…'

'King James got the loudest warning any monarch has ever had. Even his wife, the Queen, and his uncles were part of the plot. His favourites were hanged in front of him at Lauder and then he was imprisoned, while the English rampaged all over his country. His army would not fight for him and the English entered Edinburgh.'

He paused and glanced at me.

'He was humiliated, Francis, like no king has ever been.

But he was not overthrown. This was a warning, a final warning. The message was simple – be a better king or else be overthrown and suffer the consequences. Well maybe it was harsh but after that you would have thought that he would have learnt a little, wouldn't you?'

'So did the warning have its desired effect?'

Henry smiled briefly.

'If it had, Francis, I don't suppose we would be having this conversation. But no, James has not changed and now there's a move to replace him.'

I helped myself to more wine and looked at him expectantly.

'It's the English issue,' Henry began. 'Before you invaded, James wanted peace but the border lords – the Humes, the Hepworths and the Earl of Angus – wanted war. Albany encouraged them to defy the King and so the border skirmishes continued.

'Then you invaded and captured Berwick and now a lot of Scots want it back. But what does James do? Not only did he discourage war, but he made a new peace with your King Henry.'

'Not my king!'

'The English King Henry VII. He planned to marry himself and his two sons to English princesses. James' own wife died last year – a pity, she was a restraining influence on him. Well you can imagine how the talk of the royal marriages sat with the border families.'

I began to sense potential allies in Scotland.

'Are these families powerful?'

'Very. But King James has begun to force them to band together against him. The Humes had enjoyed the revenues of Coldingham Abbey for generations, but James managed to acquire them for himself and that upset them and, Francis, you do not upset that family. They're the most powerful family in the South and they are linked to the Hepworths, who have all sorts of connections to a number of other important families and none of them liked James' heavy-handed treatment.'

The fire was beginning to die away now, but Henry ignored it and fell silent as he brooded over his King's shortcomings.

'Everything he does seems clumsy or vindictive. He is alienating more and more people. But the worst thing, Francis, is that he's begun to ostracise his eldest son. He seems to prefer his younger boy. There's been no improvement in his ruling; he's still as incompetent as he ever was and just as arrogant.'

He broke off and poked at the almost dead fire.

'But there's a difference between the situation now and the time when you invaded, which King James doesn't seem to realise.'

'What is that?'

'There was a precedent set then, Francis,' he said a little grimly. 'People know now that they can hang the King's councillors and get away with it. Also, of course, they know that they can overthrow the King and imprison him because they have already done it once. But there's another change to the situation now. Back then King James' eldest son was just a wee lad but now, well, he's older and can start to think for himself. At the moment, I reckon he'll be thinking that his father means to deprive him of his natural inheritance.'

'It seems that his father's actions will push him into the rebels' camp.'

'Yes. Albany was never a credible substitute for King James but already many view young Prince James as a better alternative to his father.'

'So where do you stand?'

'I'll stand wherever my lord, the Earl of Argyll, stands,' came the prompt reply. 'I've served him for ten years and think that, out of all the lords we have, he best embodies the interests of Scotland.'

'He must be a remarkable man. Tell me all about him.'

'Colin Campbell, Earl of Argyll, is powerful. His family has extensive lands. He controls most of the Western Isles. He married well and, through his daughters' marriages, he has made strong connections with a great many influential people. He's served King James for a long time and has been his Chancellor these last five years. But you know for all that, he's still seen as his own man. Men don't link him to the King and his mistakes. They only see him acting in the best interests of Scotland. He won't take sides; nothing can influence or sway him. He has only one rule when making a decision: is the proposed action going to benefit the kingdom?'

'He sounds impressive. So, is he for or against the King?'

Henry laughed.

'He keeps his thoughts to himself and neither the King nor James' eldest son, the Prince, will know what the Earl is thinking until it is too late for one of them. But if he stays loyal to the crown the rebels are doomed. Conversely, if he joins them he'll give their revolt respectability and they can attract more support.'

He smiled at me.

'He's got a use for you, Francis, and if you help him, you may one day get your army and your money for mercenaries. But, as I said earlier, the situation here is complicated and a lot of things have to happen first.'

★ ★ ★

'And so that's the state of things,' I concluded as I briefed Broughton the next day. 'As I see it, the chances of getting any help from the present King of Scotland are non-existent. On the other hand, if there is a revolt against him which succeeds, then the successor to James III may help us.'

Broughton made a half-hearted attempt to comb his wild beard.

'Would King James' own son rebel against his father?' he asked incredulously.

I shrugged.

'It all seems to depend on the Earl of Argyll.'

'And that would be the same Earl who has smuggled you and me into Scotland and effectively imprisoned us here in Ballumbie?' he asked sourly.

'The very same, Thomas. Don't forget, too, that we are to be kept here until he reveals his purpose.'

'I wouldn't say that the chances of us getting support from the Scots were totally guaranteed at this stage,' Thomas remarked thoughtfully.

I smiled inwardly at Broughton's typical understatement.

'Well, we probably will not have to wait too long before the Earl of Argyll sends for us.'

★ ★ ★

Time dragged as there was no news from either England or Scotland and the castle was small. To make it worse,

Thomas withdrew into himself and brooded endlessly on his wife; there was little that I could say or do to comfort him. The tedium of the days affected me so badly that I was wholly unprepared on the morning when Cousin Henry burst into my chamber and asked us to be ready to leave the next day.

'Leave for where?'

He grinned at me.

'After all this time, Francis, you ask such a question. The Earl of Argyll wants to see you. We're going to Castle Gloom, of course.'

CHAPTER 9

Castle Gloom, 1488.

H enry pointed through the mist.
'Castle Gloom!' he shouted above the noise of the wind.

I peered down the slope; there did seem to be some form of blurred shape down there but I was too wet and cold to care much. The week-long journey through the constant sleet and howling winds had left me permanently wet. The peat fires in foul-smelling hovels, which served as shelter at night, did nothing to remove the damp. The problem, Henry explained, was that the Earl had instructed that on no account were we to be seen. As a result, the journey had taken longer than necessary, as we had made our way through circuitous tracks and hidden paths.

We continued to descend the steep path and I could now make out the silhouette of the castle. It looked too small to withstand a serious assault, I thought, although that big tower on the left would pose a problem for an attacker. We clattered into the courtyard where, despite the lateness of the hour, grooms were waiting. Brian Emslie approached with a smile.

'The Earl has not arrived yet, but he is expected tomorrow. No, don't take those steps; they lead up to the cellars.'

Wearily, we climbed up the other wooden staircase. A large fire in the hall was burning wood, not peat, and we clustered round it, drinking wine and spooning broth.

Morning found me on the terraced garden looking down the valley. The hills on either side and behind cloaked the castle neatly. The view was spectacular and I was watching two eagles soaring when Brian Emslie interrupted my thoughts.

'Admiring the view, my lord? The Orchil Hills – excellent for hunting.' He pointed to a raging torrent on his right. 'The Burn of Sorrows and, over there, my lord, the Burn of Care. The others are waiting for you,' Emslie continued. 'The Earl of Argyll will see you now.'

The hall itself looked much brighter than the previous night. A large window overlooked the courtyard and the bright sunshine illuminated a couple of colourful tapestries. A large fire blazed and a collection of silver cups on the table reflected its light. At the head of the table, a man sat writing and, judging by the number of sheets in front of him, he must have been so engaged for a time. He looked at us briefly and gestured to the trestle benches on either side of the table.

I studied the Earl as he went on writing. He was an older man with a lined face and dark shadows under his eyes. But his swift writing, alert eyes and sharply pointed moustache gave the impression of intelligence and impatience. At last, he threw down his pen and beckoned Henry and Brian Emslie over to him. He gestured at one set of papers.

'Brian – for the Earl of Angus.' He pointed to the second set. 'Henry, these are for Elphinstone and the King.'

They collected their papers and bowed. The Earl of Argyll, Broughton, Mulvanie and I were left together. For a few moments, the Earl stared at us and then rang a small bell. Two guards entered, but remained by the door.

'England and Scotland are officially at peace, my Lord Lovell,' the Earl began. 'The peace was signed in July two years ago, as our King wished to promote closer ties with the English. Indeed, he planned to marry Elizabeth Woodville – the mother of King Henry's own wife.'

I was puzzled.

'Well yes, but if you are going to help us…'

'Help you?' The Earl sounded surprised. 'You have rebelled against the English King Henry and he is our ally. Then I learn that you are in Scotland without the knowledge or consent of our King James. Am I correct?'

I stared at him.

'But I sought shelter in Scotland with your knowledge; you are the Chancellor. My kinsman Henry is your man.'

'With my knowledge?' Argyll asked. 'But, my lord, why should I have allowed a leading rebel against our ally, King Henry, to enter Scotland? We have a truce with England after all.'

'But…'

'And why should I have welcomed into Scotland a man who spent several years killing my countrymen on the Western March? A man who invaded Scotland with Gloucester a few years ago.'

The Earl raised his eyebrows and looked at Broughton and me.

'If none of these are reasons enough not to welcome you into Scotland, ask yourself why should I welcome the man who helped to take Berwick from us?'

I was totally dumbfounded. Broughton sat with his mouth open.

'Then what do you intend to do with us?' I asked nervously.

Mulvanie must have sensed what was going on, as he grinned openly at our discomfort. The Earl of Argyll paused and thought for a moment.

'Beneath this hall, my lord, is a wee pit prison. It's small, but it could accommodate you both easily enough and then I will gain favour with my King by handing you over to him. Now he could either give you back to Henry Tudor or sell you to him. How much do you think he'd pay?' he asked casually.

I was staggered, even a king as tight-fisted as Henry Tudor would pay a small fortune to have Broughton and myself delivered to him as captives. I looked about helplessly; Broughton was white-faced and we were both unarmed. Mulvanie looked like a formidable opponent even without his axe and there were two guards by the door. Mulvanie muttered something to the Earl who nodded gravely.

'He's asking why we have to deliver you alive. King Henry would presumably pay more for you alive, I suppose.'

He turned back to Mulvanie and began to talk in Gaelic, which I recognised but could not understand. Mulvanie nodded and gestured to the guards, who lowered their spears and advanced on us.

This was worse than Bosworth, and far worse than Stokefield. I'd trusted Henry Lovell and had lived in the hope of Scottish support these past six months. I'd believed all his talk of Colin Campbell, the great Earl of Argyll. A few moments ago, I had been thinking of advancing on England at the head of a Scottish army but now Broughton and I would be sent back to England in chains. We would be interrogated and killed, of that I had no doubt. This was the lowest treachery conceivable. Broughton looked at me and I saw that there were tears in his eyes as he knew that, whether imprisoned or killed, he could never regain his wife. My bewilderment and disbelief turned into savage anger. The realisation that I had let my friend down was the final straw.

'You're a little bastard, Colin Campbell! Doubtless the idea of selling your guests to their enemies sits well with your concept of Scottish hospitality. You may be an Earl, but your people are primitive and your country the laughing stock of Europe.'

I expected to be hauled off by the guards, but they stood back from us with spears lowered, so I thumped the table and went on.

'Even this pathetic little Castle of Gloom, with its "Burn of Sorrows" and "Burn of Care" belongs to a bygone age.' I shook Broughton's arm off my shoulder. 'Call it Castle Campbell; at least people should know who to ask for when they come to buy the guest prisoners that you're selling.'

I gestured to Broughton and rose to my feet.

'Now, if you're going to kill us – go ahead. I came here expecting to find a man of intelligence and experience with whom I could work to our mutual benefit. Instead, I've encountered Judas. Well, I won't miss you, Campbell; I won't miss the morose Mulvanie or your chattering little rat Emslie.'

Still no one moved, so I let the bitterness of my disappointment erupt completely.

'In fact, I won't miss Scotland and I won't miss its climate or its people. If I do have one regret, it's that

Richard of Gloucester merely invaded this country. What he should have done was to have thoroughly devastated the land and obliterated its entire population.' I looked at Thomas and gestured towards the door. 'Shall we leave this Garden of Gethsemane?'

'Stop!'

I turned around and, to my astonishment, I saw that Argyll and Mulvanie were still seated. Mulvanie was pouring wine into the silver goblets and the Earl was smiling broadly.

'Perfect, was it not Davie? All the arrogance and bravery, which you said he possessed, on display. I had not thought of Emslie as a rat, but Davie Mulvanie here is my chief agent. It's remarkable that behind the wild hair and rough dress dwells one of the shrewdest minds in Scotland.'

I glared at the pair of them in astonishment. Courteously, the Earl indicated that we should resume our seats. Broughton lowered himself onto the bench and immediately reached for the wine as the Earl continued.

'You see, my lord, when your cousin – I use the term loosely – Henry came to me to say that you wished to come to Scotland, I thought we might be of use to one another. But first I wished to see what type of man you were. Tell me, Davie, what you thought of Lord Lovell, on your journey to Ballumbie?'

Mulvanie looked at him.

'Lord Lovell and Sir Thomas came across Scotland by some of the roughest paths and in the worst weather. They obeyed all our instructions and did well to complete the journey. As their companion, I found Lord Lovell variously arrogant, brave and derogatory about Scotland. On one occasion, he was particularly kind to a young boy.'

'You speak English!' Broughton interrupted him.

We looked at each other in horror. The Earl laughed.

'Davie speaks Gaelic, English, French and Latin.'

Dear God! How we had been fooled by him and Emslie! We had taken care not to discuss anything in front of Brian Emslie, but Thomas and I had ignored the shambling ox as he rode next to us and had talked freely of our hopes and plans. I looked nervously at Broughton and swallowed hard; doubtless Mulvanie had passed the content of our talk onto the Earl.

'Despite the numerous insults to my servant Brian Emslie and myself, I conclude that Lord Lovell and Sir Thomas will serve our purpose.'

I was so unsettled by the sound of Mulvanie's clipped tones and embarrassed at having been so completely fooled that I could think of nothing to say. Out of habit, I looked at Broughton who glanced at the Earl and then looked back at me. He gave an imperceptible nod.

'Then my lord, we are at your service,' I said.

Argyll rose and looked serious.

'That is what I wished to hear.'

He gestured for the guards to leave the room.

'Your cousin has briefed you of developments in Scotland, I understand? Good, then let me tell you of the most recent advances and then let us see how we can assist one another. No, better still, let Davie tell you.'

He sat down and nodded at Mulvanie.

'Henry Lovell has explained to you how, by his recent actions, King James began to force men to take sides?' Mulvanie asked.

'Yes.'

'Well his latest moves have completed the process. At

the end of January, he used parliament to examine people who criticised his actions in seizing Coldingham Priory. When my Lord Argyll here told him that this was the height of folly, he dismissed him as Chancellor.'

The Earl rose and walked to the fireplace.

'Even by the standards of a totally incompetent monarch, these two actions are incredible,' continued Mulvanie. 'On top of everything else though, they were too much. The rebels have reacted. Earlier this month the Earl of Angus, the Hepworths and the Humes came to Stirling Castle, where King James' eldest son was, and released him.'

There was a laugh from Argyll.

'Davie, they bribed Shaw of Sauchie to hand him over to them.'

'And took him with them as their leader. So now there are two clear-cut parties. One led by the King and the rebels led by the Prince. Do you follow so far?' asked Mulvanie.

Broughton and I nodded.

'So what happens now?' asked Thomas.

The Earl resumed his seat and fingered his moustache pensively.

'A question for you first and then I'll answer yours.'

'Tell me,' the Earl continued, 'in the event of a civil war, who would Henry Tudor support? Would it be the King's party or the Prince's rebels?'

I thought for a moment.

'In my opinion Henry Tudor would support neither since a divided Scotland would be advantageous for England. But he might well look to reinforce the Earl of Northumberland should circumstances make it desirable to intervene in Scotland at a future date.'

There were nods from Argyll and Mulvanie, but now they both looked grim. The Earl gazed at the table and played absent-mindedly with his pen for a while. But then his bright eyes met mine.

'You asked what happens now? I'll tell you because your answer mirrors our own thinking. My mind is almost made up on which party to support but for the sake of Scottish unity I will make one final attempt. Tonight, I will return to the King and talk to him and his uncles, the Earls of Errol and Atholl. I'll even talk to Bishop Elphinstone, the new Chancellor. I'll talk to them all because, even at this late stage, there is a chance that King James may be made to see sense and civil war could be prevented.'

He sighed wearily. I felt admiration for his love of his country. He was going to humiliate himself to avert civil war. I could understand why Cousin Henry served such a man.

'Not that I hold out much hope.' the Earl continued, 'If I fail King James will ride – or to be more precise, he will travel by carriage – to the northern regions. Of course, his main support base is there: he could probably muster twenty thousand or more.'

'If his opponents can muster half that number, they'll do well,' said Mulvanie.

The situation was depressing. From what I understood, if the Earl of Argyll was unable to prevent civil war, then the forces of the pro-Tudor James III would sweep away his son's rebel army. As usual, my face betrayed my thoughts and Argyll noted it.

'There *is* a way that the Prince's party could prevail, if it came to war,' he muttered.

'There is?'

The day had already brought too many surprises.

Mulvanie grinned, his teeth very white against his black hair.

'If the two of you were prepared to support the Prince then certainly there is. Of course, if you helped the Prince he would assist you.'

At last, here was something we could discuss. We would hear why Argyll had need of us. I glanced at Broughton, who shrugged his shoulders and looked back to Mulvanie.

'You have our help,' I said.

'I'll explain first why you've been smuggled into Scotland and what needs to be done,' said the Earl happily. 'But if you don't mind, we'll start with Sir Thomas here.'

He twisted his moustache and beamed at us. Argyll and Mulvanie were involving us closer in their schemes and plans but it did not worry me. At least, by helping them, we could hope to get our army.

'I agree with you, Lord Lovell,' the Earl of Argyll began. 'If war breaks out between King James and his son, I do not believe that Henry Tudor will act immediately to support either of them. But what I fear is, if at a later stage he does take action, he will use the Earl of Northumberland. He has substantial forces after all, and is almost on our doorstep.'

'But if Northumberland comes into Scotland, it would be a disaster for the Prince,' observed Mulvanie. 'His father's support is mainly in the northern part of Scotland, whereas the bulk of the Prince's backing is from the southern regions. Now if Northumberland crosses the borders, the Prince's army, which is already smaller than his father's, will be caught between Northumberland and his father.'

He picked up a large nut from the bowl on the table and crushed it.

'So, it would serve the Prince's interests, and my own purpose, to know what the Earl of Northumberland is planning,' the Earl said.

He collected the broken pieces of shell together fastidiously.

'If we had someone in the Earl of Northumberland's retinue, perhaps that would be beneficial. Someone who could send word of when Northumberland was mustering men or gathering supplies for a campaign.' He looked as us meditatively. 'Someone who could tell us what it was that the Earl of Northumberland was planning to do.'

It was a good idea but he ignored me and looked at Broughton.

'I am advised that you were formerly a retainer of the Earl of Northumberland, Sir Thomas. Now, if I was to ask you to do it, would you or could you get yourself inserted back into his retinue?'

Broughton pulled at his beard and narrowed his eyes.

'In England, I have been declared a traitor and all my lands are forfeit. In theory, the moment I set foot in England I would be arrested and killed. But for all that, the Earl of Northumberland is short of retainers. He lost people to Richard of Gloucester when he held the power in the North. Then, after Bosworth, men were so disgusted by his actions they would not serve him.'

'You're right about the Earl of Northumberland,' I said.

'He does lack followers but remember Thomas, that Northumberland is not wholly trusted by Henry Tudor. Henry knows that while Northumberland did not fight against him at Bosworth, he did not fight for him either. Northumberland's actions in the Stokefield campaign were lacklustre. Had he been fully loyal to Henry Tudor, he would have pursued us as we marched south. As it was, he ran away from us chasing a decoy that he knew was no real threat. He knows this and Henry Tudor knows it too. If you appear in England and ask to enter his service, then he might seek to win Henry Tudor's favour by just handing you over to him.'

'It's dangerous, Thomas. Don't do it. We'll think of something else.'

Broughton shook his head.

'Francis, you know there is no other alternative. You and I both know that it's only the Scots who can help us. I'll do it for you, not just because I've always served you, but because there is a chance that it might work. The Earl of Northumberland does have men in his retinue who fought against Henry Tudor at Bosworth. Perhaps, if I were to explain that after Stokefield I fled to Ireland with the others but now wish to return, Northumberland might take me.'

'With your military expertise, he would probably accept you,' said Mulvanie. 'Your presence in his retinue would attract others into his service. Of course, to make it look realistic, you would have to arrive in England from a port in Westmoreland or Cumberland.'

'Maryport or Ravenglass,' Thomas said.

'So you'll do this for us?' Argyll asked.

Broughton eyed him firmly.

'I'll not do it for you,' he said bluntly. He pointed at me. 'I'll do it for him.'

I sighed gratefully. One day, perhaps, I could repay his loyalty.

'When do you want me to go?'

'We'll wait a few weeks,' Mulvanie told him. 'If there is to be war between the King and his son, we'll know soon enough. I would estimate that you'll be in England by the end of April.'

'One final point, Sir Thomas,' said Argyll. 'You say that you'll do this for Lord Lovell and not for us. I understand that. On the other hand, I would not wish you to think us ungrateful, as you are taking a great risk in this matter. We believe we may be able to get you something you might like.'

Broughton looked at him scornfully.

'In my own country, I am a rebel,' he said quietly. 'This has cost me my lands, my home and whatever wealth I had. All I have left is my pride.'

He ran his hand through his dishevelled beard.

'It probably means little to you, but to me it means a great deal. So, when I said that I will do what you wish me to do, it's not because of a reward from you, it's because it will help Francis. Don't try and bribe me; there's nothing that you can possibly give me.'

Argyll twisted the ends of his moustache.

'Not even your wife?' he asked quietly.

Broughton lunged forward angrily but Mulvanie was quicker and grabbed his arms from behind. He signalled for me to remain where I was. The Earl looked at Broughton, who had stopped struggling in the grip of Mulvanie.

'Sir Thomas, I do not mean to mock or anger you,' the Earl said gently. 'Oh, release him Davie!'

Broughton slumped down next to me.

'Tell me,' asked the Earl, 'after all she's done, would you still want her back?'

Broughton's shoulders slouched.

'Yes,' he said dejectedly.

'Then I have news for you,' the Earl said happily. 'After Lord Lovell told his Cousin Henry a little of what had happened, Henry mentioned it to Davie here. You'll be surprised, Sir Thomas, how much we Scots like to know about people and how useful it can be. I recall that on one occasion...'

'About my wife?' snapped Broughton.

'Ah yes.' The Earl apologised. 'Well, Davie recalled that one of his agents, who is with the Duchess Margaret in Burgundy, reported a curious story to him. It seems that there was an English lady who had returned with what was left of Martin Swartz's troops last year. So then, Davie got to wondering...'

'Go on, go on!' Broughton interrupted the Earl excitedly.

The Earl looked embarrassed.

'It seems that the lady in the story and your wife were one and the same, but now it seems that she is utterly destitute and dependent upon the charity of the Duchess.'

'What happened?'

Argyll looked down at the table.

'It would appear that the man with whom she travelled tired of her quickly. What was his name, Davie? Huttles?'

'Hans Kuttler.' I corrected him.

'Thank you. Anyway, apparently he made off with her money and left her stranded. The Duchess Margaret took her in. But according to Davie's man in Malines, she has to spend half her time in prayer and the other half being lectured by the Duchess on the solemnity of marriage.'

Broughton licked his dry lips.

'And now?'

'Well, Sir Thomas, if you agree, Davie will tell his man to pay your wife's debts and give her money to return to you. How would you like that?'

For a moment I saw Thomas wrestle with his pride. He looked at me in confusion. I nodded at him encouragingly; mercy is always more important than justice. He hesitated and then turned to the Earl.

'I would, my lord,' he said softly.

Argyll smiled at him and Broughton beamed back. I had not seen him this way for months and my heart went out to him.

'Then, Sir Thomas, Davie will arrange for her to come to Northumberland in a few weeks.' He turned to me. 'I think, my lord, we will ask these two to step outside, as they have arrangements to make. Additionally of course, there is a matter on which I would like your advice.'

The Earl motioned me to come closer after Mulvanie and Broughton had left us.

'Notwithstanding my peace-making attempt with the King's party, I need to pursue an additional strategy, so listen to me. The support for the young Prince is mainly in southern Scotland,' he began, 'whereas that of his father lies chiefly in the North. Numerically I would guess that the King's forces exceed those of the son's. Militarily, King James' wisest move would be to remain in the North and force his son to march up against him.'

'And leave the border unguarded?' I interrupted unthinkingly.

The Earl showed no sign of being offended.

'That is precisely why the son will not move against his father. So it is necessary to tempt King James down from the North to attack his son.'

I shook my head dubiously.

'Why would he leave a strong position to march south? If he does, a lot of his supporters would likely not accompany him and, anyway, the Prince has to do something to keep the momentum of his revolt going.'

The Earl of Argyll nodded.

'I agree that any sensible man would do exactly as you have said, but King James will be tempted south because he is not a sensible man and he will have the promise of English support to help him crush his rebels. He will have been told that the forces of the Earl of Northumberland will assist him to defeat his son's army.

'By the way, Francis, do you still have that ring that King Richard gave you? The one you showed Mulvanie.'

I fingered the chain around my neck.

'Do you want to see it?'

He nodded, so I passed it over. He looked at the crest.

'It's perfect!'

I frowned in puzzlement.

'How will King James know that he has English support? How will he receive such a promise from Henry Tudor?' I stammered.

He twirled the ends of that ridiculous moustache and smiled at a secret joke.

'The King will hear the news from two English heralds. He will be told that if he moves south to confront his son he will be reinforced there by six thousand men led by the Earl of Northumberland. So King James will believe that he will vastly outnumber his son's rebels. He will be tempted to come south to crush them. The King can be quite vindictive, you know,' he added cheerily.

'So, the two heralds will not be genuine and Henry Tudor will not give any real promise of support. The plan is just a ploy to get King James to come south to confront the Prince.'

'It's a neat trick isn't it? Emslie fears that the heralds will be detected as being not genuine. Mulvanie is dubious too. But I think it could work, so we'll try it.'

It would be particularly unfortunate to be the fake English herald if it did not work out, I thought. In fact, as a mission it was highly dangerous. But then I noticed the Earl was looking at me in rather a pointed way; I felt my heart sink.

'You... you want me to be one of the heralds?' I stuttered.

The Earl of Argyll smiled happily and fingered his moustache.

'Who is the other one?' I could think of nothing else to say.

It could not be Broughton since he would be in England. The Earl's smile broadened.

'Your companion is English. That will add credibility to your mission. He comes from a noble family; in fact, he is to be the next Earl of Northumberland. I'll introduce you to him when I return here from the King.'

CHAPTER 10

'Who is this next Earl of Northumberland?' asked Broughton the next day. I looked at him gloomily.

'I have no idea. It makes no sense at all.'

'Do you know what I cannot understand either? Why does Argyll believe that I will not be recognised by King James' people? If they do identify me, they'll know that I'm in rebellion against Henry Tudor. He would hardly send me as a herald, would he?'

Broughton's hand automatically reached for where his beard had been. Without it, he looked both younger and smarter. Doubtless his wife would approve of the transformation. Ironically, the idea had been recommended by the hirsute Mulvanie.

'Why would you be recognised?' he asked slowly. 'Think for a moment; when you invaded with Richard of Gloucester, where did you fight? You were at Berwick. Think about it, Francis; besides Henry Lovell, who did you meet at Berwick?'

'No one, I suppose. Then this time, we were smuggled into the country and shut up at Ballumbie.'

'Exactly. Now people may have heard of a Lord Lovell

who opposed Henry Tudor, but they would assume that either he was killed at Stokefield or fled overseas.'

'I suppose I could use one of my other titles.'

I had a sudden insight.

'They have planned all this from the beginning haven't they?' I said. 'Sending you to Northumberland and making me a herald, I mean.'

'Yes, I reckon that the Earl will shortly join the Prince's rebels. Maybe he's already with them but wants to keep a foot in both camps. Either way, by using us, the rebellion stands a better chance. We'll find out more in due course.'

This proved to be so when it became obvious that Argyll had used the intervening period to support the young Prince and not his father the King, for he sent word to me that he wished to discuss my invasion plan later that day.

Broughton grunted when I told him the news.

'Well it is obvious that he is going to back the Prince now,' he said, 'King James had a pro-Tudor policy and as Mulvanie told us if we helped the Prince he would help you.'

He stroked his chin reflectively and glanced at me.

'You'll have to be careful in your negotiations with Argyll, Francis,' he murmured. 'He must be exceptionally clever.'

'Why's that?'

'Well, how many men do you know who can plot two simultaneous rebellions in England and Scotland?'

My heart sank at the thought of negotiating with such a man. We talked more and when the time was right I presented myself to the Earl.

He led me into his hall and abruptly dismissed his

attendants. He seated himself wearily but when he looked at me his eyes were as bright as ever.

'I have heard the details of your plan Francis,' he began, 'and your demands seem reasonable enough. You require a Scottish army of ten thousand backed by five thousand Burgundian mercenary pikemen.'

I nodded.

'You envisage a swift march through England culminating in a decisive battle north of London. Thereafter you wish the Scottish and Burgundian troops to remain until Parliament approves the new monarch and his council is chosen.'

He looked at me curiously.

'But the Earl of Warwick is a young boy. Would you not head up his councillors?'

'No, my lord. There are more able men who are cleverer than I. I seek nothing for myself in this venture.'

'That is unusual but it bears out all that Davie Mulvanie found out about you; I am impressed. But Francis, will the new King's councillors agree to be bound to the terms that you and I agree?'

Even I had considered this and, with Broughton's help, had framed an answer.

'Yes, my lord. Once Henry Tudor is defeated, apart from the Earl of Northumberland, there is no other lord with sufficient troops to oppose my wishes.'

'Northumberland will not be a problem,' the Earl said cryptically. 'But Lord Stanley and his brother, Sir William might be?'

'They will have been part of Henry Tudor's defeated army and, if they are not, I have sufficient troops and support to suppress them.' I paused and looked at him.

'Whatever terms you and I agree will be honoured by Edward VI and his new government.'

'The cost of such a venture would be great.'

'Yes it would,' I said frankly, 'but to invade England with lesser numbers would be risky and, of course, if I lose, Scotland would receive nothing.'

The Earl digested this silently.

'And in return for such support?'

'I would ensure that the new King refunds all your costs and henceforth England would be a firm ally of Scotland.'

The Earl smiled.

'Come, come Francis, we are already allies.'

'Well your costs would be repaid.'

'You'll have to do better than that Francis. We're a poor country and you want us to hire – what was it – five thousand mercenaries? You want us to purchase supplies for a campaign and to provide ten thousand troops.' He eyed me thoughtfully. 'I'm not saying we can't do it but if you lose it would not be the wisest investment.'

'I won't lose.'

'There's always risk in warfare,' he said reflectively, 'but to allow me to help you, is there not a little bit more that you can offer?'

'But with the Earl of Warwick crowned Edward VI, you would have peace and both countries would be spared these costly border disputes.'

'Some of our people think they are quite lucrative.'

My shoulders dropped.

'Alright then, what do you want?'

The Earl of Argyll beamed.

'Excellent Francis, now I only have a couple of points, which will take us a few moments to discuss. First, shall we agree to have a nice little agreement written up and signed by you and I? Excellent. We'll have it witnessed by a couple of churchmen. If you have no objections, we'll ask Bishop Blacader of Glasgow and, let me see, perhaps Brown of Dunkeld?'

'I agree.'

'Good. Now these border disputes and raids are not desirable between friends and allies. So let us have a proper truce, for say, twenty-five years?'

'Yes.'

'Now we should look to join our countries closer together,' continued the Earl happily. 'Suppose we were to find a pretty, young Scottish bride for the young Earl of Warwick? When he becomes Edward VI, she will be his queen.'

I thought briefly. A French princess would have been better for England, but I had little choice.

'I agree.'

The Earl of Argyll looked delighted.

'You see how much progress can be made when men of sense and purpose sit down together?' he exclaimed merrily. 'I have only two items left now.'

I braced myself. In honesty, I could hardly say that the negotiations were going well.

'One of these Francis, you've already touched upon. I suggest that the cost of the invasion should be assessed by our people here in Scotland and will be repaid in full within three years.'

'But you could make the cost as great as you wanted!' I protested.

The Earl looked at me.

'Of course, if you could count on substantial support in

England, Francis, you would not need so many troops and supplies, so it would not be so expensive.' Then he waved a hand dismissively. 'You have my word; you'll not find us too unreasonable.'

I clenched my fists. But I had no choice but to agree.

'I suppose you will have guessed my last request?' said the Earl.

'You want Berwick back?'

It had been the only tangible achievement of the invasion, although there had been small-minded people who reckoned that it cost so much to garrison that it was not worth having. It was a wrench to surrender it so tamely, but perhaps another opportunity would arise in the future.

'Berwick, Francis?' smiled Argyll. 'For a man looking to conquer England, your vision is at times somewhat limited.'

'Well, what do you want?'

'We'll have Berwick back, of course, Francis, but there's more. The day you invade England, you'll hand over to us the whole county and Earldom of Northumberland. From that time forth, it will be a Scottish possession.'

'But that's impossible! It's part of England. It's the borders... it's... it's unthinkable.'

The Earl of Argyll smiled grimly.

'Is it? Lord Lovell, consider the whole matter. You may, or may not, have support in England, but not enough to overthrow Henry Tudor. You need allies but to whom can you turn? The French, perhaps? But they put Henry Tudor on his throne. The Irish, maybe? They will still be cursing you for their losses at Stokefield. Possibly, the Duchy of Burgundy then? Alas, as a state it is sadly weakened. Also, of course, you still owe them the cost of your last campaign.'

He looked across at me.

'So tell me, Francis, tell me from where, apart from Scotland, you can get help? You know the answer as well as I do, otherwise you would not have come here.'

He was right, of course, but to hand over Northumberland with its towns and castles would weaken England and vastly increase the strength of the Scots.

The Earl must have read my thoughts.

'We'll help you, Francis. We'll give you what you require and you'll probably succeed but consider for a moment the position of Scotland when you are victorious. England is stronger than Scotland. You could refuse to pay us our money back. You could marry your king to someone else. You could break the new truce. Militarily, we could not stop you nor could we enforce the agreement which you and I will sign.'

'But I promise that we will not do any of these.'

He smiled and relaxed a little.

'Men know that you are honest Francis, but you'll not be running the new government of your Earl of Warwick. You said that there were others more capable than yourself and I respect you for that. But, let us pretend that these other councillors do not see things the way that you do. They may well not consider themselves to be bound by an agreement that you and I have signed, so poor little Scotland must seek to protect herself against the English nobles who might not possess your honesty.'

The Earl's eyes glittered as he talked. He was a shrewd man. He knew the English and he was not prepared to trust my fellow countrymen.

'We'll need a buffer zone from you if England attacks us,' he mused. 'Northumberland, with its terrain and castles, is ideal for our purpose, as it has been for your own.'

He was right but surely not all of Northumberland was necessary. He looked at me again.

'Francis, I like you and I want to help you. You have your loyalties and I have mine to Scotland. Agree to hand over Northumberland and you'll get your army and your money for mercenaries. It will take one, perhaps two years – but I promise that you'll get them. But if you'll not agree, then leave now, for I'll not negotiate.'

I bit my lip in frustration. To agree to give up even a small part of England was wrong on almost every count, let alone an entire county but I had no alternative than to accept his terms. However, even as I brooded on this, an idea came to me.

'I agree, my lord. But if Scotland is to have the whole of Northumberland, then Scotland must pay for half of the invasion, since your country will be larger and richer than it was before.'

Argyll looked up in surprise.

'You're learning, Francis. So now it's my turn to agree.'

He got up and rang his little bell for a servant.

'Now, before I leave, I would like you to meet the next Earl of Northumberland.'

The man who entered was tall and seemingly in a thoroughly bad temper.

'At last!' he snapped to Argyll. 'Do you know how long I have been waiting in this cursed castle?'

Well, at least he was English. I had assumed the Scots would put one of their own into Northumberland.

162

'And who's this?' he demanded, looking at me arrogantly.

'Lord Lovell, may I present Sir John Egremont,' said Argyll, totally unruffled by Egremont's rudeness.

Egremont. I had heard of him but never met him. He was a cousin of Henry Percy's, the current Earl of Northumberland, and he had helped us at the time of Buckingham's revolt but had never been close to power. I wondered how he had ended up in Scotland.

Argyll beckoned us both to sit.

'Time is pressing as I must return to the court but, since I have talked to the two of you individually and we have reached agreement, I will now talk to the pair of you together, so that there can be no misunderstanding. In summary, Francis, I have promised to help Sir John gain his cousin's earldom, if he will hold it as part of the Kingdom of Scotland. He has agreed. Sir John, I have promised Lord Lovell an army to overthrow Henry Tudor, if he agrees that the Earldom of Northumberland passes into Scottish hands. He has agreed to that and certain other points. Does anyone disagree with this summary?'

We shook our heads.

'Of course, this is conditional on a number of issues, which we have also discussed. The first is that there is to be a civil war in Scotland and the young Prince will prevail and go on to become King James IV.'

We nodded.

'The second issue is that, if circumstances demand it, you both have to pretend to be envoys from Henry Tudor. It will be your job to convince our current King, James III, that he has English support, in order that he will be enticed down to Edinburgh.'

'We've already agreed that,' said Egremont in a bored tone.

Argyll slammed his hand onto the table.

'Sir John, you exist on my charity! You are additionally dependent upon me for your future prospects. I'll trouble you to remember that.'

Egremont reddened.

'My apologies, my lord.'

Argyll rang his bell and a servant appeared with a cloak.

'You'll remain in the castle until I send for you.'

Then he was gone and I was left alone with Egremont. We looked at each other and Egremont chuckled softly.

'He's clever isn't he? I don't know about you, but after a few minutes he almost had me following him around on my knees. I met your man Broughton earlier, who was singing his praises. What is your opinion of him, my lord?'

I sighed. Argyll had out-thought, out-manoeuvred and out-negotiated me from start to finish. While I had his promise of support, it was at a high cost and would be two years from now. At least I had that promise though and, more importantly, I believed it.

'I've only met one man as clever as him,' I said, 'and that was Catesby. But tell me Sir John, what is your role in my invasion?'

Egremont shrugged.

'It's whatever you wish, my lord, but the way Argyll explained it to me, it sounded simple. Prior to your invasion, I am to go into Northumberland and gather my own support against the Earl, my cousin. Then, when your army marches over the border, the whole county will be divided and will not oppose you.'

I sat up quickly. No wonder Argyll had remarked cryptically that Northumberland would not be a problem.

Dear God! I could be at York in a few days and in London two weeks later. Tudor would have virtually no time to raise his forces.

'So then my lord, while you defeat Henry Tudor,' continued Egremont, 'and go on to proclaim Edward as King, I'll pacify Northumberland and hand it over to the Scots.'

'And you'll be the next Earl of Northumberland?'

'I will be the Earl of Northumberland.'

'But why will people follow you? Your cousin, Henry Percy, has retainers, troops and commands the East March. He is established in his position. Why would men leave him to come over to you?'

I could have put it more tactfully, but I did not know how. Egremont's face was grim.

'They'll follow me for two reasons, my lord, which they will come to realise when I have the rule of them. The first is simple – my Cousin Henry has not been a good lord to his people and they know it. I, on the other hand, will protect their interests and defend their lives and property.'

'Why has he not been a good lord to them?'

'Because people do not trust him,' came the simple answer. 'Under Gloucester, when he had the rule of the North, he spoke out for the interests of the people; Henry Percy does not. Equally, when Gloucester became King, he continued to favour the North and the people there knew that they were protected. After Gloucester's death, they looked to the Earl of Northumberland for protection but he could not give it, because after Bosworth and Stokefield Henry Tudor did not completely trust him. Henry Tudor does not listen to Northumberland and men know it. So, my lord, whom do the people in the North turn to? Who will speak for them or persuade King Henry to reduce his tax demands? If their own Earl cannot do this for them, he cannot be a good lord.'

Egremont looked at me defiantly.

'You can think me as self-serving, my lord, but I do not care. I'll get support for myself in Northumberland and I'll make sure that no one lifts a finger against your army. We both have to work together. It is in your interest as much as mine that I succeed in Northumberland. At least the people there will be looked after when I am their Earl.'

I had no choice but to work with Egremont, so I made an effort to be polite.

'What is the second reason that the people in Northumberland will follow you?'

'Oh, I apologise, my lord, did I not say? It's quite simple really. The North has always been ruled by a Percy and, except for the current Earl and his son, I am the only other male Percy.'

He smiled at me but I failed to comprehend.

'Um…well, yes?'

He hastened to clarify matters.

'Well, there won't be anyone else for people to follow, will there… once I have them killed.'

In Scotland events had moved speedily. King James acted quickly against his rebellious son. After garrisoning Edinburgh and Stirling he headed to the North to win support for his cause.

'And he's taken a wagon full of money to buy allies and sent James Hommyl to England to get help from Henry

Tudor,' continued Mulvanie. He peered at the Earl of Argyll's message and looked at me. 'He wants you and Egremont to leave in a week's time. I'm to take you.'

'But everyone knows you to be in the service of the Earl of Argyll!' I objected. 'That would look too suspicious.'

'Aye.' he grunted. 'But I'll take you two near to where the King is and then I'll just fade away and bring you back later.'

I bit my lip at the thought of the hulking Mulvanie quietly fading away. He saw my reaction and grinned at me. It was odd how I was coming to like the man.

The time came when we all left Castle Gloom. Broughton was to be taken by Emslie to a small port from which he would depart for Ravenglass in Cumberland, in order to make it appear that he had arrived from Ireland. Egremont and I were to go with Mulvanie and his escort of border troops.

Thomas was concerned about the reception he would receive from the Earl of Northumberland but was more excited at the prospect of seeing his wife again. He spoke briefly to Mulvanie and came over to me.

'Be careful, Thomas,' I said. Then in a quieter tone, 'Good luck to you.'

'And to you,' he smiled. 'God keep you, Francis. I'll meet you here or in the North.'

I grinned at him and then, in obedience to one of Mulvanie's incomprehensible commands, our little party moved off.

According to Mulvanie, James III had for once moved fairly energetically around his kingdom. Whether it was down to the bribes he was lavishly dispensing, support for him was nevertheless genuine in the North and he had succeeded in gathering quite an army.

'How many men would you estimate?' I asked.

Mulvanie grunted.

'I'm not sure – thirty thousand, maybe more.'

Egremont, next to me, swallowed hard.

'Then the odds against the Prince are too high,' he said hurriedly. 'He'll be crushed.' He looked round wildly. 'There's no point to this mission now; we'll return to the South.'

He looked at me in panic. His face was white and he was starting to sweat. I looked back at him trying to suppress my contempt for my so-called fellow peer. For, in anticipation of becoming an earl, Sir John Egremont had decided to advance up the ladder of nobility and had started to style himself as Lord Egremont. Mulvanie looked at him in surprise but said nothing.

'We came to do a job for the Earl,' I said grimly, 'and we will do it. If you would prefer to return to Argyll and tell him why you saw fit to abandon the agreement you made with him, you are welcome. I will go alone. Of course, Mulvanie and his men will remain with me.'

Egremont squirmed at that. Alone and without an escort or guides, it was obvious that he would not make it to the South and he knew it. He chewed his lip and made a final appeal.

'Lovell, there's thirty thousand of them. They have no need of the English and they'll easily defeat the Prince and the Earl of Argyll.'

He looked at me, hoping I would relent but, seeing I was determined to continue, he spat on the ground and scowled.

'Alright, we'll do it,' he said grudgingly, 'but after we've done, I'll tell the Earl that I'm for running to the borders and safety. God knows how he got it so wrong.'

He turned and looked to move away. Mulvanie eyed him with distaste.

'It's possible that I made a small error earlier, Sir John – my lord, that is. I've been mulling over those numbers of King James' and, now I come to think about it, I would put his strength at around ten thousand not thirty thousand – my apologies for the mistake.'

Egremont walked away in embarrassment. Mulvanie looked at me and winked. I nearly choked. It was obvious that he had been testing us.

And so it was the next day that the Lords Egremont and Grey, the two English heralds, rode to see King James. We were escorted by the guards, who brought us up from the borders. Mulvanie remained behind but indicated the general direction of Aberdeen from where King James had left two days ago.

It was mid-afternoon when initial contact was made with the King's scouts and early evening when, with weapons sheathed, we two heralds entered the King James' camp.

'Lord Grey? Lord Egremont?' the stout grey-haired cleric enquired. 'My name is Elphinstone.'

I guessed as much, since his secretary had spent most of

the morning trying to ascertain the details of our mission, but he had little success. To ensure that the details of our message were relayed precisely and in full to the King or his Chancellor, we said little. Eventually, subdued by Egremont's hauteur and my arrogance, he had agreed that later that day we should see the King's Chancellor, Bishop Elphinstone.

We bowed and took the stools we were offered. I took my seat with relief, as while the new English cloak, tunic and hose made by the ladies of Castle Gloom fitted well enough, the hose chafed badly.

'We sent a messenger to your King Henry,' said Elphinstone. 'But surely he could not yet have arrived so soon?'

He looked as us suspiciously. I stared him down.

'My master, the King, on hearing of the trouble that his ally, the King of Scotland, was having with certain rebels and traitors, has no need of messengers. He is mindful of the support given to him by Scotland when he overthrew the usurper Richard of Gloucester. He is mindful of...' I paused, having forgotten what else he was mindful of.

'Of his duty as a friend of the King of Scotland,' Egremont added smoothly. 'Upon hearing of the situation in Scotland, he despatched us immediately to pledge his support for King James.'

'He did?' Elphinstone looked up surprised.

I nodded gravely. But Egremont, who had clearly regained his courage from the previous day, spoke again.

'King Henry is aware of the problems that insurrections and revolts can bring to even civilised countries,' he condescendingly advised the Chancellor. 'Naturally, in the case of Scotland he fears the problems will be worse but since he wishes to live in peace and tranquillity with his barbarous northern neighbour, we have been sent here.'

The Chancellor's secretary started forward angrily, but Egremont ignored him.

'Our King does not want to have bloodshed and murder spreading across the border, nor does he wish for looting, raping and pillaging to be exported from savage Scotland. Our King believes that these evils should remain confined to their natural Scottish home. Nor does he desire that the even greater Scottish plagues of...'

'What is your King proposing exactly?' snapped the Scottish Chancellor.

'He has pledged military support,' I interjected tactfully. 'Troops are to be made available from the Earldom of Northumberland.' I decided to add an authentic touch. 'Naturally, he expects the costs of this to be refunded.'

'You have a letter?' Bishop Elphinstone stretched out his arm.

Egremont looked at him in astonishment.

'My lord, my master the King, would hardly expect a mere letter to suffice on a matter as serious as this. He has sent a personal token which Lord Grey will present to you.' He smiled patronisingly at the Chancellor. 'When the token is presented, my lord bishop, it will be clear to all that it is sent directly from the King of England.'

Elphinstone held out his hand again but I decided to ape Egremont's manner. Braggart and coward though he may be, he was also very convincing.

'I am instructed to present my master's token to his Grace, King James, personally,' I said coolly. 'Lord Egremont brings letters from the Earl of Northumberland, which you are to see.'

The Chancellor's secretary, frustrated after a wasted morning with us, snatched the precious scrolls and examined it eagerly.

'Written twenty days ago, my lord,' he mumbled as his eyes scanned the letter. 'It pledges two thousand men-at-arms and four thousand archers... They can be south of Edinburgh in a month's time. We are to send word back with Lords Grey and Egremont... The length of service is to be two months... The rest of it seems to be about their costs.' He pursed his lips and gave us an angry look. 'They appear to be excessive, I would have said, even by English standards.'

His eyes flicked down.

'The seal appears genuine, my lord,' he added crossly.

Clearly he was irritated to find no deception. I raised my eyebrow at his discourtesy, but Egremont rose to the occasion and turned to me.

'Doubtless my lord, this... erm... clerk will wish to verify the letter,' he said loftily. 'Notwithstanding the instructions of His Majesty, perhaps it would be a kindly gesture to allow him to verify the King's ring as well.'

He looked at the secretary contemptuously and gave a loud sniff. After a small show of reluctance, I passed the ring over and Egremont turned to Bishop Elphinstone.

'We shall await your summons, my lord,' he said politely.

I rose with him and he looked at the secretary.

'The ring was given to Lord Grey by a King,' he told him in a patronising tone. 'Try to take care of it, as I hear you Scots are prone to thieving.'

★ ★ ★

Elphinstone hid us away in a tent and left us alone for an uncomfortable two days with a couple of sentries outside and doubtless others listening carefully to everything that we said.

The Scots would want to discuss King Henry's offer, I knew, but by the end of the second day I was beginning to wonder whether we had been detected. Surely no one could discuss such a simple offer for so long? While Egremont's performance had been masterful, the Scots were clever and there were questions which they could trip us up on. But then, why should they? We were bringers of good, albeit surprising, news and, provided no one guessed Argyll's plan and linked us to it, why should we not be believed?

I suspected that Egremont was going through the same thought process, as he was frequently helping himself to wine and pacing up and down in the small shelter. We were put out of our misery when the unsmiling secretary of the Chancellor came for us early on the third day. He advised us to prepare ourselves, as his lord would be taking us to see King James.

The King's tent was both large and noisy. We followed Elphinstone slowly, as the Chancellor made his way through the throng. Most of the looks we were given seemed hostile and the talk died away as we approached the King. While we waited for him to finish his own conversation, I studied him closely. It was then that I began to appreciate fully what separated the King from his nobles. Some of the differences were obvious. The King towered over his nobles, but lacked their solidity. Their armour and weapons contrasted oddly with his elaborately embroidered cloak with glittering brooches; the weather-beaten cheeks and rough beards of the King's men only emphasised his own pale face and thin features. King James gestured animatedly as his voice rose and I was struck by his hands. It was not the profusion of rings that caught my attention, but the length and thinness of his fingers. They were the hands of a musician.

Clearly the King had now decided to finish his talk as, with an irritated shrug, he turned slightly to face us.

'You are sent from King Henry, I believe?'

His voice was unnaturally deep and contrasted oddly with his effeminate face, thin eyebrows and full lips. He inspected the ring that Bishop Elphinstone passed to him. While less bright than the jewels he wore, the lion and crown showed it to be a King's ring.

'Your King Henry promises support, does he not?' His silver-grey eyes rested on me.

I bowed again.

'King Henry instructed the Earl of Northumberland to lead six thousand men north towards Edinburgh, Your Grace. Lord Egremont here will accompany that army, which is to be placed at your disposal. The force will arrive at the end of April and will serve for two months.'

There was a loud murmur after I had spoken and an elderly lord pushed his way forward and pointed angrily at us.

'Your Grace, we have no need of the English!' he shouted. 'We have men enough to beat Angus and Argyll.'

He stopped and jabbed his finger at the King.

'As I told you yesterday, you should force these rebels and their army to come up and face us here. We'll crush them.'

Roars of approval greeted this and, directing a snarl at us, he fell back.

'My Lord of Atholl,' said King James, 'we have indeed discussed this. We discussed it today, yesterday, the day before and, if you had your way, we'd discuss it tomorrow. But each time you raise the issue, I have told you that you are wrong. Wrong, wrong, wrong!'

'It is the correct military solution!' someone shouted.

'How can it be?' retorted King James angrily. 'With six thousand extra troops, the rebels can be crushed.' He looked at his followers impatiently. 'If you were wrong before, which you were, the news of these extra troops makes you doubly wrong.'

An unenthusiastic silence followed and then the murmurings began again. Someone spat in my direction and I saw that Egremont was deliberately jostled. King James noted it too.

'Leave our ally's envoys!' he said loudly and there were more hostile looks in our direction. King James drew himself up to his considerable height. 'Leave them, I say! With their help I shall go out and defeat these rebels. Aye, with your support and the help of the English.'

The clamour that greeted this was tremendous. Everyone seemed to try to speak simultaneously but one lord seemed even angrier than the rest; he pushed his way right up to the King, shoving Egremont aside.

'You're a fool, Your Grace!' he bellowed. 'Even though your own son heads up these rebels, this is what you should do…'

Whether it was the mention of his son or being told publicly what to do I would never know, but at that moment the King's temper got the better of him.

'You are correct my Lord of Caithness!' he snapped. 'My son does lead these rebels.' His voice rose and drowned out the babble of conversation.

'But he and all others will soon learn that, in my land, I am the King. Neither Prince, nor noble, nor bishop are beyond my power.'

His voice shook with passion and he breathed heavily as he looked around his tent.

'Make ready your men, my lords, for we march south. Lord Bothwell go to King Henry and give him my thanks.' He turned to Egremont and myself. 'My lords, thank you for your messages. Return to the Earl of Northumberland and bid him to be at Edinburgh by the end of April.'

With that he stalked out of the tent followed by Elphinstone. There was silence and with the Scottish lords glowering at us, it seemed the opportune moment for us to leave.

'And that is how matters turned out,' I said to Mulvanie, as we rode back to Castle Gloom. 'Just as you wanted.'

He grunted, which I took to be a sign of satisfaction. He pointed at Egremont riding ahead of us.

'But you say he did well.'

'Very well. He was totally convincing.'

'I suppose we'll have to give him another chance then,' said Mulvanie gloomily. 'In fairness to him, it was his idea to write the letter which you gave to Elphinstone, and he brought his cousin's seal.'

We rode for a while in silence and then he looked at me.

'Do you know the major advantage of having such a consistent King, Francis? It's simple really. The Earl, who knows King James better than anyone, worked it out when he made up the plan. He said that he believed King James would always do the opposite of what anyone who had a degree of common sense told him. And you know Francis, he was right. Right to the end, right to the bitter end, King James did not heed the advice he was given.'

He rode on and then laughed shortly.

'It'll be interesting to see how many follow him down to Edinburgh now.'

CHAPTER 11

Castle Gloom, 1488.

Back at Castle Gloom, I felt distinctly out of the action. Argyll, of course, would head the rebels. It was rumoured that he and Earl Angus were with the young Prince at Stirling. No one knew where Mulvanie was. What was known, however, was that King James had recently arrived at Blackness Castle near Edinburgh and was waiting for Northumberland's men to reinforce his army.

When King James discovered that his English allies would never arrive, he would face a difficult choice. He could return to the North and, by doing so, force his son to march up and attack him but that would mean admitting that he had been wrong to come south. Alternatively, he could try to force battle on his son in the South straight away. The frustration of not knowing what would happen was intolerable. As such, despite my dislike of Brian Emslie, I practically fell on him when he arrived at Castle Gloom. Egremont, who was as bored as I, joined in the questioning. Our eagerness for news made Emslie positively genial.

'Slow down, my Lord Lovell! You'll do yourself a mischief. Control yourself, Sir John – my lord, I mean.'

He cast a rapturous glance around him.

'Is it not beautiful here at this time of St Bride? The snow has moved away and soon we will see the wee lambs gambolling about and the flowers will...'

Restraining a violent urge to hurl the little rat down into the valley below, I pressed him for news. He clicked his fingers and preened himself.

'News, my lord? We have none. King James has come to Edinburgh and a truce was made.'

My heart sank.

'But it won't work,' he added.

'Why not?' I asked relieved.

'Because we'll never let go of the Prince,' he said happily, 'so now it's all move and counter-move. King James is sending more ambassadors to King Henry in England to request that the troops he promised him from Northumberland are sent.'

He broke off and looked at Egremont roguishly.

'A masterly performance, I hear. In the presence of – let me see – thirty thousand wild Scots I believe?' he remarked genially.

'I hear you doubted the plan would work?' Egremont retorted sourly.

'I heard at one point it almost did not, Sir John,' Emslie contended. 'But to return to the present, the rebels have sent their own messengers to King Henry. You will not need to invade England, Lord Lovell; most of Scotland is already there. My Lord Argyll was to go as well, to put forward the case of the rebels, but he is needed here.'

'So what happens to us now?' asked Egremont in his usual abrupt fashion.

'You will continue to enjoy spring in Castle Gloom,' Emslie replied cheerfully. 'I quite envy you in such

beautiful surroundings. Lord Lovell will accompany me.'
He turned to me. 'The Earl wants your advice as a soldier.'

Anything to get away from Castle Gloom and Egremont, I reflected.

'Excellent, my lord, excellent.' Emslie beamed happily. 'We will leave at once.'

★ ★ ★

I had supposed that we would head straight for Stirling where the Prince was with a number of his nobles but Emslie shook his head. We were to go to the Royal Palace of Linlithgow, where the Earls of Angus and Argyll were busy building up their contingents, ready to reinforce Prince James. Certainly as we rode round the loch to approach the palace it was easy to see that forces were being mustered. Horses were being watered at the lake and a small market had been set up to provision the soldiers.

Emslie pointed out the various contingents.

'Lord Lyle's men are over there. Lord Hailes seems to have brought most of the Hepworth contingent.'

We rode through a magnificent gateway with the royal arms proudly displayed on a shield supported by a pair of angels. I whistled at the size of the courtyard.

Emslie saw my surprise and nodded happily.

'The work was begun by the present King's grandfather,' he began. Then his face brightened at the prospect of continuing my education.

'You've not heard about the manner of his death below the floorboards?'

To his disappointment I said that I had heard the story from a lady who had been present. I added that I had marvelled at the courage of the Scottish ladies at that time, if not the men's.

'Ah well,' said Emslie uneasily, 'you know James I saw this palace as a place of pleasure. He wished to build a structure so magnificent that it would show everyone – the bishops, the nobles and the burgesses – how far above them the King was.' He gestured to the three statues inside the gate, then he dismounted and looked at me.

'The trouble, my lord, was that they didn't see matters the same way. But I suppose his grandson is of a similar mind. Shall we go to find the Earl?'

We found him with Mulvanie almost immediately. They were in a solar in what, I presumed, were the royal apartments, although they seemed small for that purpose. The Earl gestured to us to sit as he continued to listen to Mulvanie, who had obviously arrived only shortly before.

'It's quite true, my lord.' Mulvanie was saying. 'Huntley, Errol, Marischal and Glamis have left the King and returned to their lands.'

Beside me, Emslie gasped and Argyll smiled broadly.

'But hold, Davie,' he said to Mulvanie. 'Let me explain all this to Lord Lovell and you can correct me if I go wrong. Further to your mission as a herald, King James did come south to confront his enemies and to meet his promised English allies, but a lot of his supporters did not march with him, thinking he was doing the wrong thing.'

'Mind you, many did follow,' contributed Mulvanie. 'He outnumbered us.'

'Hmm… quite so,' agreed the Earl. 'But then we had two truces while we tried to persuade King James not to take the fateful step. But what does the King do?' He smiled happily. 'He foolishly breaks both and a number of his most powerful supporters are so disgusted with his treachery that they abandon him and go home.'

He looked at me, his moustache quivering with excitement.

'We are approaching the end now, Francis. In the past few weeks we've had skirmishes and truces – but nothing has been settled. In light of this news, we now outnumber the King's forces and, incredibly, he is still resolved to force battle upon us.'

I smiled happily. With the King's likely defeat and Prince James' victory, my own prospects of gaining an army for invasion were looking promising.

'You wanted my advice, my lord?' I enquired.

He signalled for Emslie to withdraw.

'Yes, indeed. Now the question I have for you is...'

But the question was not delivered as, at that same moment, the door was flung open and a vast man erupted into the small solar.

'Have you heard about Marischal and Glamis?' the giant roared at Argyll.

Argyll smiled at him.

'Yes, and Huntley and Errol, and no doubt others, will desert too in the next few days. But your timing is good, my lord, for this is Lord Lovell. I was just about to ask him that question about Bosworth. Francis, this is Earl Angus.'

I looked up at Argyll's fellow leader of the rebels. Dear God, he made Mulvanie look small. He had a wild crown of hair and a beard that straggled out in all directions, but his blue eyes were piercing and shrewd. He glanced down at me and dropped his two-handed sword on Argyll's table.

'Ah Lovell, I've heard of you,' he boomed. 'You didn't bring that coward Egremont with you, did you?'

'No, my lord.'

'Good – it's people like him who will ruin England's honour…' Angus shrugged, 'not that she had any to start with.' He looked at me meditatively. 'You killed a lot of our men in the West March, you know.'

'That was my job,' I said evenly.

He gave me a surprised look and roared with laughter.

'Aye well, we're to be allies now, so welcome my lord.' He turned to Argyll. 'Ask him that question we were discussing, Colin.'

Argyll nodded and turned to me.

'I'm sorry to ask you this, Francis, but it is important to us.' He paused for a moment while Earl Angus watched me with narrowed eyes.

'Ask me anything, my lord.'

'Thank you Francis. Had you defeated Henry Tudor at Stokefield, what would you have done with him?'

I did not hesitate.

'I would have had him killed to prevent a continuation of warfare and the loss of more lives.'

Earl Angus nodded thoughtfully.

'That makes sense.'

He turned to Argyll.

'It sounds like you'll have to persuade the young Prince that his father's death in battle will be best for the future peace of Scotland. Although I'm not sure how you'll do that.'

There was, however, little time to think of this as later that day news arrived that caused us all to leave Linlithgow Palace. Prince James had been rash and had been tempted out of Stirling Castle. He had been defeated by Lord Montgrennen and was now fleeing for his life. As we scrambled to mobilise the men and supplies to go to the aid of the fleeing Prince, more bad news arrived. Having heard of the Prince's defeat and flight, King James emerged from Edinburgh with his own forces and set out in pursuit of his son. Apparently it was Mulvanie who actually found and secured the person of the Prince, but only just in time as the King's forces were very close to him. A few days later, both armies stared at each other across the Field of Stirling.

'There's King James! Over there! On the big grey horse.'

George Brown, Bishop of Dunkeld pointed excitedly at the tall figure riding awkwardly in front of his small army. Behind him a soldier carried a sword pointed upwards and, in front of the King, the royal banners of Scotland were raised, although they also flew on our side, I noted. Meanwhile the bishop continued to point out other notable lords who were with the King.

I peered through the ranks of soldiers who were massing between us on one side and the King's army on the other. I had been instructed by Argyll not to fight and, as such, had been placed in the care of the chubby Bishop. This hardly mattered since the King's army was vastly outnumbered. Whether he was unaware of the reinforcements that Angus and Argyll had built up at Linlithgow or whether he had failed to notice the erosion of his own forces was uncertain. Either way, by forcing battle on superior forces, the King appeared to have an exaggerated belief in his army's chances.

I watched curiously as the young Prince's army deployed, for it was done in a manner that was alien to me.

An English army preparing for battle would normally be arranged in two or three separate divisions, but the Scots appeared to prefer to fight in large groups. It was true that all such bands of men were massed together in a sketchy formation but the troops seemed to be constantly changing position.

'Why do they keep on moving about?' I asked.

'They're looking for their own particular enemies who are fighting for King James,' the Bishop advised.

He pointed to a large force of spearmen who were following a knight in armour down the line.

'That's Lord Montgomery and his followers. He wants to be facing the Earl of Glencairn when the battle starts.'

'But wouldn't it be better to form the army into a more compact mass and place the archers in front?'

He gave me an amazed look.

'You'd never get anyone to fight together like that. This is an excellent chance to settle old scores and to establish once and for all who the most important lord in the region is. Look over there – Oliphant has spotted Ruthven and he's manoeuvring so he can close in on him when the time is right.'

I had no knowledge of the various rivalries of the Scottish lords but, if King James attacked while his son's army was milling around, we would be in serious trouble. Possibly Earl Angus came to the same conclusion as, with a bull-like roar, he flew into the mass of soldiery and, by sheer force of leadership, compelled them to stand still. He was joined by the Earl of Argyll with his personal force of archers, who were guarding the young Prince. The three rebel leaders watched as King James took up position in front of his own men and reached out for the sword that his attendant knight carried. At the sight of the weapon, the shouting and insults from the Prince's army slowly died away.

'That will be Robert the Bruce's very own sword,' the bishop observed. 'The very one that he used at Bannockburn to kill a goodly number of English.'

Including one of my ancestors according to Henry Lovell, I recalled. I did not respond as at that moment King James rode forward completely alone and halted about fifty paces in front of where his son stood, flanked by Argyll and the giant Angus. To this day I will never know whether, even at this late stage, the father sought to be reconciled with his son or if he wished to see him for a last time. In breathless silence, both armies awaited the Prince's response but he made none. Whether he was restrained by Argyll or whether he simply chose not to respond will never be known, but the son made no move at all while his father sat on his tall grey horse and looked at him.

With great deliberation, the King raised Bruce's sword and pointed it at the slight figure of his son. The tension snapped instantly and there was a huge roar of approval from his army. The noise from our own force answered it and, as the cacophony swelled to a crescendo, both armies seemed to leap towards each other. Neither side used cannon and there was little or no archery fire to soften up the opposition. There were no flank attacks or subtle manoeuvrings to get behind enemy lines; both sides simply rushed towards each other.

This, then, was warfare at its most brutal. Despite the unnaturalness of father fighting son and son rebelling against father, both had their own fierce partisan support and, since all attempts at reconciliation had failed, bloodshed was the only way for the issue to be resolved.

As if this was insufficient grounds for savage combat, the lords from the North who comprised much of the King's army were contemptuous of the southern nobles who formed the Prince's supporters. Also, as the bishop had pointed out, a great many lords had personal enemies in the opposing army.

Within minutes, the two armies were locked together in fierce combat with lightly armed spearmen thrusting fiercely at each other or jerking away frantically from the more heavily armed knights who occasionally could be glimpsed hacking their way inexorably through the melee.

Shrill cries mixed with savage roars – the lightly armed infantry were hugely vulnerable to the blows that fell on their backs and arms. At one point a blood-covered form stumbled out of a vicious brawl and staggered a few paces before collapsing. A moment later, as the battle swirled over the moor, a group of spearmen targeted an expensively armoured knight, positioning themselves around him. Preoccupied with despatching his victim, the knight paid them no heed until they had encircled him. Suddenly the knight realised the danger he was in and swung round ponderously to look for a line of retreat. It was too late; they were on him, jabbing wildly, their long spears easily outranging his axe.

I recognised few of the individual banners and it was hard to make out what was happening amid the billowing clouds of dust. Judging by the way that the battle was beginning to move away from us, I got the impression that the Prince's army was pushing forward. A trickle of men appeared to be slipping away in the distance.

'There goes the King.' The Bishop pointed out a large grey horse about a hundred paces away. 'Those men following him, Lord Lovell; would you say that they are his escort or his pursuers?'

'Well, he'll make for Blackness Castle now,' the Bishop muttered. 'Blackness is strong enough for him to defend and there's a natural port there for Sir Andrew Wood's ships to come and rescue him. He'll be safe there.' He glanced at me. 'Of course, the Prince has ordered that no one should kill his father, but it is better that he escapes from the battlefield I would say.'

I stared at him in consternation. My chances of getting an army were infinitely better with a dead King James and his son on the throne, but this was hardly a topic to pursue with a Bishop, even if he had witnessed the agreement that the Earl of Argyll had drawn up. Unhappily, I watched the battle degenerate into a series of small skirmishes, which spread onto the hills around us.

By noon, it was all over. The forces of King James has been routed and, while losses on both sides were slight, my Bishop was kept busy that afternoon. A messenger arrived and asked the cleric to accompany him to care for the body of the late King James III, who had been killed near a mill at Bannockburn. Curiously, no one seemed to have any idea of how it had happened or who was responsible. There was even a rumour that a priest had done the deed, but this was only one of a hundred such tales.

In the evening, Mulvanie came for me. It seemed I would not be required for a number of weeks while matters were sorted out and the new King James IV installed. The Earl wished me to return to Ballumbie. When the time was right, I would come to Linlithgow to talk to James IV and his councillors.

I was more patient than I had been six months ago. I realised that the new government would have greater priorities than me and my desired army at this time. Equally, I did not relish a lengthy period of seclusion at Ballumbie. It probably showed in my face as Mulvanie laughed at my expression.

'Both Earls and the Hepworths are grateful for your part in this. One of the first actions of the new government will be to make our papers of safe passage for you in Scotland.'

And so it was that eight days after the Field of Stirling I received my copy of safe conduct into Scotland. I was amused to see that it was signed by the new King's Chancellor, the Earl of Argyll.

I waited at Ballumbie for my summons with little confidence that it would come quickly. There would be too much for the new government to do. They needed to secure their strongholds in Edinburgh and Stirling and to start placating the more important supporters of the late King James. Above all, they needed to crown his son Cousin Henry told me wearily. He himself came infrequently to Ballumbie these days, being busy with Argyll, but I welcomed his visits for the news he brought.

He was, I knew, uneasy with the situation that had arisen in Scotland. The new King was not yet of full age, although presumably he would take up the reins of power relatively soon. In the meantime, he was surrounded by a small clique of nobles. The problem was, of course, rather like Henry Tudor after Bosworth, that this small number of nobles had only one claim through which to run the government. This sole justification was based exclusively on the fact that they had overthrown and killed the last King at Stirling Field. To make matters worse, they had simply divided up the spoils of government between themselves and had arranged for a parliament to be called in October to ratify their new power structure.

'It gives us control,' admitted Henry. 'The whole border region is in the hands of the Humes and the Hepworths, Earl Angus is sheriff of no less than four counties and Argyll is Chancellor. We're managing all right but there are an awful lot of people in the North who wished the late King James well. They are angry at his death and what they see now as a small group of southerners controlling the young King and wresting control of the government.'

He laughed after that.

'But maybe I'm just being pessimistic. Anyway Francis, in August the King will come to Linlithgow and you are to come and talk to him there.'

Linlithgow is so beautiful that even Emslie stopped chattering as we approached the palace. The thought crossed my mind that perhaps James I had been right in conceptualising a pavilion of pleasure in such a place. The Earl of Argyll walked by himself at the water's edge. I rode over, dismounted and bowed.

'Ah Francis, welcome.' He beamed at me with that ridiculous moustache bobbing up and down. 'We have news from Broughton, who is now in the service of the Earl of Northumberland. It seems that there are a few like him in the Earl's retinue. A man called Skelton presented Sir Thomas to the Earl.'

'Clement Skelton? He was with us at Stokefield.'

'Quite so, quite so. Anyway we hear from Sir Thomas that your King Henry thought we would invade England at once. Henry strengthened all the border garrisons and ordered musters at Berwick, Newcastle and Carlisle. What a frightened man he must be! But how happy he will be when we talk to the English next month and propose a proper truce between our two countries,' Argyll added.

'A truce?'

'Yes Francis, a truce – a breathing space for us to organise and plan your venture while everything is calm and peaceful. Then, when we are ready, we'll move into England – truce or no truce.'

The Earl snapped his fingers and beamed at me.

'And Broughton's wife is safely returned to him,' said the Earl with the pride of a professional matchmaker. 'Mulvanie's man brought her safely from Malines.'

I was pleased for Thomas.

'He brought letters from the Duchess Margaret, as well.'

The Earl's teasing tones interrupted my thoughts about my friend.

Things had obviously moved very fast indeed.

'Have you asked for support for the invasion plan?' I asked curiously.

He laughed.

'State secrets, state secrets, Francis! But let us say that she is sympathetic to the plan and for the right price will look to reinforce the Scottish army with a mercenary force. Her estimates of cost seem high and she makes the point that it is the Archduke Maximilian who will make the final decision. But, in principle, she seems agreeable.' He looked at me, smiling broadly. 'Perhaps you would like to meet the King now?'

I wondered, uneasily, what Burgundy's demands would be this time. They would doubtless include the unpaid costs of the Stokefield campaign, but at least Argyll seemed to be pushing ahead with the venture far quicker than I had envisaged. Still smiling, I followed the Earl past the two sentries into the royal apartments. From my experience of courts, I had expected to find the antechamber cluttered with courtiers but to my astonishment, when we entered the room, I saw only three people and one of them wore a mason's apron. All three men were intent on studying a sheet of parchment on the table. It looked like some sort of design or plan.

The Earl of Argyll bowed.

'Lord Francis Lovell, Your Grace.'

The young man in the centre of the group looked up from the drawings. He had a slightly feline face, dark hair, no beard and the beginnings of a moustache. Despite being only medium height and plainly dressed, his bearing showed him to be a King. He began to roll up the parchment and handed it to one of the men.

'We will resume later,' he said to them. 'Thank you, Master Jackson and thank you Stephen.'

The young King settled himself into his chair and gazed at me in silence for some minutes.

'Tell me your plan' he commanded.

I took him through the invasion carefully and at times slowly, since I guessed that the young King was inexperienced insofar as warfare was concerned, but I need not have bothered. It was obvious that Argyll had briefed the King. As we discussed the invasion, he nodded at each item and quickly moved the discussion onto the next point. He showed considerable interest in the role of the mercenary pikemen and then summarised the plan neatly.

'So you'll invade through Northumberland, which we know will offer no resistance. You say you'll ignore York completely and head straight to London. You say that you will not bother to have mustering points to attract support in England but advance directly to the capital.'

I bowed.

'Exactly, Your Grace.'

He frowned.

'I can foresee only two weaknesses in your plan.'

I looked up startled.

'Your Grace?'

'Surely the build-up of troops would be noted by the English? How do we assemble fifteen thousand men on the borders without it becoming common knowledge that an invasion is being planned?'

It was a fair point.

'In fact, Your Grace, I had intended to assemble men and supplies close to Edinburgh rather than on the border for the very reason you mention.'

He was satisfied.

'The essence of your plan, as I understand, is speed. Now what happens if King Henry uses part of his men to slow you down, thus giving him the chance to assemble a larger army?'

Surprisingly, the Earl of Argyll answered.

'In reality, Your Grace, the only forces capable of doing this are those of the Stanleys. However, leaving aside the question of whether they could muster their forces quickly enough to stop Lovell, there is another point.'

'What is that?' King James asked.

'The fact of the matter, Your Grace, is that they may not wish to support King Henry. Sir William Stanley feels that he was inadequately rewarded for his role at Bosworth. Additionally, Davie Mulvanie has heard that both he and his brother, Lord Stanley feel totally dissatisfied, as they received neither favours nor reward for saving King Henry at Stokefield.'

King James looked puzzled.

'How so?'

So I told His Grace the story of Stokefield.

'At the end, Your Grace, with Oxford's men defeated, it was only the reinforcements that came from Lord Stanley and Sir William that enabled Tudor to win. Without their men, we could have defeated Tudor.'

'And you say that neither of them, was rewarded for their part in the battle?' the King asked.

'It would seem not,' said the Earl of Argyll. 'Sir William, in particular, is known to feel embittered and both brothers and Lord Stanley's son, Lord Strange, usually work together.'

I sat silently trying to contain my excitement. What the Earl had failed to mention was that by placing all the Stanley troops under the command of Lord Strange at Stokefield, King Henry made it clear that he had little trust in Lord Stanley or his brother. Despite this, as at Bosworth, it had been their intervention that had decided Stokefield. If he had not rewarded or ennobled Sir William after the battle, I doubted very much whether he or his brother would support Henry Tudor for a third time.

Argyll wished to move on.

'Your Grace, I believe that we can aim to plan the invasion next year, once matters are fully settled in Scotland. Francis what is the best time for your campaign to be launched?'

'I would look to May or June, my lord. I would need nine months to organise the mercenaries and Scottish troops and for my colleague Edward Franke to arrange the supply of the force. May would be the earliest I could invade. Also, for a series of forced marches, it is better when the days are longer.'

He nodded.

'Then we will plan for May 1489, Your Grace. And by summer of next year you will rule over the largest and richest Scotland that there has ever been. The Earl of Northumberland will pay homage to you and you will have England as a friendly neighbour and true ally.'

'Francis, you have much to organise,' he continued. 'I'll give you Emslie to help and accompany you. I'll deal with the Burgundians and when I've reached an agreement with them you can go there and select the captains you want. It will be best for you to be hidden away from King Henry's spies, so base yourself at Castle Gloom and we'll use Emslie and Mulvanie as messengers between us.'

I had hoped to stay at the court but he was right. Anyway, I had much to do and, certainly, King Henry's spies in Scotland must have no inkling of what was being planned.

CHAPTER 12

Southern Scotland, 1488.

Emslie and I spent the next few weeks touring about so that I could improve my knowledge of the Scottish military capability. In the main, I was content. Their men-at-arms were reasonably well-equipped. The Scottish archers, if not so numerous as they were in England, had a good rate of fire and were accurate. Their greatest strength, as I knew from bitter experience, was in their light horse, which would prove as important as the Carlisle light horse had been at Stokefield. The absence of heavy cavalry did not bother me at all; the days of the heavily armoured knight on his steed were drawing to a close.

What impressed me most was the frugal way in which their troops operated. They seemed to require little food and scorned any form of luxury. While we had tried to make the Stokefield campaign a speedy one, we had not moved as quickly as we needed to. Once past York, provisioning had been an issue and the wagons had slowed us down. The Scottish troops, on the other hand, required so little that a rapid march to London would be fairly simple.

I was discussing this with Emslie as we returned to Castle Campbell one afternoon. I think, in our common task, we were both beginning to lose our dislike of each other. Certainly, he was proving both clever and useful. It had been his idea to establish a supply base virtually on the border so that our troops could restock with provisions just before entering England. He asked me about quantities and I was still trying to calculate what we would require as we clattered into the courtyard of the castle. Once there, I stopped in amazement; in front of me was the one man who could do such a calculation with improbable ease. He smiled at the sight of me and nodded to Brian Emslie. I dismounted quickly and moved forward to hug Edward Franke.

'How did you come to be here, Edward?' I asked excitedly. He pointed at Emslie.

'His man found me at York. Your wife, Nan, sent me to look for you after Stokefield when I had been released. I couldn't find any trace of you and returned to her. By the time I returned, she had received your message and I came north again.'

Emslie smiled and clicked his fingers happily.

'We agreed with Lord Lovell that he should not give his location in Scotland but we have been watching out for you.'

He looked at the two of us and, with surprising tact, he moved away so that we could talk. I lead Edward into the Earl's hall and poured him some wine.

'What happened to you after Stokefield?' I asked him. His honest blue eyes regarded me sombrely.

'I was caught and imprisoned. But only a few weeks later, I was released on a free pardon.'

I looked at him in astonishment.

'But why?' I asked curiously. 'You were a leading rebel and you were known to be close to me. I would have expected Tudor to have kept you in prison for much longer.' I suddenly realised how uncaring this must have sounded, so I stopped myself.

As always, Edward read my thoughts and smiled.

'It was because they knew that I was close to you that they released me,' he said dryly. 'There was a condition to my release. Do you want to hear it?'

'A heavy fine?' I speculated.

He shook his head.

'No, nothing like that. It was Archbishop Morton, Tudor's Chancellor, who arranged the whole thing. They knew that you had not been killed at Stokefield but they had no idea where you were. The condition for my release was simple; I was to find you and give you a message.'

'A message?'

'Return to England, Francis, and pay homage to Henry Tudor. Publicly acknowledge him as your overlord and openly submit to him. If you do that, you'll be placed in the Tower for a short while but then you will regain your liberty and part of your lands.'

That the offer was genuine I had no doubt. The only credible Yorkist claimant to England's throne was the young Earl of Warwick and the only person pushing his claim was myself. From Tudor's viewpoint the proposed offer of my life, liberty and lands was a good one. With my surrender, support for Warwick would evaporate and Tudor's dynasty made secure. But Tudor knew nothing of the promise I had made to Richard of Gloucester and my determination to keep it.

'Tudor certainly wants me badly' I told Edward, 'this is the second time they have made me the offer.'

He grinned.

'I take it your answer is the same; your wife said that you would not accept Tudor's offer and she told me to tell you that you will always have her full support. She sent some money and jewels for you. I'll give them to you later.'

'Thank you and I'll give you some letters to take back.'

'Right,' said Edward briskly, 'so what are you planning?'

He listened intently as I took him through the invasion plan, but when I finished he shook his head decisively.

'It won't happen,' he said shortly.

I looked at him in amazement.

'Why not?'

His explanation was both long and detailed – indeed I had forgotten quite how thorough Edward could be – but when he had completed his analysis I believed him.

'So what you are saying is that my information is out of date. Not only is Burgundy losing ground to the French, but some of their cities are in revolt against Burgundy's rulers.'

'Correct. So, under these conditions, how could Burgundy make up the manpower you require?' Edward asked. 'On top of that, Duke Francis of Brittany is dying and has no heir so the French will look to acquire that territory.'

'And Henry Tudor would not want that,' I said slowly. 'Why, it would expose the whole south coast of England to the French.'

Edward nodded gloomily.

'I have heard that he intends to take Brittany's side and has asked the Burgundians to be his allies. They would jump at the chance since England would be helping them against France.'

He looked at me keenly.

'So do you really think that the Burgundians are going to upset their powerful new allies by sending five thousand men to help overthrow Henry Tudor?'

He was right of course and for a moment I felt sick with

disappointment, but then the obvious thought struck me: if England and Burgundy were going to ally against France, why would the French not wish to help me and the young Earl of Warwick overthrow Henry Tudor? I put this excitedly to Edward.

'Is their army good enough?' asked Edward.

'It was largely French soldiers with Scottish support who won Bosworth for Henry Tudor. If they were good enough to put him on the throne, why would that same combination not be good enough to shake him off it?'

Emslie returned a few days later. He reported that, early in August, Mulvanie's agents had heard similar accounts of Burgundy's growing closeness to Henry Tudor. Anticipating my actions, the Earl had written to the Duchess more in hope than with conviction, to ask whether Burgundy would make available the mercenaries for next year's campaign. As such, Argyll believed that a meeting between himself and I would be more useful when we had the reply from Burgundy.

'But he has a request for you,' continued Emslie. 'He's already thinking of the French in case the Burgundians say they cannot help you.'

It was gratifying to know that Argyll was thinking along the same lines.

'He wants a man of yours in France to act as a go-between between ourselves and the French. He can't use Mulvanie's people; the English agents know who they are and we don't want to show our hand yet.'

I could think of no one but I mentioned the matter to

Edward Franke later in the day. He frowned in concentration.

'It's difficult,' he said at last. 'After Stokefield most people went to Ireland or Burgundy. You know Harliston, Robinson and so on.'

He fell silent and then looked up quickly.

'Francis, does this person need to have any particular skill?'

'I'm not sure. Discretion would be the most important, I suppose. Why?'

'When I was in the Tower after Stokefield, I met a fellow rebel...'

'Go on...'

'He worked for King Richard in Devon – comes from there, I understand – and helped at the time of the Buckingham revolt.' He smiled. 'He's small, enthusiastic and naïve. A little sparrow of a man, but his heart is with us'. He stopped and thought. 'Or rather it's with Clarence's son,' he corrected himself pedantically.

'But you say this fellow is in the Tower?'

'He is,' said Edward. 'His name's Taylor, by the way. But he was told that he would be released towards the end of the year on condition that he left England permanently. He talked of setting up a business in France.'

'Can we get a message to him? No, we'll tell Mulvanie and he can make contact with... who was it again?'

'Taylor, John Taylor,' said Edward.

We spoke of other matters and of previous times, as old friends are wont to do, as Edward was to leave the next day. He would report back to Archbishop Morton and give him my response and would say that I was living on the charity of the Scottish King, but no more.

★ ★ ★

It was not until late October that I was summoned to Linlithgow. Neither the King nor Argyll was there but Mulvanie welcomed me in his usual brusque fashion. He had news from Burgundy.

'So the Duchess has replied to the Earl's letter?'

He grunted.

'After a fashion. Do you want the flowery script or the simple reply?'

'Just her answer.'

'Well then,' Mulvanie began, 'the Duchess reports that Maximilian is pre-occupied with his various rebellious cities. Additionally, he is busy with France and concerned about the situation in Brittany. This being the case, he cannot see his way to diverting resources to put a Yorkist King on the throne of England at present. Next year, however, his affairs may look better and he may entertain the matter. But, at present, he believes that the struggle against France should be fought on the mainland not on the fringes of Europe.'

That was a blow, as there would never be a 'next year'. Burgundy was crumbling and Edward had been right. Ah well, it would have to be the French then. Mulvanie paused.

'The messenger the Duchess sent with the letter is known to you – I think she sent him specifically. I bade him remain here until you arrived. Will you see him now?'

I was mystified. What on earth could the Duchess want from me? Mulvanie rose.

'I'll fetch him. It was a condition that he sees you and you alone.' He looked at me thoughtfully. 'If you want to tell me after, Francis, I'll be discreet. If you tell me nothing, I'll not mind.'

I waited, intrigued, but then there was a deferential scratch on the door and Rowland Robinson appeared, grinning with pleasure, as he bowed. I rose in delight at the sight of my former bailiff and companion at Stokefield.

'Rowland!' I said happily. 'I heard that you had escaped Stokefield. But how did you get away? What have you been doing?'

He smiled back.

'It's good to see you, my lord. You're thinner, but you look well.'

'How did you survive the battle?' I asked. 'Most of the men who joined at the muster point at Middleham had fought with Lincoln's men and casualties were high.'

'After Swartz was killed, I found myself with Kuttler. He managed to extricate a number of his men and we marched off.' He smiled dryly. 'Weakened though we were, we were too tough a body for what was left of Oxford's troops to try and stop us. We got to the coast and found a ship. Lady Broughton paid for the hire of the vessel. No one else had any money.'

'What then?' I asked.

'My lord knows that I speak Flemish and some French? I offered my services to the Duchess and she was kind enough to see to my wants. So now I carry messages for her. She trusts me as I have proved myself to be discreet.' He broke off and looked at me. 'Indeed, I have a message from the Duchess for you.'

I stretched out my hand.

'Well then, let me have it.'

He shook his head.

'It is not written, my lord. Such a message cannot be written down. But may I relay it to you?'

I nodded.

He looked uneasy.

'My lord, I have served you for a long time, since you came to the West March in fact. You have treated me well and I have followed you in battle. But what I have to say is not pleasant.'

'Go on,' I said grimly. 'Whatever the Duchess and Maximilian have to say cannot alter my respect for you, Rowland.'

'Then, my lord, it is this: the Duchess knows that Burgundy cannot afford military interference in England. Equally, as you know, the Duke of Brittany died last month and England and Burgundy are allied to help keep Brittany from France. Additionally, of course, the war is not going well and there is trouble in the cities in Burgundy.'

This was common knowledge.

'Well?' I asked.

He looked at me, apprehensively.

'The Duchess says that, since you may know this, she fears that you may not wish to wait until Burgundy is in a position to help you, but you might rather be tempted to seek French help. However, if you were to do this and, with their help, place the young Earl of Warwick on England's throne, then Burgundy will be in trouble, for the Duchess believes that the combined weight of England and France would then fall on Burgundy and crush it completely.'

But what did the Duchess expect? If Burgundy would not help us, France was our only other choice.

'I have heard on several occasions that the Duchess has come to love Burgundy,' Rowland went on, 'ever since her brother, King Edward, gave her in marriage to Duke

Charles, in fact. Since that time, my lord, she has laboured to maintain the independence of the Duchy of Burgundy. Without English help though, Burgundy cannot survive against the French. Currently, of course, England and Burgundy are fighting together against the French in Brittany.

'My Lady's message is clear, my lord: if Henry Tudor is overthrown and the Earl of Warwick put on England's throne, then the Anglo-Burgundian alliance will be undone and Burgundy will be swallowed up.'

He braced himself.

'The Duchess says that if you and the Scots ally with the French to replace Tudor with Warwick she will do everything she can to stop you.'

I gazed at him in amazement.

'She's mad!' I exclaimed. 'Are you telling me that she would rather have the usurper Henry Tudor on the throne than her own nephew, the Earl of Warwick? She may be the Duchess of Burgundy, but she is of the House of York! Dear God, two of her brothers were Kings of England!'

'The independence of Burgundy is of more importance to her, my lord,' Rowland Robinson said quietly. 'She knows that the price you would pay for French support would be to agree to help the French against Burgundy or not to interfere as they overthrow the Duchy.'

'So Burgundy is more important to the Duchess than her own nephew's claim to England's throne!' I said angrily. 'She values Burgundy more than her own brother's son. I thought that she was fond of Clarence!'

Rowland shook his head decisively.

'Burgundy's survival is more important to her than her nephew's claim to the throne and she commands you to cease your efforts to win it for him.'

'So she is content to have Henry Tudor on the throne?' I asked incredulously.

A smile lit up Rowland's heavy features.

'On the contrary, my lord. The Duchess and her advisors have a plan to remove him and this is the second part of my message to you. This plan is better than your own and this is why you must cease.'

I was puzzled. On the one hand, the Duchess did not want her nephew on the throne on account of the risk this posed to Burgundy; on the other, she wanted to overthrow Henry Tudor.

'Then what is the Burgundian plan to unseat Tudor?'

'It's simple,' said Rowland. 'When Burgundy becomes strong again, it will be possible to find a youth. Now this young man can pretend to be one of the sons of King Edward. A story can readily be fabricated as to how he cheated death at the hands of his uncle, King Richard. A tale can be invented about how he escaped from the Tower. Naturally, the young Prince would make his way to his "aunt", the Duchess, for assistance. Obviously, she would recognise her "nephew" and help him with men and money to gain his throne. The Scots can assist the young Prince and, perhaps, the Irish too. Then he can invade England.'

I stared at him.

'But Rowland, this boy would be a complete fraud! He would have no royal blood in him at all!'

'But who would know?' Rowland asked. 'Henry Tudor would be overthrown and England would have a Yorkist King. Then England would help Burgundy against France.'

I shook my head in disbelief.

'Leaving aside the total immorality of the Burgundian

plan, it's completely unworkable. Everyone knows that the Princes are dead. If one had survived, I would have known about it. Who would believe the story that one of the Princes escaped from the Tower of London?'

'But why wouldn't they?' he shot back. 'Think of it, my lord. Why should people not believe the story of one of King Edward's sons surviving? After all, who witnessed the murder? Who has seen the bodies? Where are the graves?' He nodded encouragingly at me. 'Henry Tudor is not a popular King, after all. People will rise up readily for one of King Edward's sons.'

'No they won't!'

He looked surprised.

'Why is that?'

I took time to frame my words; this was important.

'Rowland, you were a good servant. Will you do me one last service?'

'Of course, my lord.'

'Then go back to the Duchess and tell her my response to her message.'

'Which is what, my lord?'

'To her first instruction that I should not support her nephew, the Earl of Warwick any longer, since it does not suit the interests of Burgundy – I reject it completely. Her nephew, whether the Duchess likes it or not, is the rightful claimant to the throne of England. It is my duty to win him his throne and I intend to do so, as I promised her brother Richard.'

Rowland looked shocked.

'What of the Duchess' own plan, my lord?' he muttered.

'It will not work, Rowland, and I will tell you why: what she and her councillors are proposing is totally dishonest and utterly immoral. It will not work for one simple reason – the moment I hear of such a pretender, I will stand up publicly and swear that he is a fake. I will swear that King Edward's sons were killed and men will believe me, as I was known to be close to Richard of Gloucester. Now, Rowland, after I have sworn that publicly, who will rise up to support the Duchess' pretender?'

He sat silently after I had spoken. At last, he raised his eyes and looked at me.

'Are you sure you will not reconsider, my lord?' he asked. 'Surely the important thing is to replace Henry Tudor?'

'Even a usurper married to a daughter of Edward IV is better than a total imposter with no royal blood in him whatsoever!' I snapped. 'In any event, Henry Tudor will not be on the throne for much longer as I will be carrying out my own design.'

I gave him some money and made him promise to convey my words accurately to the Duchess. He agreed and made to leave.

I moved to the window and looked out blankly. How on earth could a woman as devout as Margaret, Duchess of Burgundy, have come up with a plan that was so dishonest as to be positively ungodly? I heard a heavy sigh from behind me and turning I caught sight of my former retainer's saddened expression.

'Have a care, my lord; the Duchess can be vengeful,' Rowland said quietly.

★ ★ ★

I told Mulvanie about the Duchess' message the next day, since I had come to trust him and respect his mind. He listened attentively to me and sat in thought.

'It's obvious that you are the one stumbling block to the Duchess' plans, Francis,' he said at last. 'You've rebelled twice now, haven't you? At York and then at Stokefield.'

'Yes.'

'And on both occasions you've called on your supporters to help you place the Earl of Warwick on the throne?'

'I did.'

'So everyone knows that you would not have done that if you had believed that one of King Edward's sons was alive.'

'Of course not!' I agreed. 'They would have had a better claim.'

'So, by your actions, you've made it plain that you believed the Princes to be dead. Now you've threatened to stand up and denounce the Duchess' pretender,' he said with a twinkle in his eye. 'People would believe you, of course, and not just because you're honest.'

I blinked.

'What else is there?'

He roared with laughter.

'Well, can you imagine how totally unconvincing it would be if you suddenly decided to support the Duchess' pretender?'

I was intrigued.

'Why would it be so unconvincing, Davie? I mean, I could not support her pretender, but as a matter of interest...'

I was interrupted by the sound of him clapping his forehead in mock self-reproach.

'Dear God!' he mimicked me. 'Do you know that I was King Richard's Chamberlain and I simply forgot that he only killed one of the Princes? Oh, how stupid of me! I have just recalled that one of them actually escaped from the Tower of London. How careless I've been for these past three years! I should have remembered that earlier and not bothered with that whole Earl of Warwick business!'

He clapped me on the shoulder.

'Everyone knows that you are not the cleverest of men, Francis, but no one would believe that you were that stupid.'

Mulvanie had a unique way of putting things, I thought, but his point was valid.

'She cannot go ahead with her plan while you're alive, Francis. She knows that you would oppose it and denounce the false prince or, even if you swore he was genuine, you would not be believed.'

'So she wants me dead,' I said gloomily.

He nodded.

'But we'll keep you safe - never fear. Now tell me what you know of Richard Ludeley?'

'Ludeley was at Stokefield.'

'One of the Duchess' letters talks about him. Apparently he and another thirty nine men want safe conduct into Scotland. The Irish cannot afford to keep these survivors from Stokefield any longer and the Duchess writes to say that she wants no more English fugitives in Burgundy. She asks if we can give them safe conduct into Scotland. I suppose that we can use them in the invasion force.'

'The invasion force?'

Mulvanie's smile was clearly discernible beneath his hairy features.

'Well yes, Francis. The Earl decided – even before we received the Duchess' reply – that we cannot count on Burgundy. He sent a message to the French and they've sent a herald to open up discussions.'

I sat up excitedly.

'When is he expected?'

'He's already here but the fool has gone to Stirling, whereas we need him to go to Edinburgh to see the Earl and the King. Anyway, I've sent our own herald to Stirling – the French seem fond of formalities – to bring him to Edinburgh.'

'It's not an easy job being a herald,' I told him and he laughed delightedly.

'How did the Earl know that the French would want to help us?' I asked him curiously.

'My agent there sent a fairly detailed report on the situation in Burgundy. Then the Earl heard that not only were Burgundy and England assisting Brittany against France, but Spain was also opposing the French. So he reasoned that, at this time more than any other, the French would be keen to support the Scots and remove Henry Tudor.'

He looked at me thoughtfully.

'Things are beginning to move the way you wish, Francis, but we'll have to ensure that nothing happens to you. It will be better if you come and live at court.'

'Well then,' I said happily, 'shall we go?'

CHAPTER 13

Southern Scotland, 1488.

Strenuous efforts had been made to ensure that the new King's Christmas was celebrated in appropriate style. The Earl of Argyll personally took charge of all the arrangements and it was due to his natural abilities that the court glittered so spectacularly. Not only was there a whole string of themed feasts and dances to celebrate the festive season, but the musical entertainments were of such a high standard that it was rumoured that the King was responsible for many of the compositions.

There was hunting too; the new monarch made no secret of his love of the chase and his courtiers were delighted to humour him. Gradually the weather turned against us and we were forced inside, so it was that the game of courtly love thrived. Having neither the aptitude nor inclination for dalliance, I did not involve myself, but I was interested to observe that the game revealed a fine sense of romance I had not noticed before in the Scots. The nature of the exchanges themselves was inconsequential, amounting to little more than clandestine trysts and discreet kisses, but the men enjoyed these mild flirtations immensely, particularly as the ladies of the court were both graceful and beautiful, and they in turn responded willingly.

With the arrival of Mariota my life changed although I did not realise it at the time. Even in a court filled with loveliness, she easily outshone the others. Her long dark hair tumbled down to frame an angelic face, which lit up with unfeigned merriment at the slightest pretext. Such was her air of innocent provocation that she rapidly became every man's favourite. She quickly became the talk of the court. Her lightness of foot at dancing was admired and men enjoyed her lively sense of humour. Her beauty was worshipped but what really touched these hard-bitten men was her bravery.

She had recently had the misfortune of losing both her parents and the orphaned Mariota had come to court as a ward of the King. With tears in their eyes, men commiserated with her and jostled one another in their altruistic efforts to shelter the poor girl from the cruelties of the world. As normally taciturn husbands spoke so eloquently of this young angel's fortitude in the face of such a loss, so their wives tightened their lips and bitterly pointed out that court life appeared to be providing this extremely annoying girl with more than adequate compensation. In that, they appeared to be correct; Mariota threw herself into the festivities as if they had been made for her. Her fresh young beauty and boundless capacity for revelry served as a natural magnet and men gravitated to her at each entertainment and danced attendance on her while their wives seethed with impotent fury. I had some sympathy for them. After all, they had happily begun this game of courtly love imagining that they would enjoy the sport together throughout the season, but now it appeared that the only ones left on the field of play were Mariota and their own menfolk.

The Earl of Argyll was predictably sensitive to the mood of the court and, finding himself next to me one evening, gestured to the crowd surrounding Mariota and quietly enquired whether I had ever encountered a similar problem in England. I quickly realised that he did not wish to have his elaborate plans for the Christmas court to be disrupted by disharmony.

'Why don't you just send her away from court?' I asked.

'Only the King can do that,' he admitted. 'But then she would leave in disgrace and, as her father was a friend of mine, I wouldn't want that.'

'Perhaps if you spoke to her?'

He glanced at me thoughtfully.

'Aye, maybe I will. But perhaps a little bit more may be needed.'

Curiously enough, the first time I met Mariota was in church. I can recall being surprised that she had joined us for the particular service as it seemed out of character. However, as we prepared to humble ourselves by washing the feet of the twelve poor men, it did occur to me that she was one of only three ladies from the entire court who was attending.

It was not a long ceremony and, once we had played our parts, we waited for the ladies to hand over their coins for charity. Two of them did this with pitying sighs, but all the time they cast supercilious looks at Mariota, who stood awkwardly twisting her fingers. I guessed that either she had forgotten to bring her money or, more likely, the other ladies had neglected to mention that such gifts were customary. Angry at such malice being displayed in a holy place, I passed her my purse, which she took without a word. I was not offended though; while I watched her embarrassment, I had seen something that I had not expected. Her eyes were full of tears.

★ ★ ★

The Earl of Argyll poked the fire in my chamber and happily pulled his stool even closer to the inferno.

'So what do you think, Francis?' he asked.

I edged my own seat back a little. The room was small after all and, since the Earl had insisted on having the fire lit, slightly stuffy. I thought for a moment and then summarised what he had said.

'You say that Mariota has come to see you to ask your advice as a friend of her father's. She has asked you how she should deal with the situation of the ladies of the court hating her because their husbands won't leave her alone.'

'Correct.'

'She told you that she was a poor vulnerable girl unused to the sophistication of palaces and nobles, but she knew that if she was sent away for causing quarrels and fights then she would never find a husband.'

'Exactly. So what is your solution?'

I thought for a moment. Mariota's claim to be 'poor and vulnerable' did not sit too easily with my impression of a highly flirtatious girl who did not appear to have over-exerted herself in repelling the advances of her suitors. On the other hand, I am a poor judge where women are concerned and perhaps the incident at the feet-washing ceremony had brought it home to Mariota how much the ladies of the court disliked her. On balance I thought that she had just been somewhat young and foolish and said as much to the Earl. He poked the fire thoughtfully.

'You're probably right,' he mused, 'I thought so as well. So what do you propose we should do about it?'

Why on earth was he asking me?

'I'm not sure there is a solution,' I said slowly. 'If you keep her at court then matters will just get worse. Send her away in disgrace and you'll ruin her prospects. Perhaps it would be best to ask the King, after all she is his ward.'

'His Grace is perhaps still a little inexperienced in dealing with matters such as this,' the Earl interrupted. 'So you have no proposal?'

'I'm sorry but I don't think I can help you.'

He gave the fire a final prod and turned to look at me and, despite the heat of the room, I suddenly went cold – there was a keen anticipatory look on his face.

'But you can, Francis,' he murmured smoothly. 'Would you like to hear my solution?'

'It's simple really,' he explained. 'I've told her that she must be seen to have selected one of her admirers. Naturally rumours will be spread that not only has she fallen madly in love with the fortunate man but, additionally, through her adoring manner she will make it abundantly clear that the object of her affection is her one and only love.'

'So that all the other men lose interest and their wives won't hate her so much,' I said amusedly, as I could now see what was coming.

He twirled his moustache delightedly.

'Exactly Francis; this way everyone can go back to playing their ridiculous games of courtly love and Mariota can remain at court while she rebuilds her reputation.'

Was there no problem that this man couldn't solve?

'But why me?' I asked.

'Not for your romantic nature!' His warm smile took the sting out of his words. 'But Francis, don't you see? You are more than capable of dealing with a foolish young girl. Your sheer size will deter anyone else from pestering her and, because your stay in Scotland is to be of a temporary nature, the... um... affair can be quietly terminated when you depart. Now, all too conscious of your natural chivalry, I took the liberty of suggesting your name to Mariota as being eminently suitable for our mutual purpose and she readily agreed. Apparently you have already rendered her some small kindness? Then I got Brian Emslie involved.'

I waited apprehensively as he moved still closer to the fire.

'I have to admit that Brian entered into the spirit of the matter very enthusiastically. Normally his thinking is more analytical than creative but, when I heard his proposals for the rumours of how you and Mariota might have fallen in love, I was agog, but felt obliged to suppress his wilder stories about your passionate nature.'

I would kill Emslie.

'Such as?'

'Well, while I didn't doubt that physically you couldn't have killed four of your jealous rivals with your bare hands...'

'What?'

'I did believe you were too good-natured to have subsequently ripped out their still-beating hearts. So, instead, Brian was directed to concentrate more on how Mariota fell in love with you when she first saw your martial bearing and felt her heart flutter as your smouldering eyes lingered on her.'

I slammed the table.

'I'm not doing it!'

'But the story of your great love affair is already round the court Francis!' he protested. 'Brian's acted extremely quickly. If you don't help Mariota, we'll be back to where we started.'

I glared at him.

'No, we're not. In fact we are in a worse position because if I don't co-operate everyone will know that I've rejected Mariota.'

He nodded sagely.

'And that makes it infinitely worse for her, doesn't it? All the men at court will want to comfort a vulnerable young girl who has entrusted her love to you, only to have it so humiliatingly thrown back at her.'

I clenched my fists as I realise how he had trapped me, but he regarded me calmly.

'I would be grateful if you would oblige me in this, Francis,' he said, 'although, of course, in reality you'll be helping everyone.'

He was right, of course, and it would be wholly unchivalrous not to help poor Mariota. With a thin smile, I agreed to play the role of her lover.

'The task should, I imagine, be an enjoyable one', the Earl opined.

Brian Emslie had the sense to wait until evening before he approached me and, even then, he wisely refrained from making any witticisms at my expense. Instead, he was both efficient and practical.

'All you have to do is accompany her to the various entertainments and pretend to be in love with her,' he said crisply. 'Just deter any would-be suitors and make sure that Mariota only talks to women – the older the better. I've already told her what to ask them – everyone loves giving advice, don't they? I've told her to keep dancing to a minimum.'

'Attendance at church?'

'As frequently as possible. I've already covered that with her. Likewise good works for the poor should be carried out.'

★ ★ ★

But if the overall plan for Mariota's rehabilitation was simple, there seemed to me one major detail that was missing. I had been briefed about her by Argyll, but how much had he told her about me? Given the natural secretiveness of the Earl, I suspected not a great deal and yet, how convincingly could she play her role if she knew nothing about the assumed object of her affection? Clearly I would need to meet with Mariota first before we appeared in public together.

A while later, Mariota nodded thoughtfully when I raised the matter.

'That is a good point, Francis. Brian Emslie did mention your 'martial bearing' but to be truthful I was not entirely sure that by itself was wholly sufficient for me to be swept off my feet.'

She eyed me appraisingly. 'Although, that said, I would accept that it is a good starting point. So, Francis tell me about yourself so that we can make our act together appear completely realistic.'

So I did and she listened attentively, her eyes never leaving my face.

'I had not known that you were married, Francis,' she said meditatively. 'Was that why you never approached me before?'

Given the hordes of men who had surrounded Mariota, I was surprised that she had noticed my absence and, without thinking, I said as much.

She smiled lazily. 'I have heard it said that there are some women who are more attracted to men who do not seem to be bothered by them rather than the ones who are.'

It was flattering of course but equally the suggestion was wholly inappropriate to a married man. I looked at her firmly.

'Mariota, I am here to play a role,' I corrected her.

Her deep blue eyes widened. 'But of course you are, dearest Francis,' she agreed softly.

As the days passed I judged that our so-called love affair was proving reasonably convincing. I believed that Mariota found the whole charade easier but I admired the way with which she pretended to give elderly duchesses and superior countesses her undivided attention; no one could have doubted her humble sincerity when nervously she begged them for their help. Equally the adoring glances that she shot at me from her doe-like eyes and her habit of taking my arm at the slightest opportunity would have convinced even the most unromantic observer of the depths of her passion.

It was at her suggestion that we began to spend time privately together. At first I was uneasy at the notion for while I did not, for a moment, doubt my self-control, the notion of being alone with Mariota seemed vaguely improper.

'Is this not taking the pretence a bit far?' I had asked dubiously.

Mariota had shaken her head emphatically.

'On the contrary, darling Francis, it is essential. Think for a moment and reflect how unconvincing it would look if the only time we were seen together was when we were in company. Surely all couples who are in love would want to be by themselves for a lot of the time?'

'But if we are alone no one would see us,' I protested.

Mariota smiled dreamily. 'But, dearest Francis, whether we are riding together through the heather or just walking together by the loch there will always be someone around to notice us and you know how quickly gossip spreads in the court.'

Her argument was irrefutable and I had agreed to her suggestion and so it was that most days found us together by ourselves. After a while I came to view the situation as natural and, in honesty, very pleasant, for Mariota was both interesting and amusing. Her beauty of course was breathtaking but I forced myself to think of Nan each day and never once did I make any move that would have been disloyal to her.

★ ★ ★

Our time together was interrupted by Emslie's summons and curiously I sought him out, since previously, I had been briefed by either Mulvanie or Argyll himself.

Showing uncharacteristic sensitivity, Brian explained that both had left the court and, as such, it fell to him to be the bearer of news.

'So what is the problem?' I asked.

'There's trouble in the North,' he replied shortly. 'There's talk of a rebellion.'

My heart sank.

'It's only in its infancy,' Emslie continued, 'and the Earl hopes that he can prevent it. So far, all we know is that there are some who are loyal to the dead King's father...'

'...to the late James III? I thought that all of that had finished?'

'Well, it's flared up again,' Emslie snapped. 'The Earl of Buchan is in open revolt. Lord Forbes is with him; he even has the blood-stained shirt of the late King. His father is with him, of course, and I heard that the Earl of Athol is in on the plan.'

'Is the support for the insurrection mainly in the North?'

Emslie nodded.

'People there are loyal to James III but even here the new King's party is beginning to fall apart. Earl Angus was so disgusted that he did not receive more rewards, he has withdrawn from government and shut himself up in his border fortress. He's not the only one to think that he did not receive enough, Lord Lyle is another.'

Emslie paused.

'At this stage that is all we know. But the Earl is of the opinion that there will be an uprising against the King and it seems that support for him is dwindling.'

I thought hard for a while and as I did so I began to relax a little. While the rebellion was thoroughly bad news and might well delay the Scottish invasion of England it did have one major weakness: to succeed, a rebellion needed a leader. Logically if the rebels were going to fight against James IV they had to have someone to put in his place if they succeeded. Yet Emslie had spoken of no other leader and the rebels were obviously incapable of bringing his father, James III back to life. Therefore, in the long term, how could the rebels succeed?

Brian nodded when I put this to him.

'That echoes Davie Mulvanie's thinking,' he agreed, 'but he and the Earl wonder if there is not more to it. Anyway they have gone away to find out more and they told me to instruct you to come if you are sent for.'

I rose to go, but Emslie gestured to me to remain.

'You know Philippe, Sieur de Sionne, I believe?'

I nodded, De Sionne headed up the French negotiating team and Argyll had introduced us. I found him both charming and intelligent on the few occasions we had been together.

'Before the Earl left court he and De Sionne reached agreement,' Emslie went on, 'and between them they drew up a provisional treaty...'

My heart leapt. 'For the invasion of England by the Scots and the French?

'Of course,' smiled Brian. 'Anyway it has now been decided here and now all that remains is for the French government to endorse the agreement. Now clearly protocol demands that we celebrate the accord with De Sionne and his men. The Earl was unable to attend to the matter before he left here and he delegated the matter to me. Obviously your presence will be required for the occasion.'

'I'll happily attend.'

'Excellent. Now Francis I understand that on top of all this that congratulations are in order.'

I looked at Emslie apprehensively, as he grinned roguishly at me.

'For what?'

'Why for throwing yourself into your role as Mariota's lover so convincingly,' he said delightedly. 'You two are the talk of the court now.'

I swallowed apprehensively.

'Such an affair has never been heard of before!' he crowed ecstatically. 'No one here is talking about the rebels in the North or our treaty with the French. Oh no, all the gossip here is of you and Mariota.'

His gaze became misty. 'Aye, all that folk talk of is you two walking along slowly hand in hand and you were seen kissing by the loch and it is said that you were spotted...'

I held my hand up to silence him for I was angry and embarrassed. On a number of occasions Mariota had overdone her pretence of love when she sensed that others were about, but I did not need this little rat making fun of me. Furiously I stormed out of his chamber.

Oddly enough, Mariota seemed curiously interested in the news of the revolt and was concerned about the young King.

'Do you think that he will be safe, Francis?' she asked anxiously.

'I imagine that he will be,' I answered reassuringly.

'So he won't be overthrown or killed?'

I was intrigued about her worry. It seemed uncharacteristic.

'Why are you so bothered?'

She flushed.

'Well I am his ward, of course and if anything happened to him, it might affect me. But what else did Brian Emslie tell you?'

To humour her I told her about the tentative agreement with the French and then, and rather awkwardly, about how well she and I had succeeded in our pretend love match.

'So we are the talk of the court,' Mariota said thoughtfully.

'It would appear so,' I replied embarrassedly, 'it seems that everyone believes we are lovers.'

Mariota made no answer but her hand stole into mine. I made to pull mine away but she did not release her grip.

'Then why can we not be, dearest Francis?' she murmured softly.

I blinked in amazement and Mariota moved closer, her dark hair framing her lovely face.

'I have to tell you, my love,' she whispered, 'what might have started out as pretence on my part, might not perhaps by now be such an act.'

I sat numbly as her other hand reached out for mine.

'You should know by now, my darling Francis, that I am yours', she said as she laid her head on my shoulder.

Dear God it was tempting but surely, it was wrong?

'And your wife is so far away...'

That was true. Nan need never know.

'...and I have loved you ever since I first saw you...'

My arm moved round her shoulders and I bent to kiss her. Her lips rose eagerly to meet mine and in a moment we were bound in a passionate embrace. A few moments later she lay back in my arms and looked lovingly at me.

'Shall I come to your chamber tonight?' she asked softly.

For a moment I was tempted but what we had already done was sinful. Gently, I released her.

'No, Mariota,' I told her, 'I am truly sorry but I cannot be unfaithful to Nan. Moreover, I am going away soon. The Earl of Argyll may need me.'

Her blue eyes filled with tears. 'When are you going, my darling?' she sobbed. I ignored the endearment. The situation was growing worse by the moment.

'In a few days, I imagine.'

And then the crying began in earnest. Her whole body was wracked by sobbing. I tried to comfort her for I sensed that her love was real, but when her tear-streaked face moved closer to mine, I gently released her and moved to the door.

'To the Earl of Warwick!'

Jovially we clinked our goblets together and smiled at each other. So far we had already toasted the Kings of France and Scotland several times in an odd mixture of Gaelic, French and English, but now Emslie had moved onto me so I duly obliged with our next monarch.

'Did you enjoy the feast, Francis?' Philippe, Sieur De Sionne turned to me smilingly.

'Very much. And you?'

He cocked his head to one side.

'The food was excellent, of course,' he began diplomatically.

'And the wine?'

His eyes opened in amazement. 'That wasn't wine!'

I grinned at him. 'You'll get used to it, mind you I never

tasted this whisky stuff before.'

De Sionne gestured at his goblet. 'Apparently it's a local drink, although Emslie says it originated in Ireland. He also said that we should dilute it with water, but that is only for women, I have heard.'

The toasting continued for a while until De Sionne rose unsteadily to his feet. Courteously he thanked his host and with that the assembly broke up.

Having done the same I set out for my own chamber with a slightly swimming head. It took me some time to find the right corridor, but then I had dropped my candle as I negotiated the stairs. Eventually by counting the doors in the passageway I came to my room and thankfully entered it. I slid the bolt across the door and flinging off my clothes used the chink of moonlight to find the bed.

And Mariota.

Her arms were around me in an instant and her lips were on mine a second later. For an agonised moment I fought temptation, but then I succumbed.

The following day, as expected, a messenger arrived from the Earl. I was to join him, Henry Lovell and Mulvanie for urgent discussions. As an afterthought he added that both Broughton and Egremont would additionally be present. Clearly the meeting was to be of the highest importance.

My farewell to Mariota was a painful one as I had determined never to see her again and so without further delay I set off for Castle Gloom.

The hall was crowded. There was the inevitable throng around the Earl. I nodded to Egremont, who stood by the fire talking to Cousin Henry. Mulvanie and Emslie muttered together by the dais, while servants scurried around preparing the table.

'Francis!' Broughton slapped my back and smiled with delight. I returned his smile.

'You've put on weight,' I said, 'but you look happier.'

He laughed and was about to answer when the trumpet blew and we all turned to face the Earl. He looked tired and old, but his voice was still vigorous as he welcomed us. After grace had been said, he waved his hands to the benches. We would eat first and then talk, he explained, but the meal should be eaten quickly and the wine used sparingly, he added, for there was much to discuss. As usual, the Earl was correct. He got rid of his superfluous attendants after the meal and sat at the head of the table. Mulvanie sat to his right with Emslie. Broughton, Egremont and I took the other side. Henry Lovell faced the Earl.

'There are developments which affect us all,' the Earl began. 'I will start with the situation here in Scotland and then I will invite Sir Thomas Broughton to brief us on the position in England. After that, I will ask Davie Mulvanie to lead the discussion on what our next steps should be. Are we agreed?'

There were murmurs of assent, so he continued.

'The position in Scotland is bad. There are dissidents in the North whom we know about – Buchan, Huntley, Forbes, and the others. Their motives are mixed. Some believe that we are wrong to have done so little in bringing to justice the killers of King James. Others believe that the fruits of victory have not been apportioned fairly.'

He paused and took a sip of wine.

'All told these northern lords have considerable loyalty.' He sniffed dryly. 'It would appear that their support for the dead King is stronger than that which they exhibited when he was alive. Be that as it may, there is true resentment there.'

He drew breath and looked round the table at our attentive faces.

'But, if that is bad,' the Earl said grimly, 'the worst is still to come. Mulvanie here heard last month that Alexander Gordon, the son of the Earl of Huntley, has written to Henry Tudor to ask him for help in avenging the murder of James III.'

He stopped and looked at our side of the table.

'You will doubtless appreciate that not only do we face the threat of a revolt in the North, but also the possibility of the English coming up from the South to assist the rebels.'

He sipped more wine.

'It is impossible at this stage to assess the strength of the rebel forces. However, with Lennox, Huntley, Buchan and, probably Crichton, they should be able to match our numbers if it comes to war.'

A stunned silence followed his analysis.

'What about the French?' I asked. 'Would they still be interested in the invasion plan?'

Argyll smiled.

'I would judge so. England is now formally committed to assist Brittany and the French resent Henry Tudor's ingratitude. After all, they placed him on his throne and believe that they can easily unseat him to secure a friendlier England. But, let us be realistic, the French will only help if they see a united Scotland able to attack England when they invade.'

A gloomy silence followed. Everything in Scotland seemed to get pushed back. At this rate it would be years before we could invade and with each year Henry Tudor would consolidate his grasp on power. The French would probably lose interest and use their armies to capture all of Burgundy. This was news of the worse possible kind. As usual, Argyll could read my thoughts. He glanced at me.

'But when all is said and done, we can easily defeat these rebels. After all, what binds them together? It is merely a sense of injustice and loyalty to a dead King?'

I smiled inwardly and nudged Broughton. Again, Argyll guessed my thoughts.

'It does parallel your own situation, Francis,' he admitted, 'but only superficially. Our rebels here, you see, cannot agree their strategy and, as such would be incapable of forming a new government.'

He twirled his moustache and looked at me keenly.

'And unlike you, Francis their movement has no obvious leader nor do they have a monarch to put on the throne.'

This sounded more encouraging, but the Earl continued.

'We, on the other hand, have a living King. We have a government and we have strong forces in the South. If it came to a war, we would crush them and then ally with the French and plan our invasion as we intended.'

I took the wine flask which, as usual, Broughton seemed to have appropriated. The mood on our side of the table brightened visibly, as the Earl's points were valid. The potential revolt had no leader and no fixed objectives. Under these circumstances, doubtless Argyll would divide up the opposition. Some would be given posts or lands, others would be won over in other ways, and the remainder would fragment or even be crushed by the

King's forces. There would be a delay to the invasion but not an unbearable one. Reassured, I glanced sideways at Broughton, but to my astonishment he looked grim.

'Indeed,' said the Earl, 'were it not for the bigger problem we have, I would not have called you all here. Sir Thomas, will you be kind enough to explain the situation in England, and the problem that we all face?'

Broughton stood up.

'I am no public speaker,' he began, 'but hear me out, because it is important. As you know, for the best part of a year I have been in the service of the Earl of Northumberland. Now, clearly he does not confide in me, but we, who are in his service, talk between ourselves and know what is happening.'

He bent down to reach his wine.

'The Earl's situation is complex. Following his performance at Bosworth and his lack of support for Henry Tudor at Stokefield, he has lost credibility with him. Equally, his own people do not trust him, since he appears to bear them little love. Taxes levied in the last year have not been collected and attempts to collect further taxes in January were met with a blunt refusal to pay.'

'Why?' asked Emslie.

'In King Richard's day,' replied Broughton, finishing off his wine, 'the North, and York in particular, were frequently given dispensations, or reductions, in taxes. It is, after all, a poor region. But such is not the case now. The people of the North wonder whether Northumberland is pleading with the King on their behalf to lessen their tax burden. Equally, Henry Tudor is wondering where his loyalties lie and why he is not collecting the taxes.'

'But how does any of this affect our plans?' Egremont

asked rudely. 'I have been telling you all ever since I arrived here that Henry Percy has lost the trust of his people. You're merely repeating what I have already said.'

Broughton turned angrily, but Mulvanie was quicker. He stood up and, leaning over the table, he made to cuff Egremont with the back of his hand.

'Be silent!' he growled. Egremont flinched, but he subsided into an angry silence.

Satisfied, Broughton turned round to face the Earl.

'Henry Percy is no fool,' he said. 'Somehow he heard that two of the exiled Scottish lords, who were at the court of Henry Tudor, had come to the King with an idea. Apparently Montgrennan and Lord Romsay...'

'Ramsay,' the Earl corrected him.

'They had heard of the troubles in Scotland and urged Henry Tudor to send troops into southern Scotland. They argued that the new government would be squeezed between the rebels in the North of Scotland and the English in the South. Obviously, the rebels would be grateful for Tudor's assistance and England would have a friendly neighbour with a new pro-Tudor government.'

'Do we know what Henry Tudor's response was?' asked Mulvanie.

'Apparently he was keen, but he's got commitments in Brittany and the cost of a full-scale invasion would be expensive. But when the Earl of Northumberland heard of this he had an idea. Obviously his King would prefer a friendly Scotland but had not the necessary troops to invade and did not fancy the cost of raising an army. Northumberland however, as warden of the East March, already has the troops. If he took them into Scotland to support the rebels, his King would not need to do anything and he would still gain a friendly Scottish neighbour. More importantly, it would demonstrate to his King that the Earl of Northumberland was loyal and trustworthy.'

'What did he do?' I asked.

'According to Clement Skelton, he sat down and dictated a letter to the King offering to lead the force into Scotland. He assured the King of his loyalty and begged his permission to demonstrate it,' Broughton said. 'Of course, there was another point which he did not communicate to Henry Tudor, but Clement told me about it.'

'What was that?' asked Cousin Henry.

'Once he had mustered his force, he would have sufficient men to ensure that all outstanding taxes could be collected. He could easily extract every last penny. So by sending the taxes to Henry Tudor and by assisting in Scotland, suddenly Northumberland moves from being an object of suspicion to being a major asset to the Tudor regime.'

'So, in essence, he saves himself from Henry Tudor's wrath by oppressing his own people and we Scots,' said Emslie. 'What was Tudor's reply to the Earl of Northumberland's suggestion?'

Broughton looked round the table.

'That's why I'm here,' he said. 'Northumberland talked to us a few days ago. He told us that King Henry wishes him to advance his men into Scotland and has agreed to send money to pay troops. We were told to prepare ourselves for May.'

'If Henry Tudor is sending money to Northumberland then it's a genuine threat,' I told Mulvanie.

He nodded.

'So the situation is as follows – we have rebels in the North and probably, elsewhere, but we can deal with these. The real threat comes from the Earl of

Northumberland, who wishes to regain his credibility with his royal master by doing something that Henry Tudor actually wants. So with the rebels on the one hand, and the belligerent Earl on the other, we appear to be caught in a trap.'

I noticed the Earl tugging at his moustache as we all listened to Mulvanie's summary.

'Why can't we move against the rebels in the North immediately?' asked Cousin Henry. 'Once they are defeated, Northumberland would not invade.'

'Because we do not know who they all are,' Mulvanie replied. 'We know some, but not all. Also, as yet, they have not rebelled and heavy-handed action on our part would drive others into their camp.'

'And we cannot defeat the rebels and Northumberland simultaneously?' asked Broughton.

'No.' Emslie and Mulvanie spoke together.

There was a heavy silence as we tried to think of a way through all this. After a few minutes, the Earl of Argyll asked whether we had any suggestions. One by one we shook our heads but unexpectedly he smiled at us.

'There is a way if the three of you are prepared to assist,' he said looking at Egremont, Broughton and myself. 'I would say that it is possible and not only would it prevent the Earl of Northumberland's invasion, but it would also enable us to defeat our own rebels here. Of course, we will simultaneously be negotiating with the French. Naturally, once that has been done your own invasion of England could take place, Francis.'

'On the other hand,' he pointed out quietly, 'if you felt you could not assist then the Government of King James would probably collapse. You would not have your invasion Francis, because the French would not have

Scotland as an ally. Also, I regret to say that Henry Tudor would remain King of England and Henry Percy would stay as the Earl of Northumberland.'

Broughton and Egremont looked at me and I shrugged my shoulders. The way Argyll described it, it seemed we had little choice.

'What would you like us to do, my lord?' I asked and then I noticed that Broughton was looking depressed. He needed cheering up, so I looked at Argyll and added.

'Would you like us to assassinate Northumberland?'

Broughton chuckled loudly and even the sour-faced Egremont raised a thin smile. When I looked back at the Earl, I suddenly went cold; he was looking at me in surprise.

'However did you guess, Francis?'

I sat silently for a few moments. Next to me Broughton emptied the wine flask and nudged me.

'It's poisonous, this stuff,' he muttered.

I was about to agree, but Argyll began to speak.

'I have only used murder once before to solve a problem,' he began, 'but I found it to be quite a successful solution. Indeed, it is curious how beneficial it can be. Often the death of one man prevents the loss of the lives of many others. In this case, as I shall explain, the death of the Earl of Northumberland will mean that there is no English invasion. As such, countless English and Scottish lives will be saved.'

He signalled to Mulvanie to continue.

'The death of the Earl not only saves lives,' agreed Mulvanie, 'but there are two other benefits. The first one is obvious – if there is no English invasion, then our young King James will remain on the throne, as we can deal with his rebels on our own. The other benefit, of course, is that you will get your army, Francis.'

I tasted the wine again. Broughton had a point.

'Suppose Northumberland's successor decided to follow the invasion policy?'

The Earl nodded approvingly.

'A good question, Francis. But, do you accept that if there was no threat from the Earl of Northumberland we could suppress our own rebels here in Scotland?'

'I imagine so.'

'So our real danger comes from the Earl of Northumberland then,' said the Earl. 'But reflect on who the instigator of this English attack against us is. It is Northumberland himself and we know why he's doing it. His motives are selfish and shallow. He is trying to win his King's favour. Now, without Northumberland there would be no invasion and let me explain why. Tell me Francis; if you were Henry Tudor, and you knew nothing of our own plan to make Egremont the next Earl of Northumberland, who would you put in the place of Henry Percy when you heard he was dead?'

I frowned.

'It's rather difficult. In a way, it's more a question of who you would not put in the position. You see, Jasper Tudor is too old. Oxford is too incompetent and you would not want to have the Stanleys controlling the whole of the North. A bishop is no good; you need a soldier.'

Argyll nodded happily.

'But whoever was put in would be well received,' he said expectantly. 'Henry Percy, the current Earl, is neither loved nor trusted.'

I shook my head.

'Whoever Henry Tudor puts in to replace Northumberland would not be well received. The lords would not welcome an outsider and the people would still bitterly resent having to pay their taxes in full. The new man would struggle to establish himself in a hostile environment. It would take a long time before people started to follow him.'

I stopped talking, suddenly realising what was being said. For without Northumberland there would be no English move into Scotland. His successor would have no need or desire to assist the rebels for selfish motives and, even if he did, no one would follow him.

Argyll watched me closely.

'You see it now, Francis, don't you? Without Northumberland there will be no English invasion to assist the rebels here.'

I nodded. As usual, the Earl of Argyll was correct.

'The next reason to obviate the Earl of Northumberland is of benefit to both of us,' the Earl continued happily. 'It was Davie here who was kind enough to point it out to me. He observed that whoever replaced the dead Earl of Northumberland would not have the same natural authority as his predecessor, for the name of Percy commands greater respect in the North.'

'That's what I've been telling you ever since I arrived here!' Egremont burst out. 'If you only listened to me, you would realise that the name of Percy...'

He trailed off as Mulvanie had produced a large bullock knife and had risen to his feet poised to strike.

'Stop interrupting!' Mulvanie growled. 'In fact, it would be better if you left us now. I'll tell you your part in the plan tomorrow.'

Egremont flushed but faced by a hulking Mulvanie and a knife that was, by now, almost touching his face he slowly rose to his feet and walked towards the door. For a moment he hesitated, but Cousin Henry eyed him distastefully and waved him out of the room.

'Goodnight Sir John. My apologies, my lord.'

Emslie clicked his fingers happily and the door slammed behind the departing Egremont.

'To continue,' the Earl said cheerfully, 'I was remarking that with Northumberland dead and his replacement not having the same natural authority, the task of the... um... talkative Egremont becomes easier. He is after all a Percy.'

'And not much else,' said Cousin Henry.

'So, when the time is right for him to win his earldom, he will find less opposition because of his name. Now that has two advantages, Francis. One for you and one for me,' the Earl said pleasantly. 'Let's take yours first,' he added generously. 'The less opposition that Egremont faces, the easier it will be for your invading army to pass through Northumberland and onto London.'

A good point, I thought.

'And your advantage, my lord?'

He twirled the ends of his moustache.

'The less opposition that Egremont faces, the easier it is for Scotland to secure her newest piece of territory,' he said happily.

'All things considered, it's better if Henry Percy is sent to meet his maker,' my cousin observed thoughtfully.

He looked at me expectantly. Broughton glanced at him.

'I can follow all that but why does it have to be us?' he asked. 'Surely you have your own people who are... well...'

'Experts in assassination, Sir Thomas?' Henry suggested helpfully. 'If we did, we could not use them. Think for a moment. Suppose, for whatever reason, our man got caught afterwards. Regardless of the cost, regardless of his commitments in Brittany, Henry Tudor would have to take revenge on us. He would send an English army to invade Scotland immediately. The murder of one of his leading earls by the Scots would be far too great an insult to his authority for England to swallow.'

That was undoubtedly true, so we sat for a few moments in silence.

'Well Francis, will you do it?' the Earl asked.

His tone was light, but I saw lines of strain on his face. He was fighting for his political life and the position of his King and he knew it. Without doubt, his plan made total sense. Without the Earl of Northumberland, there could be no English invasion and, without that, he could crush the Scottish rebels. Equally, without the Earl of Northumberland, not only could my invasion take place but its passage would be made easier and I accepted that he dared not use the Scots to kill the Earl. It would have to be Broughton and I, so I nudged him and he nodded slightly.

'Of course, we'll help you,' I said.

Mulvanie smiled happily and Emslie clicked his fingers in satisfaction.

'Then I'll leave you two here to think of a plan,' Argyll said with a smile.

He was half way to the door when he stopped and turned around to face me.

'By the way, Francis, it was really very clever of you to think of my idea,' he said hesitantly. 'How did you guess it?'

It seemed inadvisable to tell the truth.

'Just because I am English, do you think I'm stupid?' I asked indignantly.

There was a roar of laughter from Mulvanie.

'Yes,' he wheezed, 'but obviously being in Scotland is adding to your education.'

His shoulders shook and the Earl gave a quick smile. Emslie clicked his fingers delightedly.

'Then if we are going to sit here working out how to save your regime,' I said politely, 'would you do one thing for us?'

Mulvanie nodded quickly.

'Of course.'

'Good. Ask them to bring up some better wine.' I gestured at the flagons on the table. 'This stuff is poisonous and you'll need us alive to kill the Earl of Northumberland.'

CHAPTER 14

Castle Gloom, 1489.

Mulvanie enquired sarcastically about my health the next day and asked how Broughton and I had solved the problem. I frowned.

'The problem?'

He forced a smile.

'The assassination of Northumberland. You assured me that you would work out how to kill a man whose unpopularity is such that he has to be permanently surrounded by a large escort.'

I frowned again as I tried to recall whether we had touched upon this in the course of our conversation. Thomas' stories of his adventures in France and Italy had been particularly amusing, but I think the issue had come up at some point. The trouble was that I had no recollection of what we had said.

'The Earl of Northumberland is not due to invade Scotland until May,' Mulvanie observed sardonically. 'Don't rush now, Francis.'

I looked at him in puzzlement. I was sure we had solved the problem. Anticipation and impatience showed in his face, which did not help my memory. I looked around the courtyard to try and gather inspiration. The sentry by the gatehouse was watching us keenly. He had a fiercely determined look about him, which was unusual, as most sentries merely look bored. He must be very loyal to Argyll, I thought. After a moment, I smiled happily as it all came flooding back. Seeing this, Mulvanie's face lost its strained look.

'There is a way,' I told him, 'but we are not too sure of the details; we will have to improvise as we go along.'

'Perhaps it would be best if you told me what you discussed with Sir Thomas,' Mulvanie said.

He pointed to the garden overlooking the valley.

'We will not be interrupted there and you will probably benefit from the fresh air.'

'The only way to kill him, Davie, is to detach him from his escort.'

'So how, precisely, will you do that?'

* * *

'Thomas, how many of the Earl's retinue are actually prepared to die for him?' I had asked Broughton.

He had looked puzzled when I put this question to him.

'Well, in theory, I suppose we all are. If we were in a battle against the French or the Scots, it would be our duty.'

'Yes, of course,' I said patiently, 'but suppose it was not a battle. How many of you are so loyal that you are actually prepared to die for him?'

He began to see my point.

'He's got some supporters – John Pickering and Robert Plumpton are the major ones – but there are a number of us, who previously held posts under Richard of Gloucester. You know, Francis, people like James Strangeways,

William Gascoigne. There's Eure of course.' He scratched his chin slowly, as he thought further. 'Of course, there are many in his retinue who thought that he should have supported Richard of Gloucester at Bosworth.'

'But they were prevented from fighting. Thomas, pretend that all his men were with the Earl of Northumberland...'

'They never are,' he broke in. 'There's always some of them doing something for the Earl or managing their own affairs. At any given time, Francis, I would estimate that he would only have half his retinue around him.'

He finished his wine and looked round for more. I handed over another flask.

'Thank you,' said Broughton. 'Do you know, I would say this was even better than the last one? Do you know another thing, Francis?'

'No.'

'Thinking about it,' Broughton said slowly, 'I reckon about half of the Earl's retinue would probably view his death as revenge for what he did at Bosworth.'

'Do you think we could increase that number?'

He thought for a while.

'Some of us older men could talk to the younger ones,' he said at last. 'I could get Richard Conyers to help me and then there's Thomas Ratcliffe and one or two more.'

I made no reply but watched as he made little circles in the spilled wine. At last he looked up.

'I suppose,' he slurred, 'that provided there was some manner in which we could get away ourselves, not too many of the escort would stay to defend the Earl.'

★ ★ ★

'That's the key point' I told Mulvanie. 'We know that there is unrest in the Earl of Northumberland's domain. We know that he is unpopular and heavily guarded. We now believe that the loyalty of at least part of his escort is suspect.'

'So what is your plan?' Mulvanie asked eagerly.

'We plan that Broughton should return to the Earl of Northumberland when he comes back to Scarborough from London. He will start to influence the Earl's retainers against him. Egremont should secretly move about Yorkshire to try to build up support against Northumberland. I will keep in touch with Broughton and we will look for an opportunity to dispose of the Earl.'

The Earl of Argyll saw us that evening. He did not comment on our plan but simply asked what we required to fulfil it.

'Money to influence opinion, Emslie to carry messages and a safe passage to the border,' Broughton told him.

'You'll have those,' the Earl said.

He pointed at Egremont.

'The time is not right for you to do anything except to influence opinion against Northumberland. Under no circumstances should you try to secure the earldom for yourself at this stage. The time for you to do that is when we are ready to invade England and the French are coming across the Channel. Is that perfectly clear?'

Egremont nodded. Satisfied, the Earl turned to us.

'Succeed in this and, when we've finished with our rebels, we'll invade England, Francis. That I promise you.'

We left separately. Egremont headed for the eastern part of Yorkshire, where he claimed to have good connections and was confident of winning support. Broughton departed for Scarborough to attend the Earl of Northumberland. I went to Lund near Thirsk as I had once held lands there and occupied a corner of the ramshackle hall. It had been thoroughly looted but was completely empty. Obviously, Henry Tudor's men had not completed the inventory of my lands. It was, however, a good place to base myself.

Thirsk seemed a natural place for dissidents to congregate. Suitably disguised, thanks to Emslie, I watched groups of men wandering into Thirsk and overheard their talk. How much was rumour and how much was true was hard to determine. It was said that there was to be a new tax, that there would be no concessions, and that the amount was to be collected in full. It was expected that Northumberland would use force to extract the taxes, but while the mood of the people was ugly, there were no rebel leaders. Men drifted into the town but no one seemed to have any idea of what to do. I received one brief message from Broughton. The Earl was in a foul temper; Clement Skelton had told Broughton that Northumberland had secured the promise of money from King Henry so that he could move against the Scots but apparently this was conditional on the Earl collecting all taxes in full and without delay.

I overheard that the Earl was taking his rage out on his labourers in Scarborough. He had already had a number of them flogged. It seemed that he did not like his castle renovation plans being unfavourably compared with the work that had been carried out there by Richard of Gloucester. But for all that, it was obvious to everyone that, at some stage, Northumberland would have to stop his castle-building and start getting the taxes collected.

I had resigned myself to some weeks of idleness in anticipation of this but events moved faster than I had hoped. Dressed as a simple wool trader, Emslie appeared a couple of weeks later, having completed the journey from Scarborough to Lund in three days. He shook the rain off his cap as I led him to that part of the hall that was comparatively dry. Despite the wet, he was as perky as ever.

'Your Earl's over-reached himself this time,' he said cheerfully. 'There's a whole crowd of them coming over from Ayton to Thirsk to join the others. The talk is that Northumberland is gathering his men to crush the mob here.'

'What are you talking about?' I asked him.

'Ayton,' he said excitedly. 'It's a small village close to Scarborough, but it's where quite a few of the sailors who served with the Duke of Norfolk settled. Apparently, Norfolk wanted to reward a number of them and he asked Richard of Gloucester...'

'Well, Richard was Lord of Scarborough,' I began. 'Moreover...'

'The folk of Ayton have good memories of him,' continued Emslie. 'Anyway, two weeks ago a group of Northumberland's men came to the village. They were bored and drunk. The men of the village were away. Northumberland's men raped a number of the women. When the priest tried to intervene, he was beaten.'

'But surely the Lord of Ayton can call the sheriff and have Northumberland's men brought to trial?'

'There is no lord. Ayton's a small village. It's part of the Lordship of Scarborough and Northumberland took that over when Richard of Gloucester was killed. The villagers went to the hall to protest but they were turned away by the guards. But that's not all – one of the fathers of one of the raped girls shouted out that Northumberland was not a good lord for them. Richard of Gloucester would have dealt with the matter fairly.'

I winced.

'Was he killed?'

Emslie frowned.

'No. The guards seized him and reported the matter to the Earl. He was in a fury anyway but cutting a long story short, the man, Christopher Atkinson, was returned to the village the next day.'

I was glad that Northumberland had shown some humanity.

'Minus his tongue,' added Emslie. 'So then the priest organised a meeting and Atkinson's son-in-law, John Chamber, led a number of the villagers to Thirsk. I expect they'll be here in a couple of days.'

'Did you see Broughton?'

'Briefly. He told me to tell you that he and Clement Skelton have seen Sir John Pickering, who the Earl listens to. They told him that they believe there to be two to three hundred men here. Pickering's advice to Northumberland was that he should move swiftly against them with the force that he already has before the number of rebels increases much further. Pickering thought that the Northumberland could probably muster a hundred or so knights, which would easily suffice against a mob. He also pointed out that the Earl could collect some more from Sir Robert Plumpton if he felt that they were required.'

'Did Broughton say who was in attendance on the Earl at the moment? This is important, Brian.'

Emslie frowned as he tried to remember.

'Yes, he said that they were mostly men such as

Strangeways, Grey of Horton, William Hastings; I forget the rest.'

I smiled in relief. While indentured to Northumberland, I recalled that these men had been servants of Richard of Gloucester, so I was certain that Broughton, Ratcliffe and Conyers would have already influenced their minds against the Earl.

But my relief was short lived. While Broughton had played his part excellently and had, in all likelihood, ensured that the Earl's escort would not ride to his rescue, it was now down to me to carry out the actual murder of Northumberland. I swallowed uneasily. I had killed before and doubtless would do again but that was in battle; this would be pre-meditated murder.

Oddly enough I had no concern for the danger I faced. Northumberland would be mounted in full armour and with a sword. All I had was a billhook and a knife. For all that, I had little doubt that I could manage it, provided a suitable opportunity arose. What worried me was the sheer cold-bloodedness of the business. Northumberland would be expecting trouble certainly, but not his own death. What Broughton and I were about to do was a mortal sin. I told myself that Northumberland deserved it. His betrayal of Richard at Bosworth had undoubtedly cost us the battle and the King his life, but I was still unable to convince myself – revenge rarely provides satisfaction. No, the only justification was that his death would save countless lives in Scotland and would make my own invasion of England easier. Still I found myself in an increasingly brooding mood and drinking heavily.

★ ★ ★

The aimless drifting of the tax malcontents became more focused with the arrival of a furious John Chamber, his raped wife, and his tongue-less father-in-law. The news of the atrocities in Ayton spread rapidly and indignation against the Earl of Northumberland was running high. I heard that the Earl had heeded Sir John Pickering's advice, as he arrived at his nearby manor at Maiden's Bower a couple of days later but he took no action. Emslie and I assumed that he was waiting for Plumpton and reinforcements, since Northumberland's manor was strongly guarded and the Earl did not emerge from there.

Meanwhile, the numbers of rebels swelled. I estimated that there must be seven to eight hundred and, more importantly, in John Chamber they had found a leader. I heard him speak to a large crowd by the church and his angry words boomed across the little green to where Emslie and I stood, bearded and ragged.

'He's no lord of yours... He'll not help you with your taxes... You'll pay more and more. He's not a good Lord like Gloucester was to us... Don't forget he deserted Gloucester in his hour of need. Where is his justice? His men use our women and take our possessions... See what happens when you argue...'

We were too far away to see the wronged wife and her mutilated father who must have been exhibited at each speech, but there was no doubt that Chamber was a powerful speaker. His anger boiled over into the crowd and people began to repeat his words and phrases. After two days of this, the mob fully accepted John Chamber as their leader and would have followed him anywhere.

Word of this reached Northumberland. The next day the Earl sent word that he would address the people at noon. Whether he had decided not to wait for Plumpton and to disperse the crowd on his own or whether he was going to be conciliatory neither Emslie nor I could guess. But sure enough, at the appointed hour, dressed in full armour and accompanied by about a hundred knights and men-at-arms, he rode onto the south side of the green. His escort spread themselves behind him and I spotted Broughton in the middle.

Secure in the knowledge that his heavily armed escort was sufficiently strong to deal with a crowd of peasants, Northumberland confidently pushed forward. He was met by jeers, as John Chamber had spent the morning whipping the crowd into a frenzy. Northumberland ignored the insults. For a moment he arrogantly surveyed the mob and produced a sheet of parchment.

'It's time for me to make my move,' I stammered to Emslie.

He gave me a sympathetic look and, clutching my billhook, I began to move slowly through the throng towards Northumberland. The angry mutterings of the crowd were plainly audible.

'He says we must pay all the taxes and submit to the King's will..'

My hands were sweating now; it was difficult to hold the billhook. Still I pushed forward.

'It's not the King's will. It's his will.'

Dear God! Northumberland's horse was enormous. How in hell's name was I supposed to pull him off that?

'Gloucester would never have done this…'

'Aye he was a good lord, not like that sack of…'

My whole body was shaking, as if I had a fever. I swept the sweat from my forehead irritably – I had to be able to see if I was going to do this. Northumberland had clearly finished now; he gestured to a knight on his right as I covered the last few paces to his other side. The knight shouldered his horse into the crowd.

'You heard your lord – now disperse!' he shouted.

I glanced at the Earl's escort; they were still motionless. For a moment I wondered if Broughton had failed in his mission, but then I put the thought from my mind. I trusted him as I did no other. Slowly, I raised my billhook.

A stone was thrown – then another. There was a great shout as the crowd surged forward. Northumberland's horse was skittering wildly now in fear and I had to jump away to avoid being crushed. Its rider pulled savagely at the reins and then gestured to his escort.

My billhook descended on his shoulder as his horse lurched forward and I pulled with all my strength. Surprised though he was, he struggled briefly, but I hung on and finally, with a tremendous clatter, the Earl hit the ground.

A drumming of hooves behind me told me that Northumberland's escort was deserting him. With nausea rising in me, I dropped my billhook and reached for my knife.

★ ★ ★

By the time I slunk back, the dead Earl had been stripped naked except for his hose. John Chamber picked up Northumberland's sword and waved it triumphantly.

'He was no true lord of ours!' I heard him shout. He

turned to the excited crowd. 'Let's show everyone what we thought of him.'

And so Richard of Gloucester's betrayer was tied naked over his horse and taken away by the excited crowd. Finally John Chamber selected a particularly fine old elm tree. A rope was attached to one of the branches and a noose was placed round the Earl's neck as he slumped over his horse. Unsurprisingly perhaps, it was John Chamber's father-in-law who pushed a billhook into the rear of the Earl's horse, causing it to move away sharply. Such was the end of Henry Percy, fourth Earl of Northumberland.

Our mission was accomplished. Emslie departed immediately; he wished to collect Egremont and return to Scotland in order to tell the Earl that Northumberland was no more.

'I'll wait here for Broughton,' I said. 'Where do you want us to go in Scotland? Castle Gloom?'

He thought for a moment.

'When you reach the border, I'll get them to find you and bring you to Linlithgow.' He clicked his fingers happily. 'The Earl of Argyll will be there. He'll be pleased with this news.'

'I'm glad,' I muttered dully.

He grinned and quickly departed.

Broughton arrived in a torn smock ten days later. Unkempt but cheerful, he brought food and news.

'The whole country is in an uproar at present,' he began. 'Northumberland's men have fled back to their homes but I heard that Sir Robert Plumpton, who was supposed to join the Earl, has sent word to Henry Tudor.'

'So what's happening now?'

'Groups are forming all over the county. There's one lot at Allerton and more elsewhere. There are rebels everywhere!'

'But who are they rebelling against?'

He looked at me pityingly.

'Francis, at times, you are a complete fool. Listen, the Earl of Northumberland delivers King Henry's message to his subjects. The King tells them to pay their taxes in full. Do his subjects meekly obey? No – they promptly kill his messenger. But they know that King Henry will use force to punish them and to collect the taxes, so what choice do they have other than to rebel?'

'But surely if they dispersed now and returned home they would be safe? They cannot seriously imagine that they would stand a chance against Henry Tudor's troops.'

Broughton snorted.

'I know that and you know that, but John Chamber has told them that the lords will come to their aid. Also he's promised them that the true Earl of Northumberland will lead them.'

'You don't mean that Egremont is disobeying the Earl of Argyll?'

'It seems so. Apparently, he and Chamber have said they'll force the King to cancel the taxes or they'll overthrow him. I gather that the plan is for everyone to muster at Sheriff Hutton and then they'll march south.'

I stared at him.

'Then Egremont is insane. He knows that none of the lords will join him. Precious few were prepared to take that risk at Stokefield and we had a proper army.'

'I agree but Chamber is a powerful speaker. The people are angry about the taxes and, with Northumberland dead, there's no government here. There's no one to tell the people not to rebel or to warn them of the likely consequences.' He thought for a moment. 'Shall we go to Sheriff Hutton to see for ourselves?'

★ ★ ★

There seemed to be two thousand peasants gathered at Sheriff Hutton, I estimated. Most seemed content to remain with their own groups, as they waited for John Chamber to speak to them at noon. We mingled easily among the bodies of men as people had come from far and wide. But my fears were confirmed – this was no army, it was a mob. The only weapons were billhooks and I saw only a few archers among them.

'Do you want to hear what Chamber and Egremont have to say?' muttered Thomas.

I gestured to the men about us.

'Is there nothing we can do to warn them?' I said softly. 'In a way we've caused this.'

He shook his head.

'They would think you were one of Henry Tudor's men and deal with you, accordingly,' he said quietly.

He took my arm and began to lead me through the crowd, which was beginning to converge on the little hillock where Chamber and Egremont would shortly be speaking. I cursed Egremont under my breath. These gullible peasants would have no chance against proper troops. Without the support of the local lords, his simple followers would either be shot by the King's archers or just be ridden down by his knights' horses.

Broughton sensed my mood and, as we emerged from the throng, he turned to me.

'Most of them will desert before they meet Henry Tudor's forces. The further they get from their homes, the more nervous they'll become. As soon as one lot starts deserting, others will follow. Then those who are left will start wondering why Egremont's fine friends haven't appeared and they'll leave too.'

Reassured, I nodded.

'I better start heading back to Scotland then.'

He dug me in the ribs.

'You don't get rid of me that easily,' he said jovially. He looked at my blank expression. 'I'll be coming with you. I have no reason to remain here, now that Northumberland is dead.'

'But your wife?'

'She is with her family in France until I regain my lands. After all, it won't be too long now, will it?'

It took us three months to return to Linlithgow. Egremont's revolt collapsed quickly and Tudor's men were looking everywhere for him and other rebels. Accordingly, we travelled slowly along lonely lanes and quiet paths, trying to suppress our feelings of guilt and failing completely.

CHAPTER 15

Castle Gloom, 1489.

It was evident that Mulvanie had been dealing with people of importance. His hair and beard were trimmed and his dark blue tunic with golden threads was evidently new. He looked what he was – a large, powerful and authoritative figure. He welcomed us warmly.

'So you managed it then? Or so Brian Emslie tells me. That saves a great deal of bother. The Earl of Argyll will thank you when he returns but we're certainly in your debt.'

I brushed his words away. Northumberland's murder was not a topic I wished to dwell on.

'So let me brief you on developments here,' Mulvanie continued.

'Just before that, what happened to that idiot Egremont?' asked Broughton.

Mulvanie grinned sheepishly.

'On balance, I would have to say that we made a miscalculation with that one. He arrived back here a month or so ago. He claimed credit for everything; he said he'd recruited that rabble-rouser Chamber. He said that people had flocked to support him and, despite his protests, he'd been forced into leading a revolt. Even as a reluctant leader, he did very well it seems. He feinted down towards

Doncaster and turned back cleverly to capture York.'

'He was a true hero,' Broughton said with mock solemnity.

'Made the rest of us totally superfluous,' I added.

'Anyway,' Mulvanie continued with a chortle, 'he heard that Henry Tudor's forces were advancing on his position. Obviously, he only had the interests of his people at heart, so he dismissed his followers and only just managed to escape himself by the skin of his teeth.'

'I expect, Francis, that you are struck dumb by his courage,' Broughton said sarcastically. 'To think of such nobility residing in a man's heart!'

'It's humbling to see the knightly standards that we must aspire to, Thomas.'

Mulvanie smiled grimly.

'I'm not quite sure that the Earl saw it in quite the same way as you two do. You see, Brian Emslie went to have a look at what Egremont was doing after he left you Francis. He'd heard rumours and didn't like what he heard.'

He removed a loose gold thread on his sleeve fastidiously.

'Emslie returned here two weeks after Egremont arrived and told me all that had happened. So I got Brian to tell his story to the Earl of Argyll with Egremont present and then invited Egremont to do the same.'

'That must have been interesting,' Broughton said.

'It was. He blustered a bit first. Said he might have forgotten a couple of points and omitted a few details. Then he observed that it was probable that Brian Emslie had been misled on a few facts and queried the truth of some of his story.'

'Foolish!' I said.

Mulvanie nodded.

'The Earl thought about this and pointed out that he had

known Brian Emslie for more than ten years. In all that time he had never known him to tell a lie or to be inaccurate. Then he said that he was displeased with Egremont. In fact, he was very displeased. Egremont had deliberately disobeyed his instruction and had taken advantage of the murder of Northumberland and had tried to win his earldom.'

'He behaved like an irresponsible fool!' snapped Broughton.

'I don't think Egremont realised that he had displeased the Earl of Argyll so greatly. He tried to laugh the matter off. Said he might have got a little carried away but then he more or less cut his own throat. He said the main point was that people had supported him proving that, when the invasion took place, he had the loyalty of the people. So in reality instead of criticising him, Argyll should be grateful. Egremont argued that when he was made Earl of Northumberland it would be easier for Scotland to absorb its new territory.

'The Earl looked at him and said that he was deluding himself. There would be much speculation as to what his greatest fault was. Some men would see Egremont as foolish. Many would view him as a coward. All would know him to be a liar. The Earl wondered which of these was the greatest flaw in Egremont's character and concluded that it was probably his stupidity. How could he imagine, after all that the Earl had been told, that Egremont could hope to be the Earl of Northumberland? What possible justification could there be to give a major earldom to such a man? The man was incapable of obeying instructions, had deserted his own followers, and had tried to take the credit for other men's actions.'

I could imagine the Argyll's icy tones as he spat out this damning verdict on our former colleague.

'But the Earl was merciful,' continued Mulvanie, 'he did not have him killed but pointed out that, since Egremont knew all about the invasion plan, he could hardly go free. Egremont swore that he would tell no one about it and the Earl nodded happily.

'"For once, Sir John, I am in agreement with you," he had said, "as you'll not be in a position to do so. For the next year or so you'll be imprisoned in a secure and secret place with no company, except your own. Then you'll be released but you'll have to leave Scotland."'

'He can't go back to England?' I asked.

Mulvanie shook his head.

'He'll probably go to Burgundy, but the next year will be useful for him.'

I was unable to see how solitary confinement could be productive.

'As Argyll pointed out to him, he can use the time to cure these self-deceptions of his. Now Francis, the Earl told me to tell you that our agreement still stands. In his absence, I am to work with you to ensure its success.'

He looked at me.

'Shall we walk by the loch and I'll tell you what's been happening here and when we eat later Edward Franke will advise you of what's been going on elsewhere?'

It was a beautiful day and there was much to discuss.

'There is just one thing which may be better said in private,' he said slowly. 'It would seem that the Lady Mariota is carrying your child and will give birth in two months' time.'

I stared at him. I sat stunned while I thought. Thomas

slowly rose, put his hand on my shoulder and then left the chamber. Thoughts raced through my mind; I was going to have to tell Nan now, but how was I going to do that? Then there was the danger to Mariota herself. Childbirth was always risky and could be fatal to both mother and child. Was Mariota well? Was she going to be alright?

'Where is she now?' I stammered nervously.

Mulvanie's smile was reassuring.

'The Earl attended to everything. As you know, Mariota's parents are dead and in due course she will inherit the small estate. But, at present, she is a royal ward and, despite being somewhat older than the new King, it seems that he is keen to maintain the wardship and, particularly, keep her at court.'

'Why?'

Mulvanie laughed.

'Our new King James has a comprehensive list of interests: building, poetry, music, hawking and hunting. But now he has another.' He hesitated for a moment. 'After you left for England, he and the Lady Mariota became quite close.'

I felt an irrational stab of jealousy and then the obvious thought sprang to mind: was this my child? I looked at Mulvanie enquiringly. He nodded emphatically.

'Despite the... um... friendship of King James and the Lady Mariota, Francis, the child is undoubtedly yours. So for a while Mariota has left the court for Ballumbie. When the child is strong enough, she will return to the King. Henry Lovell will care for the infant until such time as you send for it or make other arrangements.'

I nodded. Mariota's maternal instincts were likely to be readily suppressed by the lure of King James and his court.

Anyway, after the invasion I could easily provide for my child.

'I am grateful to the Earl for arranging this.'

His eyes twinkled.

'Oddly enough, Francis, both the Earl of Argyll and Henry Lovell think that you've done rather a lot for them so they both enjoyed coming up with a solution.'

He gave a sudden bellow of laughter.

'Do you know what Brian Emslie said when he heard about Mariota?'

I braced myself.

'Er... no.'

'He said how gratifying it was to know that after all this time there was actually one thing you liked about Scotland. Doubtless though you'll soon be complaining about how fickle Scottish women are!'

I winced at Emslie's quip.

'There are many things I like about Scotland!' I protested. 'I respect your Earl, I like your countryside, your new King has got good taste and, in fairness, you cannot help your climate.'

'Well, it's pleasant today. Let us go and find Broughton.' He stopped and dug me in the ribs. 'You English would be in real trouble with your womenfolk if it was not for us Scots.'

He smiled and put his arm round my shoulder.

'True Davie but at least we bring a bit of colour and excitement to the dull, grey lives of yourself and the Earl.'

So, laughing together, we walked on to where Broughton and Edward Franke were talking by the waterside. Edward smiled shyly at me as was his way while Mulvanie proposed that we discussed the situation in Scotland and how matters were progressing with the French.

'Scotland's fairly simple,' he started, 'for all our rebels have come into the open. They speak fine words and echo noble sentiments. They claim that there should be fair treatment for those who supported the late King. They say that when they fought for him he was the anointed and crowned monarch. So how can they be traitors? Why should they be penalised for fighting for their King?' Mulvanie broke off. 'It's a fair point, I suppose.'

'Can you beat them?' asked Broughton.

'Probably in the next two or three months. At the moment, the opposition is centred around Dumbarton where the Earl of Argyll confronts them. King James will go north and summon the loyal lords to support him. Then they'll attack the rebels and the issue should be decided in our favour.'

'It sounds simple enough.'

Mulvanie scowled.

'It should be but the English are supporting the rebels. Brian Emslie has heard that Henry Tudor is preparing to send munitions to Dumbarton. There's a rumour that a small English fleet is being fitted out to come north. Now clearly munitions alone cannot save the rebels at Dumbarton and Andrew Wood can deal with the English fleet, but I am glad that we don't have to worry about Northumberland as well.'

I smiled contentedly. Henry Tudor's policy of interfering in Scotland had inevitably helped our invasion of England and the prospect of a Scottish army marching south was becoming real. But what about the French?

'What news do you have Edward?' I asked.

'Much of what I have is hearsay,' he admitted. 'It comes from Taylor.'

I must have looked blank, as he hastened to explain.

'Do you recall that the Earl of Argyll wanted an agent in France? He couldn't use his own people. John Taylor was in the Tower with me after Stokefield. When he was released, he had to go into exile. I contacted him and he sends reports from Rouen from time to time.'

His synopsis was brief and to the point. Following the death of the Duke of Brittany in the previous year, the Burgundians and English had allied to help the Bretons maintain their independence. The combination of English and Burgundians had driven the French out of most of Brittany. But the coalition was a fragile one. Threatened with further unrest in Burgundy, Maximilian was looking to make peace with the French.

'Taylor reckons that in a couple of years the French will acquire Brittany,' Edward said. 'But the most interesting thing is that the French are furious with Henry Tudor.' He turned to Mulvanie. 'Perhaps you should tell Francis what the French heralds told you.'

'I'll spare you their courtly speeches,' said Mulvanie. 'Essentially their message was short and simple – they bitterly regret putting Henry Tudor on the throne and they see him as totally ungrateful.'

'Why is that?' I asked.

He grinned.

'The French helped him when he was in exile. Then they helped him with an army and fleet to defeat Gloucester. How does he repay them? He allies with the Burgundians against them, so the French are thoroughly annoyed.'

Excellent news, I thought.

'The French propose that Scotland and France formally renew their previous alliance,' continued Mulvanie, 'after all, they want a friendly England to the North and we want a friendly England to the South. They have military resources. We have military resources. Let us invade England in conjunction, they say, and the sooner the better.'

Broughton and I smiled at each other. We were almost there now.

'We have gone so far as to plan for May next year,' Mulvanie added. 'You'll need to go to France and agree terms, but they won't be too difficult. From what I hear, you'll be able to keep Calais. All you will need to do is make a contribution towards their costs and promise that you'll not aid Burgundy, once the Earl of Warwick is King.'

I nodded happily and turned to go, but Mulvanie gestured for me to accompany him. He remained silent until we were back in his chamber.

'Tell me Francis;' he began, 'now that you have the support of both Scotland and France, what are your plans?'

I went to the window and looked out. With so much news arriving at the same time, it was hard to think properly. Still, I concentrated hard and he waited patiently as we were used to each other by now.

'I'll go to France and agree terms with the French. We will need to discuss the types of troops they'll be using, landing points in England, and the issue of supplies, of course. There is a great deal to plan before next May.'

'And then?' asked Mulvanie.

'We co-ordinate timings and you come over the border at the same time as we cross the Channel. Both our armies converge on London, where I'll proclaim Edward, Earl of Warwick, the lawful King.'

He nodded.

'In fairness, that is the way the Earl and I had been

thinking. Maybe with everything else that's been going on in Scotland we didn't think it through properly.'

'Why is that?' I asked nervously.

'It was stupid of us to miss the blindingly obvious,' Mulvanie added.

My hands started to sweat.

'Which is what?' I stuttered

'It was the Sieur de Sionne who pointed it out to the Earl,' Mulvanie said moodily. 'Do you know it's the first time I've ever seen Argyll totally surprised and admit he was wrong?'

I thumped the table in frustration. 'About what?' I yelled.

He looked up surprised.

'I'm sorry Francis, let me just take you through the Sieur de Sionne's thinking. He said that he had been giving the invasion plan considerable thought. He regretted that he could detect a possible weakness in it. Naturally, the Earl of Argyll asked him what it was. I'll summarise his speech, Francis, but essentially it boiled down to this: Henry Tudor knows you're in Scotland. He has got a good network of agents, almost as good as my own in fact. Presently, he'll know you are in France.'

I was puzzled.

'What of it?' I asked.

'That is more or less what I said,' admitted Mulvanie. 'But the Sieur de Sionne made another point. He said that it would be inevitable that Henry Tudor's agents would start to detect the build-up of forces both in Scotland and in France.'

'There is that risk, I admit, but again what of it? Henry Tudor would not know the date of the invasions nor the routes of marches.' I thought for a few moments. 'Even if he did, Davie, what could he do about it? The French and the Scottish forces outnumber any force that Tudor could summon and you are both invading England from different directions. What is Tudor supposed to do?'

Mulvanie grimaced.

'That is what I said. But de Sionne's answer was simple. He said that if he were in Henry Tudor's position and heard about the twin invasions he would have to take action.'

'But how? What could he do?' I stammered.

Mulvanie smiled sadly.

'It's simple Francis: he would just have to remove the young Earl of Warwick.'

'To where?'

'Into the next world...'

I sat stunned for a long time. Without Edward, Earl of Warwick there was no serious Yorkist claimant. It was, of course, the simplest solution for Henry Tudor but then a thought struck me:

'Do you really believe that Henry Tudor would murder a child?' I asked. 'His own wife's cousin.'

I regretted saying it the moment I had spoken.

'Your last King killed two children who were in a much closer relationship,' Mulvanie observed. 'Our own King James may repent his father's death daily and wear a metal belt to remind him of his sin but the moment he rebelled against his father he would have known that it would result in the death of one of them.'

He looked down at the table.

'When it comes to acquiring power or retaining it,

Francis, both kings and princes can be quite brutal with their families.'

'But such a murder would make Henry Tudor loathed in England,' I said quickly. 'Men would not stand for it; he would be overthrown.'

'And replaced by whom?' Mulvanie asked gently. 'Would your country really wish to re-embark on civil war?'

I wondered. With Warwick dead, the only other claimants for the throne from the House of York would be Lincoln's brothers. Would men support one of them? It was possible but unlikely, I concluded.

'That said,' Mulvanie broke into my thoughts, 'Henry Tudor is less impetuous than Richard of Gloucester. Warwick's death would not be perceived as murder. There would be a trumped-up accusation of treason. The Earl of Warwick would be charged of plotting with the French. There would be an attempted escape by the young Earl, but he would be recaptured. Then there would be a fair trial populated with the supporters of Henry Tudor, followed by a discreet execution on Tower Green.'

'And with the Earl of Warwick dead, the French would not invade?' I asked.

He shook his head.

'To what end?'

I smiled bitterly at him. He shook his head again.

'Nor would we invade.'

I slumped back in my chair. This was the end, I thought miserably. To think that we had all missed such an obvious solution to Henry Tudor's problem. Mulvanie eyed me sympathetically.

'Don't imagine that either Scotland or the French are any less disappointed than you. We have our eyes on

Northumberland and the French want England to stop meddling in Brittany and Burgundy.'

I grunted. Their disappointment was no consolation.

'So between the Earl, myself and the Sieur de Sionne we have come up with a scheme to get round this,' said Mulvanie briskly. I sat up quickly.

Mulvanie eyed me carefully.

'If you accept our plan, then all the agreements between you, the French and the Scots stand and we can go ahead exactly as we originally envisaged.'

'And if I don't?'

'Then, with mutual regret, neither we nor the French will proceed, since we are certain that Henry Tudor will kill the young Earl of Warwick.'

'So what are you proposing?' I asked.

'If you accept that Henry Tudor will dispose of the Earl of Warwick the moment he is aware of the invasions, there is only one solution,' Mulvanie replied.

'What is it?' I demanded.

'What you need to do is to extract the Earl of Warwick from the Tower of London. Then you have to get him to France. It will be safer than Scotland. The French will help you establish a court in exile for the young Prince and you can look to win support for him from England. Some lords may come to join you in France, as they joined Henry Tudor before he invaded England and overthrew King Richard.'

I started to speak, but he lifted his hand.

'Hear me out, Francis. It looks better for you if you invade England with at least a few English nobles in the front of the French army. It will divide up the opposition to you.'

Mulvanie paused and looked at me.

'So that's what will happen if you invade with the Earl of Warwick. But let's look at the other side for a moment. If you don't secure the young Earl, Henry Tudor will undoubtedly kill him and there will be no French or Scottish invasions because there would be no benefit for either of us. So you need to get hold of young Warwick.'

I nodded glumly.

'You're fine when you talk in theory Davie, but you're useless when you speak of reality. The Earl of Warwick was closely guarded before Stokefield and he'll be even better protected now. I cannot use a pretender; no one would believe me. Nor can I get the Earl of Warwick out of the Tower.'

'The Earl of Argyll believes that you can,' Mulvanie said quietly.

I stared at Mulvanie in amazement.

'How?'

'He made one key point and one suggestion. The first point is that you have the element of surprise. Two years ago, your army was defeated at Stokefield. Since that time no one knows what you and Broughton have been up to.'

'Henry Tudor knows I'm in Scotland!' I pointed out.

'True but he will assume that you are just existing on the charity of the Scots. After all, he has Scottish rebels at his own court. Henry Tudor will not – at this stage – suspect that a major invasion of England is planned, and no one will be expecting you to rescue the Earl of Warwick.'

He paused and looked at me.

'Think about it Francis, if you were a guard at the Tower of London two years after the Yorkists have been defeated, would you be expecting a rescue attempt?'

I considered his point. There was a certain logic to his

argument. The sheer strength of the Tower of London would deter anyone. There would be a high degree of boredom involved in guarding the young Earl and complacency would have crept in after Stokefield.

'All right,' I nodded grudgingly. 'But what was his suggestion?'

'It's a "who" and not a "what,"' Mulvanie said quietly. 'He told me who I should use to help you. You'll meet him tomorrow.'

'One of your agents?'

Mulvanie nodded.

'He's good Francis; very good indeed.'

I sat silently, while I mulled this over. Clearly we had to rescue the Earl of Warwick and, if we could do that, then, without doubt, Henry Tudor was finished. He could never withstand a simultaneous invasion from Scotland and France headed up by the future King Edward VI. But the Tower of London was formidable in the extreme and the only advantages we had were the element of surprise and one of the Earl's agents.

'And that,' I told Broughton and Edward Franke, 'is why the Earl of Warwick needs to be rescued from the Tower.'

'We have done many things together,' I went on awkwardly, 'but this one I'll do on my own. You will both remain here and come to England with the Scottish army. Meanwhile, I'll get Warwick out of the Tower and take him to France. I'll bring him back over with the French army.'

There was a short silence and Broughton and Edward looked at each other.

'Selfish to the end, wouldn't you say Edward?' grinned Broughton.

'Francis never had any consideration for his followers,' Edward agreed smilingly.

'Even those who have spent their lives trailing after him with unflagging devotion, risking their lives for him in one lunatic venture after the other,' Broughton continued. 'Oh yes, when men talk of selfishness the name Lovell comes readily to mind.'

'Dear God! What are you talking about?' I demanded.

Broughton jabbed a finger at me.

'You!'

'But I don't understand.' I was totally confused.

'You are leaving Edward and me here in the cold and the damp. You're abandoning us in a land of indifferent food...'

'But you never stop eating and drinking!' I protested.

'And worse wine with no company to speak of. And where are you going? A brief jaunt to London so that you can collect the young Earl and then on to France, a land where it's always sunny. The women are unbelievable – and I know because I married one – their food is superb and their wine is to die for.'

'So Francis gets all that France has to offer and we are just left here,' chimed in Edward. 'It doesn't sound that fair, does it?'

They looked at me and I felt tears welling up in my eyes.

'But the Tower will be almost impossible!' I protested. 'I can't ask you to join me.'

Broughton jabbed his finger at me.

'Stop being so selfish, Francis. First France and now this! Listen, I dare say the Tower is impregnable. But it will be interesting to try, don't you agree Edward?'

Edward nodded.

'Why should Francis have all the excitement?'

Broughton looked at me.

'So stop arguing Francis; we're coming with you!'

CHAPTER 16

Castle Gloom, 1489.

I insisted that Broughton and Edward Franke were present the next day when I met Mulvanie. He made no objection, but greeted us sardonically.

'No doubt your sorry appearance is due to the fact that you have spent the night planning what, to mere mortals like myself, seems impossible,' he said with a smile. 'Personally, I have never heard of anyone escaping from the Tower, let alone breaking in and then escaping. Do feel free to share your plan with me.'

The blank faces of the other two suggested that we had not devised any plan the previous night during our carousing. I vaguely recalled that both of them had agreed to serve as godfathers to my son and to care for him if anything ever happened to me for, as Broughton had put it so tactfully, 'You can hardly expect your wife to bring up your other woman's child.' But my recollection of the remainder of the evening was hazy.

Mulvanie, still in his smart blue tunic, looked relaxed. Occasionally he glanced towards the door, as if he were expecting someone. At last, there were the sounds of footsteps, a scratch at the door and a tall, long-haired man dressed entirely in black entered. He made a small bow to

Mulvanie, and nodded to the three of us. Mulvanie smiled at him.

'Be seated Thomas,' he told him and, looking at us, waved his hand at the newcomer. 'This is Thomas Rothwell. Before that he was Thomas Even and, before that, Thomas Someone Else. Like you, he is English, but for many years now he has been my principal agent in England. Of all my people, I would judge him to be the best.'

Rothwell eyed us keenly and picked me out.

'You have no recollection of me then, Lord Lovell?'

If anything, my headache was getting worse.

'No,' I told him shortly.

Mulvanie laughed.

'Then it is obvious that you play your part well in England,' Mulvanie said delightedly. 'Tell him, Thomas.'

Rothwell shook his long hair.

'I was a priest at court, my lord, firstly under King Edward and then under King Richard. There were many prelates there, so who would notice another one?' He gave a little smile. 'Of course, under King Henry there are even more, so my task is much easier.'

He looked at Mulvanie, who nodded for him to proceed.

'Master Mulvanie has told me of your wish to free the Earl of Warwick from the Tower of London and to carry him to France. He has asked me to accompany you and advise you.' He broke off and looked at the three of us. 'I take it you do not already have a plan?'

We shook our heads.

'In that case,' continued Rothwell, 'there are three possible ways of achieving our objective. I will outline them all.' He consulted a scrap of parchment.

'The first method is the most obvious way. You would

simply storm the Tower. Given the strength of the fortification with its outer and inner walls, you have a choice. You can assemble a large number of armed men and try to batter your way through the western or eastern gates. However, if you succeeded in achieving this, you would still have to penetrate the inner part of the Tower. Naturally you would be under constant attack from its defenders at all times.'

He gave us a thin smile.

'Of course, you could simply besiege the Tower to avoid direct assault. But I believe that the troops of Henry Tudor would defeat your men fairly quickly.'

'Can we move onto the second way?' Broughton said irritably.

'The second option is to arrange shipping and land your force directly on the wharf in front of the Tower on the south side. But again, you would somehow have to break through the outer defences and penetrate the inner part of the Tower while under constant assault.'

'Either of those two approaches would be suicidal!' I told Rothwell. 'It would take at least five hundred well-armed men to penetrate the outer defences. I do not have such an army and, even if I did, I would not use them for a frontal attack on the Tower of London. I would not ask men to sacrifice their lives in such a reckless fashion.'

'It would not work even if the attack succeeded,' added Broughton. 'Not that it would, of course. But imagine you did succeed, Francis – where exactly is the Earl of Warwick in the Tower? Are you going to look for him while we are under attack from all sides?'

'It's worse than that,' Edward Franke pointed out. 'How could we get the boy out of the Tower safely while a battle is going on?'

I turned to Rothwell.

'You can forget the idea of a direct assault on the Tower. It would not work whether we came at it from the west, east or south. The place is impregnable.'

Rothwell smiled fully for the first time.

'I agree wholeheartedly, my lord. In fact, had you wished to adopt either of the two methods that I have just described I would not have joined you.'

'You would disobey the Earl of Argyll?' asked Mulvanie.

Rothwell looked indignant.

'Of course I would. The Earl told me to assist Lord Lovell, not to commit suicide! But there is a third method. It uses stealth, not brute force, and guile in place of weapons. There is one other major difference between it and the first two ways of which I have talked.'

'What is that?' I asked.

'It will work, my lord,' Rothwell said quietly. 'The task is difficult but by no means impossible. However, we will require a number of things in order to guarantee its success.'

Mulvanie reached for a pen.

'What will you need?'

Rothwell looked thoughtful.

'Starting at the end and working backwards, we will need a ship to take us to France, but it has to ready for us, since we cannot afford to linger in England. Secondly, we need horses and a guide to be ready to take us to the east coast once we have the Earl.'

'Surely the south coast would be nearer to France?' observed Edward Franke.

'That is exactly what I trust our pursuers will think,'

Rothwell pointed out, 'so we'll head for the east coast. But first we will need somewhere to stay in London for a few nights and money.'

'I can see why we need somewhere to stay in London that is safe,' said Broughton, 'but why do we need the money?'

'For bribes, Sir Thomas,' answered Rothwell. 'We need to find out where the Earl of Warwick is lodged in the Tower and guards will need to be bribed to assist us.'

'With regard to the shipping, I'll arrange that with Andrew Wood,' Mulvanie volunteered. 'He can provide you with two ships and we'll give you an escort of a hundred troops. They can guard you on the journey and be ceremonial protection for the young Earl once he's in France. We'll have to think of some place where the ships can stand off the coast until you're ready.'

'In the middle of winter?' Broughton queried. 'They would be broken up in the North Sea. Besides, how would they know that we were ready for them? It would be better if they could lie in a port looking as if they had been damaged in a storm and needed to make repairs.'

Mulvanie nodded.

'That would be better.'

Then I smiled very broadly, as I suddenly saw how we could solve three out of the four requirements very simply.

'Ipswich!' I said. 'Let the ships lie there.' I turned to Rothwell. 'I know a man who is an exceptional organiser. He was my deputy at Ipswich when I held the post of Chief Butler. Not only does he know all the people at the port, but he can arrange horses and a guide for us there.'

'Where is he now?' asked Edward.

My smile grew larger.

'He did well in his job and so I helped him establish himself in business in London. He bought himself a house there.'

Edward looked at the others.

'Henry Davy was grateful to Francis. Apparently, no one else would employ a man with a devil's mark.'

'What's that?' asked Mulvanie.

'It's a purple mark on his wrist,' I told him briefly. 'Anyway, we can lodge at his house.'

'A large place, London,' Broughton said pointedly.

I thought hard. The place where Henry Davy had bought his house had something to do with God; he still longed for a cure for his disfigurement. It was not near St. Paul's, since that had been too expensive. The others looked at me and then I remembered.

'Bishop's Gate!' I said triumphantly. 'It's by the side of St Ethelburgh Church.'

Mulvanie smiled.

'Well that's three out of four problems solved. Now let us come to the money. We could give you some, but you'll be travelling through England in disguise and you will not be able to carry too much securely.'

We looked at each other. He was right; it would be impossible to travel the length of England clutching bags of coins.

'John Sante?' asked Edward.

'Who is he?' asked Mulvanie.

'The Abbot of Our Lady in Abingdon. He has known Francis a long time; the abbey is close to Minster Lovell. He helped us before Stokefield. He would have the money. I'll get that fellow who was so useful before to approach him. What was his name again, Francis?'

'Mayne. John Mayne. But Edward, it will be better if you tell him the whole story like we did before Stokefield.'

We were making good progress that morning. It was agreed that Mulvanie would continue to finalise arrangements with the French and plan the Scottish invasion. He estimated that Argyll would have completed the destruction of the Scottish rebels by the end of November. This gave him adequate time to organise matters before the invasion of England in May of next year.

'Edward, you can travel freely in England, can't you?' I asked. 'Good. Now will you find Henry Davy near the Bishop's Gate and tell him that we have need of his house? Again, tell him the whole plan; he will feel more involved and I know we can trust him. Then make contact with Abbot Sante.'

Rothwell looked up.

'I'll go to see the Abbot as well. Now, with regard to the timing of the mission, it would be best to secure the person of the young Earl of Warwick before any hint of the invasions reach Henry Tudor. My gut instinct is to try in December. At that time the nights are at their longest and the sentries less keen to leave the comparative warmth of their towers. I would suggest that we meet at Henry Davy's house at the end of November.'

I thought for a moment. If I allowed myself a month to travel to London that would give me sufficient time to see my child. I looked at Broughton who appeared worn and tired.

'Will you stay here, Thomas?' I asked him. 'At least for a while before you come south.'

I believe he guessed my own intentions, as he grunted his agreement. I turned to Edward.

'When you go south, will you see Nan?' I asked him.

He nodded slowly, as I think he was embarrassed about the situation with Mariota.

'Then tell her to be at her favourite place in October and we may have some time together,' I told him.

He and Rothwell stood up to depart. Rothwell paused briefly.

'Until November then,' he said and they were gone.

Finally Broughton got up and clasped my hand.

'I will see you then too, Francis. In the meanwhile, have a care with your women.'

With a roguish grin, he too departed. I was left with Mulvanie.

★ ★ ★

I was impressed by Rothwell and said so. Mulvanie looked at me meditatively.

'He's the best there is, Francis. The Earl insisted on you having him and no other. He'll arrange things at the Tower for you, never fear.'

He spread his hands.

'Mind you, it's probably as well that Rothwell is out of Scotland for a while anyway. Now that he's done the job that the Earl wanted him to do that is.'

It was difficult to think of a job that Argyll required doing that could not have been managed by either Mulvanie or Emslie and I said as much. Mulvanie smiled at the compliment.

'Ah well, Francis, this particular job had to be done by someone whom no one knew. Brian Emslie and I are known to be the Earl of Argyll's men. Rothwell, of course, has been in England these past ten years and no one in Scotland knows who he is or that he works for the Earl. So that is why the Earl brought him up from England.'

I was intrigued.

'What was the job?'

Mulvanie looked surprised.

'You don't know Francis? It was your idea.'

He stared at me.

'Rothwell was brought back to Scotland to ensure that the late King James did not leave the Field of Stirling alive. You'll recall that the Earl sent for you before the battle and asked you a question about Henry Tudor and Stokefield?'

I could not remember, so I looked at him hopefully.

'You told him that, had you defeated Henry Tudor at Stokefield, you would have executed him in order to prevent the war from continuing. Well, maybe Earl Angus was content to let matters take their own course in battle, but the Earl of Argyll was more conscientious. In his view, a continuing civil war in Scotland was totally detrimental to the interests of the country. As such, he reasoned that either the Prince or the King had to be disposed of.'

'So Rothwell was brought to Scotland to get rid of one of them?' I asked curiously.

'Quite so.' Mulvanie toyed with a ring on his finger. 'In the end, the Earl decided that Scotland would have a better future with the young Prince so Rothwell was instructed to ensure that King James died either in battle or in flight.'

I recalled Argyll saying that he had only used assassination on one previous occasion but I had not appreciated the scale of it.

'So by using Rothwell, who no one knew in Scotland, it could not be traced back to the Earl. Given that he was Chancellor to King James, and now to his son, I'm sure you'll agree that it was a prudent way to arrange matters.'

'I'm not sure that "prudent" is the best word to describe an assassination, Davie.'

'No?' he asked curiously. 'Tell me Francis, what word would you use to describe killing the Earl of Northumberland?'

'The word "justified" springs to mind, Davie.'

Mulvanie shrugged.

'Have it your own way then, but what's done is done. With James IV, Scotland has a fine new King and you get your help with the invasion so we have all gained in one way or another. Let's leave it at that.'

He stretched his arms.

'Now, I suppose you'll be in a hurry to see your child, so I'll give you a guide to take you to Ballumbie. Then presently I'll send Brian Emslie to lead you to the border.'

We rose slowly together.

'Just think of it, Francis, the next time we'll see each other will be when our two young kings face each other across a table and sign the peace treaty. Then we'll drink together and boast how we have both established new monarchs in our two countries.'

His lips twitched.

'We'll both end up as dukes!'

I was going to miss this clever giant of a man; I respected him and was proud to have him as a friend.

'I'll look forward to that day, Davie.'

Then a happy thought struck me.

'If the two new kings are there, Davie, you'll have to produce some decent wine for a change. Something different to the stuff you've been serving up all these months.'

He gave a great roar of laughter and I was roughly embraced by his two strong arms.

★ ★ ★

The old man's welcome to Ballumbie was in keeping with his character.

''Tis no time for a man to be about when a babe is being born,' he muttered darkly. 'No wonder Henry rushed off to join the others at Dumbarton.'

His wife Katherine bustled about cheerfully.

'Is not the Lady Mariota beautiful, Francis? How exciting her life at court is.'

Her eyes twinkled as she looked at me.

'Do you know that she reminds me a little of myself when I was a young girl. Isn't the little boy good-looking though? He'll break some hearts when he grows up.'

A boy! So my instincts were right; I had a son! But I had missed a question from Lady Katherine. I begged her pardon.

'Is it true that Mariota is a good friend of the young King James?' she asked excitedly.

Until a younger or prettier Mariota is noticed by His Grace, I reflected, but it was not a thought that should be spoken aloud so I nodded and asked if I could see my son and his mother.

'They have both been waiting for you,' smiled Lady Katherine.

As a mother, Mariota was even more beautiful than before. Propped up in bed, her long dark hair tumbled down, and her face lit up at the sight of me. By the bed stood the crib and within it lay a tiny bundle: my son.

'The child was born early, Francis, but he is well and healthy.'

'And you, Mariota?'

'Every day I grow stronger – I sleep, I eat. Yes, I am well.'

We looked at each other uncertainly.

'May I see the boy?'

'Of course, but try not to wake him.'

So I bent over the crib and looked at the angry, red face of my son. For an instant, he opened his eyes and I saw that they were the same colour as my own. Then with a tiny sigh, he closed them again and resumed his slumber. Gently, I straightened the coverlet over him, marvelling at his tiny hands and fingers and then I turned to Mariota.

'So what now?'

She smiled gently at me.

'Francis, we need to be honest with each other. We have never truly loved each other and we'll go our separate ways. I'll carry a little piece of you in my heart and maybe you'll do the same for me, but we need to decide what we will do with the child.'

'You'll stay with him until a suitable nurse can be found for him surely?'

'Of course,' agreed Mariota, 'but will you provide for him in due course? Lady Katherine has said that he can remain here and they will care for him.' She looked at me anxiously. 'But you can raise him up in life, Francis, as befits his rank? You will provide for him, won't you?'

'The boy will be provided for Mariota, now and always,' I said firmly. 'But I would like him to be raised in England. He'll live in a place of peace and security, where he'll be cared for and loved.'

She looked at me steadily.

'You promise?'

'That, Mariota, I promise you.'

She sighed and moved her hand down to adjust the coverlet.

'Then I am happy both for him and for you,' she said simply. 'You do understand, Francis, why I cannot raise the child?'

Tears came to her eyes.

'You'll think me unnatural, I know, but I have my own dreams... and hopes.'

She tailed off.

'Will you wish to see your son?' I asked abruptly.

Mariota smiled bitterly.

'To what end?' she asked. 'Francis, I'm selfish I know, but there's so much ahead of me. So much I have to look forward to.'

Her lovely blue eyes looked sadly at me.

'You do understand, don't you?'

'Of course,' I reassured her. 'You can trust me to look after the boy's future.'

Mariota nodded soberly.

'Everyone trusts you; the Earl of Argyll told me that. Davie Mulvanie said that you were the only man he knew who, once he had agreed to do something, would see it through to the end no matter what happened, how much it cost you, or how much it hurt you.'

I started to speak, but she gestured to the sleeping child.

'You're known to all as being truthful and completely trustworthy, so I know that my son will be safe in your care.'

It was, in a way, a compliment but for a moment I felt sorrowful that we could not be the boy's parents together. Of course that was impossible though. Mariota must have sensed my mood, as she sought to distract me.

'And now, tell me about the King and the court, Francis,' she said gaily. 'For while Ballumbie is beautiful, it is distant from the events there and after five months here I feel as if I am living in a different country.'

So to please her I sat down and told her all that had happened. King James had called his loyal lords to meet him at Dumbarton, although the war was expected to be over soon. Clearly this cheered Mariota; while all this military activity was taking place she would not be missed. I imagined her making plans to return triumphantly at a suitably victorious moment.

We talked more over the next few days and became friends. Despite myself it might, perhaps, have developed into a form of love, so it was probably as well that Emslie and Henry Lovell appeared at the beginning of September. The final battle against the rebels, they explained, was expected shortly and there was little doubt that the forces of the King would prevail. Mariota smiled happily at the news – but there was more. Messages from France confirmed the plan for the simultaneous invasion of England. The French were fully prepared to set up a court in exile for the young Earl of Warwick and they eagerly awaited his arrival.

It was clearly time to depart, yet I felt oddly sad at the prospect of leaving. Perhaps the others shared my mood as the castle was subdued the day before Emslie and I set off for the border. Mariota and I said our farewells in private. Regret was offset in both our cases by expectation. She was, after all, like me, planning to secure a King. Still, our farewells were tearful and it was with sadness that I held my son before we parted.

Later that evening, I walked with Cousin Henry. He

spoke of the invasion and asked if I was confident of the venture's success.

'The hardest part is actually securing the Earl of Warwick,' I told him frankly.

'But if you can get him?' he persisted.

'If we can grab the boy, then I know that both invasions will succeed and Tudor will be swept from his throne.' I gave him an embarrassed look. 'But Henry, if I fail, there's the boy.'

'He can he brought up here, if necessary,' my cousin replied.

'Thank you. What might happen is that Thomas Broughton or Edward Franke come for him though. I would ideally like him raised in England.'

He nodded.

'Alright. If something happens to you, I'll release the boy either to Broughton or to Franke. If none of you come back, we'll manage here as best we can.' He paused and looked earnestly at me.

'Thank you Henry,' I said, 'but I have another favour to ask.'

'Anything,' he said immediately.

'I wish to leave some things with you for the boy, in case luck goes against me – my sword, some money and jewels that I have. Finally, I have a chest with some parchment sheets, which will tell the boy about the father he may never know.'

His eyebrows rose and I shrugged.

'Think about it Henry. His mother does not want him but between you, Broughton or Edward Franke, he'll learn a little about me. With the aid of the parchment, he'll know his ancestry and blood.'

He gave me a sharp glance.

'He'll also know what it is that you believed in and why you died fighting to achieve it. Alright, if none of you return, we will tell him about his family, when he's old enough to understand, and give him your papers to read. But if either Franke or Broughton come for the boy then I'll give both the boy and the papers to them and they can do the job themselves.'

I nodded gratefully.

'What names do you want for the lad?' he asked.

'Surely you can guess?' I said.

Part III

1489 - 1491

From the papers of
Sir Thomas Broughton

CHAPTER 17

London, 1489.

The arrival of yet another pedlar at the Bishop's Gate of the City of London attracted no undue attention from the guards. Thus it was that I came to London filthy for the first time in my life. It was dirtier than Paris, I reflected, and noisier than Rome, but it seemed to share the constant bustle and stench of all great cities. With a longing for Cumberland, I pushed my way through the crowd and, after several enquiries, found the Church of St Ethelburgh. At length, despite Francis' totally inaccurate directions, I came to the house of Henry Davy.

Edward Franke and Francis were already there, bearded and roughly dressed. With them were two others – one was small with a mark on his wrist whom I supposed to be our host, Henry Davy.

'And this is John Mayne of Abingdon,' Francis smiled. 'You remember, Thomas; he helped Lincoln to come to Burgundy.'

I looked at Mayne with interest. He was a large, powerfully built man, but he reddened as Francis spoke of him.

'It was only as you commanded, my lord,' he muttered.

Francis clapped him on the shoulder.

'Well, it was well managed.' He laughed and the man went a deeper shade of red at these words. 'Now John, tell Sir Thomas what you have achieved with our mutual friend the Abbot.'

The big man thought for a moment and then looked at me.

'Edward Franke and Rothwell contacted me and I met them in Oxford,' he began. 'They explained that Lord Lovell had a message for the Abbot and I should pass it to him, as it could not be written. So I went to see John Sante and told him that it was the wish of my lord to free the young Earl of Warwick from the Tower. Once freed, he would be taken to France where he would be proclaimed King of England. Then he would invade England with a French army while the Scots attacked at the same time. The twin invasions would unseat the usurper, Henry Tudor.'

He paused and rubbed his head.

'Sir Thomas, I have worked with the Abbot before. He knows my lord and his family well. Therefore, I expected my request for funds to facilitate the escape to be readily forthcoming, but to my surprise the Abbot refused me.'

'But why?' I asked puzzled. 'He's helped you before.'

'That was the problem,' said John Mayne. 'Abbot John Sante said that had he not helped the Earl of Lincoln to escape, countless lives would have been spared, since there would not have been a battle at Stokefield. The deaths were on his conscience, despite confessing his sins every day. How could he possibly add to these sins by giving money to fund more warfare, he reasoned. In the end, he flatly refused to have anything to do with the matter.'

John Mayne shrugged his shoulders.

'I am not a clever man, Sir Thomas, and I could not argue with him on this count. I have neither the intellect nor the words, but I said that I had explained the matter badly. Then I asked the Abbot if I could bring Lord Lovell's friend Edward Franke and the priest Rothwell to him, as both were clever people and could explain the matter better.'

'That was quick thinking,' I said.

'Thank you but alas it had no effect. The Abbot seemed to lose his temper. He barked that he had not the slightest desire to meet a mere priest. Priests were simple people and he doubted that one could tell him more about the wishes of God than he already knew. Neither did he have any wish to see Edward Franke. He said that if Franke persisted in this matter he would be putting his immortal soul in danger and should desist from it altogether. He even said that when he was next in London he would speak to him about this. Then he ordered me out and I returned to Oxford to ask the others what I should do next.'

Mayne smiled at us.

'That priest Rothwell is a clever fellow though. He listened to my story and observed that it would be impossible to change the Abbot's mind quickly; he is obviously a stubborn man. He would think of a solution, but he must have time to reflect.'

'In all the years that I have known John Sante I have seldom known him to change his mind,' Francis agreed slowly.

He glanced at Mayne's excited face. 'But this is going to be one of those rare occasions, so please go on.'

'Two weeks later, I returned to the Abbot,' John Mayne continued his tale. 'I had with me a letter from Edward Franke. I knew the contents, as Rothwell had dictated it in my presence. In essence, Franke claimed that all the Abbot had said to me was true, but his argument did not balance the scales of justice. Where was the fairness in allowing a small child to be imprisoned for life merely because he had Plantagenet blood? The child had already lost both his parents, so why, additionally, should he be denied all that was natural in life – education, the companionship of others his own age, love and affection? The letter went on to speculate that the boy's life was probably in danger from the King. Henry Tudor might well fear that the young Earl could escape or be rescued. As such, he might be tempted to follow the example of his predecessor and kill the boy before he can stir up trouble against him. This being the case, the letter continued, surely there was an even greater burden on the Abbot's conscience.

'On the subject of guilt, the letter pointed out, no one had been physically compelled to fight at Stokefield. As such, it was incorrect for the Abbot to blame himself. The Stokefield campaign would have been fought even if John, Earl of Lincoln had not joined it. The objective of the campaign was to place the Earl of Warwick, not Lincoln, on the throne. As such, the Abbot had nothing to blame himself for.

'What he would carry the blame for though, was if he permitted an innocent child to be incarcerated and killed while he could prevent it. Rather than dwelling on the past, surely the Abbot should look to the future and help preserve an innocent's life.'

It was a good argument and typical of the intelligence of Mulvanie's agents.

'What happened?' I asked.

Francis broke in.

'John Sante pointed out that, if the Earl of Warwick was free, he might still look to gain the throne and there would be more deaths, but he acknowledged the point that there could only be bloodshed if men chose to fight for or against Warwick. It would be their own choice and they, not he, would be answerable to God for their actions. He said that he had not appreciated that the Stokefield campaign would have taken place even if the Earl of Lincoln had not joined it. Then he retired to pray. When he returned, he said that he had been told very clearly where his duty lay and he would do what was right.'

'Indeed he got quite excited,' said Mayne. 'He said it would be difficult to rescue Warwick from the Tower and wondered whether it might not be easier if we smuggled a message to the young Earl urging him to escape. He could go to Colchester – I think he meant Ipswich – whereupon we could meet him and take the Scottish ships to France.'

I smiled at the ridiculous notion of a young boy single-handedly breaking out of the Tower, alone and friendless, making his way along unknown paths without money, but then doubtless the Abbot was an unworldly man.

'So anyway, he went off to see a fellow cleric, Miles Salley, and they arranged the money. Then he gave me one of his monks to help us.'

'Why?' I asked.

'The Abbot pointed out that you, Lord Lovell and Edward Franke, are known to people. Additionally, you two,' he indicated Francis and myself, 'are traitors and would be arrested if you were seen. So it would require someone else to look at ways of getting into the Tower, speaking to the guards and arranging matters. No one would notice or question a monk.'

Perhaps the Abbot was not so unworldly, I thought.

'But a monk is not going to be able to do all that,' I said dubiously.

'An ordinary monk, no,' Francis reassured me, 'but Christopher Swan was formerly a soldier and after that he became the bailiff of Abingdon. It was only after he tired of feathering his nest and his conscience overtook him that he became a monk. Anyway, so far, he's been very useful. He brought the money from our Benedictine friends and gave it to John Mayne and now Rothwell has it.'

'So Rothwell and Christopher Swan are already in the Tower?' I asked.

There had clearly been no time wasted.

'Of course,' said Francis quickly, 'they are looking at ways in which we can enter the Tower. They are also trying to establish where precisely the young Earl is lodged. Henry Davy here is preparing horses for us.' The little man smiled proudly as his former master clasped him on the shoulder. 'And we should have a plan fairly soon.'

'So in the meantime we wait here?' I asked.

Francis nodded.

'Henry has offered us hospitality. It's crowded, but we'll manage and he will feed us.'

'And wine?' I asked hopefully.

Francis grinned.

'Well, now that you're here, of course.'

It was two days later when Rothwell returned dressed in his priest's robes. With him was a monk, presumably Brother Christopher. We greeted each other courteously, as Francis introduced us. Then Rothwell moved to the table and extracted a roll of parchment from his clothing. Carefully, he unrolled it and laid it on the table. We weighed down the corners with coins. Rothwell looked at us keenly.

'Before we tell you our plan to rescue the Earl of Warwick,' he began, 'I should tell you that for these past few weeks Brother Christopher and I have been in the Tower. Besides yourself, my lord,' he nodded at Francis, 'are any of you familiar with it?'

We shook our heads but I was curious.

'How could the two of you just wander round the Tower?' I asked.

Rothwell shrugged.

'The Tower is a thriving place, thronging with servants and many people supplying all of its needs. Who would pay heed to a solitary monk or an individual priest in the daytime? Besides which, I am known to some of the older staff as I was in service there at the time of King Richard.' He gave a thin smile. 'But in those days I had another name, not Thomas Rothwell.'

He nodded to his colleague.

'Brother Christopher, please show us your drawing.'

We looked down at the parchment. It was a mass of lines and circles; it was evidently some form of replication of the Tower, but while monks are used to writing and drawing, it made little sense to me. Brother Christopher looked at our bemused faces and smiled briefly at us.

'Imagine, for a moment, you were a bird in the air and flying over the Tower,' he began, 'this is how it would look. Let's start at the bottom here. Here is the River Thames.' A grimy fingernail traced the river and then moved upwards and round. 'And here are the outer walls and the moat that surrounds the Tower.'

So the straight lines were walls and the circles were

towers. I followed the monk's finger as it moved inwards.

'These are the inner walls. Naturally they are higher than the outer walls.'

'What are these?' Edward Franke indicated the circles on the outer walls.

'Those are the twelve great towers, which protect the perimeter walls,' Brother Christopher answered patiently. He pointed to a large square shape right in the centre of the Tower. 'This is the White Tower. It is the strongest part; it's a castle in its own right.'

'And that is where the Earl of Warwick is?' asked Francis.

'Why do you say that, my lord?' Rothwell asked him.

'It's where Richard kept the two Princes,' muttered Francis, 'for the reason that Brother Christopher has already stated.'

Rothwell nodded.

'Originally, the Earl of Warwick was put in the White Tower, but a year after Stokefield he began to sicken. His cousin, Queen Elizabeth, prevailed upon the King to move him to the royal apartments.'

He pointed on the parchment.

'See. Here they are.'

I looked down at a line of buildings which started near the south-east corner of the White Tower and ran to the inner wall. Another row came down from the White Tower. A similar line of buildings ran along the bottom to create a crude rectangle.

'In the centre of the square is a small garden,' Rothwell explained. 'The boy can get light and air there as he plays.' He pointed to the four towers that overlooked the garden. 'Naturally, the young Earl is visible at all times and, as such, he is judged to be secure. Anyway, in his new lodgings the boy's health improved and he is still there to this day.'

'Alright,' Francis said impatiently. 'Now we know where Warwick is, how do we get into the Tower?'

Edward Franke had been studying the drawings in silence. He rubbed his head and frowned in concentration.

'There only seem to be three entrances to the Tower,' he observed. 'Moreover, each of them looks extremely difficult. They all have gate after gate.'

Rothwell moved back to the chart.

'All three entrances appear impossible,' he said quietly. 'Let us look at them one by one.'

We all crowded back round the table.

'If you came at the Tower from the west, somehow you would need to pass the Bulwark Gate. If you got through that, you would then have to cross totally exposed land to reach the Lion Gate. If you got through that, you would have to pass through the massive Middle Tower. If you accomplished that, you would then have to run the gauntlet between the outer and inner wall. Even then, you would still have to pass the Hall Tower, climb over a high wall and get through the Landthorn Tower.'

'Shall we look at the other entrances,' said Francis dryly. 'Obviously this route is impossible; even if we were to gain entry, we could not get out with the Earl of Warwick.'

'They are no better,' said Rothwell. 'The eastern entrance is admittedly shorter, but it is no less difficult. You would need to pass through the Iron Gate and get through the tower above it, and then somehow you would need to get through the Well Tower.'

'The south entrance?' I asked, dispiritedly.

'Aptly asked, Sir Thomas,' said Rothwell. 'St Thomas' Tower is separated from the wharf by water. But let us suppose you could cross that. You would have to pass through the largest and heaviest portcullis in the country. Of course, all the defences of the southern wall are centred in St Thomas' Tower, so that is where the majority of troops are, but if you managed to break through, you would still have to penetrate the inner walls.'

Francis looked at Rothwell.

'Clearly you have a plan,' he said slowly, 'because otherwise you would have said at the outset that it is impossible. Why don't you just tell us how it can be done? Tell us what you are thinking of. Are you planning to disguise us and smuggle us into the Tower?'

I was surprised at how confident he sounded. Rothwell gave him an apologetic look.

'I beg your pardon, my lord, but we wanted you all to look at the three most obvious ways of entering the Tower. After all, it is possible that you might have disagreed with the conclusions of Brother Christopher and myself. You might have spotted some defensive fault, which we had totally overlooked.'

Francis nodded.

'I think we all agree with you that to enter the Tower through the obvious routes would be impossible.'

He looked round at us and we muttered our assent.

'So what are you planning?' asked Francis.

Rothwell shook his head.

'Not disguises, my lord. Forget for a moment how we enter the Tower and think instead of the bigger problem. How do we persuade the young Earl to leave the Tower with us? He knows none of us. He thinks of the Tower as his home and would be fearful to leave it, let alone with strangers.'

'It would not require much force to compel him to accompany us,' I observed.

'Would his shouts not attract the attention of the guards?' asked Brother Christopher.

'We could grab him at night,' I persisted.

'The gates of the Tower are locked at night, Sir Thomas,' Rothwell retorted. 'Even if we got in, we could never get out.'

'Perhaps we could drug the boy?' suggested Edward.

'A drug would take time to work,' Brother Christopher pointed out. 'The boy's cries would be heard by the guards.'

'Even if he were not to cry out,' Henry Davy said, 'how do we walk out of the Tower with a child?'

He looked at the floor in embarrassment, as we turned to stare at him. His point was a good one. It would be difficult to escape with the boy, whether he was willing or not.

'That's a very good point Henry, but we'll leave that for now,' Francis said comfortingly. 'Now then Rothwell, why don't you show us why Mulvanie regards you as his best agent?'

Rothwell laughed.

'After what Brother Christopher has done, I suspect that Davie Mulvanie would sooner have him than myself,' he admitted. 'There is a plan and it's a good one but it's his idea. He spotted what I missed and none of you have thought of it yet.'

'Well, Brother Christopher, please tell us your plan,' Edward Franke said curiously.

We all looked expectantly at the tonsured monk, who stood with his eyes modestly cast down.

'It is not my plan but the will of God,' he said quietly and crossed himself. 'For my Holy Abbot has interpreted the will of God and assigned me a role in it. Who am I to argue with what the Abbot tells me? But I ventured to enquire what help I could give to the child's rescuers.'

'What did he reply?' I asked curiously.

'The Abbot reassured me, Sir Thomas. He believes that which I must do is the Lord's will and He will guide me. So I say that this plan is not mine but the Lord's.'

We nodded but all our eyes followed his fingers to a small tower on the outer wall of the south-eastern part of the Tower.

'This is the Cradle Tower,' Brother Christopher said gently. 'It seems an appropriate name for the rescue of a young boy, do you not think?'

He looked round at our expectant faces.

'Can any of you tell me what makes the Cradle Tower different from any of the other outer towers?' he asked.

Complete silence followed his question.

'The Cradle Tower was built at the time of King Edward III,' said Brother Christopher. 'At that time the King used to have his private chamber here.' He pointed to the nearby Landthorn Tower. 'It is said that from time to time King Edward wished to receive guests who he did not want others to know about so the nearby Cradle Tower has a door that opens out onto the moat. Visitors could arrive by boat and be conducted from the Cradle Tower to the King.'

Rothwell leant forward and calmly Brother Christopher stepped back. It was evident that the two had worked closely together.

'The Cradle Tower is therefore accessible from the moat,' he confirmed. 'It is guarded by two men and has two portcullises, but one has not been working for a long time. Indeed, it looks rusted up. I will ensure the other is open.'

I glanced sideways at Francis. His gaze was focused on the south-east corner of the Tower and his frown of concentration was deep. But I could see he was having difficulty in visualising what Rothwell was describing. I turned to Rothwell.

'Could you describe where we would go once we got to the Cradle Tower?' I said.

Francis's brow cleared and he glanced at Brother Christopher.

'Let's say that we've crossed the moat, shall we? We can come back to that part later. We are in the Cradle Tower and you'll see a small room on the right side of the passage; there's a fire there.'

'The guards?' Edward Franke interrupted.

'They have already been bribed with the Abbot's gold. They'll be trussed up in the chamber on the other side of the passage. I'll have weapons in there for you as well. Now outside the Cradle Tower we go up a slight slope veering to the right to this door.'

His finger pointed to an entrance in the centre of the buildings, which formed the south side of the quadrangle of royal apartments.

'That doesn't look too far,' I said.

'Twenty paces, Sir Thomas.'

'Dear God!' Francis burst out. 'Do you realise that we can break into the Tower at almost the closest point to the Earl of Warwick!' He looked at us, totally amazed. 'It's nothing short of miraculous that the one tower with access to the moat should be so near to him.'

'It is miraculous,' Brother Christopher agreed, 'but it is what God has arranged.'

Francis nodded quickly.

'I believe you. Now here we are at the entrance to the royal apartments; where do we go?'

Rothwell pointed to the doorway.

'On the night that we approach, this doorway will not be locked. We will pass through it and find ourselves in a small passage way, which takes us to the garden of the royal apartments. The lodgings of the Earl of Warwick are on the west side, to our left.'

Francis gestured at the parchment.

'Davie Mulvanie would have known the exact door,' he teased Rothwell.

'Indeed he would,' Rothwell agreed seriously, 'and it would have taken him less time to discover it. But see here, my lord, we will enter through the second door and turn right into a passageway. The Earl of Warwick's sleeping chamber is the third room.'

He straightened himself and looked round at us.

'Once inside, we will overpower his servant. I have given my promise to Brother Christopher that he will not be killed. The boy will be bound and suppressed, of course.'

He looked at us defiantly, as if expecting dissent, but he found none. It was obvious that the moment a number of strangers entered the boy's room in the middle of the night, he would shout out in fear and confusion. He would have to be bound and gagged to allow us to secure him and extract him from the Tower without attracting the attention of the sentries. Indeed, it seemed safest to keep him tied up until we were at Ipswich and on the Scottish ships. There would be time to explain everything once we were on board and sailing to France.

'Just come back to the moat a minute,' Edward Franke asked. 'How deep and how wide is it?'

'From the wharf to the Cradle Tower is about eight paces. With all the rubbish that has been cast in it, I would guess that it is chest height,' said Rothwell.

Francis nodded absently.

'Let's move back to the royal apartments. How is the Earl guarded?'

'A servant sleeps at the foot of his bed and there is a sentry who is supposed to patrol the garden,' replied Brother Christopher. 'In reality, he sits in the Salt Tower and only looks busy when the Captain of the Guard appears.'

'How do you two know all this?' I asked quietly.

Rothwell and Brother Christopher had done an exceptional job in locating the Earl and identifying the Cradle Tower. But during their research, they would have needed to have left the Tower before the gates closed at night. How could they know the movements of the guards at night? Rothwell raised an eyebrow.

'Mulvanie said you were the suspicious one, Sir Thomas, but I'll not take offence. I have friends in the Tower, whom I told you of before. They tell me what I need to know, but ask Brother Christopher how he came by his information.'

He waved his hand generously in the direction of the monk, who stood quietly. Clearly, it was not a subject he wished to discuss and I realised that I had probably upset him with my suspicions. Francis looked approvingly at Brother Christopher.

'You have obviously been extremely clever, Brother. Your Abbot will be delighted with what you have achieved. How did you manage it?'

The secret of Francis' charm was in his complete honesty. I had yet to meet a man who did not highly value praise from Lovell because the listener knew instinctively that it came from the heart. Nor was Brother Christopher an exception. For the first time since we had met him, he smiled broadly as he slid his hood off his head. He looked openly at Francis.

'I have some skills with herbs, my lord, and have offered my services freely. Men tend to trust a monk who treats them', he paused modestly, 'particularly, if the treatment seems to improve their condition.'

I apologised to Rothwell and Brother Christopher for my ill-judged suspicions. Rothwell smilingly waved his hand.

'It was a fair question, Sir Thomas,' he said.

I pointed to the picture of the Tower.

'Tell me – can the men on top of those two towers see into the garden?'

Brother Christopher looked at my finger.

'Those are the Broad Arrow and Salt Towers, Sir Thomas. In theory, the sentries can see into the garden. In reality, they seldom venture out in winter and, if they do, they would look outside the Tower and not back into it.'

Rothwell began to roll the parchment up.

'So providing only a small number of us enter the garden and move slowly and separately, it would be hard for anyone to see us. This is particularly true if the night is cloudy.'

'Don't forget, no one is expecting to see anyone.'

So gradually the plan was finalised. It took time as Edward Franke was meticulous in probing every aspect of the scheme.

'The worst part will be crossing the moat,' I said gloomily. 'The water will be both freezing and filthy.'

'It's only eight paces,' Edward said mildly, 'and there's a fire in the Cradle Tower.' He thought for a moment. 'Actually, it will be worse on the way back since there will be no fire.'

'It will be marvellous on the way back!' Francis said encouragingly. 'Anyway Thomas, it can't be any colder or wetter in the moat than it was in Scotland.'

Despite myself I laughed, as did the others.

'Mayne here can stay at the Cradle Tower to protect our escape route,' said Francis. 'Edward, will you guard our rear? That will leave Broughton, Rothwell and me to seize the Earl.'

We all nodded slowly. Rothwell raised his hand.

'Now we need to think of how to approach the Tower and when,' he said quietly. 'Master Davy, I believe that you had undertaken to look into that side of our operation, while Brother Christopher and I worked on the plan for the Tower.'

He tied the roll lightly.

We all looked at Francis' former deputy, who was clearly embarrassed by all the attention. He twisted his hands and glanced at us. Noticing Francis' encouraging smile, he drew breath and straightened his shoulders.

'It is all planned,' he said softly. 'I have already established how it will all be managed. Let us first assume we are successful. To proceed from the Tower to Ipswich, we have already acquired the horses we will need. Therefore, on the morning prior to our operation, John Mayne will take them to St Katherine's hospital and remain there. He will have with him, additionally, some food, money and cloaks.'

Reconstruction of a Sketch of the South East Corner of the Tower of London at the End of C15th Showing Lovell's Route

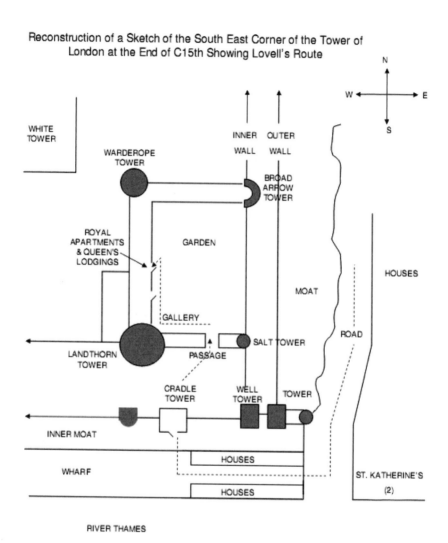

1) ------→   LOVELL'S ROUTE DEC 1489.

2)   APPROXIMATE LOCATION OF HENRY DAVY & BROTHER CHRISTOPHER

It was beginning to sound as it Henry Davy knew his business.

'With regard to approaching the Tower, we will proceed there in two groups,' continued Henry Davy. 'The primary purpose of this is to ensure that at least one group reaches there undetected. Brother Christopher will take Sir Thomas and Edward Franke. I myself will take my lord.'

'What about you?' I asked Rothwell.

'I will already be in the Tower,' he said. 'I will remain there while the gates are locked for the night and will ensure that the two guards in the Cradle Tower are still to be relied upon. I will stay in there, open the door out to the moat and you will cross once you see my candle.'

'It will be difficult to move through London,' Edward Franke muttered.

Henry Davy looked serious.

'It will be indeed. However, fortunately the best route is to be found by leaving the city. I have assessed all routes to ensure our safety and have found the best way. Accordingly, we will leave the city before the gates close. I will take my lord though the Bishop's Gate and a few minutes later Brother Christopher will take you and Sir Thomas the same way. We will proceed into White Chapel, past Portspoken and East Smithfield, and finally we will come to St Katherine's.'

'What is the hardest part?' I asked.

He considered the question. All trace of awkwardness had left him and there was an air of complete assurance about him.

'On the journey to the Tower, Sir Thomas, there is no difficulty to speak of. By going quietly and under the cover of darkness, the risk of detection is small. Ironically, the most difficult part will be in leaving this house, which we must do by daylight. The street is busy and I am known to live alone. How do I explain the presence of three other men and a monk as I emerge onto the street?'

'Well, how do you?' Francis demanded.

'I don't, my lord,' Henry Davy said quietly. 'I will take you first and the others will remain here for a short while. Doubtless, it will be somewhat uncomfortable for them.'

'Why is that?' I asked apprehensively.

'On account of the fire, Sir Thomas,' he answered calmly. 'Prior to departing with Lord Lovell, I will light a large fire in the back. As the fire spreads to the neighbouring buildings and smoke billows out onto the street, you will emerge with Edward Franke and Brother Christopher supporting you. In the confusion, it will naturally be assumed that they have rescued you. In reality, with the mayhem and looting that accompanies a sizeable fire, no one will question the presence of any of you.'

'A good plan.' Rothwell nodded. 'It will, additionally, distract the guards at Bishop's Gate.'

'But where will you live?' asked Brother Christopher, 'and what of the poor people whose homes you will have destroyed?'

Henry Davy looked at him for a moment.

'Doubtless, my lord will compensate and assist them when we return from France. With regard to myself, I have total confidence that my lord will procure me another house when we come back. We must have a distraction when we emerge from this dwelling and approach Bishop's Gate. While there are other ways, this will undoubtedly prove the most effective.'

Edward Franke and I exchanged glances. There was a

ruthless efficiency about Henry Davy, which would have endeared him to the Earl of Argyll.

'Tell us how we shall get to Ipswich,' Edward Franke asked after a minute.

Listening to Henry Davy, I was amazed at his diligence. Having described the route that we would take, he told us how he and John Mayne would take us to the point where he judged the Scottish ships would lie.

'What happens if the Scots are not there?' Edward Franke interrupted Henry Davy's description of the port of Ipswich.

'They'll be there,' Rothwell said with certainty and I nodded. Mulvanie would have personally ensured it.

'But we ought to have an alternative plan,' Edward insisted. He had great persistence where matters of detail were concerned. Henry Davy stepped forward.

'If the Scottish ships are not there then I will arrange alternative shipping for us.'

His air of confidence was now so great that not even Edward bothered to prolong the discussion. Francis looked grimly at us all.

'Well then, we have no need to talk further. We'll seize Warwick tonight.'

CHAPTER 18

East London, December 1489.

The small row of houses on either side of the eastern
end of the wharf afforded little protection against
the driving rain, which had lashed us ceaselessly
since we had left St Katherine's hospital. Just ahead lay the
open expanse of the wharf. Behind the houses to our right
lay the dark bulk of the Tower. Gesturing for Edward
Franke and Mayne to remain where they were, Francis led
me to the last house. We huddled by its side.

'Thomas, we have a few moments together before we
can hope to see Rothwell's light,' he muttered.

It was unlike Francis to sound uneasy.

'What is it Francis?'

I could not make out his expression but the stiffness of
his posture told me that he was worried about something.

'Tell me,' I told him firmly.

'You'll remember your promise to care for the boy if
something happens to me. You and Edward swore to care
for him. You'll keep your promise won't you?'

'Of course we will!' It seemed pointless to state that if
something happened to Francis, the same fate would befall
Edward and I. A thought occurred to me: 'Did you tell Nan
about Mariota?'

'Of course I did!' he said indignantly.

'And?'

'If I survive we'll raise the child as our own,' he said quietly. 'Such is her love, which I don't deserve. But if something happens to me, she wishes to enter a nunnery.'

'As we agreed, then, the boy will be brought up by me or Edward, Francis,' I told him. 'If we all perish, then Henry Lovell will raise him.'

I felt his arm round my shoulder as an expression of his gratitude. Then I nudged him.

'Rothwell's light!' I hissed.

We waved to Edward Franke and Mayne and moved towards the edge of the wharf, opposite to where the light could be seen.

The order of our crossing had been agreed before; Francis was first. He turned his back to the Tower and lowered himself into the water. For a moment I saw his white face grimace with cold and shock. But then, half swimming, half wading, he made his way across. Edward and John Mayne followed him separately.

Finally, it was my turn. I had to bite my tongue so as not to cry out as I lowered myself into the freezing water. Fright made me move faster than I should have done. I slipped and went under, but strong hands grasped me and, looking up, I made out the tousled hair of John Mayne.

The Cradle Tower was both small and dark, but the fire was burning. Shivering and panting, we crowded round it. Rothwell wrapped a cloak around me and then returned to the inner door to watch. It had been agreed beforehand that it would be prudent to wait for a short time before proceeding further. Presently Rothwell returned.

'Your entrance appears to have gone unnoticed. In a few moments we will move forward. Sir Thomas, in the chamber opposite are weapons. Will you come and show me what you need for yourself and the others?'

I moved across the passage to the other chamber. My eyes fell on an assortment of weapons. A crossbow – no use, it would be too slow. A spear – useful for Edward, I thought. I picked it up and reached for the swords and shuddered. There in the corner, neatly propped up against the wall, were two men-at-arms. Both appeared to have had their throats cut.

I looked at Rothwell.

'I thought you had bribed them?'

He nodded.

'I did Sir Thomas.' He picked up two of the swords. 'But as Davie Mulvanie always says: "How far do you trust a man who's already proved that he can be bribed?"'

He cocked his head and listened.

'It's all quiet,' he muttered. 'They will all be inside in this rain. Let us go now.'

Mayne took one of the swords and looked at Francis.

'I'll be waiting for you here, my lord.'

The rest of us followed Rothwell who gestured ahead.

'Now follow me, one after the other. When it is your turn, count to five before you move on.'

He went swiftly up the slight slope to the row of buildings, which lay at the southern end of the royal apartments. We followed him and left Edward Franke at the small door to guard our retreat. In total silence, we crept along a narrow passageway illuminated by sconces in brackets on the walls. Ahead I could hear, rather than see, the torrential rain, which poured down on the open space that must have been the central garden.

Rothwell paused and silently indicated a door on the western side. Hugging the side of the buildings, we edged ourselves slowly round the garden. The rain felt harder than ever; no sentry could possibly see through the murk. Indeed, I doubted whether there was anyone who was sufficiently foolish to be up on top of the towers. Quietly Rothwell lifted the catch on a door and we followed him inside. Directly ahead of us, lit by spluttering sconces, lay a small passage.

We followed Rothwell as he turned right into another such corridor. It was completely silent, so the sound of a man's cough in one of the chambers further ahead made me jump. Rothwell paused outside a small oak door. Glancing sideways, I saw Francis take a deep breath. As the largest of us, it was his job to overpower the servant, while Rothwell and I would bind and gag the young Earl.

I heard a shout but Francis ignored it. Very slowly, he lifted the catch and, with a tiny creak, the door opened a fraction. There must have been a candle lit in the chamber; I saw a shaft of light grow larger as the door slowly opened.

We rushed in after Francis but then stopped. We looked at each other in total bewilderment. While this was undoubtedly the bedchamber of a nobleman – the furnishings and tapestries proclaimed as much – it was completely empty.

The shouts were much closer now. White-faced, Rothwell swung round to Francis and grabbed his arm, pulling him to the doorway. We stopped. Immediately in front of us in the corridor a group of soldiers clattered towards us in half-armour. Rothwell wheeled to his right, preparing to flee further up the corridor, but at the sound of a shouted command, doors were flung open and, with swords outstretched, troops erupted into the passageway. Between the two groups, we were totally trapped.

Francis and I looked at each other; for an instant I glimpsed the look of anguish on his face. Without armour and in a narrow corridor we had no chance. He threw down his sword in despair. I followed his example and, one by one our weapons clanged noisily on the stone floor.

CHAPTER 19

The Tower of London, 1489.

There was no attempt to harm us. We were separated and led away. I was taken to a chamber where a fire burned and was given fresh clothes. Afterwards my hands were tied and two guards remained with me in the chamber. I guessed that Francis would have been even more heavily guarded.

To my surprise, I was reasonably treated. The chamber had an arrow slit for light, wood was provided for the fire and fresh straw for the floor. Food and water were proffered through a grill in the door, but I had little appetite. But then who would when facing death by hanging, drawing and castration?

That we would all die, in this manner, was inevitable. We were all guilty of treason in attempting to rescue the Earl and have him proclaimed King. I guessed that Edward Franke was already dead; he would have been killed as the guards closed in on us. At least he would be spared the torment of a traitor's death, I thought grimly.

Days passed. My initial panic at the thought of death began to subside. You cannot, after all, remain frightened forever. As an old man, I felt I was likely to meet my maker soon, but I grieved for Francis, who four years and more after Bosworth, had come as close as he could possibly could to keeping his promise to Richard of Gloucester. What he, and indeed I, had been through in those years to honour that promise I shuddered to recall.

Inevitably, my thoughts turned to whom among us was the traitor. I was convinced that we had been betrayed. We had walked into a trap so well organised that it reeked of treachery. The empty room where the Earl should have been and the guards concealed in the nearby rooms were hardly coincidences. Indeed, the more that I thought, the cleverer the trap appeared; in that narrow corridor there had been no chance of any of us escaping.

Again and again, I went through the suspects. Francis and Edward I discarded immediately. That left Rothwell, John Mayne, Henry Davy and Brother Christopher. Rothwell was the immediate suspect. He had been in the Tower before our attempt on numerous occasions and he had had many opportunities to betray us, but he had no apparent motive. Indeed, it was in his interest and that of his master, Davie Mulvanie that the Earl of Warwick should escape.

The same argument applied to Brother Christopher. He too had been in the Tower and had ample opportunity to betray us. But again, he had no motive. He was with us, after all, because his superior had instructed him. His Abbot had believed that, in assisting us, he was fulfilling God's will and had funded the venture for this reason. Was it credible to believe that a monk would work against the wishes of his Abbot and his God? I could not believe it.

Equally, John Mayne had no motive. He too had worked for the Abbot at the time of Stokefield, when he had helped the Earl of Lincoln. Besides this, he had been with us, or Henry Davy, all the time since he had arrived in London. John Mayne had not had the opportunity to betray us, nor, except money, had he any motive.

That left Henry Davy. Was it possible that his devotion to Francis was already a pretence? He had been out of the house many times and could have passed on word of our plans, but again his only motive could have been money and he could have betrayed Francis earlier had he wished to. Instead of doing so, he had actually burned down his own house to help Francis escape. The more I thought about Henry Davy the more I rejected him as a suspect. I was suspicious, but Davy's devotion to Francis was genuine. While none of our group had a reason to betray Francis, the fact was that one of us had. No one else had known the method by which or the time when we had planned to enter the Tower.

The dreary days passed with these brooding meditations until, at last, the day I expected finally arrived. Four guards entered my chamber and my wrists were bound. I made no struggle. I was going to die and I had long resolved to do so with whatever dignity I could muster. There would undoubtedly be a large crowd outside the Tower to watch. I would be hanged by the neck until I almost suffocated. The clamour would increase as, half-conscious, I would be cut down to be laid on my back. There would be a great cry as my belly was cut open and yelling as my innards were drawn out. Finally, the screams would reach a crescendo as the bullock knife would be plunged into me. For all my feigned courage, I began to shiver as I was led out of the chamber and down the steps.

To my complete astonishment, we halted on the ground floor and, instead of going outside, I was led into a small hall. My puzzlement increased, as I was taken to a dais where a tiny man with wispy white hair and a rich gown was busy studying a parchment. Two attendant priests stood behind him.

'The prisoner, Thomas Broughton, Your Grace.'

Your Grace? I thought quickly. Henry Tudor was addressed as Majesty; the only people referred to in such a manner now were dukes and archbishops. The two attendant priests suggested the latter – ah yes, this must be John Morton, long-serving royal councillor and now Chancellor and Archbishop of Canterbury. His eyes rose up from his papers and he studied me silently. His face was a mass of wrinkles surrounding those dark eyes that swiftly appraised me. I guessed that I was to be interrogated before my death. I resolved to say nothing, after all, given the death I faced, with what else could he threaten me?

Morton signalled the guards to withdraw and, seeing this, the two clerics moved off the dais and went to join them. Clearly, the content of the interrogation was to be kept secret from the others, now clustered at the far end of the hall.

'Without doubt, you are expecting death?'

His voice was surprisingly strong for such a tiny old man. I nodded.

'Yet His Majesty has decreed otherwise,' Morton continued. I gasped in amazement. 'Not for you the rope, the knife and the full penalty due to a traitor.' I sagged with relief, as he paused to consult his papers. 'Nor any other form of death whatsoever.'

I drew in my breath sharply. The room suddenly became blurred and I found myself shivering violently. Then my heart sank; instead I would be a prisoner for the remainder of my life. I would be a beast in a cage, a man isolated from all others until I went insane. Was this really preferable to a few brief moments of pain?

'In fact, His Majesty has decreed that, in a while, you are to be given your liberty.'

I was too stunned to make any response. This was unbelievable. But then I felt a surge of anger as I sensed he was playing with me as a cat plays with a wounded bird. Forgetting that my wrists were bound, I moved angrily towards him and the guards rushed at me.

Morton raised his arm and they halted. I stopped and took a few paces back. Cautiously, the guards raised their halberds and slowly moved back up the hall, away from the dais. Morton's wrinkled face peered at me.

'In your position, Sir Thomas, it is probable that I would not believe the news either, but I assure you that it is the truth. Your life is to be spared and you will go free. Naturally, you will have no lands. You will not be permitted to travel more than a few miles from the small manor that Lord Stanley will graciously provide for you.' He peered down at me. 'Of course, he has all your lands now and you will be in his care, but you will be free.'

He leant forward.

'All this the King has decreed. Life and liberty will be yours, Sir Thomas, but on three conditions.'

I stared at him defiantly.

'If any of them affects the interest of Lord Lovell, I will not accept. Do with me, as you wish.'

A look of surprise came to his face.

'If only all our servants were so loyal,' he said thoughtfully. 'But the answer is simple enough: none of the conditions can harm Lord Lovell.'

I looked at him suspiciously for John Morton was reported to be both extremely clever and devious. He saw my look and seemed to understand.

'They cannot affect Lovell', he said simply, 'as he is dead. He was hanged on Tower Hill five days ago together with Rothwell and John Mayne. There was another one, but his name escapes me.'

It was not until I saw him cross himself that the impact of his news hit me. My tears came quickly and, with my wrists bound, I could do nothing to wipe away the water. It was foolish because I knew that Francis would be killed – it was inevitable but it made Morton's news no more bearable.

'They were hanged three days after your attempted seizure of the Earl of Warwick. It was done in the early morning so not as to attract too many onlookers. But now, Sir Thomas, we need to continue. The three conditions you have to honour are as follows: firstly, you will swear to refrain from doing anything contrary to the interests of your sovereign lord, King Henry. Secondly, you will swear that anything which I tell you will not be discussed with a living soul. Thirdly, you will promise to answer truthfully, one specific question I will put to you later.'

With Francis dead, there was no point in continuing the struggle, I thought dourly. Without him, whatever remained of the House of York would be without a champion and doomed to failure. But I needed to check one point first.

'Your Grace will swear that Lord Lovell is dead?' I asked.

Morton's eyebrows rose in astonishment at the impudence of hearing his word questioned, but he swiftly mastered his emotion.

'I can assure you that Lovell is indeed dead,' he said coldly.

I sighed.

'Then I agree to all three conditions, Your Grace,' I said and read out the oath that one of the attendant priests brought to me.

Both priests then left the room together with the guards. I noted that the door was left slightly ajar, and there was a small bell on the table. Even though I had my hands tightly bound, Morton was not prepared to take any chances. At the same time, my mind was completely muddled. I had been expecting death, now I had been granted life. Not only that, but I was to have liberty. In some manner this must be connected with Francis' death, but I could not see how. I waited for the Archbishop to satisfy himself that no one was within hearing distance and, at length, his gaze left the door and focused on me.

'Before commencing, Sir Thomas, let me say that personally I find it both unwise and unnatural to be discussing state affairs with you. Not only have you schemed and plotted against His Majesty but, additionally, you have fought against him.' The tortoise-like head peered at me myopically. 'However, rebel and traitor that you are, there is one piece of information that we require from you.'

I could not imagine what this was; I hoped it had no bearing on the death of the Earl of Northumberland.

'Left to me, I would have used torture to drag the answer from you,' the Archbishop continued. 'However, His Majesty made a promise to Lovell and, against my better judgement, he has insisted that I keep it. I am to tell you how and why you were betrayed.'

It made little sense to me, so I kept silent.

'I will start, Sir Thomas, by confirming that you are to

have life and liberty. Your freedom will, however, not come for at least one year. While you have given your promise not to rebel further, there is a danger that certain malcontents may see you as their leader.' He eyed me grimly. 'Following the death of Lovell, there is a void in the leadership of such traitors and I would hate to expose you to temptation.'

'With the death of Francis Lovell, I doubt whether there will be any further revolts, Your Grace.'

Morton looked at his parchment for a moment and then at me.

'It would be pleasant to believe that,' he said mildly, 'but it is strange that despite the benevolence and love that His Majesty bears for his subjects, there are still those who oppose him.'

He paused, as if to contemplate the ingratitude of certain sections of the population.

'Worse still, there are some in positions of authority who would take their instructions from foreign rulers.' He rubbed his fingers together. 'We know the Abbot of Our Lady at Abingdon to be such a one.' He consulted his parchment. 'We are also aware that he assisted Francis Lovell before Stokefield and perhaps more recently. Sir Thomas you can confirm this?'

I remained silent. I would not betray John Sante, Abbot of Abingdon. Morton eyed me thoughtfully.

'His Majesty values loyalty too, Sir Thomas but only when it is given to him and not another.'

Doubtless I would be killed or sent back to my cell for the rest of my life, but I would not betray the man who helped us.

Morton waited a while longer.

'Are you certain that you do not wish to assist us?' he asked politely. 'You must be aware of the alternative fate which awaits you?'

His hand began to stretch out to the bell on the table. I stared back defiantly, and in silence. The little bell rang and two soldiers in their green and white livery appeared quickly. Wearily, I turned towards them; all I wished for now was for this to be finished.

'Untie his hands and bring him a stool!' Morton commanded.

I turned bewildered and I saw that he was smiling. Then I swore: my hands were suddenly very painful. Morton indicated the stool and motioned for the guards to withdraw. I sat mystified.

'You will forgive an old man's little deception,' Morton said pleasantly. 'But it seemed an excellent way of testing how silent you could be, if you wished.'

I stared back at him, uncomprehending.

'You will recall your oath not to discuss anything I told you, Sir Thomas?' he asked.

'Of course,' I replied.

'I thought to test you. However, now that I know you can honour my confidence and remain silent, I shall return to the subject of the not-so-good Abbot. We know that he assisted you before Stokefield. We know that his man Mayne helped the late Earl of Lincoln out of the country. We also know that he provided money to help you to try and free the Earl of Warwick. We know that he sent one of his monks to assist you. Am I correct?'

I supposed Mayne had been tortured before he was hanged. Clearly Morton knew everything.

'You are correct,' I said flatly.

He nodded in a satisfied manner.

'Of course, he has been punished for his treason.'

God help him then, I thought, for his fate must have been the very one which I had been dreading myself. My thoughts must have shown in my expression, as Morton gave me a wintery smile.

'Clearly you know the penalty for treason, Sir Thomas, and naturally you would expect the Abbot to suffer it?' he enquired.

I nodded but made no comment.

'However, in the Abbot's case, the penalty for treason was quite mild. He'll lose the lands that his abbey owns in Westminster. They'll pass to the crown and, additionally, the Abbot is obliged to pray for the health of His Majesty each day.'

He gave a small noise, almost like a chuckle. I frowned thoughtfully. By any standards this was supreme clemency, but another matter puzzled me:

'Why were Francis and the others hanged, instead of receiving the full penalties for treason?'

Henry Tudor was not renowned for his clemency and nor was Archbishop Morton. Francis' sentence and the fate of the Abbot seemed totally out of Tudor character. Morton smiled.

'I'll come back to why Lovell was hanged later but you must agree that the punishment for the Abbot was very mild. Now, why do you think that was?'

I shrugged my shoulders.

'Because he was a churchman?' I hazarded.

Morton shook his head.

'Try again, Sir Thomas,' he invited me. 'Think very hard. You know that John Sante, Abbot of Abingdon committed treason two years ago. For that he deserved a traitor's death. He was as guilty as any of the other rebels, who fought against His Majesty at Stokefield. But was he killed? No. Did he lose his post as the Abbot? Again, no. Was there a crippling fine placed upon him? Again, no. Is he now to be punished for helping you to rescue the Earl of Warwick? Also, not the case.'

He paused and looked at me patiently.

'Now, Sir Thomas, both the Abbot and His Majesty know that he committed treason two years ago, yet there is no real punishment. Why should that be? Surely the only logical conclusion a man of sense such as yourself can derive from this is that in some way the Abbot made amends sufficient to please His Majesty; sufficient to enable the Abbot not to suffer as you thought he would.'

I closed my eyes to try to block out the incomprehensible truth.

'So Sir Thomas, how you do you think he made amends?' asked Morton.

There was no other explanation.

'He betrayed us,' I said slowly.

Morton nodded his head, as I buried my face in my hands.

'You all assumed that the Abbot was helping you,' he continued a few moments later, 'whereas, in reality, he destroyed you for it was from him that we heard of Lovell's plan to invade from Scotland and France. We had known that you and Lovell were in Scotland. We feared that one day the danger could come from there, particularly given the state of disarray in the North, but we had no idea of a potential French invasion as well.'

He rang his bell and called for water.

'It was a clever plan and undoubtedly it would have

succeeded. We could not have withstood two invasions coming from different directions at the same time.'

Coming from a man of Morton's calibre, this was probably the finest praise Francis would ever receive, I thought grimly.

'It was also from the Abbot that we learned of your plan to rescue the Earl of Warwick,' said Morton, 'but he harmed you far more than that. He sent one of his more worldly monks to assist you, didn't he?'

'The fourth man hanged with Francis, Rothwell and John Mayne was Henry Davy, was he not?'

'The little man? Yes, you're correct, Sir Thomas. I recall his name now.' In reality, he had known all along. 'He specifically asked for the honour of dying next to Lord Lovell. Anyway, to return to our Abbot, he sent Brother Christopher to assist you'

'Correct.'

'And it was he who gave you directions of how you might enter the Tower?' enquired Morton smoothly.

I remembered Rothwell crediting Brother Christopher with the idea of the Cradle Tower. How stupid we had been to believe that a monk could have come up with such an idea. But then Brother Christopher had been so convincing with his talk of performing God's will. What we had all failed to appreciate was that in this case the Abbot had taken God's will to mean betraying us rather than assisting us. He had briefed Brother Christopher accordingly.

'But why would the Abbot have wished to betray us?' I asked confused.

Morton rubbed his tiny hands in excitement.

'Now we come to the heart of the matter, Sir Thomas.

My initial thought was that he betrayed you because he became aware that we knew of his previous treason, thus he was prepared to sacrifice you all to save himself. What is your opinion?'

'I doubt that was his reason. For a start, what proof do you have that he was involved in Stokefield?'

'Enough,' said Morton cryptically. 'But I agree with you, he did not betray you in order to save himself. I heard from Mayne how the Abbot tried to warn you off at first. He would not have done this if he was acting to save himself. He faked a fit of conscience for his actions at Stokefield and refused to get involved in your plan, didn't he? But you persisted, did you not? It was only when it became obvious to the Abbot that you were going to mount your invasions and rescue the Earl of Warwick with or without him that he communicated with us.'

I sat shocked. John Sante, Abbot of our Lady at Abingdon had betrayed us. Worse still, he had used Brother Christopher to ensure that we were all caught. He had no reason to do it; he was a friend of Francis. Morton watched me closely.

'Yes, Sir Thomas. That is what interested me as well. Why was it so crucial to the Abbot that you were all caught? Merely notifying us of your plans would have removed any odium of his past misdeeds. We knew this and he knew this. So I became convinced that the Abbot did not betray you merely to save his own life. We did not ask him to send Brother Christopher along to betray you while you were in London. Indeed it was Brother Christopher acting on his Abbot's instructions who told the Captain of the Guards at the Tower of your intent. Now why should your arrests be so important to the Abbot?'

I had no answer. I could see how we had been betrayed. Abbot John Sante had communicated with the government. Doubtless the authorities had received a shock when Brother Christopher presented himself at the Tower and told them his story, but however surprised they would have been at the manner in which the last rebel, Lovell, was to be delivered up to them, they would have been quick to take advantage of the situation. Despite this, I could still find no reason for our betrayal.

'I suspect, Sir Thomas, that your thoughts mirror my own. Clearly, the Abbot was not moved by a love of King Henry or else he would not have tried to warn you off at first. For the same reason, he was not acting out of self-preservation. If we discount the idea that he was motivated by money, we are left with only one conclusion.'

'We are?'

He nodded.

'Clearly yes. That conclusion, Sir Thomas, is a logical one. John Sante was acting on the instructions of someone who wanted Francis Lovell stopped from rescuing the Earl of Warwick even more than ourselves.'

I sat silently. I knew the answer.

'So to ensure that I was correct,' continued Morton, 'I sent a message to the Abbot. I said simply that all his misdeeds would be forgiven if he would tell me the contents of the message he had received from... you can guess the source of his instructions can't you, Sir Thomas?'

'Margaret, Duchess of Burgundy,' I said bitterly. 'But how did John Sante know her?'

'He is, in his own way, a deeply religious man. He visited the Duchess over fifteen years ago and regards her as a godly person. They have communicated over the years on a number of occasions. The Abbot deeply values her advice and has the highest respect for her morality and deep spiritual values. This I discovered after Stokefield.'

'But why should he follow her instructions?' I asked, confused.

'He is an elderly man, Sir Thomas, and thinks more of the next world than the current one. He is easily impressed by spirituality and he knew that the Duchess Margaret's instructions were sent to a number of prominent clergymen. He declined to volunteer who they were nor will I press him to reveal them just yet.'

'So what was the content of the message that the Duchess sent to all these clergy?'

He gave a little laugh.

'Can you not guess Sir Thomas? I am sure you already know. Well, it was a simple message: under no circumstances should anyone who received such a message, aid or assist Lord Lovell in any way. His actions, in supporting the Earl of Warwick, were imperilling the Duchy of Burgundy. Were he to succeed, his actions would lead to its total destruction. As such, it was essential that he was stopped since his works were not Christian. If necessary, he was to be handed over to the authorities.'

He paused and peered down at me.

'Do you have any idea why Duchess Margaret should have written such a message?'

There was no point in holding anything back.

'Originally, we had planned to invade England with a Scottish army reinforced with five thousand mercenary troops supplied from Burgundy. However, when it became clear that Burgundy was not in a position to supply the troops, we decided to use the French instead. The Duchess sent a message to Francis telling him not to use the French, since a French-backed invasion of England would threaten Burgundy's existence.'

'Did she threaten Lovell personally, if he persisted?' asked Morton.

I thought back to what Francis had told me about Rowland Robinson's message.

'Yes, she did but Francis defied her.'

'To his cost. Nevertheless, I am grateful to you for saying this, Sir Thomas as it confirms what I had assumed. I thought that somehow the Duchess had got wind of your alliance with France and feared for Burgundy's survival. Doubtless, the price of assistance from the French for your invasion of England was the promise that, when you succeeded, England would help France acquire Burgundy?'

'Negotiations had not got that far but they probably would have done so.'

Morton nodded.

'That was my conclusion and I was satisfied with it. It all hung together very neatly. The Duchess of Burgundy did not want her nephew, the Earl of Warwick, on the throne of England if it was done with French backing. Then the French and their English allies would attack the already weakened Burgundy and swallow it up. I guessed that Lovell had foolishly, albeit honestly, made it clear that he regarded the Earl of Warwick as the rightful King of England. Moreover, he would persist in this. If Burgundy could not assist him, he would use the French. Lovell had to be stopped or else Burgundy was finished.'

'And the Abbot acted on her instructions!' I groaned.

'So it seems, Sir Thomas. And in the same way Brother Christopher acted on the Abbot's instructions. I was, initially, quite satisfied by this explanation.'

'Initially?' I asked.

He looked slightly embarrassed.

'To me, this explanation was entirely logical, so I reported it to His Majesty who accepted it readily. But his mother, who is a source of great comfort and wisdom to him, ventured to disagree. Having reflected deeply on the matter, she observed that there might be another reason why the Duchess of Burgundy did not want her nephew, the Earl of Warwick to be set free and to gain the throne of England.'

He broke off and looked sadly at me.

'I must confess,' he said wistfully, 'I had not thought of it.'

'What other explanation could there be?'

'King Henry's mother, Sir Thomas, argued that even with France and England allied against Burgundy, its defeat was not certain. Some territories might be lost but Burgundy might possibly call on all the resources of the Holy Roman Empire to assist it. Moreover, the King's mother pointed out, just because the French had helped to put a new King on England's throne, there was no reason to believe that he would help the French.'

'That is a fair point. There is...'

'Be silent, Sir Thomas!' Morton cut me off. 'His Majesty's mother observed that her own son had not done so. Indeed, he was doing precisely the opposite. Why should a new King plunge his country into warfare with Burgundy? It would be unpopular, more taxes would be unwelcome and trade would be harmed. His Majesty's mother observed that the Duchess of Burgundy would be aware of all these things. Therefore, it was obvious to even the most stupid individual that there was another reason why the Duchess wished to stop Lord Lovell. Moreover, it was equally obvious that my own explanation was...' He coughed and looked embarrassed, 'Um... superficial.'

Despite everything, I made a sympathetic sound. Henry Tudor's mother sounded extremely formidable.

'In short, Sir Thomas, she believed that the Duchess of Burgundy had, or hoped to have, a claimant to the English throne of her own. That claimant, backed by Burgundy, the Holy Roman Empire, and Scotland and Ireland, might succeed to the throne of England. Were that to occur, England and Burgundy would then ally against France. Then it would be France's turn to suffer,' Morton said slowly.

I frowned for this made no sense at all.

'But Your Grace knows that there is no one with a better claim to the throne of England than the Earl of Warwick.'

'Except His Majesty King Henry,' contradicted Morton with a wry smile. 'But think again, Sir Thomas, who else could possibly have a better claim to the throne of England than Edward, Earl of Warwick?'

'There is no one,' I said shortly.

He paused and looked hard at me.

'Not even one or both of the sons of the late King Edward?' he asked. 'The Princes allegedly killed in the Tower by Richard of Gloucester.'

'But they are dead.'

Francis had told me, therefore it must be true.

Archbishop Morton raised his eyebrows in surprise.

'Are they, Sir Thomas? Are you quite sure?'

CHAPTER 20

My new cell was far more pleasant than the one in which I had previously been lodged. I welcomed the solitude as there was much to think through.

I sat on the pallet for some time grieving Francis. My thoughts turned to the manner of his betrayal and I felt a savage hatred for Margaret, Duchess of Burgundy. She was truly loathsome with a ruthlessness which seemed unbelievable. Her love for Burgundy appeared so deep that it even suggested a degree of insanity. What she had done defied credibility yet I should not have been surprised; I had heard that she was mad and fanatical not only from Francis but from my own wife Marguerite.

I smiled, as I thought back. Mulvanie's man had brought Marguerite back to me from Burgundy in accordance with the Earl of Argyll's instructions. We had been reconciled quickly. She had been foolish she admitted and, in turn, I agreed that I had neglected her. Indeed, we were only uneasy with each other for a few days. I loved her and always will, and I believed that she would not stray again. We returned to that comfortable state of familiarity between husband and wife who have been married for some time. It is a time when you know your spouse as well as you know yourself and no longer blind yourself to the other's imperfections. You accept them as being perfectly natural. Equally, because you know that your spouse feels the same, you feel unembarrassed by your own faults, and even make gentle fun of them. I knew that we had arrived at this happy condition when Marguerite spoke with regret about her brief affair with Kuttler. Her eyes twinkled up at me; she knew that I had forgiven her.

'Just don't go and leave me again,' I said freely.

'I never will Thomas. Do you wish to know why?' she asked.

'Because you are happy with me?' I returned her smile.

'Of course and without your beard you are so much more handsome,' she replied, shaking her hair. She put her finger to my lips. 'Now Thomas, I will be truly honest and tell you the real reason I could never leave you again.'

She was teasing me, I knew, but I was happy.

'Well then?'

Marguerite dramatically covered her face with her hands and peeped through her fingers to see if I was watching her.

'The real reason I could never leave you again, Thomas, my love, is that I might find myself back in Malines.'

'Malines?'

'At the court of the Duchess Margaret,' my wife said in mock terror.

I slid my arm round her waist.

'Was it really so terrible?" I asked good-humouredly.

'It was worse,' said Marguerite sliding back against my shoulder as if for protection. 'I was bored.'

I laughed, since Marguerite at times was very much like a child.

'I always heard that courts were lively places. How could you be bored?'

'I was dependent on the Duchess for everything,' she replied dolefully, 'and her court is not lively, I can assure you. Everyone does what the Duchess does each and every day and Thomas…' her voice rose in mock horror, '… the woman is mad!'

'How so?'

Marguerite thought for a moment.

'She loves only two things: God and the Duchy. All the talk has to be about one of them.' She tossed her hair again and frowned at the memory of the tedium. 'I had to spend all my time praying and there were no young men at the services. The rest of the time I spent attending her while she talked with these old men – that is all she ever did. No dancing, no music, nothing but talk, talk, talk.'

I bit off a natural retort, for I had resolved to be more considerate.

'What did she talk about?'

Marguerite rolled her eyes.

'Politics, always politics. How could we profit from this situation here? What of this opportunity there? Supposing this was to occur, what could we do? Day and night it was talk, talk, talk.'

'Well, you managed to get away,' I said smiling at the notion of Marguerite enduring the tedium while the Duchess' councillors debated weighty matters.

A look of pure happiness came to her face.

'Thanks to you,' she said and then kissed me. 'So that is why I will never leave you – I fear that I might find myself back in that terrible place with that insane old woman. I tell you Thomas, she is crazed. She is a …..' She searched for the English word and could not find, so to help her I said: 'fanatic?'

I reflected bitterly on the Duchess' ruthlessness but then I put her from my mind as I reviewed the rest of what Archbishop Morton had told me. I came to the conclusion that what he had said was probably true. But there were still some questions that I could not answer. Predictably, perhaps, the next two days passed slowly.

I was brought by the guards to the same hall where we had talked before. Morton seemed to have defied nature by adding even more lines to his face in such a short space of time, but he seemed cheerful enough. I was surprised that a priest remained with him.

'We had established that only the sons of King Edward would have a better claim to the throne of England than the Earl of Warwick,' he began. 'Naturally, we accept that neither of them has a claim since, in reality, His Majesty King Henry is the King of England. But, I regret to say, there are those who support the House of York and who will always look for an alternative monarch.'

'Until I discovered how we were betrayed, Your Grace, I was such a one,' I replied grimly.

Unexpectedly, he emitted a cackle of high-pitched laughter and jabbed the attendant priest.

'The repentant sinner!' he exclaimed happily and even I had to smirk.

Then he looked at me seriously.

'Doubtless, you have had time to dwell on our discussion. Do you have any questions?'

I nodded.

'I have some. I do not understand why I am to have my life and liberty. I do not understand what you mean about the sons of King Edward and I also do not understand why you are telling me all that has happened.'

I would have also liked to have asked why I had escaped a traitor's death but it seemed an unwise subject to raise.

He smiled slowly.

'I have heard that you were both shrewd and suspicious. I like that in a man. But you will remember the third of my conditions? So I will answer all your questions and, in return, you will answer a specific one of mine.'

Clearly, I would have to give a truthful answer but I would be in considerable trouble if Morton's question dealt with the fate of the late Earl of Northumberland.

'I will, Your Grace.' I braced myself.

'I will ask it at the end, I think. It will make better sense to you then.'

I failed to understand but made the oath to the attendant priest. Morton dismissed him with a wave of his hand and settled back in his chair.

'To a supporter of the House of York, the sons of King Edward, undoubtedly, have the best claim to England's throne.'

'But they are dead,' I said impatiently.

He peered down at me.

'The problem, Sir Thomas, is that they are reported dead or assumed dead. At Brecknoch Castle the Duke of Buckingham assured me that they were dead but he was unstable. Apparently, after Catesby was captured at Bosworth, he swore that they were dead. He even produced two of his followers, whom he claimed had done the deed but that fool Oxford had them all killed.'

He broke off to drink some water.

'Even the Queen's mother, Elizabeth Woodville, was stupid enough to confide in His Majesty's mother. She said she wondered, sometimes, whether Richard of Gloucester had allowed one of the boys to live,' he said angrily. 'Still, no doubt she has ample time to reflect on her foolishness in the nunnery.'

He cupped his chin in his hands and narrowed his eyes.

'The fact is, Sir Thomas, we are now in the fifth year of His Majesty's reign. Despite the resources available to us, we have no idea of whether the Princes are alive or dead. The only information we have is from people whom we do not trust, or who seek to please us.'

I looked at him incredulously.

'But since Bosworth, Francis has championed the cause of Edward, Earl of Warwick. Why would he have done that if the Princes were alive? He was an honest man and they had a better right to the throne.'

'He could have been bluffing,' said Morton. 'He could have mounted a revolt and subsequently produced one of King Edward's sons from a place of safety. But I will agree with you: Lovell was honest.'

I grunted. Had he been less honest with the Duchess of Burgundy, he might still be alive, I thought.

'In fact, the only person whose answer on the Princes His Majesty would trust was Lovell's,' Morton continued. 'That is why we sought him out after Bosworth and again after Stokefield. We knew that Lovell was aware of what fate had befallen the Princes and that he would give a truthful answer. Until we heard Lovell's answer, if one – let alone two – Princes sprang up claiming to be the sons of King

Edward, we would not believe them, but we could not disprove them. Worse still, others might believe them.'

I stared at Morton.

'But Francis would have never done anything to assist Henry Tudor,' I said without even thinking. 'There was nothing that you could have bribed him with. Why do you think he turned down your envoys after Bosworth and Stokefield?'

Morton leant forward.

'Perhaps you're right, Sir Thomas. But then, perhaps you're wrong. Maybe, there was one thing that Lovell wanted or maybe there were several things. Now, would you care to hear the story of our discussion with Lord Lovell, since that will answer your questions?'

'Of course, Your Grace.'

'The day after your capture,' began Morton, 'Lovell was brought before us in this very hall.'

'Us?' I interjected.

'His Majesty and myself. The hall was cleared of all servants and guards save two. Being trusted Welsh servants of the Duke of Bedford and speaking no English, they alone were permitted to remain.

'His Majesty regarded Lovell with great interest. Doubtless, he was relieved to have his persistent opponent finally secured. Equally, he was keen to hear the answer to the question that was troubling him.'

It was hard to imagine Francis standing where I sat now. I was saddened at the thought of it.

'His Majesty observed that Lovell must have been aware

that he faced death. However, were Lovell to answer one question then not only would he be spared the penalties of death for treason but Lovell's wife would also be protected. Additionally, His Majesty guaranteed that she would be provided with a pension and not forced into a marriage she might not desire.'

'Lovell seemed to stare into space, for a considerable time,' Morton went on, 'so I pointed out to him that such a display of obstinacy could not assist him. He looked at me in a surprised fashion and apologised. He had not meant to be discourteous, he said, it was just that his thoughts were elsewhere.'

I smiled to myself. I could imagine Francis saying it.

'Thinking His Majesty's offer to Lovell might have been misunderstood, I tried again,' said Morton. 'I repeated that in return for telling us what had happened to the sons of King Edward, Lovell would not suffer a traitor's death. Indeed he would not face death from us by any means. That was our offer.'

If anything this seemed even more generous, I thought.

'He rejected it.'

Morton looked crossly at me.

'You are correct. Lovell said he appreciated the offer, but he could not accept it. Henry Tudor was a usurper to the throne of England and he would do nothing to help him. Moreover, any attempt by ourselves to torture the answer out of him would be useless since we would never know whether the answer given was correct or not.

'His Majesty and I looked at each other when we heard his defiance. The point made by Lovell was a good one. An answer given under torture can never carry the same conviction as a voluntary one. We knew Lovell to be honest and we would only believe his answer if it was freely given.'

'So what did you do?'

'I increased our offer. I said, if His Majesty would spare Lovell's life, would he acknowledge His Majesty to be his King? Furthermore, in return for Lovell's life and a partial restoration of his estates, would he answer our questions?'

'I suppose he rejected that too.'

I was beginning to enjoy this.

'Again, you are correct Sir Thomas. Lovell said that he regretted that he could never serve a man who he perceived had little or no claim to the throne of England. It would be totally dishonest to pretend to do so merely to preserve his own life. As such, our offer had to be refused.'

Morton paused and scowled.

'It seemed that we had reached a total impasse. Lovell seemed to view death with equanimity and was seemingly unconcerned about the method of his demise.'

'That was unfortunate for you.'

Morton pulled his cloak further round him.

'It was but fortunately His Majesty, whose mind is sometimes sharper than my own, came up with a solution. Was there anything, anything at all, which Lovell wanted to persuade him to answer the question that we wished to put to him? He again appeared to look at the wall for some time. At last, he looked at us and enquired after the fate of his friend, Edward Franke. Neither of us knew, so a physician was summoned. The news was bad, however. Edward Franke had suffered numerous wounds and, regrettably, his death was expected imminently.

'Lovell relapsed into silence and resumed his examination of the wall. Suddenly, he smiled broadly. Under the circumstances, it was so surprising that His

Majesty commented on it afterwards. Lovell then looked at us and thanked us for our patience. He had reflected on the matter and would answer the question we would put to him. He had but three requests. We invited him to tell us his conditions.

'Lovell said that he knew he faced death. Had the position been reversed, he would have had Henry Tudor killed, for clearly Henry Tudor could no more serve under the Earl of Warwick than he could serve under Henry Tudor.'

'What were Francis' requests?' I asked with rare tact.

'Firstly, since to his mind death was inevitable, he wished his death, and those of his companions, to be as quick as possible. To this, we agreed readily. Secondly, he was grateful to the King for his offer to protect his wife, as had been already described. Would he honour that promise? Lovell wondered. This again was speedily agreed. Finally, he wished to thank his fellow captive and friend of so many years, Thomas Broughton. He asked that Broughton should be set free and given a piece of land and a small manor, preferably in his former estates. Additionally, he should be permitted to live there with his wife for the remainder of his life. He should be told the manner by which we had been betrayed and how he came to be released. Finally, Sir Thomas should be permitted to make one brief journey to Scotland to collect a valuable possession of Lord Lovell's. That possession he should care for.'

Tears came to my eyes and Morton viewed me sympathetically.

'His Majesty and I looked at each other cautiously. Clearly, this last demand of Lovell's was both hard and unwelcome. Scotland was preparing to invade England along with the French and you, Sir Thomas, could have been the figurehead. On the other hand, as His Majesty pointed out, without the Earl of Warwick in France or Scotland, there was little chance of the invasions materialising.

'Could this possession harm His Majesty?' I asked Lovell.

'"No," was his flat response.

'Sir Thomas would need to swear publicly not to work against His Majesty or his heirs,' I told Lovell.

'"Broughton will swear to that readily when he knows how we were betrayed," Lovell replied. "If he does not, then I will have already given you the answer to your question."

'His Majesty observed that the rebellion, which Lovell had instigated, would take time to be settled. Even if you swore your loyalty to the Tudors, Sir Thomas, we could not release you for at least one year, but Lovell accepted that. He asked that, if you were to be kept in prison, you should be well looked after.

'His Majesty and I exchanged glances. Lovell's demands were risky but manageable. I turned to Lovell and told him, that we agreed to it.'

'And then, you asked Lovell your question?' I said slowly. Morton nodded.

'Lovell turned to me and asked me what was the question we wished to put to him. He must have known what it would be. So I asked him, simply, whether Richard of Gloucester had caused his two nephews, the sons of King Edward, to be put to death.

'Lovell did not hesitate: "Yes," he said, "he did."

'"And their bodies?"

'He shook his head. "I do not know precisely, but the two boys were kept in the White Tower. I doubt whether they were moved far."

'His Majesty visibly relaxed. He turned to Lovell and

thanked him for his honest replies. He swore that he would honour the agreement that we had made. Then he asked Lovell if he wished to know how and why he had been betrayed.

'To my astonishment, Lovell shook his head. "Even to me," he said, "it is obvious that the betrayal of our plan comes, directly or indirectly, from the Duchess of Burgundy." He thought for a few moments then. "She wishes to place her own claimant on the throne of England and she knows that I could never support such a youth."

'Ignoring me, Lovell looked straight at His Majesty. "I could not have supported him; indeed, I would have denounced him for the real sons of King Edward are dead."

'Plainly His Majesty was wholly convinced by Lovell and believed him to be telling the truth,' Morton told me, 'but I found myself increasingly concerned about his mysterious possession in Scotland.'

'Why was that?'

He looked at me steadily.

'For all his famed truthfulness it occurred to me that Lovell might possibly have lied to His Majesty and myself. We had no means of confirming that he had spoken the truth after all.'

I blinked in surprise. Morton's suspicious nature greatly exceeded my own.

'So I began to ponder what this possession might be. Of course it would have to be a particularly valuable item, would it not, for Lovell to request that you specifically collect and care for it, Sir Thomas? But then why you, Sir Thomas? What could the item be that Lovell would entrust to a committed Yorkist and fellow traitor?'

I kept silent as he eyed me speculatively.

'Eventually it occurred to me,' continued Morton, 'that the mysterious item might not be an object but a person – or, to be more specific, a boy.'

I sat up sharply.

He eyed me shrewdly.

'You see, despite everything that Lovell had said, I thought he might have been concealing the presence of one of King Edward's sons.'

'After he had broken into the Tower of London to rescue the Earl of Warwick?' I asked incredulously.

Morton's obsession amazed me.

'I owed it to His Majesty to be certain,' he replied, 'so I asked Lovell directly what the possession was that he had left in Scotland.'

'And?'

'Lovell replied that we had made an agreement. He had already provided an answer to the question posed to him. As such, he declined to answer any more. However, he did say that if His Majesty promised to make known to you the whole story of how and why you had been betrayed, then you would supply the answer. His Majesty enquired whether I wished him to do so and I ventured the opinion that, while distasteful, it would be a prudent act.'

He looked down at me.

'So now, Sir Thomas, you will understand why – against my better judgement – I have told you about your betrayal. A King's oath cannot be broken it would appear.'

'I believe that you have a question for me?'

Morton licked dry lips.

'Remember that you are under oath, Sir Thomas,' he cautioned me.

'I will.'

'What is this possession Lovell wishes you to collect from Scotland?'

For an instant I sensed Francis' presence and recalled his irrepressible sense of humour.

'A young boy,' I told Morton with a straight face.

He paled quickly and dabbed at his forehead.

'Who is he?'

'Lovell's infant son. He's less than a year old and base born.'

'The mother?'

'She does not want the child.'

'So Lovell wanted you to raise the boy?' Morton was more relaxed now, with colour in his cheeks.

'Yes.'

He pondered on it for a while, doubtless relieved by my revelation.

'May I raise Francis' son?'

'The House of Tudor does not wage war on infants, Sir Thomas!' he snapped and shuffled his papers. 'Raise the boy and when he is older we will bring him to court. If we failed to bind his father to England's new dynasty, we will succeed with the son.'

That was both generous and prudent of Morton, I reflected. There was no point in raising Francis' son to fight his father's battles – the conflict was now over.

'I believe that my explanation has answered all your questions, Sir Thomas.'

I hesitated.

'I can understand why I am to be set free and why you

have told me all this– you believe that at some stage in the future a pretender may come from Burgundy claiming to be one of those Princes.'

He looked at me shrewdly.

'Yet something else is troubling you?'

'Then why did you not keep Francis Lovell alive?' I asked bitterly. 'The moment such a pretender appeared you could have used Lovell to stand up and denounce him. He would have confirmed that the real Princes were killed by Richard of Gloucester.'

Morton looked amazed.

'But to do so would be to surrender a major advantage,' he pointed out. 'We can use this situation. After all, now that we know that any future pretender cannot be genuine, we can observe men. We can see whether they are loyal to us or would prefer to have someone they believe to be the son of King Edward crowned. If Lovell was alive and denied the authenticity of the pretender, then who would stand up to support such a youth?'

I nodded sadly in acknowledgement of Morton's political acumen.

'Then the war is over now.'

He smiled, a little grimly.

'If only all men thought so. We will part now, Sir Thomas. We will not meet again in this lifetime, but I cannot but feel that our acquaintanceship has been mutually beneficial.'

The little bell rang again and I was led away.

CHAPTER 21

Tower of London, 1490.

My stay in the Tower was not wholly unpleasant. I was kept in the Beauchamp Tower where, apparently, the last Earl of Northumberland had been lodged after Bosworth. In such a small community, news seemed to travel almost by itself. I was immensely saddened to hear that, when his wounds had healed sufficiently, Edward Franke was hanged just before Easter Sunday on Tower Hill. Of all the plotters, only I remained. I discounted Brother Christopher for he had betrayed us and was only kept in the Tower to prevent the news of our attempt to rescue the Earl of Warwick from becoming common knowledge. I did hear, however, that he had ceased to be a monk, since he blamed himself for causing the deaths of the others.

I knew that I was to be kept captive, so that there was no danger of my being tempted to break my promise. I would not have done; I would not rebel again.

Over a year later, it was decided that I no longer was a danger and was granted my freedom. In accordance with my discussion with Archbishop Morton, I returned to Ballumbie to collect Lovell's son.

My visit to Scotland was brief. I had promised not to work against King Henry or to reveal what Morton had told me. As such, all I could explain to Henry Lovell was that I was under oath but Francis and the others were dead. He expressed great sorrow at the news and was certain that Mulvanie and the Earl of Argyll would share this grief. I told him additionally that, while the plot had failed, Francis had saved my life and wished me to raise his son. To this, Henry readily agreed and said that Francis had spoken to him about this.

Since Edward Franke too was dead, I invited Henry Lovell to be the child's other godfather to which he willingly assented. He did request, though, that a simple service of blessing was done to mark the end of his direct responsibility for Francis' son. I naturally agreed and a few days later we were fortunate to find a simple priest returning to York. He duly performed the ceremony on the new Lord Lovell, as Henry called him.

I was touched to hear the names that Francis had selected for the boy and, when it was time, Henry and his men took young Thomas Edward and myself all the way back to the Debateable Land. As I looked at the familiar empty wasteland, I could not but reflect on all that had occurred since we had first entered Scotland from this place.

I returned to the small manor at Witherslack which was allocated to me. Lord Stanley's bailiff visits monthly to check on me and, rather than attempt to conceal the boy, Marguerite and I pass him off as our own son. There is already much of Francis about him and my prayer is that I shall live long enough to see him grow into manhood. When he is old enough, I shall tell him of his father and give him these papers so that he may learn of his lineage and his father. With that knowledge, his father's sword, money and jewels, he will be set up for whichever path in life he chooses to follow. Until that time, I will give him the same love and service that I gave to his father.